Slow Death by Quicksilver

A Murray of Letho Mystery

by

Lexie Conyngham

Lexie Conyngham

With thanks to John, who first told me about the students and their travels.

Dramatis Personae

In Kirkwelland:
Mr. Herkless, the benevolent laird
Kitty Herkless, his daughter, perfect in every way
Mr. Pringle, whose excellent opinion of himself is not
    necessarily shared by …
Mrs. Pringle, or indeed …
Anna Pringle, his pretty daughter
Mr. Coulter, the minister, recently bereaved
Charles Murray of Letho in Fifeshire, his guest

The Students:
John McCullough, a mother hen
James Adair, a chick with problems
Joseph Gibson, not quite of this world
Adam Nugent, born to be unhappy

The Mutual Improvement Society:
John Innes, a shoemaker and meteorologist, and his intelligent
    wife (member by association)
Gourlay, farmer and fancier of optics
Old Pearce and his son Norrie, who prefer chemicals that go
    bang
Raffan, the smith, fancier of Sarah Burns
Mr. Burns, general merchant

Sundry Others:
Mrs. Veitch, housekeeper at the manse
Walter Fenwick, servant to Murray of Letho
Thomson, the sheriff's officer
Two horses, one of a mildly depressive character

Lexie Conyngham

Slow Death by Quicksilver

Chapter One

'Yer pal's no waking up. Is there somethin' wrang wi' him?'

The woman, in her middle years, wore a cap and apron in a matching dirt-grey, adorned with a number of tantalisingly unidentifiable stains in contrasting colours. Along with them, to complete the look, she sported an unsympathetic scowl and a lingering aroma of grease. McCullough had never seen a French fashion plate, but he was fairly sure she did not resemble one.

He tried to favour her with a winning smile, and edged past her forbidding figure to the doorway of the parlour in which he and his three friends had spent the night. They had already opened the shutters and rolled up their packs, ready to depart, and McCullough had tipped the requisite small coins into the hand of that angel of loveliness who had been their hostess. It was as he, Nugent and Gibson had been organising themselves outside in the refreshing sunshine, deciding the important matter of breakfast, that they noticed that Adair had not yet joined them.

From the parlour door, McCullough could see that Adair's long black coat was over the back of a chair on the other side of the central table, and as he squeezed round the table he saw that the coat was hanging with one sleeve touching the floor and the other tucked into itself. Over it was cast Adair's yellowing neckcloth, and one boot was in the fireplace, which fortunately their hostess had not seen fit to fill and light. Adair himself was sprawled on the floor, half-wrapped in his own blanket like a decadent Roman senator, one stocking sole under the table and the other, still clad in its boot, in the coal scuttle. He was snoring with a noise like a bullock-cart on a stone road. His long-drawn face had a faint sheen of sweat, visible even in the dim parlour. McCullough went and knelt by him, his own plump face creased with anxiety. He rose quickly and with a reassuring nod at their landlady, went outside.

'Lads, with the spirit on that there man's breath you could pickle an entire sheep's head in the Anatomy School, so you could. We'll not be rousing him before midday.'

'He's been at the whisky?' demanded Nugent, snapping almost before he knew what to snap at. 'Where did he get yon devil's brew from this time? You said you were watching him!'

'McCullough cannot be watching him the whole time,' said Gibson gently, stooping to touch Nugent on the arm. McCullough waved his hands as if to deflect Gibson's kind words.

'Nugent's dead on, I should have had my eye on him. I took all the stuff off him he'd brought from Glasgow, and he swore to me he wouldn't touch another drop from there to Portpatrick. How he finds more I don't know. I wish I did.'

The landlady had come to the cottage door and was observing them, one hip solidly against the frame, arms folded to reinforce her argument before she even spoke.

'You canna leave that loon here,' she stated. 'The way he is, likely he'll boke on my good clean floorboards the minute he wakes up.'

'If he could find your good clean floorboards amidst the rest of them, no doubt he would,' muttered Nugent.

'We'll have to carry him out between us, lads,' sighed McCullough, moving fast before the landlady could react to Nugent. 'Come on,' he added, against the rumble of Nugent's grumbling, 'let's get the job done before he bokes.'

'If it doesn't make him boke itself,' Nugent added darkly.

Adair struggled a bit in his spirit-fuelled dreams as they tried to straighten out his blanket and roll the sides of it against him to act as a stretcher. The landlady watched like a hawk, pointedly holding a tin pail close at hand. McCullough handed Gibson the coat, neck cloth and boot, and tucked the remains of Adair's pack under his own arm before awkwardly lifting his end of the blanket. Nugent did not move.

'What's the matter?'

'Why do we have to do all the work? Why does Gibson get away with just dandering out with a wee bit of a coat over his arm?'

McCullough bit his lip.

'There's no way three of us are going to get round the table here in the middle carrying Adair with us and not drop him, not with the length of him, and we're the strongest, aye?' He added the last bit trying to adorn it with blandishment, not pleading. The landlady tapped her foot on the dusty floorboards.

'And I've got the heavy end as usual, I see,' said Nugent, still not bending to the task. He nudged their friend with his toe, and Adair's snoring changed key. 'We could save ourselves the trouble and see if he wakes up.'

'I'll take the head end, then,' said McCullough, ignoring that, 'and you take the feet.' He circumnavigated the table and urged Nugent to step down to the foot end, then crouched once again to clutch the folds of the blanket. 'One, two, three!'

'He should never be allowed to take his boots off,' grumbled Nugent, averting his nose, but he lifted nevertheless. They raised Adair above table height and wriggled him round the backs of the hard chairs, and out into the kitchen, then readjusted and guided him as carefully as they could into the road outside where Gibson hovered. The landlady had the door closed almost before they were through it: McCullough thought for a second his coat tails had been caught in the doorway.

Outside they carried Adair as far as a grassy bank by the side of the road, out of sight of their erstwhile hostess, and laid him down. His feet bounced as Nugent let go of the blanket a moment early, but McCullough tucked its edges around him, turned him on his side in case he did vomit, and did his best to make him comfortable with his pack at his back.

'I doubt we'll not get to Stranraer the night,' he said quietly to Gibson, watching Nugent in case he was provoked into more anger.

'It's as God wills it,' said Gibson, with a smile. He spread his long, gingery fingers wide. 'Who knows but that we can be of service to someone along the way, whom we would never meet if we were half a day earlier?'

'Aye, well, maybe so,' said McCullough, unable to help smiling back. 'If it's to be, it'll be, right enough.'

'Dear Lord,' said Gibson, folding his hands and bowing his head, 'bless and preserve our dear weak friend here, Jamesie Adair, and keep from him all thoughts of liquor.'

'At least until we get him home,' added McCullough, practically.

'And dear Lord, if it be thy will, guide and direct the wrath of our dear friend Adam Nugent here, so that it be used only for thy service and in righteous smiting of the foes of the just.'

'Or if thy will is otherwise, could you go some way to calming him down a wee bit?' put in McCullough again. 'Before he gets us all into trouble?'

'Look down with mercy, O Lord, on all thy servants, faithful and flawed, now and in time to come. Amen.'

'Amen,' repeated McCullough with feeling. Gibson paused a moment and then opened his eyes to meet McCullough's. It was like a blessing.

The peaceful moment was interrupted by Nugent, leaping back into the conversation with fury.

'I tell you, if this happens again I'm going to swing for that man! If I don't get back by the Sabbath, my mother'll skin me alive!'

Not that many miles south, a well set-up man of a certain age was strolling amongst a stand of birch trees, on a headland overlooking a broad bay glinting with the morning's sun. It would have been hard to be displeased by his surroundings: chaffinches, wrens and blackbirds filled the branches with song, and as the woods delicately stepped down the soft slope behind him, tousled by the light wind off the bay, oak and elm mingled with the birch to point up their creamy white trunks, and the incredible green of young beech glowed where the sun's beams reached tentatively through the canopy. It would be harder underfoot here, where there were brambles and bracken, so the man, who was not roughly dressed, kept to the upper headland, where the view of the bay and the circling seabirds seemed to draw him. He removed his hat, put his back comfortably to one of the broader birches and relaxed, inhaling the bright breeze dizzy with salt air and leaf mould.

Anyone watching would not have thought him displeased when the pretty woman appeared, tiptoeing along the headland path with her head down, for the path could be rough. Her bonnet was between blue and green, hard to define against the sapphire bay and glittering sky beyond, but no mistake could be made about her hair, the golden red of beech leaves in autumn, curling into ringlets around her little face. When she saw him, though, she took a jump back, her hands whipping up in front of her as if to ward him off.

The old man in the trees at the foot of the slope smiled to himself, settling into his stick. Really, it was as good as a mime.

The man pushed himself away from the tree with a twitch of his strong shoulders, and spoke, his words slithering away on the breeze. The woman's neck and arms relaxed, her hands slowly clasped and folded in front of her as she turned away and gazed out over the bay. The man came closer, reaching out to her. She turned back to him, her hands motionless. They did not quite touch. For a moment, neither of them seemed to speak, and the old man held his breath, grinning. Then he seemed struck by a thought, and with gnarled hands pulled an old-fashioned pair of wax tablets out of his satchel. He made a few marks awkwardly on the first tablet, smirking to himself, glancing up again once or twice at the couple on the headland as if he could sketch them in that position.

By the time he had finished making his notes, the couple had moved apart, and were both staring fixedly at the coast on the other side of the broad bay, as if fascinated by something there. By the movements of their heads, he guessed they were talking again, but stiffly, as if each were not quite sure of the other or perhaps of themselves. The old man, taking advantage of them looking the other way, eased himself off his good but tired leg, taking the weight for a moment on his bad leg and the stick, then wobbled back to the good leg, stretching his arms and shoulders instead. The breeze might have been spring-like, but it was chilly, and he pulled his old tweed collar up around a knitted shawl wound about his neck. He should be in his own home, which if not exactly warm was at least sheltered. He began to think longingly of his box bed, where he had laboriously over the years plugged all the draughts with bits of rag long-saved, and where the old blankets still gave some warmth. Had he seen all there was to see here? Would there be something more juicy to come? He stretched his loose old lips wide at the thought, almost licking them, as he watched the couple closely.

There was the crack of a branch, and a blackbird shot out of a bramble, squawking alarm. The man on the headland turned as if it had been a gunshot. The woman was away, slipping and tripping down the path in the direction from which she had come, clutching her bonnet with one hand, the other arm swinging wildly to steady herself. The old man froze: he knew he had made no sound, but the man on the headland was not to know that and the noise could equally lead to the old man as to another. He turned unsteadily with his stick, pulled up his collar even further and slid quietly into a patch of denser woodland, crouching down as fast as he could with the aid of his stick and a young beech tree. He heard the man's footsteps as he lunged down from the headland and into the woods. Was he heading this way? Had the beech tree's shining round leaves shaken and betrayed him?

Then he heard running footsteps, lighter than the man's, and breaking twigs as someone fled north, away from him and from the path the woman had taken. There followed the heavy thump of the man's boots giving pursuit. The old man breathed out, only then aware that he had been holding his breath as hard as he clutched the beech tree's smooth trunk, and only then realising how his poor old legs were aching after only a moment in that cramped position. He was not to be caught today, then: he would be able to head back to that cosy box bed after all.

Well, he would when he managed to get up.

'A most remarkable child! Which no doubt comes as no surprise to the ears of a fond father.'

Charles Murray of Letho grinned. Mrs. Helliwell, who lived in Letho village, wrote a good letter, which was why he had asked her to report on Miss Augusta Murray, left at home by her father for the first time in her eight months of life. Nursemaids and housekeepers were all very well, but it was good to have an outsider's view of what his daughter was doing every day.

'Yesterday when I called, she was sitting up against a cushion on the nursery floor, when she found that her rag doll, her favourite toy at present, had unaccountably been left some feet away on a blanket. Instead of crying and calling, she simply leaned forward and tugged the blanket towards her until Dollie was within reach. She has twice pulled herself up to stand, and even let go of the table leg to reach for my hand! And when I left today, she waved me goodbye quite imperiously.'

That Augusta was capable of so doing Murray knew: he had received the same imperious wave himself when he had dragged himself away from her a week ago. He bit his lip.

'Her teeth (none new since you left) are causing her little

trouble and she is sleeping very well, though yesterday when the maid awoke she reports that Madam was lying quite happily awake in her cradle, lifting the sheets and peering at the underside of them, then laying them flat to study the upper side, as if making a comparison of them. She has great curiosity, and has enjoyed some time in the garden in the last couple of days when the sunshine has been very pleasant, encountering flowers and insects. Her appetite continues exceeding healthy and indeed she often tries to feed herself, though the result is not always pretty!'

He laid down the letter and closed his eyes, happily picturing his daughter. He wondered when he should look out for Mrs. Helliwell's next letter. It was quiet in the manse before breakfast, but he had to be careful. He roused himself to fold and put away this letter before his friend Coulter might appear. He did not want to cause any upset, when he was supposed to be here to soothe and comfort.

The letter safely in his coat pocket, he turned on the windowseat to see what the morning was to bring. It was a pleasant spring day here, too: the little front garden of the manse was bright with flowers, and from here, somewhat higher than the rest of the village, he could see the luscious blue of Loch Ryan beyond, the sun making the well-kept white of the village cottages dazzle against it. Fishing boats dotted the water, and he could see figures by the shore, too, perhaps gathering seaweed. He had not been here long: did they work kelp here? The west coast of Scotland was not familiar to him at all, he thought, but at least the workings of church and manse were much the same as on the east coast of his birth. The kirkyard beyond the manse wall to one side was rich and green: a new grave near the kirk door was already beginning to vanish under thick grass. Perhaps that would ease Coulter's pain, though to have one's dearest ones buried just at one's own place of work could not be pleasant.

Along the road came, slowly, five or six young men with packs on their backs and an air of youthful respectability about them. He watched them as they seemed to be setting out from a cottage not far away, settling their packs and arranging their cloaks. Could they be students? It was a long way from Glasgow, which would be the nearest university. And where could they be walking to from here? As he let his eyes follow them lazily along the road, they were joined by a couple more of the same type, with a moment's greeting, then they quickly found a steady stride and soon disappeared, along the road that led, so Murray believed, to Stranraer.

'Good morning, Murray,' came a voice from the parlour doorway, and he jumped up.

'Good morning, Coulter. I hope you slept well?'

He regretted the words as soon as he had said them, for Coulter looked like a wrung-out dishclout that had happened to remember to dress and brush its hair.

'Alas, no,' said Coulter shortly. 'Have you breakfasted?'

'Not yet.'

Coulter rang the bell.

'I hope I haven't kept you waiting.' He drew a heavy breath, and sat hard on a chair at the parlour table, which had been laid for breakfast. He pushed away the cutlery, making room for his elbows, and sank his face in his hands.

'Bad dreams again?' Murray asked, with slightly reluctant sympathy.

'No, no!' Coulter stared at the table. 'Good dreams. Lovely dreams. In my dreams, Bessie is still alive, and sometimes even the child lives. But then I wake, cast out, back to the darkness of the real world. *You* know,' he said, meeting Murray's eye with his own drooping gaze.

Murray nodded slowly, thinking that he did, but perhaps not quite in the way that Coulter thought. There were sometimes dreams about someone who had died, who he had rather had lived, but they were fading. She was years dead now, and far away, though he had cared for her so very much. There were other dreams, too, not so pleasant, in which he thought his dead wife was still alive. He was usually very glad to wake from those.

'Well …' he began, trying to find something both honest and useful. At that instant, though, the door opened and Mrs. Veitch came in with the breakfast, appraising Coulter's haggard appearance with one practised glance as she laid the hot dishes out.

'I'll bring the chocolate,' she added, with a kind of defiant curtsey.

'No, no, Mrs. Veitch, no chocolate!' Coulter protested, but she was already away and returned in a moment with the chocolate pot.

'And may it please you, sir,' she added to Murray, 'see he gets a good cup of it down him, the state he's in the morn.' The curtsey was repeated, and she vanished.

'Well,' said Murray, 'you'd better drink it, or you'll be responsible for whatever consequences come upon me for not making sure you do.'

Coulter shuddered, but he sipped at the sweet cupful and gradually seemed to become a little more human. Murray let him come to himself with only a few unchallenging remarks about the weather, then asked,

'What are your plans for the day, then?'

'I had thought,' said Coulter, 'to go into Stranraer and carry on some of my work amongst the poor there, but I hear there are some sick parishioners who require visits here, so I shall stay and do that. And I have a talk to write, or to think about writing, and perhaps some reading to do for that.'

Murray had been there for three days: each day Coulter had expressed an intention to go into Stranraer and yet he had always found some excuse not to. Murray was beginning to wonder if Coulter would ever leave the village again, or if perhaps Stranraer was mythical and not real at all.

'What do you intend to talk about? And to whom?' he asked, leaving his doubts of Stranraer to one side.

'They prefer a science subject, generally,' said Coulter. 'We have in the village a species of mutual improvement society, which the tradesmen have started with the laird's encouragement. And mine, indeed, for they cannot better themselves and their families without education, and the parish school, competent though it is, can only take them so far.'

'So what do they do, this mutual improvement society?'

'They meet once a week, on a Saturday evening, and give little talks about their mineral collections, or their observations of the weather or of animals. Sometimes someone will talk about a book they've read, or about some current matter abroad if they have read about it in the newspapers. The laird gives them his newspaper when he's finished with it, of course, so they can all have a look at that. Sometimes they even perform little experiments and make notes on them: again the laird is happy to purchase or donate odd pieces of equipment from his own extensive collection, and between them they are rather good at knocking up whatever they need. Of course they are restricted in financial terms, but there is little now that restricts their imagination.'

'And on what are you to talk to them?' Murray was thrilled to find this topic: it was the first that Coulter had embarked upon with anything like enthusiasm since he had arrived.

'Um, well, I have been reading about optics in the *Encyclopaedia Britannica*, and David Brewster seems to be making interesting progress on those lines …'

'I see.' Murray reflected for a moment. 'You weren't that interested in natural philosophy at university, as I recall?'

Coulter blushed.

'No, not at all. But in the country of the blind …'

'The one-eyed man knows more about optics. Well, good luck!'

'Thank you – I may need it!' The forgotten shadow of a smile nipped across his face, as if afraid to be caught there. Murray grinned at him, hoping to encourage it.

'It's a grand thing to have in a village,' he went on. 'I'd like to see them, if I may, so as to learn more about it for starting something similar in Letho.'

'The education of the poorer classes is always in need of improvement,' Coulter agreed, earnestly.

'The education of the richer classes is often wanting, too,' said Murray, 'though for different reasons. Where do they meet?'

'In the schoolroom. They have a kist there with all their equipment in it, and a shelf for their books. I say the tradesmen started it, but there are few of them in a village this size and so they have started to bring in some of the farmers. That can only be to the benefit of all, for there are so many so-called improvements in farming these days that it is better to have the farmers educated so that they can assess which improvements are genuine and which are quackery.'

'That would be extremely useful,' Murray agreed, thinking of the improvement works on his own estate. His little black cattle seemed like toys beside the big Galloway creatures he had seen here, but he had seen no sheep yet at all. It was almost like visiting a different country.

'Well, they will be meeting on Saturday as usual, and the laird and I frequently attend even when we are not called upon to speak. I shall take you to see them, if you wish.'

Chapter Two

Coulter had vanished into his study after a sketchy breakfast, leaving Murray to read and to answer his letters in his own room. In the afternoon, Coulter went out to visit his sick parishioners, while Murray sat in the parlour twiddling his thumbs and wondering when he could reasonably go home to Fife.

Coulter's wife had died in childbirth, along with their son, a month ago. Through some mysterious web of communication across North Britain, Murray's minister in Letho, Mr. Helliwell, had reported to Coulter (once his own assistant at Letho) that Murray himself had lost his wife the previous autumn, in similar circumstances – although Murray's child lived. Coulter had been at St. Andrews University at the same time as Murray, and though they had known each other only slightly Mr. Helliwell had found it sufficient grounds to arrange an invitation for Murray to the little village of Kirkwelland. Mr. Helliwell had taken Murray aside before he answered the invitation to explain that Coulter had taken his losses particularly badly, and some concern had been expressed in the presbytery over his health. Murray, briefly and awfully imagining life without little Augusta, had agreed to accept, but in the three days he had been there he had no feeling of progress or any idea as to how to proceed to achieve any. Coulter seemed to have little will to recover.

His mention at breakfast of the local mutual improvement society had been Murray's first glint of hope, the first interest in anything beyond basic duties that Coulter had shown. Murray was determined to follow it up. He decided, for want of any other way of doing so, to take a walk into the village on this beautiful spring morning and see if he could make contact with anyone who

21

belonged to the society with a view to being mutually improved.

He ventured to the back of the house to find his servant, Walter. Walter, a lad of twelve or thirteen with a nut-shaped cap of hair clamped to his head and a serious expression, was thoughtfully consuming a bannock when Murray knocked and put his head round the kitchen door, enjoying the freedom of not having to make a formal call to the servants' quarters.

'Oh, Mr. Murray, what is your will?' asked Mrs. Veitch easily, then turned anxious. 'It's not the minister, is it?'

'No, he's out, visiting the sick,' Murray reassured her. 'I'm off out for a walk myself, so I'm seeking Walter.'

'Aye, sir,' said Walter, who had risen from his stool at Murray's arrival. He brushed the bannock crumbs off his livery coat and presented himself for duty, receiving with aplomb the pat on the head and fond glance given by Mrs. Veitch as he passed.

'There's a lad who likes his food,' she said with approval.

'How are you finding the quarters, Walter?' Murray asked as they walked down to the bulk of the village by the shore. In truth there was not much to look at: a few boats pulled up on the pebbly beach, more out in the bay, and a dozen or two small white cottages with only five or six buildings of more substance amongst them. Behind the village, beyond the kirk and manse, small fields were dragged from between boulders and gorse, flung against the hillside. The breeze whipped off the bay and washed them in a bracing bath of salt and fish.

'The bed's lumpy but the food is grand, sir,' said Walter after some thought.

'That sounds fair.'

'It's no bad for a wee while,' Walter agreed. 'But foreign travel aye has its drawbacks.' Walter had once been to Edinburgh, and considered that to have been quite far enough.

'At least there's not much of a town for you to lose yourself in, here.'

'But all the houses look the same,' Walter complained. His sense of direction was well known for its complete absence.

The main street, such as it was, formed part of the road to Stranraer, so at least it was broad and well maintained. There was no inn, but there was a small premises which sold, apparently, a considered selection of anything one could not be bothered to travel to Stranraer for and in addition served as an office for the local carrier. Next to it was the school and schoolhouse, the former the meeting place for the mutual improvement society and storage site for their equipment. Murray was intrigued to see what they might have collected and fashioned for their use, but did not feel he could simply march into the schoolroom on a Wednesday morning and investigate.

He and Walter wandered to the south end of the village, where a few passersby nodded a greeting uncuriously. They smelled before they found it a busy tanner's yard at the foot of the Welland burn there. The burn's water, sparkling where the reedwarblers croaked further upstream, was here diverted to fill a number of pools, fresh, salty, or brown-black with dung, surrounded by hefty wooden frames where the hides would drain and be worked. Walter watched intrigued for a few minutes, hand over his face, while a massive cow's hide, peat-brown from its soaking, was swiftly stripped of its coarse hairs. Murray thought the tanner might have been capable of mutual improvement, but did not fancy approaching him through the dark fluids of his trade. He turned back towards the north.

The north end of the village was the more prosperous, and here the few greetings came with more reserve. However, outside a pleasant rendered house with railings to its front garden he saw Coulter, paused in the roadway to talk with a plump little woman at the gate, and two figures on horseback, a middle-aged gentleman and a younger lady, sitting a neat sidesaddle. Murray approached and removed his hat, bowing to Coulter who nodded back.

'May I present my friend from Fife, Charles Murray of Letho? Mrs. Black, the widow of our late doctor,' he gestured to the plump woman, 'and Miss Herkless, and Mr. Herkless of Kirkwelland, the laird.'

Murray bowed, Mrs. Black curtseyed, and the Herklesses dipped their heads in greeting. Herkless was a handsome man, well turned out with boots buffed to a particularly enviable chestnut polish. His hair and whiskers were crisply curled and sandy, his face long and bony, and his voice a pleasant, very slightly drawling baritone.

'Welcome to our village, Mr. Murray. I hope we shall see you up at the house in the course of your visit to the manse?'

'Very kind of you, sir,' said Murray.

'Oh, yes, that would be very good of you! We love having visitors!' added Miss Herkless, and Murray, for whom she had been a shadow against the morning sun, turned a little to see her better.

He was very glad he had.

She had eschewed her father's sandy hair for shining black curls and deep blue eyes, with a narrow, elfin face and high cheekbones. The sea breeze had brought a healthy glow to her cheeks and lips as she smiled down at him. He could not resist smiling back, and hoping really quite hard that Coulter would accept such an invitation if it came.

'And what brings you to stay in Kirkwelland?' asked Mrs. Black briskly, breaking into his brief dwam.

'Coulter and I were acquainted at St. Andrews University, Mrs. Black, and he very kindly asked me to visit him and benefit from a few weeks on the coast of this lovely bay,' said Murray. Mrs. Black, whose hair was dark but rigorously straight under its lace cap, nodded approval, though she exchanged a look with the Herklesses, too.

'It is indeed a healthy place: my late husband always said so,' she agreed.

'Not the ideal home, then, for a medical professional?' suggested Herkless with sardonic eyebrows. Mrs. Black blushed.

'Physicians are always of use, even in healthy places!' she said quickly, with a wave of her finger. 'The best air in the world cannot set a broken leg, Mr. Herkless!' She gave him a teasing smile. She was certainly a good enough advertisement for the air herself, with a shining face and clear eyes and her fair share of the stoutness that comes with a few decades of good food.

'Now, now, Father, do not quarrel!' said Miss Herkless, well used to laughing with him. 'Let us make an engagement with these gentlemen before they escape. Mr. Murray, Mr. Coulter, are you free this evening? Could I tempt you to supper at Kirkwelland House?'

With that smile, she could have tempted him to fire and brimstone at Kirkwelland House, thought Murray, but he turned politely to his host for Coulter's response. Unsmiling, Coulter bowed.

'That would be delightful, I'm sure,' he said, unconvincingly, but it was acceptance.

'Mrs. Black, I include you in the invitation, of course,' said Miss Herkless smoothly. 'Do come, won't you?'

'I'd be delighted, Kitty! I shall bring some of my sweetmeats.'

Kitty, thought Murray. Catherine, presumably. A pretty name, and it suited her well.

'Till this evening, then, gentlemen,' said Herkless, putting his heels to his horse. 'Come along, Kitty: I want to see what's happening along the shore.'

Murray watched them go, until Mrs. Black said, a little sharply,

'A bonny girl, is she not?'

'I was rather envying her father's horse,' said Murray a little too readily. 'I have left my horses at home, coming here by postchaise, and miss the exercise.'

'He'll no doubt lend you something if you ask him,' said Mrs. Black. 'He's the most generous of men.'

'And he has a fine stable, not like mine,' added Coulter, miserably.

'I didn't mean to criticise,' said Murray. 'It was a moment's thought, that's all.' It was true, though, that he had come by post knowing that Coulter had nowhere for him to put his own carriage and horses. It had felt curiously liberating, but now he did miss them.

'Well, I must get on with my letters, Mr. Coulter, Mr. Murray, and look forward to becoming better acquainted with you this evening. Adieu!' she said winningly, and retreated to her own front door with a little wave of her hand.

'Your society seems charming,' said Murray when she had gone.

'It's a little limited,' Coulter admitted. 'You've met two thirds of it already, I believe. And that includes me in it.'

'No wonder they were so quick with an invitation, then,' said Murray. 'Are you busy? Am I keeping you back from your visiting?'

'There's no hurry,' said Coulter, and stood there as if uncertain where to go next.

'I came into the village in the hope of meeting one of your mutual improvement society, though I confess I have no idea where to find them. Your description of them intrigued me.'

It worked again: Coulter's eyes took on a little lift, and he straightened his shoulders and pulled out his watch.

'No doubt we could call in on John Innes, the shoemaker,' he said. 'He's back up nearer the manse.'

'I don't want to take you back out of your way,' said Murray, though he very much did if it was going to do Coulter any good.

'Not at all, not at all.' He led Murray and Walter up a little muddy lane that served as a short cut from the north end of the village back towards the manse on its slight rise. Cottages lined it, but set a little apart from each other, and Coulter took them past nearly all of them until they reached the corner of the lane, where it became the road down which Murray had seen the strange walkers that morning. At the corner, Coulter paused.

'This is his house here,' he said, pointing to the one on the inside corner and reaching in the same gesture for the risp by the door. A sound from the other side of the lane made him turn. 'Oh, but there he is.'

John Innes, if it were he, was emerging from a cottage door on the outside corner of the lane, still talking to someone within. He was tallish, with a hunch which at least enabled him to clear the low doorway relatively easily, and he seemed to have been disturbed in his work for he wore a well-fitted leather apron over his shirt, waistcoat and breeches, and no coat.

'Aye, you'll be fine the now,' he was saying, and was answered by a grumble from inside the cottage. 'You'd no feel them if there was something outside you were keen to see, would you? You'd be out there gawking and never a mind for your poor old legs.'

'You could bring me a pinch of tobacco if you were a Christian,' whined the voice from within, more clearly now. A shuffling was audible: the occupant must have put his poor old legs to work.

'If you were a Christian you'd pay me for all the other pinches of tobacco I'd brought you, you scourie oul coof,' said Innes.

'You ungrateful wee skite,' replied the inhabitant of the cottage, who now reached the door to reveal himself as an unshaven, unsavoury elderly man with a stick. 'After all I've done for you over the years …'

'Dinna give me that,' retorted Innes. 'The only good thing you ever gave me was your daughter, and the more I look at you the more I think she was never your daughter at all.'

'Would you besmirch her mother's good name?' demanded the old man querulously.

'You've never been too slow to besmirch it yourself. And anyway, I'd think it a tribute to her mother's good name that she had the wit to bear no child to you!'

'Ye filthy-mouthed – oh, minister, is it yourself?'

A nasty yellow smile spread over the old man's face, as his son-in-law Innes spun round and gaped at the minister and the gentleman behind him.

'You'll have to forgive Mr. Innes here,' said the old man greasily. 'It's an awfu' shame, but he canna seem to help being an ill-mannered clyte. I think his mother must have dropped him on his heid when he was a wean.'

'I beg pardon, minister,' said Innes, who seemed to have been carrying out a quick review of what the minister might have overheard. 'Were you waiting to see me?'

'If we could have a word, please, John,' said Coulter, a little coldly. Innes turned his back on his father-in-law and guided Coulter and Murray into his cottage, while the old man stood easy in his cottage door, still grinning, and eyeing Murray and Coulter with deep interest. Murray did not care much for his expression.

'I'm sorry, gentlemen,' said Innes again when they were inside with the door shut. The cottage smelled sweetly of new leather, and there were signs of his work everywhere in the front room. The kitchen appeared, wisely, to be separate, but a woman with neat brown hair under a clean white cap poked her head around the door and then hurried forward to greet the minister.

'Mr. Coulter, sir,' she said with a decent curtsey, 'what can we do for you?'

'The gentlemen caught me coming out of your father's cottage,' said Innes contritely. She evidently knew exactly what to read into this.

'And what kind of language were you using this time, John Innes?'

'Not the best, Maggie, not the best.'

'I'm gey sorry, Mr. Coulter,' said Maggie Innes to the minister, 'but you ken well what my faither's like. He would drive the Moderator of the General Assembly himself into a temper, and John's only human.'

Murray felt his lips twitch, and thought he saw Coulter's face twist a little, too.

'Nonetheless,' Coulter knew what was expected of him, 'you should moderate your language, particularly in the street. You know that you are in a position to set an example to the weaker members of the community. But remember, too, that God hears you whether you are in the street or not, and will judge according to your behaviour – and your heart.'

John Innes looked suitably apologetic, a look which his hunched shoulders only emphasised.

'Right,' said Coulter, duty done. 'This here's Mr. Murray of Letho, come all the way from Fife to visit us here, and I've been telling him about your mutual improvement society.'

'It sounds very much like the kind of thing I should like to help set up in my own village,' said Murray. 'I understand you find it quite valuable.'

Just like Coulter, Innes' eyes had lit up at the first mention of the society, and he glanced at his wife again now with greater assurance.

'Oh, aye, sir, it's a grand thing!'

'And what do you do at your meetings? I gather you meet weekly?'

'We do, sir, aye. On a Saturday night at the schoolroom. Well, sir, it's hard to tell sometimes what we do for there are a few of us and whiles we do different things altogether. See, I like to keep a wee log of the weather. Would you be at all interested in seeing it?' His shoulders hunched slightly again, wary of plying this stranger too much with his own enthusiasm.

'I should like to see it very much, if I may,' said Murray. Without further encouragement, Innes whipped a leather notebook off the mantelpiece and handed it to him. Inside were pages dedicated to temperature, wind strength and direction, remarks on rain or snow, and descriptions of clouds, all laboriously laid out in careful ink.

'I been keeping it a year now, and that makes it even more interesting because you can go back a year, see?' he reached out a shy finger and flicked the pages, 'and see what the weather was doing this exact time last year.'

'Fascinating,' said Murray. 'And you have a thermometer, then?'

'The laird gived me one,' said Innes, in awe. 'I'm gey careful with it and all. Maggie here reads off the wee figures, and I write it all down. And Raffan the smith, he made me a wee flap thing to work out the wind speed, with numbers marked on it so I know if it's one, or two, or three, or more, and of course I can say the direction too. And I have a bucket at the back for the rain.'

'This is all very impressive,' said Murray, and meant it: at very little outlay except in terms of dedication to his science, the shoemaker had made some very thorough observations. 'And what do the others do?'

'Well, we've a couple that like rocks. Geology, they cry it, no? And one body who's a farmer, he's just joined us, and he's comparing the soil on all different parts of his farm and how the crops grow in each place. And Rab Smith, he's interested in seaweed, and his brother Dod likes fish – well, he's a fisherman, but even so. And then the minister here or the laird will come and give us a wee talk now and again, and we learn something new again.' He nodded acknowledgement to Coulter. 'Once even one of yon students frae Glasgow has stopped and given us a wee word or two, and it's all grand, all new information for us, ken, sir?'

'Indeed: it all sounds excellent. May I attend your next meeting? Would my presence be inconvenient at all?'

'You'd be gey welcome, sir,' said Innes at once. 'We're proud to welcome anyone who is informed or interested in being informed.'

'And the bannocks are fine, too,' added his wife, with a little smile.

'I hope you weren't offended by that,' said Coulter as they walked back down the lane, a sideways anxious glance at Murray.

'Offended? I've heard worse language,' said Murray, more amused than anything.

'No, not his language – though his wife's right, old Newell

would drive anyone to an early grave. He's a nasty piece of work. No, I meant Innes' rather grand invitation to you. You didn't take ill his manners?'

'Not at all!' said Murray. 'I as good as invited myself to his meeting, and he was very polite.'

'Good, good.' Coulter seemed to be slipping back into his doldrums, and Murray hurried to snatch him up again.

'I'm impressed with his weather diary. What a deal of work to put into it!'

'It's a fine thing,' agreed Coulter. 'He's very proud of it, and rightly so. And the fact that the laird gave him an old thermometer was nearly the end of him. Did you see it pinned up by his front door, there for all the street to read? I daren't tell him, but Herkless has a new barometer coming from London, and he plans to give the old one to the society. Herkless is nearly as interested in science as Innes is: he has a microscope and a telescope at the big house. No doubt he'll be more than ready to show them to you.'

'I've seen several telescopes, but rarely a microscope,' said Murray thoughtfully. Kirkwelland House seemed full of delights.

'He has brought them down in the past to show the mutual improvement society. John Innes was particularly enthusiastic about them.'

'Then they are very lucky to have each other as neighbours,' said Murray. 'It seems to me to be a splendid idea in any village, and to have the laird and the minister so closely involved, too, must only encourage it.'

They had returned to the main street, and paused together, each waiting to see where the other was going and how soon they would break away. Coulter presumably had calls to make on his sickly parishioners, but Murray, outside his task of trying to cheer his old acquaintance, had nothing to hand to occupy him until dinner time, certainly not without a horse.

'How do you feel about a little stroll along the shore, Walter?' he asked. Coulter seemed relieved.

'And I must away and pay my visits. I shall see you back at the manse for dinner, shall I?'

'Of course.' They bowed, and Coulter hurried away, probably as relieved to be spared the effort of being cheered as Murray was of cheering. Murray guided Walter towards a lane that led seawards, but as they reached it they met four young men, footsore and weighed down with their packs, pacing steadily into the village. Immediately he remembered the young men he had seen that morning: these seemed to be very much of the same type.

'Excuse me,' he said, curiosity defeating him as one approached with ginger hair and a friendly look about him, 'may I ask whither you are bound, and from where?'

The ginger-haired man blinked and smiled.

'Aye, surely you can, sir, though it's well seen you're a stranger in these parts or you'd likely know already what we're doing here. We're students from the college in Glasgow, heading home for the summer.'

'Heading home to where?' asked Murray. He was not sure he had heard the man's accent before.

'To Ireland, sir. By way of a boat at Portpatrick.'

'Oh, of course! A long walk, then.'

'Long enough,' said the man with a cheerful smile.

'Too long,' added another, less amiable. 'Longer than any sane man would think necessary.'

'Och, now, Nugent! We'll catch up on ourselves the morrow. Never you mind him, sir, he was born sour.'

'But if you'll excuse us, sir,' said another of them, one with a long, ill-looking face, 'we must go to see if our usual stopping-place is still available. My friend here is weary from the walk and not as well as he might be.' Indeed the tallest of them, a freckle-faced lad, had not spoken and seemed to weave on his feet. The first man he had spoken to stepped quickly to his side, and supported him with a hand under his arm, though he had to reach up a little to do it.

'Are you going far? Can I help at all?' asked Murray. The surly one had made no effort to help the tall one, and the long-faced fellow did not seem strong enough to be of any use. The first student seemed to come to the same conclusion.

'Aye, that'd be great, so it would. If you could get round the other side of him, sir, and hold his arm like this. It's being so tall, you see – I think he outgrew his own strength.'

'Where are we taking him?' Murray nodded to the student's pack and Walter scooped it up, following in solemn procession.

'Just up this wee lane here: it's the wee house at the top,' said the first man.

With a strange sense of inevitability, Murray realised that the wee house at the top was the cottage where Innes' father-in-law had been so welcoming earlier. He was reluctant to meet the man again, but was saved by the long-faced student turning to him, just short of the cottage.

'Sir, we are more than grateful. My name is James Adair, of County Down and the University of Glasgow. May I know the name of our helper?'

'I am Charles Murray of Letho, in Fife.'

'Then God be with you, sir, you are a kind man.' He bowed with some refinement.

'I'm John McCullough,' said the cheery student, 'and this is Joseph Gibson and Adam Nugent.' The sour-faced man bowed under the weight of his pack. Gibson nodded, his eyes vague.

'I'll wish you a safe and quiet rest, then,' said Murray, seeing that he was no longer needed. Walter set the pack down by the door and folded his hands behind his back, coming to stand just at bidding distance as he did when he wanted to impress.

'And the same to you, sir, the same to you,' the students echoed politely, and watched him as he turned away and descended the lane once again to the main street.

Chapter Three

'There's time, Walter,' said Murray patiently. 'You could have another go.'

'Could you show me again, sir?'

Murray undid the interesting knot in his black neckcloth, and slowly retied it, showing Walter each move as he went. He was used enough to tending to himself in matters of dress, but Walter needed training. Walter watched intently, nodding his shiny head and biting his lips in concentration.

'See?' said Murray.

'Yes, sir, of course. It's easy when you do it, sir.'

'Now,' Murray pulled it loose again, 'your turn.'

Walter took the two ends of the neckcloth, which was beginning to show signs of overuse, and contemplated his first move.

'Sir,' he said, beginning his manoeuvres, 'what happens if I'm never good enough to be a manservant?' Being Walter he asked the question with no apparent anxiety.

'You'll have to run away to sea, Walter.'

He thought about this.

'I dinna think I'd fancy that, sir.'

'No, I suspect it's not your vocation. What would you like to do, Walter, if you had the choice?'

Walter answered without hesitation.

'I'd like fine to be a scientist, sir.'

'A scientist? What makes you say that?' But even as he asked, he remembered Walter's fascination with any scientific exhibit he had ever had the chance to see – there had been a whale in Edinburgh, for example, and even its peculiar aroma had failed to put him off that.

'Yon Mr. Innes today, and all his work,' Walter was saying. 'And Mr. Blair who comes to visit Letho – he has a microscope in his pocket, and he let me look at leaves through it and flies' legs and all sorts.'

'Does he indeed?' asked Murray thoughtfully. His old friend Blair had a knack of finding out the real interests of those around him. In the mirror he watched Walter weaving his neckcloth into another aesthetic disaster. It was true that he was not destined to be a natural manservant, though he was better than he had been.

'It's gone peculiar again, sir,' said Walter, as if the neckcloth had done it deliberately.

'Well, that's probably enough for today, anyway. Run along and wash your face and hands, and be ready to attend us to the big house: I'll see to this.'

Walter left, and Murray shook off the mangled neckcloth and gave it a bit of a stretch to pull it straight. He examined himself in the mirror as he retied it. It was some time since he had gone among so many strangers all at once, and he wondered what they would see – a tall man, certainly, already in his thirties, with long hands and a big nose. That was enough to start with. And he wore mourning, his neckcloth black instead of the usual white he would have worn for a supper engagement, waistcoat black too, with dull buttons. Coulter would be the same. But in Coulter's case the mourning was in his eyes, too. Murray stared into the reflection of his own brown eyes – no, no grief there. He was past even regretting the time he had spent married to Lady Agostinella. He was happy simply to move on, and appreciate the gift of his daughter.

Murray, Coulter and Walter walked from the manse to Kirkwelland House, which snuggled in a nest against the hill north of the village. The approach, up a driveway leafy with trees glowing spring green in the dusk, was easy and well-maintained if not grand, and the house when they saw it was of a piece, a low villa rendered and coloured a reddish ochre, warm and inviting. Small lawns set it off neatly, and a set of shallow steps led to the front door, flung open now to entice them with golden candlelight. Herkless and his daughter had come to the hall to greet them, and as far as Murray was concerned the effect could not have been bettered.

'Welcome!' said Kitty Herkless. 'No cloaks, gentlemen?'

'It's a mild night,' said Murray, handing his hat to the maid.

'I'm led to believe it's an effect called 'spring',' said Herkless, with a smile, 'though I grant we don't see it often in these parts.'

'And I thought the west coast was always like this – I'm gravely disappointed!' said Murray.

'Anyway, it's cool enough down here,' said Kitty, rubbing her bare arms above her long gloves. 'I've left my shawl upstairs in my eagerness to greet you! The least you can do is to hurry back up to the drawing room and the warmth for my sake.'

Laughing (and even Coulter smiled), they followed her up the central staircase to the drawing room on the first floor.

'Here they are – last to arrive just to tantalise us!' announced Kitty. 'Now, you've met Mrs. Black,' she went on, as the doctor's widow stood from her seat by the fire, rosy-cheeked in its warmth, and made her curtsey. 'But here we have some new acquaintances for you, Mr. Murray: this is Mrs. Pringle and her daughter, and here is Mr. Pringle. Mr. Pringle is our local man of law. This is Mr. Murray of Letho, in Fifeshire, I believe you said?'

Murray concurred and bowed. Mrs. Pringle and Miss Pringle curtseyed, and Mr. Pringle, who was on the stout side of handsome, nodded his head, too round, Murray suspected, to make much of a bend any lower. He had an aggressive jaw and favoured longish hair, perhaps feeling his dignity worthy of a wig, had he been an older man. Miss Pringle, who fortunately took after her mother, was a slim girl with a creamy complexion and finely arched eyebrows over pretty blue eyes, but these were as nothing when compared with the glory of her red hair. Murray had never had a prejudice against red hair, but he had met people who did – he suspected that Miss Pringle would override all their hostility with one sweep of her curls. What extraordinary fortune, he thought to himself, to travel so far to such a small village, to spend the evening in the company of two such pretty girls: he wondered if the village had even more of them to offer.

'From Fifeshire, sir?' asked Mrs. Pringle as they all settled themselves down again. 'That is a prodigious long way.'

'It is not too bad on the roads we have these days, madam,' said Murray. 'I came by post and had a tolerable journey.'

'Do you not keep your own carriage, sir?' demanded Mr. Pringle with a curl of one fine nostril. 'I assure you that every gentleman in these parts keeps at least one.'

Murray glimpsed, sideways, Miss Pringle rolling her eyes. Mrs. Pringle nudged her sharply, but her own face was stoney. He stifled a laugh.

'Perhaps Mr. Murray is one of these eccentric gentlemen who intends to write a novel on the condition of the common man,' said Herkless smoothly, 'and is conducting research on the matter. Is that not the case, Mr. Murray?'

'I wish I could say that it was, sir!' said Murray, much amused. 'But I chose not to have the trouble of bringing my own horses and coachman with me for once, and enjoy the liberty of travelling only with a little luggage and one servant. It was quite refreshing.'

'Oh, and of course there is no coach house at the manse,' added Mr. Pringle, slapping his lips together as if the whole situation were most unsatisfactory.

'That is the fault of us heritors, then,' said Herkless, 'for we have not provided one.'

'There is no need, really,' said Coulter hurriedly. 'Please do not trouble on my account. A single stable is plenty for a man who has no horse. I have no need of a carriage.'

'Not at present, perhaps,' said Herkless, 'but you may in the future.'

'Well, no sense building one until it's needed,' said Pringle, 'and leaving it to stand and rot, as no doubt your stable is doing, Mr. Coulter. The sea air, Mr. Murray, is no respecter of buildings.'

'I can imagine.'

'And what like is your estate, Mr. Murray?' Pringle carried on, removing, as he did so, a fragment of dinner from the corner of his lapel. 'You no doubt have a surplus of sheep.'

'Not a surplus, sir, but a good number. More of the pasture land is given over to cattle.'

'To cattle?' Pringle regarded him with small eyes. 'You must be mistaken, sir. There are very few cattle on the east coast.'

'We are greatly blessed, Mr. Murray, as you can see, to have such an agricultural authority as Mr. Pringle in our midst,' Herkless remarked. Murray glanced at him, but he was entirely straight-faced – perhaps too much so. 'Perhaps you have mistaken your sheep for very small cattle?'

'Certainly they are smaller than your cattle here in the west, but I believe I'm right in saying that much of the land of my estate is taken up with cattle,' said Murray carefully, not quite used to being so summarily contradicted about his own business.

'Indeed our cattle are unusually large,' agreed Herkless, nodding solemnly. 'I have heard that the same breed is used in India, but there goes under the name of 'elephant'. A man used to these would have difficulty in distinguishing any normal size of cow, I should think.'

This time there was a definite twinkle in his eye, though Pringle remained completely solemn. Murray realised that he himself was not the one being teased here.

'The contrast is certainly striking,' Murray agreed, with a smile, 'and I speak as one who has ridden an elephant – for rather longer than I wished, as I recall.'

'You have been to India, Mr. Murray?' Kitty Herkless leaned forward in her chair in excitement.

'I have.'

'You see, I knew you would bring us all kinds of exotic entertainment! India! Good gracious!'

'And what was your business there?' asked Mr. Pringle sharply.

'I was visiting an acquaintance,' said Murray.

'An acquaintance of some standing, then,' Mr. Pringle remarked. Murray ignored what seemed to be some kind of insinuation of immorality in his tone. 'The country is entirely hazardous, with heat and disease and violence of all kinds.'

'It was a fascinating country, though I did not enjoy the voyage there and back overmuch.'

'Not a good seafarer, then,' said Pringle with satisfaction. 'You would have found that a steady consumption of brandy and eggs would have settled your stomach, for a certainty. It is infallible.'

'I had not realised, sir, that I was in the presence of an experienced traveller.' Murray bowed his head.

'Oh, yes, I believe that Mr. Pringle has been twice to Glasgow!' said Herkless.

'I have.' Pringle nodded with dignity. 'Once in the winter.'

'Not the happiest of times to travel, perhaps?' Murray

suggested politely.

'It was a matter of great urgency – a business matter.' Pringle was stately. 'And preparation is the key in all these things. I can tell you that I know exactly how to travel, in any conditions. Any Wigtownshire gentleman does.'

'Mr. Murray,' said Miss Herkless with a bright smile, 'I wish to play the piano. Would you be so good as to come and turn the pages for me?'

'Of course.'

The pianoforte stood in the corner, and Miss Herkless quickly settled herself behind it, showing Murray where he should stand. They were at a little distance from the others, and under the cover of sorting through a few music books, Miss Herkless murmured,

'I beg you will not think his remarks personal. He is perfectly odious to everyone.'

'I shall be guided by you, of course,' said Murray politely. In fact he had found Mr. Pringle amusing so far, but he was sure that a little of his conversation would go a long way.

'Here: plenty of pages to turn on this one, back and forth for the repeats, too. Are you musical, Mr. Murray?'

'I like music – and can follow the odd repeat,' he assured her with a smile.

'Then let us test you,' she said brightly, and began to play.

She was indeed accomplished, and if Murray almost missed a page turn it was only because he had not heard such good playing for months. She played with a light touch and a sympathetic air that made her seem at one with the music: the few minutes the piece lasted were a delight. At the end, everyone applauded, and she rose and made a little bow.

'Now, Anna,' she said, and Miss Pringle took her turn. Murray stayed on out of courtesy to turn the pages again, while Mr. Pringle glowered at him across the room as if suspecting him of impropriety behind the piano. Miss Pringle's playing was pleasant enough, though her hands were too small to stretch far and she sang a little sharp. Murray was quite prepared to enjoy it, too, so he smiled at Mr. Pringle and then focussed on the music.

After Miss Pringle, there was a little pause, before Kitty and Mr. Herkless spoke at once.

'Mrs. Black, will you play?' asked Kitty, just as her father was leaning over to usher Mrs. Pringle to the piano. Mrs. Black was already on her feet, but stepping back uncertainly.

'No, no,' said Mrs. Pringle with a sweet smile. 'After you, dear Mrs. Black.'

'If you are sure?' Mrs. Black teetered on the spot.

'Absolutely. I have no intention of playing this evening,' said Mrs. Pringle. Mrs. Black shot her a look like a dagger, but took her chance and hurried to the piano.

'Though I have scarcely played since my marriage,' she began excusing herself before she had even sat down. 'Mr. Murray, I declare you must be exhausted, and you will want to escort Miss Pringle to her seat. Dear Mr. Herkless, I fear you must supply the place!'

'Of course, madam,' said Herkless, though his smile was a little twisted, Murray thought. He did as he had been bid and took Miss Pringle back to sit by her mother on the sopha, then returned to sit beside Coulter.

Mrs. Black also sang, and her playing showed no sign of rustiness. Either her marriage had been remarkably short, or she had indeed been practising. Her black mourning suited her well, and she had a touch of white in her cap and at her neck, which set off her rosy complexion and black hair very prettily. If she was flirting with Herkless, she was at least off to a good start, Murray thought, watching her glance up at him as she sang.

There was no dancing, in deference, Murray suspected, to the fact that three of the party were in mourning. He regretted it, but dwelt for a little on the idea of dancing with either Miss Pringle or Miss Herkless, a pleasant reflection. When Mrs. Black had played, Miss Herkless rang for supper and the company once again turned to conversation, which carried on seamlessly after they had eaten: Mr. Herkless drew Mr. Pringle over to examine some old book he drew out from a selection about the room. Coulter was drawn into a discussion with Mrs. Black and Miss Herkless concerning the provision of some charitable supplies. Murray leaned towards the Pringle ladies and subjected himself to a series of questions about Fife and his family which held little remarkable in it, but was nevertheless pleasant. As the night drew on, Miss Herkless rang the bell again and herself served rum punch to the company, curtseying with a laugh as she did so. It was as delightful an evening, notwithstanding Mr. Pringle, as Murray had spent for a long time.

He woke next day with a smile on his face, after a good night's sleep, and stretched his rested limbs comfortably. It was later than he would usually rise and he felt the benefit, for once, leaving it another few minutes before he rang for Walter.

No letter had arrived from Mrs. Helliwell that morning, but he reassured himself that she would have sent an express if anything was amiss. When he had breakfasted – alone, for Coulter had already retired to his study for whatever lonely meditations he indulged in – he stayed in the parlour with its interesting view down to the village and wrote to his daughter (nonsense, he would be the first to admit). Then he availed himself of an interesting looking book, stretched his legs out towards the fire, and wallowed luxuriously in reading for the rest of the morning.

Coulter had not made an appearance by the afternoon and when Murray enquired of Mrs. Veitch he discovered that his host had gone out at some point without seeking him out. Murray decided he needed at least some exercise, put away his book and called for his hat and gloves. That his feet led him up towards the north of the town was surely a coincidence, but he felt that should he happen to meet Kitty Herkless – or even Miss Anna Pringle – neither encounter would be unpleasant.

However, in this hope he was to be disappointed. He strolled past the smarter houses but not even Mrs. Black appeared to while away a few minutes with him, and he found himself without distraction, leaving the north end of the town on the road, presumably, to Cairnryan and other coastal villages. The road was fair in itself, being the toll road from Glasgow to Portpatrick, but it rose steeply out of the little Kirkwelland Bay on to the headland, taking off abruptly like a startled blackbird. He enjoyed feeling the backs of his legs working hard up the hill, and when he reached the top he was glad enough to pause by the side of the road and enjoy the view of the bay and the village below him. Further around the headland was light woodland, but here there were only gorse and boulders, and he propped himself against a warm rock to take in the spring sunshine. Below to his left he could see the tide was well out, the muddy foreshore littered with seabirds: he picked out curlews with their curving beaks, noisy oystercatchers, and wigeons feeding where patches of eel grass spread uninvitingly. Above him terns wheeled, busy in the bright sky, weaving him into a waking doze. When ten minutes later or so he heard footsteps behind him, it took him a moment to clear his vision and see who was passing. It was one of the students he had met yesterday, the tall, dark one with the pale face.

'Oh, Mr. Murray!' said the man, with a loose bow.

'Mr. Adair, wasn't it?' He returned the bow.

'A beautiful day, is it not?' said Adair. 'I find this coastline particularly charming.'

'I take it you're familiar with it, if you have been travelling back and forth to Glasgow. It is my first visit, and I'm very impressed.'

'Oh, yes, up and down for years!' Adair grinned. His eyes were dark brown and kindly, though his face looked old, for a student.

'How long do you plan to stay here on your way?'

'Ah.' Adair's smile slid away. 'That is a moot point. One of our number is not at his best today – the man you helped yesterday, Gibson - so we are to wait until tomorrow to continue. Usually we prefer to stay only one night, particularly here.' He tailed off thoughtfully.

'Particularly here?' Murray's curiosity was aroused.

'Oh!' Adair shook himself. 'Well, it's so near to Portpatrick that we are eager to get on and find a boat.'

'Surely it's another two days or more from here?'

'Yes, yes, but when you've walked from Glasgow ...' He smiled again, lopsidedly, not sure he was convincing. Murray decided to leave it.

'It's a long way to walk, anyway,' he said. 'I thought there was a college in Ireland? In Dublin? Would it not be easier to go there?'

Adair settled himself against the boulder next to Murray and blinked into the sunshine.

'Well, aye, there is. There's Trinity College, but to study there you have to be Anglican – Church of Ireland, the Episcopalians, you know? And we're all Presbyterians. And we want to be ordained, and so we have to have a few terms at a Scottish college or one in the Low Countries before we'll be considered.'

'Just a few terms? Not a degree?'

'No.' Adair shrugged. 'Standards are a wee bit low at the minute. We're lucky, the four of us: we've all graduated now, but we're the rare ones. In a few years things might be different, for there's a new college set up in Belfast, but it's hardly even started yet and well, we had three years under our belts already in Glasgow.' He stopped, and squinted down the hill. 'Oh, aye, there's Gibson, sitting on a rock down on the beach.'

Murray looked where he gestured, and saw a bare-headed but well-happed-up figure perched on a boulder down on the shoreline, staring out to sea.

'If he's ill, why is he not resting at your lodgings?'

Adair laughed briefly.

'Our landlord was going out, and did not want any of us in the house while he was out. Besides, I think we all wanted a bit of fresh air. And anyway, when Gibson's not – himself – it's usually best if he goes out somewhere and just sits quiet for a wee bit.'

'Is it something he can take something for? Does he need medication?'

'No, no. He's just – he's just a bit closer to Heaven than the rest of us,' said Adair obscurely. 'Well, I'll take up no more of your time, Mr. Murray: I'm just dandering up the road a wee bit, not far and then back again. I'll leave you to your fine view.'

He bowed and meandered on to the north of the headland, into the trees and out of sight. It occurred to Murray to wonder why someone who had walked all the way from Glasgow and still had two days' walk to go should walk for recreation, but then, perhaps it was a relief simply not to walk with his pack.

He pushed himself away from his rock, and stretched, took off his hat and rubbed his fingers through his hair, then set off back down the hill towards the village. By the time he had once again strolled through the north end he felt he had still not quite had enough air, so he began again down the main street: he glanced up the lane he had visited yesterday, assuring himself that it was the one that led, past Innes' house, to the manse. Though it was no proof, he was reassured to see Coulter up the lane, talking with Herkless who was propped comfortably on his cane, other elbow on his hip, at ease with his minister. Murray smiled at the memory of the previous evening, as he walked the length of the main street, nodding to a few people who had greeted him the day before. Among them were two more of the students, the tubby one and the one with the short temper. He bowed.

'Mr. Murray! Thank you again for your help yesterday!' said the tubby one – McCullough, he had said his name was.

'I am sorry to hear the gentleman in question is still unwell today. I gather you have been detained on your journey?'

'Again!' said the other student. 'This journey is cursed. I should have travelled with some other party.'

'We did say you could go on ahead if you wanted,' said McCullough earnestly. 'If you had left early you might have caught up with the men who left yesterday.'

The other student muttered to himself, and kicked a stone along the road.

'Anyway,' he said, suddenly turning back to them, 'I think we should go back and see if that oul fella has come back home. If we're not there looking at him he'll have every last bit of a thing out of our bags to see if he can find anything he fancies. Or something he can make use of ...' He met McCullough's eye with some meaning Murray missed.

'Aye, well, I suppose so,' said McCullough with a shrug.

'I'm heading back that way myself,' said Murray amiably. 'I'll walk with you, if you don't mind.'

'Oh, aye, by all means!' McCullough managed a smile at him, which Murray felt was genuine. 'You're staying in the village, then, sir?'

'That's right, with the minister.'

'Mr. Coulter? Oh, he's a grand man. He and his wife usually have us for a meal if they know we're coming.'

'His wife died a month ago, in childbirth,' said Murray gently. 'The child was lost, too.'

'Och no! The poor man!' McCullough stopped in his tracks, clearly upset. 'Did you hear that, Ishmael?'

Nugent turned from a few paces ahead of them.

'What now?'

'Yon Mrs. Coulter's with her maker! And a wean with her. We should go and pay our respects. I hadn't done it before now with Gibson not well, but we'll have to go. Imagine that fine woman dead and us none the wiser! That's desperate, so it is.' He lapsed into silence, walking again towards the other end of the village. 'Poor man, poor man,' he murmured eventually, as they turned into the end of their lane.

'We should pick up our decent neckcloths before we go and see him,' said Nugent. 'Even old Newell wouldn't want us going to condole with the minister with these rags on. Come on, let's see if he's back.' Nugent hurried ahead, and McCullough trotted to catch up. Nugent reached the door of the cottage just as McCullough caught him up, Murray a few paces behind. He knocked, then pushed the door open.

'Och, what now!' he shouted, and plunged into the cottage.

'Och no!' McCullough echoed, and vanished after him. Murray reached the door and peered in, his eyes quickly adapting to the dim light inside. 'What's wrong with him?'

Newell, groaning hoarsely, was on the dirt floor, curled up tight and clutching his stomach. His whole body was twitching in a most alarming way.

'I'll fetch his daughter,' said Murray at once, and in two paces was across the lane, hammering on the door of Innes' cottage.

'Who the – ' Innes snatched open the door as if he had been just behind it.

'Mr. Newell has taken ill, sir,' said Murray rapidly. 'Will Mrs. Innes come?'

Mrs. Innes was by the fire with a cloth in her hand, wiping something on the mantelpiece. She shot an anguished look at her husband, seized up her shawl, and came to the door.

'Is he at home, sir?'

'Yes.' Murray crossed back with her. 'The students had just come back, and found him on the floor.'

Nugent and McCullough backed off as Mrs. Innes hurried in and knelt by her father, taking his hand and feeling his forehead in one movement.

'Father! Father! What's wrang with you this time, eh?'

Newell opened his eyes, but they did not seem to focus. His mouth moved and sound came out, but no words were formed.

'Has he had a stroke?' asked McCullough. 'My granny had a stroke,' he explained, as if it had been an odd question.

'It seems the most likely thing.'

'Unless he's drunk,' added Nugent, with less sympathy.

'There's a smell of whisky off him, right enough,' said Mrs. Innes, 'but I've never seen him like this before. Gentlemen, could you help me get him into the bed?'

McCullough darted forward, taking Newell's legs, and after a moment Nugent sighed and took his head.

'You always give me the heavy end,' he muttered at McCullough, who shushed him anxiously. They stood back to make room for Mrs. Innes.

'Is there a doctor I could go for?' asked Murray.

'There's no doctor in the village since Dr. Black died,' she said, trying to pull blankets up around her father's shoulders. He was still shaking, trying to help her with hands that would not work properly. 'Mrs. Black might know something,' she added. She glanced back, and Murray could see fear in her eyes. 'Could you fetch her, please, sir? I don't know who else to ask for this. I don't know what this is.'

'Of course.' Murray turned, but Nugent was there first.

'Let me go, sir: I'm fast, and I know where it is.' He cast a glance back at the bed, as if he was keen to be far from the sights there.

'Of course.' Murray let him past. Nugent vanished down the lane, slamming the door behind him, and a stone whisky flask spun, grating, on the floor as he went.

Chapter Four

The next few hours were chaotic. Newell squirmed and shook on the bed, making appalling noises as he struggled to speak, to grasp at his daughter's sleeve, to scratch, fumbling and useless, at his own skin. McCullough did what he could to help Mrs. Innes as she in turn tried to help her father. Innes himself appeared at the door, ready to quarrel again with his father-in-law only to find him genuinely ill, and retreated, confused. Gibson, the wan student whose illness had delayed them, returned, and finding what was going on fell down on his knees in the middle of the cottage floor and began to pray loudly. Nugent returned with Mrs. Black, plump and self-important at her summons, but she set to quickly to try bring some relief, directing McCullough to heat water and stones. Murray, Nugent and Innes backed out of the cottage, trying to make room for the action but somehow unable to leave entirely. The stone whisky bottle was kicked again under a bench, but Murray, who was nearest the door, noted its fall and reached in to retrieve it, not quite sure why.

'You said he went out this morning,' he finally said to Nugent. 'Did he say where?'

Nugent was usefully employed nervously kicking render off the base of the cottage wall. He scowled.

'Nah, he said nothing.'

'He went out every morning,' said Innes, hunched under the eaves. 'I dinna think he had a fixed path: he's aye nosing into other folks' business wherever it's most like to be able to be nosed into.'

'Did you see him this morning?' Murray asked him.

'I seen him go by the window, just as I was settling down to work after doing my observations. When I get up, see, I do a bit of work about dawn, then I have a bite to eat and then do my observations when the sun's up, then back to work.'

'I see. So that would be half an hour or so after dawn, then?'

'Aye, that'd be right.'

'Aye, aye it would,' said Nugent, taking some more interest in the conversation. 'He chucked us out at sun-up, with all our bags still unpacked across the floor, and Gibson having all sorts of strange notions and nobody with more than an hour's sleep.' The wall received another hearty kick. 'I'm never going to get home, am I?' he demanded.

'Gibson was having strange notions?' Murray asked, curious.

'Aye, just his usual ones. He gets … well, visions, I suppose you could call it. And dreams.' He fell silent, and Murray met Innes' eyes in puzzlement. Innes shrugged politely.

'He would have gone to get his sweetmeats from Mrs. Black,' said Innes suddenly, but they were interrupted by a cry from inside the cottage. Innes thrust his head indoors.

'He's gone!' came a wail from Mrs. Innes.

'What? So fast?' said Innes. Murray pushed in after him.

Newell lay on the bed, still on his side. His hands, clawing in front of him, had finally relaxed, the skin loose and peeling on the fingertips. Saliva trailed from his open mouth on to his shoulder and the blankets, which reeked with bodily odours. Mrs. Black and Mrs. Innes, one at his head and one at the foot, sat like shocked angels attending him, their hands still in the air as if they had sat up suddenly.

'He couldn't breathe,' Mrs. Innes whispered, as Gibson sank down on the floor, exhausted, and McCullough set down a pail of water with a thud. Mrs. Black drew a long breath, and stood to take Mrs. Innes into a large hug.

'We did what we could, my dear,' she murmured, and Mrs. Innes nodded, before leaving for her husband's embrace. Innes looked over her head at his unloved father-in-law, with an expression not of unmixed sorrow.

'Come, gentlemen,' said Murray, 'perhaps we had better leave here. I'll see if Mr. Coulter can think of a place for you to stay.'

McCullough went to help Gibson up off the floor, and absently brushed down his knees and elbows, black with dirt.

'Aye, there's nothing we can do here, now. Come on, let's gather up our things, lads.'

He and Nugent gathered the packs that had been rolled up roughly against the cottage wall, lifting two each. As they emerged from the cottage, with Murray behind them, Adair came up the lane, smiling in greeting.

'Surely you're not planning to leave without me?' he asked. 'Or have we been evicted?'

'Old Newell's dead,' said Nugent.

'Dead?' Adair reeled on his feet. 'How?'

'Some kind of fit,' said McCullough, with a kindly hand on Adair's arm. 'He couldn't say anything.'

'Then that's – that's very sudden,' said Adair, his mind not entirely on his words. 'His family must be sorely grieved.'

'Aye, surely,' said Nugent sarcastically, but McCullough nudged him hard.

'I was just suggesting,' said Murray, 'unless you have some alternative, that I ask Mr. Coulter where you could stay. I assume you are not heading on tonight.'

Coulter, already bewildered at Murray's lateness for dinner, agreed that the students should stay in his other spare bedroom for the night. McCullough scurried about with blankets and pillows, making sure that they would all be as comfortable as was consistent with not putting out the minister and his housekeeper. The housekeeper, challenged, rose up and provided plenty of food for four extra guests with a look on her face that might well have been satisfaction.

The students had retired for the night, much later, after plenty of shocked discussion of the afternoon's events, when the housekeeper brought in brandy and lemons for Coulter and Murray. She curtseyed in a manner that said she had more to tell them, and Coulter nodded to her.

'Young Walter tells me, sir, that Mr. Murray here has something of a reputation for looking into unexpected deaths,' she said, and curtseyed again to leave the room. The door closed, and Coulter turned to eye Murray in confusion.

'Unexpected deaths?' he repeated. Murray pursed his lips and frowned.

'Your housekeeper has a talent for drama. I must mention discretion to Walter some time, though whether he will pay attention is another matter,' he muttered.

'Unexpected deaths?' said Coulter again. 'Why would you

consider it worthwhile to look into old Newell's death? Clearly he had a stroke. His style of living, and his age, make it highly probable.'

'I don't know what Walter has in mind,' said Murray, 'for he was not even there this afternoon, but I did find Newell's death a little odd.'

'In what way?' demanded Coulter. 'Remember these are my parishioners you are examining!'

'Yes, of course. I intend no offence,' said Murray quickly. 'I may be altogether wrong. Mrs. Innes said he had been drinking, but he did not seem drunk. He kept trying to grasp at things, but could not quite make his hands do what he wanted – I have seen people when they have suffered a stroke, and it was not quite the same. Newell's hands moved, but as if they were numb, almost. Then whatever it was affected both sides of his body, and strokes generally only attack one side at a time. And then there was the skin: it had peeled from his fingers, even in the time since we had found him on the floor. I remember him reaching out for something as he lay there, and his skin was whole then.'

'Some kind of poisoning?' asked Coulter, now quite focussed on the matter.

'I did wonder.'

'Something he ate by accident, or drank,' Coulter mused.

'He was not a popular man, I gather,' said Murray carefully. He had had some experience of murder, but he should be wary, he told himself, not to see it everywhere.

'I cannot offhand think of anyone who liked him,' Coulter admitted. 'He was quite obnoxious.'

'Yet to dislike someone is only the very first step to murder, and few progress down that path,' said Murray. 'I just wonder. I'm sorry, I should not sow such ideas in your head!'

'It was your servant who sowed the idea. Or mine, gossiping with him.' Coulter sat back in his chair and poured Murray a glass of the warmed brandy. 'Newell had no family but for the daughter and son-in-law you have met. His wife died years ago, which was a wise move on her part. The daughter stayed on to keep house for him and then as soon as she could she married Innes. They are well suited: it is not one of these marriages that has been randomly selected as a refuge and turns out to be as bad as the original.'

Murray remembered seeing Innes and his wife embrace in the little cottage that evening: he was sure Coulter was right. 'Innes cordially hates his father-in-law. You saw them yesterday: that exchange was fairly typical of their relationship. I have never seen Innes angry at anyone else.'

'You seem to be making out that if murder has been done, we should only look across the lane for a culprit,' said Murray.

'Not at all. I cannot see Innes doing himself so much damage, or his wife either. Both are sensible, clever people: they would know the consequences.'

They stared into the fire, thinking, both of them, about Newell and the Inneses. Murray also noted, silently, that Coulter had mentioned a dead wife without apparent upset: perhaps he was indeed beginning to recover.

Next morning the students were at breakfast bright and early, with Gibson apparently recovered from whatever fit had taken him the day before. McCullough mothered him a little, mashing an egg on to a piece of toasted bread for him, but the others treated him quite as if nothing had happened and tucked in heartily.

'It's not everywhere we stay that we can break our fast before we set off,' Adair explained. His face was flushed, presumably straight from scrubbing. 'This is a rare luxury.'

'Which I hope does not make us late again,' put in Nugent, though even he seemed lighter this morning. 'We must be on our way soon.'

'Aye, aye,' agreed McCullough, now slicing his own ham with enthusiasm. 'We won't have to stop till after Stranraer. If we shift ourselves, we might even make Portpatrick by nightfall.'

'Well, I hope the rest of your journey passes uneventfully,' said Coulter, who was himself eating a little more healthily this morning. 'We'll walk you to the end of the village and put you on your way.'

'That would be most courteous,' said Adair, and the others nodded.

Mrs. Veitch provided food for their midday meal, Coulter and Murray took a pack each to give them a rest, and they set off, reminiscing about their own college days at the students' encouragement. It was not long before they put them on the

Stranraer road, and bade them farewell, Coulter urging them to keep in touch and let him know, as soon-to-be-brother clergy, when they were to be ordained. All shook hands and bowed, and waved until the turn in the road, and then Coulter and Murray, light in their hearts, headed back towards the manse.

It was a couple of hours later that Murray, glancing out the parlour window as he read his book, saw four weary travellers return with their bundles past the front gate, accompanied by a personage in black on a short horse. Nugent, even at the length of the garden, seemed fit to be tied, and the others were wide-eyed with fright. Murray hurried outside.

'Whatever's the matter?' he asked. 'Why are you back?'

'Do you know these fellows?' asked the personage on the horse.

'I am acquainted with them, yes. They are students from Glasgow college, heading home to Ireland by Portpatrick.'

'And did they bide the night before last in the house of one Thomas Newell?'

'I believe so, yes.'

'And is said Thomas Newell now,' the man licked his lips, 'deceased?'

'Well, yes.'

'I,' said the man, 'am the Sheriff's officer for these parts. I have been requested to make enquiry into the death of said Thomas Newell, and I have apprehended these four persons as valuable witnesses in the case.'

'You've what?' came Coulter's voice, and Murray turned to see him hurry down the manse garden path behind him. The sheriff's officer straightened in his saddle, and repeated his charge. He was a shiny man: his face shone, his boots shone, his horse shone, and his buttons glinted in the sunlight. Even his whiskers, dark though they were, shone, and his hat seemed to have been polished for the occasion.

'You are the minister, are you not?' he asked. 'Coulter, by name?'

'Yes, you know me, Thomson,' said Coulter, a little crossly.

'And this gentleman?' He looked Murray up and down as if expecting to see concealed corpses fall from his coat pockets.

'Charles Murray of Letho, in Fifeshire, at your service,' said

Murray politely. The man nodded, then turned about at the sound of approaching hooves. Murray's heart lifted when he saw Mr. Herkless appear at the head of the lane by Newell's cottage – unfortunately, however, Miss Herkless did not follow.

'Good day to you all,' said Herkless, tilting his hat. 'Have I heard aright? Has there been foul play here?'

'That is what I am here to make out, Mr. Herkless, sir,' said Thomson humbly. 'And I have apprehended these persons as witnesses and possible suspects.'

'Hi!' cried Nugent. 'Suspects?'

'But he was ill when we found him,' said McCullough, alarmed.

'That's all very well,' said Thomson. 'All your stories will be taken down and considered in the fullness of time.'

'But they have to get home!' said Coulter.

'That's as may be. But there's a fine line,' said Thomson roundly, 'between getting home and fleeing from justice!'

'All right, Thomson,' said Herkless, soothingly. 'I tell you what: Newell's house is no good for keeping them and questioning them. Why don't you bring them up to the big house? I can easily put them up if you want them here for longer than today, and there are rooms for you to talk to them without the others overhearing, and so on. All your usual routine, no doubt.'

'At the big house?' Thomson considered the offer. His weighing up between the situation being taken out of his hands, and having a base at Kirkwelland House, was almost visible on his face. 'Aye, aye, that might be handy enough. But I'll have to examine the cottage and the body first, like.'

'Of course. Shall we stay here and guard these men while you do that?' asked Herkless.

'Aye, aye,' Thomson agreed. He slid off his horse and tied it solemnly to the gatepost of the manse. 'I'll make my way from here.'

'Will you all come in? Come in at once?' Coulter was saying, tidying the poor students and the laird off the road, but Murray, with a nod at his host, took a couple of long strides and caught up with the sheriff's man before he reached the end of the lane.

'How did you hear about Newell's death?' he asked the man.

'I was called out by the family,' said Thomson. 'A Mr. Innes attended the sheriff's office this morning. Ah, here he is.'

Innes was at his own front door, alert for the sound of visitors.

'See this?' he said, as soon as he saw them turn the corner. 'My thermometer's smashed! Do you think it might all be part of the same business?' He fingered the long wooden frame of his precious thermometer, his face full of grief as it had not been for his father-in-law. 'What am I to do?' he whispered, as if to the broken glass in its brackets.

'I'm here about your father-in-law,' said Thomson unsympathetically, 'no about some barometer thing.'

'*Therm*ometer,' said Innes automatically, but he hunched himself across the lane to Newell's door. 'He's in here, of course.'

He waved Thomson in, and Murray glimpsed Mrs. Innes sitting by the bed, where Newell's body had been straightened and smoothed for burial. He was about to follow, when Thomson turned back at him.

'What's your business here, Mr. – Murray, was it?'

'Ah, none,' Murray admitted. 'Oh, except for this.'

He took the stone whisky bottle from his coat pocket, where he had been guarding it.

'And where did that come from?' asked Thomson suspiciously.

'That was here,' said Innes. 'I saw the gentleman pick it up off the floor yesterday evening.'

'And why would you do a thing like that, sir?' asked Thomson.

'I thought it might be significant, because it had been beside Newell where he was lying. It was being kicked around in the crowd and I feared it might be lost or damaged.'

Thomson snorted.

'The fellow had been drinking, no doubt: small mystery there.'

'I'd never seen him drunk like this, sir,' Innes insisted. 'My wife said there was whisky on his breath, true, but he didn't act as if he was drunk.'

'I agree,' said Murray. 'It was more like a stroke, but not quite like that, either.'

Thomson turned down the corners of his shiny lips in disbelief.

'What do you think you're saying, the pair of you?'

'Well, that's why I went to Stranraer to find you,' said Innes, reasonably. 'It didna seem like a natural death to me, or my wife, and I didna want blamed for it.'

'Plenty of others disliked the man, from what I've heard,' said Murray, nodding.

'And why would you be blamed?' asked Thomson, as if he had already made up his mind.

'Because I was always quarrelling with the man. It's common knowledge we hated the sight of each other,' said Innes frankly. 'But if I'd killed him I'd have throttled him – and I've often come close, I'd be the first to admit. I'd not have done – whatever it was – to him.'

'It looked like some kind of poison,' Murray added, 'which is why I thought this might be useful.' He proffered the stone bottle again. It was the kind, now he examined it more closely, that you took to your local dealer to be refilled: Newell might have had it for years. 'Do you recognise it?' he asked Innes. 'Was it his?'

'Aye, he's that on a shelf in his bed recess.' Innes took the bottle and sniffed at the open mouth. 'Smells like good stuff.'

Murray tried, but it did not appeal to him.

'Give it here, then,' said Thomson, with his hand out. 'It was by him when he was taken ill, you say?'

'That's right. Oh, no!'

Thomson had misjudged, and Murray tried to catch the bottle again as it fell, but it was too late. It cracked in three on the stone door sill.

'What's that?' said Thomson suddenly. All three men crouched down, staring at the spilt dregs of the bottle. There was spirit, no doubt, trickling away, but not much of it. Amongst its drops was a silvery thread of fluid, as fine as a spider's web where it caught the late morning sunlight.

'Can we save that bit in the corner of the bottle?' asked Murray. 'You might want to show it to a physician if you get someone to examine the body.'

Thomson gave him an unfriendly look, but he carefully lifted the broken base, tipped to keep the last few drops of whisky and silver safe.

'How am I going to hold this?' he demanded.

'No doubt my wife will have a clean jar in her kitchen if I stay with her father a wee minute,' said Innes, still staring at the odd mixture. He ducked into the cottage, and in a moment Mrs. Innes appeared in the lane. She, too, studied the fluid in the broken bottle.

'There's a thing,' she remarked cryptically, and hurried off to fetch a jar. Thomson inspected it, tilting it to the sun, before he decanted the fluid carefully into it and pressed down the cork lid. He lowered the jar into his wide pockets.

'Wait there,' he said firmly to Murray. 'You, madam, come on in with me.'

He drew Mrs. Innes back into her father's cottage and flung a glare over his shoulder at Murray, daring him to follow. In a moment, Innes himself came back out.

'You're too tall, man,' came Thomson's voice from within. 'You take up more space than the box bed.'

There was a moment's silence, both in the house and in the lane. Then Innes gave an apologetic twitch of his shoulders.

'I had to fetch him, hadn't I?'

'No choice, I should say,' Murray reassured him.

'Right,' said Thomson, emerging suddenly from the cottage like a shiny cork from a less than savoury bottle. He brushed dust from his sleeves in a business-like fashion. 'I want to talk to those students. Where have they gone?'

'I believe they're at the manse,' said Murray helpfully. 'Unless they've already gone up to Kirkwelland House.'

Thomson ignored him, and marched off along the lane. Innes waved his arms uncertainly.

'I should stay here,' he said. 'The wife's on her own.'

'It's all right. I'll see if I can keep an eye on him. Not very friendly, though, is he?'

Innes shook his head, a slight grin flitting across his face.

'Seems right, then, him enquiring in to old Newell's death. They'd suit each other rightly.'

Murray hurried along the lane to catch up with Thomson. Thomson wore a frock coat that, from the style, might have been a legacy from his grandfather, with mighty pockets and a wide skirt. His legs were so bandy that from behind, under the coat skirts, they seemed as if they might well belong to two different people. As he approached the manse gate, his horse, still tethered there, jerked his head up with a quizzical look that almost made Murray laugh out loud: his horse thought no more of him than anyone else, then. Someone had brought a pail of water out for the poor animal, he noticed, just as Thomson spun round at him again.

'Have you a manservant with you, that I could send back to Stranraer for a physician?'

'I have a manservant,' said Murray mildly, 'but I would not send him to Stranraer on his own.'

'Well, the physician was your idea,' snapped Thomson. 'The least you could do is send your man for him.'

'I'm very willing to go myself, if necessary,' said Murray, 'but if I sent my manservant we might never see him again. He could not be relied upon to find his way to the end of the street and back.'

Thomson made a face, as if suspecting him of obstruction.

'You're a stranger around here, Mr. Murray, are you not?'

'It's my first visit to these parts,' Murray agreed.

'And you did not know Newell personally?'

'I met him yesterday for the first time.'

'Nor Innes?'

'The same.'

'Then what, may I ask, is your interest in this matter?'

'It's a reasonable question,' Murray admitted. 'I was there when Newell died, and however unpleasant he seems to have been, I do not like the thought of someone taking it upon him – or her – self to take another's life before their time. It makes me want to find out what happened and make matters as straight as they can be made.'

'And this has – you have met such instances before?'

'Several times.'

'That seems to me to be a very curious circumstance. To have met unnatural death "several times", that might be considered suspicious in itself.'

'I would be more inclined to call it unfortunate,' said Murray with a smile, 'and of course, when one has a little experience in the field, sometimes acquaintances ask for one's advice, and that means that one is more likely to be involved in such matters. I don't go about seeking out murders, if that's what you think.'

'Nor encouraging them, nor committing them, I hope,' said

Thomson, fixing him with a stern look.

'I'd hardly admit it to you if I did,' said Murray, feeling no compulsion to be particularly polite.

Thomson kept his gaze on Murray for a long moment, as if expecting him to break down and confess all. Murray held his gaze, until Thomson shook his head crossly.

'You'll interfere whatever I do,' he decided.

'I'll try not to,' Murray conceded, 'but curiosity is bound to get the better of me. It's a particular weakness.'

'Then I'd sooner keep you close than have you poking your nose in where I cannot see you,' said Thomson. 'I'm going to question the students now. I gather you're a little acquainted with them, too. You'd better come and sit in with me, for if you don't know doubt you'll find everything out some other way, anyway. Come on.'

It was as gracious an invitation as he was likely to receive, so Murray followed him up the path to the manse door.

Chapter Five

The students had not yet moved from the manse to the big house, but were sitting about the parlour in a silence that felt well-developed and mature. Adair, the long unhealthy looking one, was the only man you could call anything near relaxed. Gibson appeared to be praying, eyes closed, hands clasped but twitching expressively. Nugent was flexing his fists, as if ready for a fight, his face white and set. Coulter and Herkless had found that talk had defeated even them, and sat at the table staring at the cloth, smothered by the atmosphere. McCullough, from his perch on the edge of the windowseat, had seen Murray and Thomson the sheriff's man coming, and was first on his feet the minute the door opened.

'I want to question these yins separate. One at a time,' Thomson clarified to Coulter, as if they had thought they might go like animals into the Ark. 'You first,' he added, pointing to Gibson. Gibson barely nodded.

'I'd like to be there, if I may,' said Coulter, rising from the table. 'They are but young, and they are, or will shortly be, my fellow clergy.'

'Oh, will they indeed?' Thomson regarded them with, if anything, more distrust than before. 'Oh, and have you such a thing as a reliable manservant who could go to Stranraer for a physician? Mr. Murray here claims his is not to be trusted.'

'Only in point of his sense of direction,' said Murray, quick to defend his servants.

'That's true,' said Coulter. 'No, I keep no man here.'

'I'll go myself,' said Herkless easily. 'Is it Dr. Forbes you want?'

'Aye, sir. That would be very kind of you, sir,' said Thomson, who evidently drew a distinction between Wigtownshire gentry and the lesser sort.

'If I have time, Coulter,' said Herkless aside to the minister,

'I'll call in and see how our work is progressing.'

'Of course: I hope you find it successful,' said Coulter quickly. 'I have been intending to go, but I have been so busy here …'

Herkless nodded, a kindly look on his face as he left. Murray noticed it and remembered the times he had noted already during his stay when Coulter had announced his intention to go to Stranraer but in the end had failed to leave the village. Herkless seemed to have seen it, too. Murray was pleased that the laird had an eye to his minister's welfare.

'Where can I talk to these fellows privately?' Thomson asked impatiently.

'Come through to my study,' said Coulter. 'Gibson, will you be all right?' he asked, concerned. Gibson pulled himself back from wherever he seemed to have been, and nodded, though Murray was not quite sure he knew what was going on. He followed Coulter, Gibson and Thomson into the hall and back to the little study behind the dining room.

The dining room itself would have been better, he thought. There were two seats in the study, one the desk chair, the other an armchair by the fire, which was unlit. Coulter, attentive to the needs of his junior brothers, gestured Gibson to the armchair, then hesitantly allowed Thomson the desk chair. He edged his own hip on to the desk, leaving Murray to lean against the bookcase, which gave an uncertain wobble at his touch.

'Right,' said Thomson, taking out a pair of slates. 'What's your name?'

'Joseph Gibson, sir,' said Gibson, eyes wide as if he could take in more of the situation through them.

'Where do you hail from?'

'From Ballyclare, sir, in the County Antrim.'

'Your father's name?'

'Joseph Gibson, farmer.' Gibson was pulling himself slowly together.

'And your reason for being here?'

'You know that, Thomson,' Coulter interrupted.

'I have to put it in my records,' Thomson explained as if to a fool.

'I'm on my way back home from the term at the college in

Glasgow, with my friends, by God's grace.'

'By God's grace? Something has been stopping you?'

Gibson looked confused.

'No, no, I just meant that like everything else, it's by God's grace we are here.'

'Where you could murder Newell?'

'Murder Newell? Was he murdered?' Gibson's confusion deepened. 'I was there when he died. I saw no one do him any violence, I'm sure.'

'Mr. Newell may have been poisoned,' Coulter put in, and backed off at Thomson's scowl.

'Then his illness was not – natural?'

'That's the theory,' Thomson grudgingly admitted. 'Can you think of anyone who might have had reason to kill him?'

'To kill Mr. Newell?'

'Yes!' Thomson was not a patient man.

'Murder is a terrible sin,' said Gibson reasonably. 'Who would do such a thing?'

'That's what I'm asking you. Did you like Mr. Newell?'

'Mr. Newell was not an easy man to like, but I did my best,' said Gibson, frowning. 'I'm not perfect, of course, who is? I may have failed.'

'Failed and killed him?'

'No, no. Failed and allowed an uncharitable dislike to enter my heart. Mr. Newell was not blessed with a likeable character, but that should not prevent us from trying to like him.'

'I'm not sure I like you,' muttered Thomson.

'Then I am truly sorry, and will strive to be better,' said Gibson sincerely.

Thomson snorted.

'When did you get here?'

'The night before last, I believe.'

'And why did you stay with Mr. Newell?'

'Because that's where we stay. McCullough arranges all that kind of thing.'

'So you've known Mr. Newell for a while, then?'

'This is our fourth year so yes, four years. But we only see him for a night on each journey.'

'You stay a night each way?'

'That's right.'

'So why are you here today?' asked Thomson in triumph, as if he had solved the whole thing. 'You said you came the night before last.'

'Oh. That was my fault. Poor Ishmael was not happy, though I believe McCullough urged him to go on on his own.'

'Your fault?'

'I … was weak yesterday morning. I could not manage …' He trailed off, vague again, his gaze somewhere further than the study would normally permit.

'What do you mean, weak?'

'I mean I was unable to face the walk, the next part of the walk. I had not slept well for two nights. I have dreams, sometimes.'

'Dreams.' The notion was dismissed. 'You didn't sleep well so you all stayed here an extra day, is that the story?'

'That's the fact.'

'In Newell's cottage?'

'No, no, Mr. Newell had to go out, so we had to go, too. I went to the shore. To me it was this morning the Sea of Galilee, and in truth I saw our Lord walk upon the golden waters, speaking with the fishermen.'

'What?' Thomson looked aghast.

'Gibson has visions, Mr. Thomson,' Coulter explained, and he went to stand beside Gibson's chair. 'Are you all right, Joseph?' he asked gently.

'Certainly, Mr. Coulter,' said Gibson, smiling. 'The Lord is very good to me.'

'This man is wud,' said Thomson succinctly. 'Bring me one of the others. This fellow can go as soon as he likes. Sooner, maybe.'

Coulter helped Gibson from the armchair and led him from the room, a hand on his arm. Murray watched them go. He had not met anyone before who had had visions, but Gibson seemed entirely sincere. Coulter trusted him, too, it appeared. In the age of reason such things were not trusted, but Murray had seen some curious things himself in the last few months, and was beginning to feel that reason sometimes had its limitations.

Coulter returned with Adair, who greeted the sheriff's man with graceful politeness.

'Aye, aye, sit down there,' was the rather less graceful response. 'What do they cry you?'

'James Adair, sir.'

'From?'

'Hillsborough, County Down, and the college of Glasgow.'

'And your faither?'

'Robert Adair, also of Hillsborough, merchant.' Adair crossed his long legs and made a net of his fingers on his lap. Thomson regarded him with disdain and wrote the information on his slates, making, Murray thought, a deliberately slow job of it.

'I gather,' he said, 'that you stayed with Newell each time you travelled to and from Glasgow.'

'We did. He charged a very reasonable rate, and as divinity students we are, of course, deeply conscious of very reasonable rates for any commodity.' He smiled sweetly at Thomson. Thomson pursed his lips.

'So you knew the old man well?'

'I'd hardly say that. Mr. Newell was also deeply conscious of his very reasonable rates and did not, for example, entertain us to an evening meal, or break his fast with us. Rather he closed himself in his box bed with our money, and allowed us to go to our rest undisturbed by any dazzling crusie lamps or tallow candles. He said he was anxious that we might set fire to the place.'

'Surely there were other places to stay, even in the village?' asked Murray. Adair turned to see him against his bookcase.

'Not many in this village, and you see, one always stays in the same place. It's like a kind of predestination.' He smiled again, and though Coulter gave a little frown at the irreverent joke, he said nothing. 'A custom, anyway,' Adair amended, his soft brown eyes apologetic.

'How did you spend the day, when Mr. Newell asked you to leave the cottage?' Thomson asked. 'Were you on the shore sharing Mr. Gibson's visions?'

'Not at all: I chose to take some exercise. I took a walk over the headland, did I not, Mr. Murray?' His head on its long neck snaked around again to see that he had Murray's confirmation.

'I did meet Mr. Adair up on the headland to the north,' Murray agreed. 'He was walking further north, and I came back to the village.'

'Were you on your ain?' Thomson asked Adair. Adair spread his hands wide.

'My fellow students had taken a different direction. I'm sure Mr. Murray will verify that I was alone.'

Up to a point, thought Murray suddenly. It seemed like a very careful answer. Thomson however seemed satisfied with its veracity for now.

'So you could have slipped the poison into his whisky, and then left him to drink it at his leisure,' he said thoughtfully.

'He was poisoned, was he?' said Adair, and his expression sharpened. 'He had whisky? I had no idea.'

'Aye, aye,' said Thomson, expecting a denial. 'If it wasna you, who was it?'

'Well, it wasna me,' said Adair, neatly imitating him, 'for I had no reason to kill him, though I may not have found him a congenial host. As to who might have done the deed, I cannot imagine. No doubt he was the kind of character who was capable of making many enemies, of different grades. Only seeing him a few times a year allowed us a certain space to recover from our encounters with him, so dislike could not really build up to any dangerous levels.'

Thomson blinked at him, sure he was being mocked but not quite able to put his finger on the precise mockery in question.

'Did you see him argifying with his son-in-law?'

'That's the scientific gentleman across the lane? Once or twice certainly I have heard them exchange words one might call hasty, but that's not to say that Mr. Innes would be capable of murdering the man. I certainly never saw him give Mr. Newell whisky, or any other spirit.'

'And did anybody else call on Mr. Newell while you were in the house?'

'Not a soul.'

'Right, then, Mr. Adair. Away you go, and send in that red-haired one with the pasty face.'

'At your service, sir,' said Adair, rising and bowing smoothly. He left the room.

'Yon one's hiding something, nae doubt,' Thomson observed. Murray thought that was quite possible.

In a moment, McCullough knocked the door softly and came

in, his expression eager to please. Thomson waved him to the armchair without looking much at him, and McCullough perched on the edge of it, his hands clutching his knees, his smile dancing from Coulter to Thomson to Murray and round again.

'Name?' sighed Thomson.

'John McCullough.'

'Where are you from and who's your faither?'

'My father's a tailor in Larne: we live there, of course. His name's Isaac McCullough and it's a good wee business he has there or he wouldn't be able to send me over here, not that we're rolling in it, mind you, I wouldn't want you to think that for it wouldn't be true, so it wouldn't, but he's comfortable enough and my brothers have both gone into the business now with him, Jimmy, he's the grand one for picking out the colours, never met a man with such an eye for colour, but Patrick, now, he's the one with the business head on his shoulders, so we're hoping between the two of them they might do well enough, with a following wind, if they stay together which they're likely to do to be honest for they get along all right most days and even if they do quarrel now and again it's only what anyone does when they're working together all day every day, isn't it?'

He drew breath and found Thomson staring at him.

'And what about your mother and your aunts and uncles?' he asked.

'Oh, my ma's great, so she is, she's a hard worker and a good church woman –'

'I think he's joking, McCullough,' interrupted Coulter gently. McCullough blinked, and reddened.

'Am I talking too much?' he asked, clearly trying to slow down. 'I get like that when I'm nervous.'

'And what have you to be nervous about?' asked Thomson, in a manner calculated to make him worse, if anything.

'Nothing! Well, nothing only a man's died and you've brought us back here to question us and I'd say that would make anyone nervous, innocent or guilty, and even though I hadn't a button to do with it except that I tried to help when his daughter came over to nurse him and all I did was heat water that was hardly used and heat stones that he tried to push away, and the place left in a state and our stuff all over the floor and poor Mrs. Innes left with it all to clear up except our stuff, of course, we gathered that up as far as we could but –'

'Johnnie, Johnnie,' said Coulter soothingly.

'Oh, aye, right.' He subsided again.

'Where did you go this morning when Mr. Newell asked you to leave his cottage?' asked Thomson, his fingers tight on his slates. 'And if you could restrict your answer to five minutes or so, that would be appreciated.'

McCullough shot him a desperate look.

'Ishmael Nugent and I went for a walk together. Jamesie Adair wanted to go off on his own, he said, for a wee break, which is fair enough for we've seen plenty of each other these last few days and it was friendly meant, and Hugh Gibson wanted to sit on the shore and said he didn't need us to tend to him, he would be fine.' He snapped his mouth shut, eyes wide.

'Well done,' said Thomson sourly. 'Did you see Mr. Newell at all on your travels? Which way did you go?'

'We went down to the south of the village, where the tannery is. There's a pool at the stream there and we like to shy stones into it.'

Coulter nodded, clearly recognising the description.

'Did you see Mr. Newell?'

'I can't think that we did, sir, not at all. Not that we were looking, either.'

'I see.' Thomson made their omission sound ominous. He let the silence lie for a moment, contemplating his slates, though Murray was sure he was not reading them. 'What do you know of a stone whisky bottle that Mr. Newell might have had around the cottage?

'A whisky bottle?' McCullough blinked, alarmed. 'There was a whisky bottle in the cottage?'

'There was: did you not see it?'

'No! No, I didn't – oh, wait a wee minute. Was there one down beside him on the floor? I remember something …'

'That's the one,' agreed Thomson. 'Had you no seen it before?'

'Never. I'd seen Mr. Newell with drink taken before, but I'd never seen him drinking in the cottage. That's why … That's why it's a good place to stay, a decent house, with no spirits in it.' He tailed away, not quite convincing his listeners. Why should McCullough be so alarmed at the thought of whisky in the cottage? Was he a committed abstainer?

'So if I told you,' said Thomson slowly, 'that the bottle likely had poison in it, you would tell me you wouldn't know how it might have got there?'

'Yes,' said McCullough, after a moment.

'You know how it got there?' asked Thomson, pouncing.

'No, I'd tell you that I wouldn't know how it might have got there. I don't know how it got there. I didn't know there was a bottle and even if I had known I wouldn't have put poison in it, and I don't know anyone who would!' He finished in a rush, his eyes flicking again from one to another of them.

'I hadna asked you if you knew anyone who would,' said Thomson.

'But it's what you were going to ask me, wasn't it?' McCullough replied quickly. 'It's what I would ask, in the case.'

Thomson pursed his lips, frowning.

'Then you know of no enemies the old man might have had?'

'No!' McCullough considered for a moment. 'Well, he wasn't very nice, that's true. But that's not to say someone would want to poison him. And whatever it was they used, it was horrible! Who would wish that on anyone? I mean, you hear about poisons, don't you, ones that are quick and don't give you time to set your affairs straight or condemn your murderer or make your peace, and that's bad enough, but to lie there for hours, not able to speak properly, not able to move properly, squirming and moaning and – and -' His face had taken on a greenish tinge as he remembered the awful afternoon. 'The smell ...' he murmured.

'You tried your best to help,' said Murray, for he seemed in some need of comfort. Thomson gave him a scathing look.

'But was he the one who caused it, all the same?'

McCullough's eyes filled with tears.

'I did not!' he insisted. 'I did not! I'd no call to kill him, and I would not have made him suffer like that!'

'Aye, away with you, and send in the last fellow,' said Thomson, unfeeling, not even glancing up as McCullough lurched from the chair and staggered out, cheeks wet and hand clasped to his mouth.

In a moment Nugent slammed in to the room, and stood, furious.

'I hear you're accusing all of us of murder?' he started.

'Ah, come on in, Mr. Nugent, and make yourself comfortable,' said Thomson, superficially friendly. 'Let's not start like that, eh? Now, it's Ishmael Nugent, isn't it?'

'Ishmael? No, that's what the others call me. It's Adam, Adam Nugent.'

'Then why Ishmael?' asked Thomson.

Nugent paused.

'It's after Ishmael in Genesis. The son of Hagar.'

'"And he will be a wild man;"' quoted Coulter quietly, '"his hand will be against every man, and every man's hand against him."'

'Well, the second bit's true enough,' said Nugent with bitterness.

'Where do you come from, then, and what's your faither?' asked Thomson, skating over this.

'I'm from Portaferry, in the County Down, and my father's dead.'

'Aye, aye, but what was his name?'

'David Nugent,' said Nugent, as if the words were being torn from him. 'Presbyterian clergyman.'

'David Nugent,' repeated Thomson, writing it down.

'A child of the manse, then? Me too,' said Coulter cheerfully. Nugent did not respond.

'Right, well,' said Thomson, finishing his notes. 'Where did you go this morning when Newell asked you to leave the house?'

'Threw us out, more like,' said Nugent. 'I went with McCullough down to the tanner's pool to play skipping stones. He beat me.'

'What about Adair and Gibson?'

'Gibson was on the shore, shaking himself back out of his heavenly visions. Adair went off somewhere – up on the headland, I think he said.'

'Did you see Newell at all when you were out?'

'Newell?' Nugent made a derogatory sound. 'He said he was going out, but I'd wager, if I were a betting man, that he was through every stitch we owned the minute we were out the door.'

'What for?'

'For anything useful he might find.'

'You mean he stole from you?' Coulter was shocked.

'Not stole. Not usually, though that's not to say I don't think he wouldn't have taken spirits or meat or something if he had found it. No, what he wanted was information.'

'Information?' Thomson for once was puzzled.

'Do you mean,' said Murray, 'that Newell was a blackmailer?' Nugent nodded sharply.

'Famous for it.'

'Good heavens!' Coulter was beyond shocked. 'That is dreadful!'

'That's why none of the students wanted to stay with him,' Nugent explained. 'But we all have our routes, and we all have the parties we travel with, and for one thing he's cheap, and for another, we were late leaving the last place and then Gibson had one of his fairy fits and so we couldn't get on any further, we had to stay here. I say he's cheap: he's cheap if you keep yourself well away from his blackmailing. Otherwise he could be very expensive indeed.'

'And was he blackmailing you?' asked Thomson.

'No!' Nugent gave a snort of a laugh. 'I have more wit – and nothing to hide.'

'But your friends?'

'Look,' said Nugent quickly, 'we're the odd ones, the ones no one else much wants to travel with. There's Gibson with his visions, and me with my temper – aye, I'll admit it, if every man's hand is against me sometimes maybe I draw them on myself. McCullough sorts out our accommodation and our food, and he does things cheaply, and I'm grateful enough for that, for I haven't much myself – you'll see I'm a bit older than the others, no doubt, and I've had to save to go to college. But none of us is foolish enough to lay ourselves open to a man like Newell: we had no reason to kill him. I'm just saying, though, that if he was blackmailing students, likely he had fingers in other pies, too.'

'The odd ones,' Murray repeated, when Nugent had been dismissed. 'He didn't say what made McCullough or Adair odd, though, did he?'

'No.' Coulter tapped the arm of the chair, into which he had flung himself when Nugent left. Thomson still sat at the desk, tidying his slates. 'Newell a blackmailer! I wish I had known: perhaps I could have put a stop to it, and saved his life.'

'If he was killed for that. There are strong links, then, between the church here and the Presbyterians in Ireland?'

'Oh, aye, of course.' Coulter pulled himself up a little to direct his explanation to Murray. 'They're mostly amongst the Scottish settlers in the north, anyway. Then during the Glorious Revolution numbers of their clergy took refuge in Scotland – often they had family here, too, and the General Assembly allowed them to be presented to parishes, if the opportunity arose. And then they study here or in the Low Countries, for there's no college in Ireland that will take them.'

'Adair says there's a new one now,' Murray remarked.

'Does he? Then that might change things, if it's a success. The people around here will miss them travelling through: sometimes great friendships grow up over those brief visits, and students stay longer or someone from here will travel part of the way with them. It doesn't seem that Newell fell into that pattern, though, does it?'

'So do you think one of them did it?' asked Thomson, more as if he were thinking aloud than as if he truly valued their opinions.

'I hope not,' said Coulter.

'But if not them, then who?' asked Murray. 'Innes? His wife? Some other local person who was being blackmailed by Newell?'

'It hardly bears thinking about,' said Coulter, with a desperate wave of his fingers. 'These are my parishioners, or they are my brothers in the church. How could I wish any of them to be guilty?'

'Well, it's not your wishing that will make it so,' said Murray, pushing himself warily from the wobbly bookcase. 'Someone already is guilty. And whether it's one of the students or not, I'm quite sure there isn't one of them yet that has told us the whole truth.'

Chapter Six

As Herkless the laird had not returned from Stranraer by dinner time that Friday evening, the students once again ate at the manse. It was not a particularly easy meal as Coulter felt obliged to offer hospitality to Thomson, the sheriff's man, as well. After dinner they retired in a body to the parlour, and Murray offered to play the box piano. The offer was seized upon with almost indecent enthusiasm by Coulter, McCullough and Adair, and Thomson composed himself, hands firmly on his knees, to listen as if it were another painful duty he had to assume for the sake of the sheriff. Murray had been playing for twenty minutes or so when they heard the risp rattle and Mrs. Veitch's solemn tread in the hall. Coulter took the chance to slide over to Murray.

'That piano has not been touched since Bessie died. I thought I should never want to hear it again – thank you for proving me wrong.'

'I think you may thank the circumstances,' Murray murmured in return. 'I feared the awful silence otherwise!'

Coulter grinned in agreement, and turned as Mrs. Veitch entered the parlour and announced Mr. Herkless. The laird strode in, followed by a stranger to Murray.

'Dr. Forbes has arrived,' said Herkless, gesturing to him. Thomson rose.

'I'm right glad to see you, Dr. Forbes. Will you be wanting the corpus straight away?'

'Or would you like to partake of a little dinner?' asked Coulter, the pair of them like angel and devil on the doctor's shoulders.

'I dined early, I thank you,' said Dr. Forbes with a species of bow to the company. 'I'd sooner do the body without a full stomach, if you're ready.'

'Then let us go,' said Thomson, with a grim smile.

'I'm more than ready for my dinner,' said Herkless, 'but it'll be waiting for me at the big house. Are you ready to come with me, gentlemen? No doubt you'll have had a tiring day: I don't imagine that being questioned on a murder is something they teach you much about even at Glasgow college.' He gathered the students together, with their packs, and led them to the door where they thanked Coulter again for dinner and his help. Dr. Forbes and Thomson hung back a moment to let them leave, and in the confusion Herkless managed to double back to Murray.

'You might want to keep a wary eye on our worthy physician there,' he remarked, sotto voce. 'If you can do so without remark, take a sniff at his breath.' Herkless caught Murray's eye and winked significantly at him, before following the students out on to the road. Murray blinked, and snatched his hat from the hall table, and with a wave to Coulter he followed the doctor and Thomson out as well. They seemed not to notice Murray tagging along behind them as they returned to Newell's dark cottage. No doubt it was behaviour unworthy of a Wigtownshire gentleman, but Murray had to admit to himself that his curiosity was prodigiously stimulated.

At the cottage, the Inneses still waked old Newell's corpse unaccompanied by any friends or neighbours. Innes rose and stretched before bowing to the sheriff's man again.

'This is Dr. Forbes up frae Stranraer,' Thomson announced with little formality. 'I need him to examine the corpus.'

Dr. Forbes stepped forward into the candlelight past Murray, who inhaled delicately. There was little need for discretion: the physician exuded the aroma of ale from every generous pore. He removed his hat to display a broad lick of gingery brown hair, and a profusion of true ginger whiskers which framed his face like lambrequin and met under one of his chins. His eyes were oily.

'I'd be much obliged by a look at your late relative, madam,' he said, in a surprisingly charming manner. Mrs. Innes gathered up her skirts and curtseyed, shifting readily out of his way so that he could examine Newell's body more conveniently where it still lay on the edge of the box bed. The old head, whiskery and flaccid in death, already had a cloth tied about it to hold the jaw closed but the yellowing skin had slid down from the sharp nose and brows, and gravity tugged at the corners of the closed eyelids. Thomson closed in, so that Murray could catch only glimpses as Dr. Forbes slipped the sheet down and undid Newell's clothing. More patches of yellow-grey skin were revealed, spattered unattractively with grey-black hairs.

'May I watch what you are doing, sir?' asked Innes politely. 'He was my father-in-law.'

'Will you swoon?' asked Dr. Forbes.

'I don't believe so, sir,' said Innes. Forbes looked him up and down, and seemed to come to some decision about him, for he made room for him on his other side, away from Thomson. Innes latched his fingers behind his back, and bent attentively. Thomson stiffened, displeased, and Murray could see slightly less.

Whatever his breath smelled like, and however much ale he might have consumed, Dr. Forbes set to with efficiency. He examined Newell's face, skin, eyes, teeth and hair, and even peered inside his hairy ears, though he could not have seen much there. Then he poked and prodded at Newell's puny ribcage and stomach, in a manner that made Thomson pull back to catch his breath. Lastly he studied Newell's hands and fingers, and, having laid them reverently back across Newell's pigeon chest, slid the sheet back further and nudged Thomson along so that he could work at the corpse's feet. He set them back, too, and spread the sheet back over the body, adjusting the clothing as he went. All in all he seemed both thorough and respectful, and Murray wondered if Herkless knew something else of the man, to be suspicious.

'You'll have cleaned him, madam,' he said to Mrs. Innes, taking the cloth she offered to wipe his hands.

'Of course, sir.'

'But there would have been a deal of soiling, I imagine.'

'Yes, sir,' she replied, going pink. 'He lost control of himself before he died.'

'Of course, of course. No shame in that, madam. We are all human.' He tapped his teeth with a thoughtful finger.

'So was it a stroke?' asked Thomson. 'Or was it poison? Arsenic, maybe?' He said the word with flair, one professional to another. The doctor tutted.

'No arsenic. No a stroke, either, I'm bound. I'd say he was poisoned, right enough. And I'd say the poison was a mercury compound. He's lost skin on his fingers and toes, and – well, I'll no go into the rest in present company.' Innes, the scientist, seemed faintly disappointed. 'Was he taking mercury for anything? Asthma, maybe?'

The Inneses shook their heads, eyes wide.

'The only thing he complained of was his legs. And he couldna remember things the way he used to so well.'

'But would that explain this?' asked Thomson, producing from the tent of his coatskirts the jar into which he had poured the dregs of the stone whisky bottle. Dr. Forbes took it, opened it, and tilted it to the candlelight. He whistled.

'Aye, that looks very much like mercury. In his whisky, eh? That would be a bold move.'

'Why's that?' asked Murray.

'Well, for one, the mercury's heavier than the whisky - it would sink to the bottom. Likely if he drank it he'd still drink enough to kill him, but the chances of him seeing it and not drinking the stuff at all would be quite high. And then, he wouldn't die at once. How long was he sick?'

'A few hours,' said Mrs. Innes.

'We don't know exactly,' said Innes, standing close to her. 'The students found him already ill.'

'A few hours. I'm guessing he couldn't speak? Fumbled his words? And clumsy in his movements?'

'That's right, sir,' agreed Mrs. Innes.

'That's the way it goes. But there's nothing to say he couldn't have made himself understood, if he was lucky, before he went. He might, for example, have told you who gave him the whisky.'

'But he didn't!' said Innes.

'But that's what I mean: it was chancy. He might have been able to tell you: it's somebody's very good luck that he could not, I'd say.'

'We've been wondering,' Murray said, trying to sound as unobtrusive as possible, 'where he went in the morning, but several people have said it looks like his own whisky bottle. Could someone have sneaked into the cottage in his absence and filled it with the mercury?'

'They could indeed,' Thomson admitted with a scowl. 'Or they could have gived it to him when he was out.'

'Yes, either,' Murray agreed, keen to keep the peace.

Thomson sighed, and turned to Innes.

'Is there anything else in the cottage you wouldna expect?'

'The whisky was unexpected,' said Innes. 'I didna know he'd the flask full.'

'Could someone have done it earlier than yesterday, and he hadn't noticed?'

The Inneses exchanged glances.

'Mebbe,' said Mrs. Innes slowly. 'If it had been full he wouldna have drunk it all the one day.'

'Would he no?' said Innes, darkly.

'But is there anything else bar the whisky? We ken that's strange,' said Thomson impatiently.

'Or is there anything missing?' Murray added.

Innes stared at his wife, and shrugged.

'He hadna much stuff, and what was dear to him he kept here on that shelf in the box bed. And there's a wee cupboard behind it, and all. That's where he kept his wee bit money.'

His wee bit money, thought Murray. I wonder how much the wee bit was, if he was blackmailing students?

'Let's see,' said Thomson, but he could not quite reach the cupboard or the shelf with Newell's body arranged on the edge of the bed. Innes went to lean over, but Thomson stopped him.

'I'd sooner it wasna you looking.' He pursed his lips. 'Mr. Murray, you're a tall man.' He made it sound like something else uncharacteristic of a decent Wigtownshire gentleman. 'Would you do the job?'

'Gladly,' said Murray, ignoring his tone, and leaned over Newell to the shelf, which contained a dry crusie lamp and a piece of elderly bacon on a pewter plate. He passed them back to Thomson.

'He'll have been keeping that there in case the students ate it,' said Mrs. Innes wryly. Murray leaned over again, one balancing finger against the shelf, and opened the little cupboard door in the wooden wall. The door opened towards him and did not flatten back against the wall, so he had to feel inside, very tentatively. The cupboard formed a cubic space, approximately a foot each way. The floor of it was wooden, and dusty, and the sides, back and roof were the same. It was empty.

'Empty?' echoed Innes, and looked as if he would like to have jumped on to the bed to check for himself. Murray reached in again, quartering the space with his long fingers. It was definitely empty.

'Then where's his money?' asked Innes. 'Dinna tell me the old miser's going to make us pay to put him in the ground and all!'

The doctor and the sheriff's man retreated for the night to Stranraer and their own homes, as there was no inn to stay in. The doctor had brought a gig, and Thomson's horse had been fed and watered, so there was no impediment to their departure and Murray and Coulter at last relaxed in the manse parlour, with the usual brandy punch. Murray stretched out his legs towards the fire.

'So tell me, Murray: what did your servant mean about you investigating unexpected deaths?' said Coulter, one eyebrow raised at him. 'You listened very attentively to all the students' accounts today, and then I find you have nipped off to spy on the examination of Newell's body, which cannot have been for any aesthetic reasons. What have you been up to, and what are you up to now?'

Murray pushed a hand through his hair and took a strong sip of punch.

'It's a long enough story, if I tell all,' he said. 'Remember when Professor Keith died when we were at St. Andrews?'

'Oh … yes. I was away that term, but I heard something about it.'

'Well, that was the start, I suppose,' said Murray. 'And with one thing and another, I suppose I have some familiarity with sudden deaths. My late wife thought I sought them out, but I really don't: it's only that I find that if I am confronted by an unexpected death, I feel a compulsion to discover what I can about it, to allow, if you'll permit the superstition, the victim to rest in peace, and to save the innocent from any suspicion that might have fallen upon them.'

'In this case the students? Innes?' Coulter suggested.

'That I don't know. I don't know at all. Yes, I like Innes, and the students are an interesting set, but as to whether any of them deliberately or accidentally killed Newell, that I don't know. Yet.'

The mail the following day brought another reassuring and

entertaining letter from Mrs. Helliwell concerning Augusta, and there was as yet no sign of the surly and shiny Thomson, so Murray was already well disposed to enjoy the day when a note came down from Kirkwelland House inviting Coulter and Murray to spend the afternoon there and dine with the family and the students. Coulter scowled.

'I have not yet written my sermon for tomorrow,' he explained. 'I always leave it till Saturday, in case any event occurs that I feel I need to address – in this case, perhaps Newell's death, indeed. Oh, but Gibson is here …'

'What has that to do with it?' Murray was reluctant to let anything stand in the way of a day with Miss Herkless.

'Oh, Gibson is an excellent, an extraordinary preacher. Perhaps I could ask him if he would be prepared to do it, if he is feeling strong enough.'

'He has visions, Nugent said,' Murray remembered. 'Dreams, perhaps?'

'He sees something, certainly. I think Gibson lives in two worlds,' said Coulter thoughtfully. 'He sees the world about him, and then as if layered between the features of our world like tissue, he sees wonders. He is a remarkable young man. He also has the virtue of preaching extempore, so he will not struggle with words on the page, like us lesser mortals. He will retire to pray, and then speak.'

'Impressive, indeed, particularly in one so young. Well, that being the case, would it be a good idea to accept this invitation and then you can ask him?'

Coulter permitted himself a small smile.

'Miss Herkless is very charming, is she not?' he asked, and Murray grinned. 'I cannot imagine myself considering another woman. You are fortunate, Charles, to be able to think of such things after your wife's death.'

Murray felt his face twist.

'It is longer since my wife died,' he said quietly. 'And perhaps … perhaps …' He could not think of a way of going on that would suit the occasion. 'Suffice it to say,' he said at last, 'that I could see myself marrying again, if I thought it would bring happiness to both parties.' If there was rather more emphasis on the last part of the sentence, Coulter did not seem to notice. Murray laid a hand on his friend's arm, unable to tell him whether or not he would ever feel the same way: Bessie Coulter had by all accounts been a lovely woman.

When Coulter had gone out to see the Inneses, Murray rang for Mrs. Veitch.

'I wonder if you could help me, Mrs. Veitch,' he said. 'I think I heard someone say yesterday or the day before that Mrs. Black, the doctor's widow, sells sweetmeats?'

'That's right, sir,' Mrs. Veitch agreed. 'When Dr. Black died she found herself in a bit of a guddle, sir, in money terms, and she's no seamstress – and anyway, Mrs. Innes is the seamstress in the town and it would be hard enough to compete with her. So she turned to making sweetmeats and bonbons and the like, as being an occupation suitable for a gentlewoman, I suppose.'

'Does she do well?'

'I believe so, sir. The boys at the school are ready customers, of course, when they have a penny or two, and there are a few others about the place who make a point of buying one or two of her kinds of things each week. I have a sweet tooth myself, Mr. Murray, but I'm a cake hand, I'm no a sweet hand. I hear she's very well liked in the line.'

'I see. Could you send Walter in, please?'

Walter appeared readily.

'I'd like you to go to Mrs. Black's – do you remember the doctor's widow, in the north of the village?'

'I remember the look of the house, sir,' said Walter dubiously.

'I'll draw you a little plan,' said Murray, scribbling on a piece of paper. 'I want you to go there with this shilling, and buy a little of each of her sweetmeats, please.' Walter's face lit up with an unearthly glow, and Murray laughed. 'Don't eat any of them! Or not till I've seen them, anyway. Bring them back safely here in the first place. All right?' He handed Walter the plan, and showed him his path on it. Walter's face dimmed again, but he nodded resolutely, and set out. Murray waited anxiously at the window until he reappeared.

'I kenned I'd gone wrong when I reached the tannery again,' he explained, knocking the mud off his boots at the door. 'But I went back and tried again, and here I am – and here are the sweetmeats,' he said in triumph, handing over a large bag.

'Well done, Walter!' Murray took the bag and tipped it carefully out on to the parlour table, while Walter hovered, inhaling the sugary scent. The sweets made a pretty little heap on the cloth: there were two marzipan birds coloured red and green, a few sugared almonds, a piece of sticky jellied something, which immediately stuck to the cloth, one tiny square of chocolate conserve, and a twist of paper containing a lump of soft toffee. Nothing, not even the chocolate, had any decoration that appeared to be shiny or metallic.

'This is a sample of everything she had?' Murray asked.

'That's right, sir. But she said they were made fresh most days, so maybe she had something different yesterday or the day before.'

'Good point. Was she busy?'

'There were two other people waiting, sir. They go round the back of the house to the kitchen and it's laid out there at the window. It's not like a sweetmeat shop in Edinburgh, sir: there's nowhere for anybody to sit and eat and there were no big puddings. Everyone just took what they wanted and paid for it and went.'

'Interesting. Do you fancy any of these, Walter?'

'Oh, yes, sir!'

'Well,' Murray fished out the toffee and slid the rest of the sweets back into the poke, detaching the jelly carefully. 'Here you are. Don't eat them all at once!'

Walter vanished with his prize at unaccustomed speed, and Murray popped the toffee into his mouth. It was soft and buttery and almost immediately out of control: he hoped that no one would call for at least the next half hour as he tried to chew with any dignity at all. He remembered Newell's old yellow teeth: what had been his sweetmeat of choice?

In the early afternoon, they strolled up to Kirkwelland House in the midst of a misty spring shower, the kind of rain that does not fall but imbues the whole air with droplets that find their way down collars and up cuffs. The weather had apparently chased the company in from the garden, and they were now trapped in the drawing room where Murray had been before, turning their backs on the rain or gazing out at it resentfully. A fire had been freshly lit, but the south-facing windows allowed plenty of light to cheer the scene, too. Murray was a little dismayed to find the Pringles already there, along with Mrs. Black, but Mrs. Black and Mr. and Mrs. Pringle were already settled at cards. Adair and Herkless were chatting easily while Nugent and Gibson were reading, and Miss Pringle and Kitty Herkless were at a table, sewing and talking in low voices. McCullough beamed when he saw Coulter and Murray announced, and as soon as Kitty and her father had greeted the new guests he too hurried forward.

'I'm delighted to see you, sir! Is there any news of poor Mr. Newell's family? How are they?'

'They are tolerably well, thank you, McCullough.'

'Could I visit them, do you think? Is there any comfort I could offer them?'

'I'm sure they would appreciate any company,' said Coulter, 'for Newell was not popular amongst the neighbours and they have had only a few people come to wake with them. Mr. Thomson has not yet given them permission to have the funeral.'

'That makes it very difficult for them,' agreed McCullough.

'Aye,' said Herkless, 'it would be reassuring to have the old man safely into the ground. He was never fragrant, but he cannot be improving.'

'Father!' Kitty shook her head at him. It was not a girlish toss of the head, but her curls still caught the light enticingly.

'It's a practical point,' he told her. 'I'm sure Thomson is well aware of it. No sign of him yet today? I so look forward to our amicable exchanges of opinion.'

'Nothing that I've seen or heard,' said Coulter.

'It will be found to have been an accident,' said Pringle with authority, addressing them from the midst of his cards. Murray noticed with interest that Mrs. Black's little stack of counters was the largest at the table. 'It is patently ridiculous, this rumour of murder and violence.'

'Why do you think so, sir?' Murray asked humbly.

'Firstly,' said Pringle, fixing Murray with a superior stare, 'to imagine that anyone in this village would murder anyone is highly improbable. Secondly, no one in the village would have the first idea where to obtain mercury. Thirdly, no one amongst the villagers would have any idea that mercury was poisonous or that it might be a suitable method for murder. These points are irrefutable.'

'I see. Thank you,' Murray replied dutifully, disagreeing completely.

'Your arguments are most telling, as always, Pringle. We are lucky to have such good sense spoken amongst us,' said Herkless, but Murray caught his daughter flashing him another warning look, even as her eyes danced. Pringle glowed.

'Nevertheless, sir,' said Adair from the windowseat, 'Mr. Thomson seems to think that one of us would be perfectly capable of murder, and presumably he does not find the method unlikely. He subjected us to some questioning yesterday, and demanded we remain during his investigation.'

'Good heavens!' Miss Pringle stared up from her work, quite pale. 'He cannot think that you have anything to do with Newell's death, can he?'

'That at least,' said her father, 'is a more reasonable theory. We know much less of our visiting students than we do of our fellow villagers. Any one of you might be capable of violence.'

Anna Pringle squeaked in alarm.

'Father, surely we know these gentlemen? And more charming gentlemen could not be found!'

'Do not be taken in by appearances, my dear,' said Pringle firmly, oblivious to any offence he might be causing.

'Whatever our violent proclivities,' said Adair with a smile, 'surely it is much less likely that we should have reason to murder Mr. Newell? If you do not know us, then we also do not know you.'

'You could have struck him down for his money,' said Herkless, with a grin. 'A notably wealthy man, Newell.'

'He's joking,' Kitty Herkless explained quickly, just in case.

'Nevertheless, his savings have disappeared,' said Murray. 'The Inneses said he had some money hidden in his box bed, and it has gone.'

'There you are, then,' said Pringle comfortably. 'No need to be well acquainted with someone to murder them for their money.'

'I admit defeat, then, sir,' said Adair.

'No doubt you'll hand yourself over to the sheriff's man as soon as he reappears?' asked Herkless. Adair smiled.

'Of course!'

'I pray you do no such thing!' cried Anna Pringle. 'How could you even think of it? Horrid Mr. Newell is dead and Papa says it must be an accident, so we should just leave it at that, should we not?' She glanced uncertainly from her father to Adair and on to Herkless, seeking reassurance.

'I'm sure Mr. Adair will never do anything so foolish, Anna,' said Kitty soothingly. 'He is joking, too.'

'He cannot be joking about such a thing!' Anna stared wide-eyed at Adair, whose smile faltered a little. He let his attention be caught by something outside the wet windows and turned away. 'I declare you are all much too clever for me,' she finished a little sadly.

'Not at all: the gentlemen are being very unfair,' said Kitty, with a glare at her father. 'You are quite right: it is not a matter to be joked about. Do not make yourself anxious over it: no doubt Mr. Pringle is quite right and it has all been a terrible accident.' She met Murray's eye and shot him a warning look: he knew he should take it as advice not to pursue the subject, and that the same look was no doubt directed at others in the room, but the moment's connexion pleased him very much. Kitty turned away to soothe Anna, and Murray moved to ask Herkless about his estate, but he still felt the connexion, invisible across the room, and wondered how he might make it stronger.

Chapter Seven

'Oh, good heavens,' said Herkless as the brandy circled the table. 'I'd forgotten the rude mechanicals.'

Adair poured himself a tiny glass and slid the bottle on to Murray. McCullough was frowning absently.

'Oh, no!' said Coulter. 'So had I.' He looked contrite. 'Do you think we could go now? Would the ladies mind?'

'I think we probably ought to go,' said Herkless. 'I'm supposed to be talking to them about rocks.' He smiled round the table.

'Is this the mutual improvement society?' Murray asked. 'If there is a general invitation, may I make one of the party?'

'It is a tedious business,' said Pringle. He flared his nostrils at the table's perfect polish, and speared a marzipan flower with his knife. Murray wondered if Mrs. Black had made them.

'Not at all, Mr. Pringle,' said Coulter. 'Even if the subjects themselves are not of sufficient interest, surely observing the broadening of minds and feeding of intellectual curiosity is reward enough for attending.'

'There are plenty of minds that should never be broadened,' said Pringle, chewing the marzipan in a stately fashion.

'Not amongst our villagers, I am sure!' Coulter was defensive.

'Certainly you are very welcome to make one with us,' said Herkless. 'Though I admit my talk is poorly prepared and your own mind might not be much broadened by it.'

'I'll take that risk, sir,' said Murray with a smile.

'The ladies no doubt will stay here,' Herkless went on. 'Coulter, you'll come of course. Gentlemen? Who will join us?'

'I should like …' began Gibson hesitantly.

'But if you are to preach tomorrow, Hugh,' McCullough interrupted him gently, 'should you not see to it that you have a good night's rest?'

Gibson's face turned up in concern for an instant, then relaxed.

'Of course. You are quite right. Forgive me, I forget that I am not as strong as others.'

'Strong in other things, perhaps,' said McCullough. 'Perhaps I should also stay here,' he added.

'I'd like to go, if I may,' said Nugent, who had been quiet that evening. 'Since we can get no further yet, I'd like to make my time useful, and I always liked natural philosophy at the college.'

'You'd be most welcome. Adair?'

'I'm not sure,' said Adair, sipping his brandy with the air of a connoisseur. 'You have made your home so comfortable and welcoming that it would take a considerable charm to lure me from its warmth this evening.' Nugent scowled at him.

'Well, I'm staying here,' said Pringle firmly. 'The school room on a wet evening, filled with the uneducated, holds no delights for me.'

'Then I encourage you to help yourself to more brandy, Pringle,' said the laird generously, 'and we'll go and excuse ourselves to the ladies.'

Pringle gulped down the spirit and rose with the rest of them to return to the drawing room, where the ladies were waiting. Kitty smiled as her father came in, smoothing down her pale blue silk dress. A simple necklace winked at her throat, and her black curls had matching combs holding them in check. Murray had found it hard to keep his eyes from her at dinner, and now began to regret promising to go out again.

'My dear,' said Herkless to Kitty, 'you must forgive us – I had forgotten the rude mechanicals this evening.'

'Oh, Father! You are quite hopeless.' Kitty frowned at him. 'I reminded you this morning at breakfast. I suppose you don't even remember where your box of rocks is!'

'Oh! Good gracious, yes, I should have forgotten that, too. Whatever should I do without you?'

'Survive very nicely, I daresay,' said Kitty, with a grin. 'They are on the hall table.'

'I am not going,' Pringle announced, as if all he lacked was a herald with a trumpet. He seated himself on a chair by the fire. Mrs. Pringle's face was blank, but her lips seemed a little tight.

'Are the rest of you all to abandon us?' asked Kitty. 'Mr. Murray, I am sure you will be fascinated by the mutual improvers. They have a great spirit of curiosity.'

'Since you encourage me to leave, madam, I shall!' He bowed, and she laughed.

'Would that others were so quick to take hints!' she murmured, then turned away. 'And Mr. Coulter, of course you must go, we understand.'

'Gibson and I will remain,' said McCullough with a little bow, perhaps feeling that he ought to emulate Murray.

'But I must retire early,' said Gibson.

'I had no intention of placing such a restriction on your evening when I asked you to preach,' said Coulter guiltily.

'Not at all: I thank you heartily for the privilege,' said Gibson. 'I am sure if I had to preach weekly I should have to build up my stamina as you have done.'

'That's right, that's right,' said McCullough. He edged towards a sopha and Murray wondered if the unaccustomed richness of the meal and the accompanying wines had taken its effect on him.

'But I'm going,' said Nugent, when Kitty turned to him. 'I'm looking forward to it.'

'And you, Mr. Adair?' called Anna Pringle, already organising herself at the pianoforte. The candlelight painted her red hair and cream skin most beautifully against the dark polished wood. 'Are you to go, or will you come and turn the music for me?'

Adair glanced at her, and coughed slightly.

'You must forgive me, Miss Pringle, for I have already promised to go to the mutual improvement meeting.' He bowed, more elegantly than McCullough, though his cheeks were flushed. Murray was surprised: surely there was nothing in Miss Pringle's invitation to make him change his mind – and even to lie? Adair's response was so smoothly done that for a moment Murray thought that he himself had misremembered Adair's words in the dining room, but he had definitely said he was inclined to stay at Kirkwelland House. Perhaps the presence of Pringle put him off – it was not unlikely.

'Pringle, you will have observed, is a man who has progressed further in life by looks and stature than by any more cerebral aptitude,' Herkless said as they followed servants with lanterns down the drive to the village. One of them was Walter, but as he kept close to Herkless's servant Murray was less worried than he might have been. 'And as the looks decline, of course, the stature increases.'

'Why is he so reluctant to see the villagers better educated?' Murray asked.

'I should think he knows that most of them are cleverer than he is already, and with a little education might render him entirely superfluous,' said Herkless. 'Wouldn't you say, Coulter?'

'He is not perhaps the best informed of men,' Coulter agreed. 'And not everyone wants to see the lower classes benefit from education and information.'

'Surely it depends on what they do with it?' asked Adair. 'If they find that they can make their political arguments clear, will some of them not rise in revolution, like the French did?'

'But if they are educated,' said Coulter, diffidently, 'then perhaps they are less likely to rise in revolution unless it is with good reason? Less likely to be swayed by some bold orator?'

'Education is just a good thing in itself,' said Nugent unexpectedly. 'Anything that stretches your mind, that gets you thinking beyond the next shoe, the next ditch, the next nail. Even if you have to keep on making the shoe and digging the ditch and hammering the nail.'

'I see you are of my own mind, Mr. Nugent,' said Herkless, turning to look at him. 'Perhaps you would like to carry this box of rocks for a little?'

Nugent gave a brief, snorting laugh, and took the box.

'Aye,' he said, 'but I'll be thinking while I'm carrying it.'

They all chuckled at that. The lantern light misted through the rain, and Murray pulled his collar a little higher under the brim of his hat. There was a reason why the west coast was so green, he remembered.

Herkless adjusted his step to walk with him.

'The students say you were present at their talks with Thomson yesterday,' he began, 'and I noted myself your interest in the case. Were you acquainted with Newell previously? Or with Innes?'

'Not at all,' said Murray. 'I met them only the day before Newell died.'

'He likes unexplained deaths,' Coulter put in from Murray's other side.

'"Like" is not the word I would have chosen,' said Murray. 'In fact, I dislike them to the extent that I wish to see whatever was the cause exposed and explained.'

'You have studied such things before?' asked Herkless, interested.

'Once or twice,' said Murray. 'Last autumn, an old woman in my village was found dead. Of course, I felt responsible for finding out what had happened to her.'

'Pringle would declare it to be natural causes, unless your villagers are unusually ill-disposed and intelligent. Though of course, you live on the east coast and are deceived as to the possibility of farming cattle: presumably anything unnatural could happen in your village.'

They laughed again.

'Our cattle are very small!' Murray agreed. 'Or perhaps I have confused them with sheep.'

'Here is the schoolhouse,' said Coulter, as Herkless's servant grabbed Walter's shoulder to stop him at the school gate. 'I see it is already well lit.'

'I trust we are not too late,' said Herkless. 'I should hate poor Nugent here to have carried the box of rocks for nothing!'

'Me too, sir,' agreed Nugent, and followed Herkless into the schoolhouse.

The schoolhouse was not extensive, and contained six or eight desks with low benches attached to them, designed to seat three small children or two larger ones. The air was ripe with a proliferation of tallow candles to illuminate the scientific endeavour therein, and already busy with a dozen or so men, some in their best coats, some in shirt sleeves, gathered around the master's desk at the front of the room and eagerly discussing something that lay before them. At the sound of the door, one tallish figure turned round and Murray recognised Innes, a black neckcloth casual at his collar. Innes' face fell at the sight of the laird.

'I think perhaps they were hoping I would have forgotten!' said Herkless quietly to Murray and Coulter, but Innes was across the room in three strides, hands out placatingly.

'Mr. Herkless! Sir, I must tell you at once. The thermometer you so generously gave me – it has been broken!'

'Oh!' Herkless's eyes widened, struggling to pitch his regret correctly.

'Of course, so you said,' said Murray quickly, to give him time. 'You haven't found out what happened to it?'

'No, sir, I have not. Forgive me interrupting your conversation, sir, but I had to tell Mr. Herkless straightaway. Sir, I cannot begin to apologise enough for this terrible accident,' he went on to Herkless.

'Well, accidents do happen, Innes,' said Herkless. 'Was it on its bracket in the lane?'

'Yes, sir.'

'And the bracket did not give way?'

'No, sir. The bulb was broken off the bottom of the tube, sir. Something must have hit it as it went down the lane – maybe someone carrying a box or the like.'

'I don't suppose,' said Murray thoughtfully, 'that Mr. Newell ever left his whisky flask on the ground there, under the thermometer?'

'Oh! I see what you mean, Murray. The mercury! Well, would he have done such a thing, Innes?'

Innes rubbed his eyes.

'You're saying maybe the mercury came out of my thermometer and went into Newell's whisky? Well, I'm not saying it didn't, but it wasn't me that put it there. And I doubt it was an accident, for Newell would never have left his whisky bottle unattended in the lane, I can tell you that.'

'And you heard nothing, I suppose?' Murray went on, sure that it would have taken a great deal of provocation on Innes' part to make him break his precious thermometer. 'No breaking glass, no sound of a collision outside your door?'

'Nothing, sir.' Innes shrugged his hunched shoulders. 'I wish I could say I had, but to be truthful I did not.'

Herkless met Murray's eye.

'Curious,' he said. 'Well, there's one of Pringle's statements neatly refuted. The villagers could not get mercury. Mercury has disappeared in the village. Ergo, a villager could get mercury.'

'And not just a villager, of course,' added Adair, though Murray thought his words were very slightly slurred. 'A student would have been able to do that, too, that.'

'You're quite determined to be arrested, Adair, aren't you?' asked Herkless with amusement.

'Be careful,' said Coulter. 'I'm not sure Thomson would share your sense of humour. He might take you all too seriously.'

''Sfunny being back in school again,' said Adair, leaning on a nearby desk. 'Makes me feel very old.' He wobbled.

'I think perhaps you ought to sit down, at your advanced age,' said Murray, and took him gently by the elbow. McCullough was not the only one who had apparently overdone the wines. Adair must be unused to them, or surely the walk down from Kirkwelland House would have worn off the effects a little. He eased Adair on to the bench attached to the desk, where his knees stuck up like a Jenny Meggie. Innes, still fretting about his thermometer, watched him absently.

'Well, I have come ready to give my little talk,' said Herkless, with a glance at Adair. 'Would you like me to give it, or to leave it for another evening?'

'Oh, aye, aye sir, please come up to the front,' said Innes, and he coughed to draw the attention of the company. They moved away reluctantly from the master's desk, where Murray could see – and smell – a selection of seaweeds laid out for comparison. He wondered if the schoolmaster would be grateful. Innes pushed them to one side and invited Herkless up on to the shallow platform, while the other members of the group arranged themselves easily on the school benches. A younger man, nudged into action, lounged forward with four chairs and set them along the back of the room, bowing to Murray, Coulter and Nugent, who sat as directed.

'Surely it would be hard enough to collect mercury falling from a thermometer on a wall?' Coulter asked Murray, leaning to his ear.

'I'm not sure: I've never really considered it before,' said Murray. 'Adair, do you want to move to this chair? I'm sure you'd be more comfortable.'

'No, no, 'sfine,' said Adair, leaning back against the desk. 'This is remarkably comfable. More comfable than I remember from when I was at school.'

'Is he drunk?' asked Coulter, eyes wide.

'I hope so – if not I'm not sure what's wrong with him.'

'But that's very bad,' said Coulter. 'I don't remember seeing him drink that much at dinner.'

'No,' said Murray thoughtfully. 'He may not be accustomed to it.'

Adair settled back, folded his hands on his lap and closed his eyes.

'Now, then, friends.' Innes raised his voice at the front of the schoolroom, and the members quietened at their desks, even when they were squashed into place. 'Mr. Herkless has very generously come to talk to us this evening, on the subject of – have I got this right, sir? 'The Geology of Kirkwelland'.

'That's the thing, Innes. Many thanks. And thank you, men, for allowing me to talk to you this evening. I have brought some rocks with me and I shall pass them around for you all to see as I'm talking – though of course you will all have seen the like around the village and the parish, and no doubt there are some here who know much more about this than I do. But these are some of my own observations on the subject. Now, I shall start, as it were, at the top of the parish – for to start up on the hill suited my temperament well, for it meant that in preparation for this part of the talk I had to stray only a very short distance indeed from my own front door.'

The audience laughed a little and settled back, prepared to enjoy themselves. Adair emitted a tiny snore.

Herkless's talk, which he made without any more aid to memory than the rocks he produced from his box and passed around, was both intelligent and entertaining. He had pitched it perfectly to appeal to his audience's desire for education and their local knowledge, and layered it with little local jokes and occasional teasing of village figures amongst their number, but in such a way that even strangers like Murray and Nugent laughed along with the others. It all went down very well, and fortunately Adair's continued snoring was mostly masked by the laughter and applause. Herkless left the platform and returned to the back of the schoolroom grinning around the room, and took the fourth seat by the wall.

'Well done, sir!' said Murray. 'I feel I have learned a great deal!'

'No more than you would have learned in a quick perusal of the encyclopaedia, I promise you,' Herkless said. 'The day this society finds themselves a copy, I shall be entirely redundant.'

'I'm sure the encyclopaedia is nowhere near as entertaining a read,' said Murray sincerely. Herkless grinned again.

'That takes only knowledge of the fine people of Kirkwelland.'

The members of the society had now risen from their desks and were about the room, some back with the seaweed, others discussing a pamphlet apparently concerned with improved plough shares. Murray, looking about, was startled to see Thomson, the sheriff's man, standing to attention by the door and watching proceedings with a grim air. Innes apparently did not notice him, but followed Herkless to the back of the room, and bowed to Murray.

'Would you care, sir, to see something of the scientific equipment we've been fortunate enough to gather together? Since you so kindly expressed an interest in my weather records the other day.'

'I'd be delighted,' said Murray, and rose to follow him. Along the wall from their seats was a solid wooden chest with a hasp but no padlock or keyhole. Innes swung it open with a jerk, and Murray and Nugent, with Coulter and Herkless nearby, peered inside.

'We have,' said Innes, in tones of some awe, 'two microscopes!' He drew out a battered brass tube with a plate attached to the bottom by curling brackets. 'Of which,' he added proudly, 'this is the lesser. The greater is in use, as you may see more closely shortly, up there on the desk.' He waved at the master's desk where, as Murray could now see, there was the tilting brass apparatus on longer legs which he had seen before – his friend Blair had one. One of the members was carving the seaweed into long, fine strips while another squinted down the eyepiece, and a third held a candle none too steadily near the other end, dripping tallow on to the desk.

'Mr. Herkless gave us the wee one, which is handy for the field, and the other we bought when Dr. Black died. Here's a compass that was gived us by one of the students passing through. We dinna use that that much, for we've all lived here all our lives and we ken well which way is which. But no doubt it'll come in useful one of these days. Then this is a chartometer,' he said the word carefully. 'There's none of us kens what you do with it except only Mr. Gourlay up at the mains farm – and I'm no sure he kens either,' he admitted. 'But one day we'll learn, nae doubt. Then there's these wee tiny scales, only one of the weights is missing. Are they no bonny?' He lifted them out of the kist by their centre point and turned them delicately in his hand, admiring them.

'Very bonny,' agreed Murray. 'So tiny.'

'Aye, you couldna weigh your bag of flour on them,' said Innes with a little smile. 'Then Raffan down at the smithy, he's gey clever wi' his hands and he's made us these wee tiny tweezers.' He opened a wooden box to show a cloth lining and a row of graded tweezers slipped into it neatly. 'They get a lot of use: I'm waiting for one or two of them to go astray.'

'So your members can borrow these and take them out and around to carry out their own observations?' Murray asked.

'That's right. Or they can use them here on Saturday nights. See, we have a wee book to say who has what: Mr. Gourlay has a pocket sundial at the minute, for he wants to make a big one and he needs it to copy.'

'What's this?' asked Nugent, who had been poking around amongst the kist's contents. He fingered a long rod of iron with brackets attached to it.

'It's cried a – now, what was it? A retort stand, aye. See, we can attach things to it and then heat them up with the end of a candle, maybe, or look at the light through them to see if the light goes sideways – have you heard tell of David Brewster? He does all that kind of thing. Who knows, one of us here might make some michty discovery! Only, we only have the one wee glass tube to use, so we need to be careful.'

'What are these books?' Murray asked, for the equipment only filled the top of the kist.

'Well, here's Raffan's book: he likes wee flowers, and he collects them and flattens them out like this and glues them into the book. See?'

Each page had a few flowers pressed on to it, with notes underneath as to where and when they had been found.

'A botanist,' said Murray. 'A very useful skill. Every physician must learn it.'

'Well, I hope he stays a smith,' said Innes frankly. 'He's mair use to us that way, in an everyday kind of way. These ones are just pamphlets that we find here and there, mostly on farming,' he went on, pulling out a couple of them and showing the covers to the gentlemen.

'And the box at the bottom?' asked Nugent, not wanting to miss anything.

'Oh,' said Innes, 'that's our chemicals box!'

'May I see?' asked Nugent eagerly. Innes moved the pamphlets aside and hooked his hands under the wooden box, pulling it out with care and balancing it on the corner of the kist.

'I'd be better on the desk, maybe. Or one of those chairs,' he said uncertainly, and Murray spun a chair quickly round for him to slip the box on to. They crowded in to watch as he opened the close-fitting lid.

The inside was designed like a travelling medicine chest: Murray had one himself back at the manse. There were twelve sections, most with bottles slipped snugly into them, others with folds of paper.

'What do you have, then?' Murray asked. He glanced up and saw that Walter, who had been sitting quietly on a stool during the proceedings, had now irresistibly approached and was staring into the kist in deep fascination. Behind him Thomson lurked, watching every move Innes made.

'There's lead,' said Innes, pulling out a fold of paper, 'and some iron filings, thanks to Raffan, of course. We have a magnet somewhere but I think someone has that out. Then this is saltpetre.'

'That they use for gunpowder?' asked Coulter, slightly alarmed. Walter's eyes widened.

'Aye, that's where we got it, from the gunsmith in Stranraer. This is a bit of copper, you'll see. This bottle's vitriol, as far as we know – there's none of us wants to open it in case it is. Mr. Gourlay, he got a look once in Glasgow at a book called the

Edinburgh New Dispensatory, and while he was there he bought a few wee bits and pieces he read about in it – this is sulphur, here, too. No, dinna open that, sir!' He jumped, but it was too late: Nugent had pulled out the stopper from a bottle and they all reeled back.

'Ammonia! Sorry!' said Nugent, choking. He shoved the stopper back quickly.

'Hm,' said Innes, trying to contain some annoyance. 'Chalk, there, that's not so bad. And sea salt. Arsenic – ca' canny with that one, then, sir. What's this? Oh, mercury, of course. Oh.'

He lifted the little bottle clear of the box, and eyed it distrustfully. It was only half full.

Chapter Eight

'I hope Adair is feeling better this morning,' said Coulter at breakfast.

'He was very much under the weather last night,' said Murray, who had helped to support him most of the way back to Kirkwelland House. It had been a long hill to climb, and though Adair had proved a very courteous drunk, he was tall and unwieldy.

'Or under the bottle.' Coulter gave a brief laugh. 'I don't think I've seen a man so drunk since we were at college ourselves. He must indeed be unaccustomed to it.'

'Poor fellow: still, his friend McCullough had sobered up and soon took him under his wing.'

'As long as he did not disturb Gibson! My preacher is too fragile to have drunken songs sung to him late on a Saturday night!'

'Is it a relief not to have to preach?' Murray asked. 'Or just not to have to write a sermon?'

Coulter made a wry face.

'I've written one anyway, just in case,' he said. 'If Gibson preaches, that's a mixed blessing. On the plus side, he's excellent, and I'm sure my congregation will benefit from hearing a different voice in the pulpit. He has preached here before, and is extremely popular. On the minus side, his delicacy of health can cause him to be unreliable – hence my own sermon – and then when he preaches he can be so wonderful I feel inadequate the next week, and my preaching goes very flat and self-conscious. And then if he preaches I feel guilty that I'm shirking my duty and not doing my own preaching, even though I am sure his sermon will be to the spiritual benefit of the parish. You see, it can be difficult. It's complicated.'

'Good heavens, yes. I had no idea. But he has permission to

preach, from the Presbytery, I suppose?'

'Yes: he has permission to preach, I believe, from every presbytery he passes through between Glasgow and Portpatrick. He talks of building up his stamina but he must already have to depend on serious inner strength, to meet all the demands of those he preaches for. He is a remarkable young man.'

'I'm looking forward to hearing him.'

Murray went across early to the church with Coulter, who wanted to make his preparations before the congregation began to arrive. Murray sat in the front pew, where the manse family would normally sit, at Coulter's direction, though Murray had seen how bleak his eyes went at that and at his wife's grave just outside the church door. It would take time yet, no doubt, though he was seeing less of the worrying depths of grief that had caused Mr. Helliwell to ask him to visit. Soon he would be able to go home to Augusta – once the matter of Newell's death was settled. It was the first time he had felt pulled in two directions so strongly: he longed to go home to his daughter, but the thought of breaking away from the village before the murder was solved made his head ache.

Soon the villagers began to arrive and settle themselves in their accustomed pews, or on stools they had brought to the back of the church – Murray checked to see that Walter was there, with Mrs. Veitch. Mrs. Black, rounded and dull in her mourning, sat halfway up, with the Pringles in front of her: all of them nodded to Murray with varying degrees of friendliness, Mrs. Black the most enthusiastic. Coulter poked his head out of the vestry now and again, looking anxious but resigned, but it was only just before the service was due to start that the party arrived from Kirkwelland House. Murray's pulse gave a little thump as Mr. Herkless and Kitty, with a long-tailed, leaf-green pelisse over her cloud-white gown, led the way to the front pew on the other side from Murray. The students filed in after them, Adair washed out, Nugent scrubbed, leaving Gibson last and McCullough beside him, watching him like a mother bird waiting for the first flight of its chick.

The service began, and Murray glanced across a couple of times at Gibson. The student spent much of it on his knees, his face screwed up in concentration, eyes tightly closed. When the time came for him to preach, he lurched from his seat as if dizzy, but caught the end of the pew and steadied himself for the climb to the pulpit. The beadle, a little man with fuzzy white hair whom Murray remembered from the mutual improvement society, turned over the hourglass, and Gibson drew himself up, fastened his freckled hands on the ledge of the pulpit, and began.

For the hour for which Gibson preached, Murray could have sworn not one of the congregation moved a muscle, not even to breathe. He took the text 'And I shall make ye fishers of men,' and wove it into a speech of such great power that by the end there was more than one person dabbing a handkerchief to his eyes. The pictures he conjured, from the bay outside to the Sea of Galilee, the glittering fish in their nets and the gathering up of souls into the glory of heaven, swam even before their open gaze as if they had been cast into the air, fashioned from the dust by Gibson's mystical hands, and hovered before them in the spring sunlight. Murray finally drew breath as Gibson staggered back down to his seat, white and shaking, and McCullough turned on him a face shining with awe. And not just with awe, Murray suddenly realised: there was something else there, too, that took Murray aback. He looked away quickly and tried to focus on the psalter, putting what he had seen to the back of his mind.

The golden light of Gibson's sermon stayed with him – with them all, he thought probable – throughout the rest of the service. As the familiar words of psalms echoed around him he relished the feeling. There was nothing the age of reason could do to replace this kind of sensation, he thought. And sometimes reason made no sense at all. Last autumn he had thought his own villagers irrational when they began to talk of witches in their midst, but he himself had seen a few things, even in Letho, that he could not explain away, had allowed himself to panic. He could not dismiss his villagers' irrational beliefs in such a high-handed way if he found himself believing in things for which there was no rational explanation.

In the afternoon, his head still humming with the brightness of the service, he took himself out for a walk with Walter. Coulter had to preach at a little chapel of ease up in the hills behind Kirkwelland House but the day was very fair, and Murray could not resist it in his present mood. The headland he had found the other day lured him with its fine view of the loch, and he wondered if he would meet other villagers there, also enjoying the weather, who might easily submit to discreet questions about Newell, mercury and the old man's whereabouts the morning before his death.

Pringle's decided views on the availability of mercury in the village were being washed away with the tide. Not only was there a bottle of it at the popular mutual improvement society, where almost any member could have taken and used it, but Innes' large thermometer must have contained enough to poison anyone and though it was broken, there had been no trace of mercury on the ground below it. Who knew but that there might be other sources, too? Dr. Black, for example, might have had medicines containing quicksilver of which his widow had not disposed. Could Newell have obtained the whisky from her that morning, when he went to buy sweetmeats from her? The mercury might even have entered it by accident in Mrs. Black's house.

He glanced at Walter, hoping he had not put the boy in any danger with those sweetmeats. Then he remembered the look of delight on Walter's face: at least he would have suffered in a good cause. He smiled to himself, and called to Walter who had missed the turning for the headland road.

If Newell was a blackmailer, he went on in his head, who were his victims? Nugent had said that he was not one, but he had neatly avoided answering the same question about his fellow students. He had accused Newell of going through their packs, hunting for information. What might he have found? Or what might he have seen or heard, over the years, squatting in his dingy little box bed, listening and watching at the cracks as his students came and went? Murray shivered. The image was not a comfortable one, for anyone with something to hide.

But surely, as Nugent had suggested, if Newell had discovered the advantages of being a blackmailer he would not have limited his scope to the students, who, even if they had something they were prepared to pay to hide, only appeared a few times a year. He must also have at least thought about the possibility of his fellow villagers. Murray knew all too well that small communities had as many secrets, sometimes more, than larger ones, and individuals as eager to keep them. Was that what Newell had been seeking on his morning walks? New sources of income? And what had happened to that money?

He had been thinking and walking, staring at the ground unseeing as he went, when he realised that he had gone beyond the rocky outcrop at which he had intended to stop, where he had enjoyed the view a few days ago and talked with Adair. Instead the road now wound down slightly, still curling around the higher ground to his right and making for the north closer to the shore. Breaking off from the road to his right and mounting that higher ground to another headland was a broadish, sandy path. He stopped for a moment and gestured ahead.

'Well, Walter? Up or down?'

Walter considered.

'If we go down we'll have to come up again, sir,' he said at last. 'And forbye, the soles of my Sunday boots would likely slither if we went down on to that sand by those rocks.'

'Very well, then,' said Murray, not reluctant to climb up again to a good view. 'Let's go up.'

The path was easier than it looked, and they were soon high again. This time there were few rocks of any size between the path and the steep slope back down to the road, but on the landward side of the path was light woodland, mostly birch, leaning away from the prevailing winds. It was a pleasant spot on a sunny day, with gulls calling high in the sky and a goldfinch putting his heart into his song in the birches, and they stood for a long moment, gazing out at the loch below. It was flat and calm today, with no fishing boats out on the Sabbath anyway, the sapphire blue of the water and the turquoise of the sky pressing the far side of the loch between them in a broad green wedge, all dazzling with the intensity of their colours.

'Oh!' came a voice behind them. Murray spun round, to find Miss Anna Pringle on the path, one hand out, an expression of confusion on her pretty face.

'I beg your pardon, Miss Pringle,' said Murray, bowing. 'I hope I did not startle you.'

'Oh, Mr. Murray, no, not at all.' She curtseyed delicately. 'Um, I hope you are enjoying your walk?'

'Very much so, thank you. You have some beautiful views in

this part of the world, have you not?'

'I admire them very much,' said Miss Pringle, 'though I fear I have nothing to compare them to. I have never travelled further than Stranraer in all my life.'

'Well, I'm sure you have plenty of time yet, Miss Pringle. And you will have met plenty of people from outside Wigtownshire, and their talk must have broadened your experiences by proxy, surely?' He smiled, for he had the impression she was not entirely at ease. She held her bonnet in her hand, her glorious red hair uncovered, and he wondered if perhaps she felt this impropriety and was alarmed at what he might think.

'You have travelled very far, I think, sir?' she asked, seeming to gain courage.

'Quite far, from time to time.'

'Even from Fife – that is a long way! I hope, maybe, some day, I might travel a little.'

'Where would you most like to go?'

'Oh! Well … It always seems so unfair, that here we are so close to Ireland, and yet I have never been there. A whole other country!'

'That must certainly be tantalising. I have never been to Ireland, myself.'

'I am told it is a fair land, or the north is, anyway.'

'Of course, you will have had plenty of informants passing through the village who can give you a good account of it. No wonder it attracts you!'

Miss Pringle blushed.

'It is certainly refreshing to speak with people from elsewhere,' she murmured, not quite as if her mind were on her words.

'The students must broaden the social circle here,' said Murray, feeling he was doing nothing to make the conversation any more interesting.

'They do,' she said with sudden decision. 'And while the poor students are to be kept back here, we should make the most of it, and ensure they do not feel the time drag, should we not?'

'That's true enough,' said Murray, a little taken aback. 'Particularly if the weather holds fair like this.'

'A picnic!' she cried. 'We should have a picnic. A spring

picnic is so pleasant, much better than a summer one where everyone is over-heated and sleepy. That's what we must do! I think I must go and ask my mother at once. Please, do not let me hold you back from your lovely walk, Mr. Murray!' With a fleeting curtsey and a skip, she was away down the hill, before Murray even had the chance to think about bowing back.

'Good gracious, Walter, it seems we were present at a moment of inspiration.'

'Aye, sir. Sir?'

'Yes, Walter?'

'See those men last night?'

'Which – oh, the men at the mutual improvement society?'

'Aye, sir. Will we be staying here long, sir? In Kirkwelland, I mean, not up here on the hill.'

'I'm not sure. Not too long, I think.'

'Oh. But while we're here, sir, would it be all right if I went along to their meetings?'

'It depends if they'll let you.'

'I asked Mr. Innes last night, sir, and he said I could go if you would give me leave.'

'Oh, did you indeed?' Murray hid a smile. Walter had ways of getting what he wanted, but what he wanted was usually no bad thing, for his general education. 'Yes, Walter, you may go.'

'Thank you, sir!' Walter beamed. Murray wondered if he thought the next meeting would involve sweetmeats.

A thin breeze ruffled the trees and Murray looked up at the sound, only to see Herkless strolling towards them through the birch trees.

'Good afternoon, Mr. Murray,' he called, and bowed when he neared them. 'Thank you for helping with Adair last night: I'm only pleased the Pringles had already left, or we should have had the benefit of Pringle's wisdom on the subject, no doubt.'

'These things happen, particularly to students, I seem to remember!' said Murray.

'That is true enough,' Herkless agreed. 'I am sure I remember incidents during my own couple of years at the college in Glasgow – of course, they had no direct connection to me.' He grinned, giving himself the lie, and Murray nodded solemnly as if believing him. 'Gibson, however, is a different sort. What did you make of his sermon this morning?'

'Extraordinary. I never saw a congregation so clearly inspired,' said Murray sincerely.

'It is true: he is a rare beast. Whether he has the strength to maintain such a career is another question. He almost collapsed on the way back to the big house, even in our carriage, and went straight to bed when we reached home.'

'It would not bode well for tending to a parish. Perhaps an academic life would suit him better.'

'Well, that is up to him. McCullough looks after him devotedly, and mothers the rest of them into the bargain. You should have seen him clucking around Adair last night!'

Another swell of wind buffeted the trees, and Murray hunched his shoulders.

'Is that the kind of breeze that announces rain?' he asked. 'I hope not: someone was speaking of picnics to keep the students amused while they are here.'

'You'd be best to ask Innes, of course, our local weather expert. But I think not: this fine weather should hold for another few days, I should say. A picnic is an excellent idea. I like to eat out of doors, don't you?'

'Very much so,' agreed Murray. 'I should say you have some delightful sites to eat in, too – is this your land?'

Herkless surveyed the birches briefly, as if making sure.

'Yes, all these woods down to that burn there.' He pointed to a broad, shallow river running down into the rocky shoreline that Walter had chosen not to tackle in his Sunday boots.

'It is fine woodland,' said Murray, who took a keen interest in his own woods at Letho. 'Pleasantly mixed, I see, which is useful, too.'

'Plenty of game, but we have had some trouble with poachers lately. They are becoming so bold I half expect to see them come up the drive and lift the rabbits off our plates in the dining room.'

'Your gamekeeper can't find them?'

'He says not. It may be time to find a new gamekeeper, I suppose. This one is about as much use as a sugar umbrella.'

Murray had no recommendations to make, and fell silent. He wanted very much to ask after Kitty Herkless, but could not think how to do it without arousing a teasing suspicion on the part of her father.

'Well,' said Herkless at last, 'it's Newell's funeral tomorrow, and I daresay with your mysterious interest in the case you'll want to attend that – and much joy may you have of it! If we perhaps say Tuesday for the picnic? To be sure of the weather before it breaks again – and that's not to say it won't rain on Tuesday anyway. If one can be sure of anything in this part of the world, it is that we are unlikely to suffer the traumas of drought.'

'Tuesday should be fine, but I shall have to ask Coulter, of course. What about the students? If Thomson allows the Inneses to bury Newell, will he also let them go? It seems a shame to have a picnic for them just after they leave.'

'You saw Thomson at the meeting last night?'

'Yes.'

'I had a word. He is no nearer being sure who, if anyone, killed Newell, but he is also very far from losing hope over the matter. I should say the students are safely here for another week, at least.'

'They will not like that!'

'No. So a picnic to distract them for at least one afternoon is a splendid idea. I hope Coulter can come too!' He glanced about, half as if expecting to see Coulter emerge from the trees. 'Thought I heard something – perhaps the poachers are working by daylight now, so as not to spoil their night's sleep! I must do my lairdly bit and stride through the woods with authority, reminding them whose land they are on. Perhaps I could get Pringle to help? He always walks about as if he thinks he owns the place. He would convince them any time, much more than I seem to! No doubt I shall see you tomorrow about the village, but if not, ask Coulter to be kind enough to send a note up? And I shall get Kitty to write to the Pringles and Mrs. Black – the usual set. Thank heavens for the students and you, Mr. Murray!' He bowed, and hurried off in pursuit of whatever sound he had heard. Once again Murray was left standing on the headland with Walter, abruptly abandoned.

'This breeze is growing chilly, Walter. I think we should begin to head back,' he began to say, when they heard another step on the path leading up from the road, and Mrs. Black appeared, a pale grey shawl flying around her, and very short of breath.

'Mrs. Black!'

She jumped, and tried to gather the tails of her shawl about her and breathe through her nose at the same time. She managed a decent curtsey and Murray bowed.

'Lovely day, is it not?' she gasped.

'Delightful, though I am glad to see you are clever enough to be prepared for the wind with that shawl,' said Murray in a leisurely fashion, to give her the chance to recover. 'I was just remarking to my servant that it was growing chilly, though it makes a pretty effect amongst the birch leaves.'

'Very pretty,' she managed.

'Are you going far? Do you require an escort?' he asked.

'No, not at all! I try to take a little exercise each day, when the weather permits it.' She took another deep breath. 'A brisk walk up here helps me sleep, I find.'

'And the view is charming,' added Murray, for what seemed like the twentieth time on that headland. 'In that case, when you are ready may I walk you home?'

She paused, as if trying to think of a reason to decline him.

'That would be very kind of you, Mr. Murray. I had not realised until my husband died how useful a man was for that kind of thing – of course, I miss him in many ways but I had never been without someone to escort me until then. It felt very limiting at first.'

'May I enquire how long ago you suffered his loss?'

'Two years today, Mr. Murray. Two years today.'

A flash of envy passed across his mind: two years of full mourning for a spouse, and from tomorrow she could wear what colours she wanted, and dance till dawn if someone would play. He still had eighteen months to go.

Mrs. Black was gazing out to sea, remembering.

'He was a fine man, and a good doctor. I was lucky, for I loved him dearly and he treated me well, and left me well respected in the village.' Not so well off, though, Murray remembered, and wondered if she resented that at all. 'And people have been extremely kind ever since: I spend half my time up at Kirkwelland House, you know! It is a second home to me. Mr. Herkless and Kitty are like family.' The loch attracted her attention again, and she stared out over the darkening blue, flecked now with the white frills of wavelets in the rising breeze.

'I suppose you find you still have all kinds of things of your husband's around the house,' said Murray carefully. 'I know it took me some time to arrange my wife's affairs, and of course the life of a doctor would be rather more complicated. Medicines and apparatus and books to think of, I imagine?'

'Oh, you have no idea! Of course I rid myself of all the medicines and apparatus, except for a few things that were useful for my own medicine chest. Dr. Forbes from Stranraer purchased all those at a very generous price ... Books, now, he said he had most of what my husband kept, so I am left with some of those still.'

'He wouldn't have had,' said Murray, suddenly struck by a thought, 'a copy of the *New Edinburgh Dispensatory*, would he? Someone mentioned it last night and I have a fancy to see a copy.'

'Do you know, it does sound familiar?' said Mrs. Black. 'Perhaps, when you have walked me home, we can take a little look.' She favoured him with a girlish smile, and Murray blinked, wondering if she were in the market for another husband. On the other hand, he thought, she seemed very keen to spend time with Herkless. And it occurred to him that he had had the feeling, earlier, that he and Walter had perhaps interrupted a tryst, there on the headland by the birch woods. The question was, who were the couple trysting?

Lexie Conyngham

Chapter Nine

It took Murray a little time to find mercury in the materia medica of the *New Edinburgh Dispensatory*, chiefly since he looked it up first under M, then under Q for quicksilver, and then, with a moment's long forgotten inspiration, he found it under Hygrargyrus 'sive Argentum vivum', it added, 'or quicksilver'. 'The ancients considered it as a corrosive poison,' he read, 'though of itself perfectly void of acrimony, taste and smell.' On its own, he found, it would pass harmlessly through the body: it was only as fumes or in certain mixtures that it cured skin or venereal diseases, or indeed became harmful as well as healing. That agreed with what Dr. Forbes had said. The question was, would any of the other chemicals in the mutual improvement society's precious collection produce any of these mixtures, and if so, who would know how to mix them? Someone called Gourlay, a farmer, Innes had said, had seen a copy of this very book, and who knew if he had taken notes, or was perhaps one of Newell's blackmailing victims. How easy would it be to produce a medicinal form of mercury compound? Murray wanted to talk with Dr. Forbes again.

Perhaps Newell had been taking mercury for some medical complaint? Murray read that it was sometimes prescribed in its pure state for an obstruction of the bowel, in the hope that the weight of the metal would push out the obstacle, but it was not generally met with much success. But Mrs. Innes said that her father had not complained of anything beyond forgetfulness and bad legs, and by all reports he seemed unlikely to spend money unnecessarily, except on Mrs. Black's sweetmeats.

It was an easy matter to prepare for Newell's funeral on Monday morning, for Murray was used to – and weary of – his mourning clothes. Walter had laid them out without question, alongside Murray's shaving equipment: he was allowed to soap Murray's chin, but Murray was not confident enough in his abilities yet to permit him the use of the razors. A boy who need not yet shave himself, Murray felt, and particularly not Walter, should not be allowed near another man's throat with a sharp object.

'Where are you off to?' asked Coulter, meeting Murray in the hallway with something almost approaching cheerfulness.

'To Newell's funeral, to pay my respects.'

'You'll need to have plenty of respects to pay,' remarked Coulter, 'to be going this early. I'll be along around noon to say a prayer over the kisting. Come with me then.'

'Ah, well,' said Murray, 'when I say 'pay my respects', I also mean to try to find out where exactly Newell was on the morning of his death, whom he visited, to whom he spoke, and who might have visited him – and refilled his whisky flask. Who were his cronies, for instance? No one has mentioned them.'

'I suspect that'll be because he had none,' said Coulter frankly. 'He was not a man for friends. It is a hard thing to say about the dead, but he was a man disinclined to share anything with anyone else, not his money, nor his hospitality, nor even his time. Anyone there today will, I suspect, be there to support Innes and his wife, and not for their fond memories of Newell.'

'There must be someone, or must have been someone. Surely in his youth – he was born here, was he not? Lived here all his life? Some childhood playmate, even for the sake of old times?'

Coulter considered.

'Perhaps old Pearce,' he said at last. 'If nothing else, they had a similar outlook on life: take what you can get, and keep it close when you have it.'

Murray frowned in concern.

'I worry about you, Coulter: you are so blindly attached to your parishioners you see none of their faults!'

Coulter gave a wry smile.

'Best to be realistic about some people, at least,' he said, 'for the sake of one's sanity, if nothing else.'

Murray grinned, and said he would see Coulter at noon.

If the mourners attended Newell's cottage to support the Inneses, the Inneses had plenty of support, to judge by the crowd at the cottage door. To say that they were there simply out of curiosity, Murray thought sternly to himself, would doubtless be doing them a disservice. The cottage was far too small for the numbers who were eager to see Newell buried, for whatever reason, and Murray hovered in the lane, half in the queue to go in and pay his respects, half hesitant, hoping to hear something useful in the lane where conversation was likely to flow more freely.

The Inneses had taken advantage of the proximity of the two households, and were holding the greater part of the wake in their own house. Once Murray had taken his turn entering Newell's cottage and touching the corpse, bowing to Mrs. Innes and to Mrs. Black who sat with her, he wormed his way outside again and was crossing to be given ale in the shoemaker's house when he heard hoofbeats smart on the cobbles. He looked down the lane to see Thomson, shining in funereal black, dismounting to lead his horse up to the door.

'Here, too, of course, Mr. Murray,' he said, by way of greeting. 'Learned anything useful you'd care to share with me?'

'I don't think so,' said Murray. 'And you?'

'Not an iota,' said Thomson smugly. 'I've had more important matters on my hands, anyway. You may think that an old man's death ranks highly in my daily business, Mr. Murray, but with an important port like Portpatrick on my doorstep, and Irish beggars camped around Stranraer like a besieging army (excepting only that usually it's the besiegers who starve out the inhabitants, and not the besiegers who are begging), and reports of the French rising up again to take the country by surprise and free Bonaparte from St. Helena, I have plenty to do without considering old men falling down dead in their cups.'

'I had no idea you were so high in matters of state,' said Murray in awe. 'I met Henry Dundas a few times, Lord Melville, but clearly you are more powerful by far.'

Thomson opened his polished lips to reply, but at that moment a welcome and familiar voice called out,

'Mr. Murray!'

Murray turned to find Herkless, accompanied by his daughter and Mrs. Pringle with Anna, all sombre in black and joining the queue to pay their respects in Newell's cottage. Gratefully, he hurried to greet them: there was something about Thomson that drove all thought of good manners out of Murray's head. He bowed to the party.

'Have you been in?' Herkless said, nodding his head towards the low doorway.

'Yes: they have a sensible arrangement, I think,' Murray said, pointing to the Innes' house. 'I was about to go in for ale and oatcakes.'

'Oh, if you can wait for us, Mr. Murray, that would be so kind!' said Mrs. Pringle. She was still a very handsome woman, Murray thought, her looks not unlike her daughter's, but her eyes with a finer understanding in them. 'My husband is caught up with his business, and cannot hope to join us until nearer the kisting.'

'I should be happy to wait for you,' he said with a bow. The queue was moving more freely now than it had done at first, and in a moment or two the Herklesses and the Pringles had vanished into the cottage. Murray stood in the lane, avoiding Thomson's eye as he, too, joined the queue, leaving his horse tethered to the hook where Innes' thermometer had been. Murray sent Walter to find a pail of water for the poor beast, which seemed resigned to being abandoned in odd places. As Walter left, Murray told himself firmly not to be distracted by the Pringles and the Herklesses: he must find out about Newell's friends and Newell's movements, and not think he was there to enjoy himself. That was clearly not what funerals were for.

He edged nearer the door of the Innes' house, and peered inside as discreetly as he could. He recognised some of the faces: the wiry, white-haired beadle from the church, along with an old red-faced man and a younger one crowned with a slab of fair hair who must be his son, he remembered from the mutual improvement society. Innes, at least, had friends, he thought.

'Mrs. Black is talking with my father,' said a voice behind him, and Murray turned from his peering to find Kitty Herkless emerging from the cottage, 'and Mrs. Pringle is discussing a dress for Anna with Mrs. Innes. She's a seamstress, you know: we are all indebted to her in this village! But I have escaped, and I wanted to ask you something.'

She looked severely at him, up and down, her dark eyebrows firm, and he waited with some trepidation to hear her question.

'My father says that you are interesting yourself in the matter of Newell's death.'

'It is a matter that interests me, yes,' he concurred.

'Then you believe,' she dropped her voice, and glanced about her before continuing, 'you believe that he may not have died a natural death? That is, that someone helped him on his way?'

'I'm not yet sure.' Murray thought of the materia medica he had been reading that morning. 'I think it is a possibility.'

'Then it is a possibility that someone killed him? Yes. Then that someone would have good reason, if he thought you clever enough – and I suspect you are indeed quite clever, Mr. Murray - to do you some damage, too?'

'That would indeed be the inevitable concomitant, I think,' said Murray.

Kitty raised an eyebrow at him. She was all black and white, black bonnet and gown, black hair, pale face, white fichu, her eyes dark.

'I should take it quite ill if someone from our village should do you any damage,' she said precisely. His head swam a little.

'I am glad to find you so loyal to your village,' he said with a slight struggle. 'Presumably the students can do me any damage they like?' he went on, forcing lightness. 'Where are they this morning? Are they to attend here?'

She smiled and turned away.

'They are on their way, I believe,' she said coolly. 'Mr. McCullough is an early riser, and Mr. Nugent does not stay long abed, but Mr. Gibson and Mr. Adair are less … robust.'

'Who is robust?' came a voice. 'I vow it is not I!'

Miss Pringle did not suit black: that was to say, it was less flattering to her than other colours, but still could not detract from the flames of her hair.

'Not at all, dear,' said Kitty Herkless. 'I should never insult you in such a way! To say a lady is robust conjures up all kinds of images of sturdy self-sufficiency of which you, at least, have never been guilty. We were talking of Mr. Gibson and Mr. Adair, the frailer of our four captive students.'

'Why, are they ill? I hope they are well!' cried Anna, alarmed, blue eyes blinking rapidly.

'They are quite well, if you take into account Mr. Gibson's nervous exhaustion after preaching yesterday. They will be here shortly: they all felt that the walk would benefit them, while we came on horseback.'

'Are those idleset individuals not here yet?' asked her father easily, emerging from the cottage.

'No, father: we should just go on without them,' said Kitty, glancing at Anna.

'I should wait for Mamma,' said Anna, but her mother appeared and the five of them moved on into the Innes' house, which enticed them in a most unfunereal manner with the smell of fresh oatcakes.

Inside extra benches had been brought in, and the place was cramped. Innes, in charge of the oatcakes, seeing the gentry arrive hurried forward in alarm.

'Please, please be seated,' he gabbled, hunting desperately about for space. He waved at some women on one bench and caused way to be made for the Pringle ladies and Kitty, and shuffled two children off a broad wooden armchair to dust it down for Mr. Herkless. Murray heard a sigh behind him and turned to find that some men had squashed themselves more tightly on to a bench to make way for him. He sat.

'Thank you so much,' he said to the youngish man next to him. 'We have not been introduced, but I believe I know your face from the meeting of the mutual improvement society on Saturday? My name is Murray.'

'Aye, I seen you there, sir. I'm Pearce, Norrie Pearce.' They nodded in lieu of bows. Pearce had a rough, outdoor complexion and that slab of greasy fair hair, which, with his prominent upper teeth, gave him the look of a sleek rodent in a hat.

'Are you a regular member of the society? I believe they meet frequently.'

'Aye. Gets you out the house, see? Nothing much else going on around here.'

'Have you a particular scientific interest, then?'

The young man thought about it.

'Aye, I like chemicals, like.'

'The society has a good range in that kist of theirs, hasn't it?'

'No so much the ones I'm interested in. I like the ones that explode, gunpowder and the like.'

'Oh.' Murray raised his eyebrows. 'Do you get to use them much, in your line of work?'

'Aye. I'm gamekeeper to the laird.'

'Oh, I see! Of course.' This, then, was the sugar umbrella so despaired of by Mr. Herkless. Innes appeared at the kitchen door with plates of oatcakes and handed them to the two children who had lost their seat to Herkless, and they distributed them with more enthusiasm than accuracy around the room: Murray's portion was mostly crumbled over his lap, but what he was able to eat was fresh and delicious. Innes poured the ale himself, perhaps fearing a similar level of competence from the children. It, too, was good.

'So you're here to support poor Innes and his wife, then?' Murray casually asked his neighbour when the ale had gone down.

'Aye, I suppose,' said Pearce. 'My faither here's the oul fella's oldest friend, are you no?'

He turned to the old man at his other side, whose receding hairline was deeper and greyer than the gamekeeper's but whose face, though lopsided, was still rosy.

'Oh, aye, me and him goes back a gey lang way,' agreed Mr. Pearce elder. He had a sour mouth and eyes that took in everything – and probably priced it, too, Murray thought. He had something wrong with his mouth, and one eye drooped, as if he had suffered a stroke.

'You'll be sad to see him go, then,' said Murray sympathetically. 'Do you live in the village here? You probably saw him every day.'

'Or every ither day,' the old man nodded.

'He was always there if he had a'thing to crow about,' said Norrie Pearce. 'Never let it be said he was ungenerous with his company if he could swank.'

'Now, now,' said his father, 'less impidence to your elders and betters, Norrie.' His upper lip twisted in irritation, displaying long yellowing teeth like a sheep's.

'Does that make you the last of the circle, then?' asked Murray quickly. 'Do you have other friends in common?'

'Nah, it was just the two of us were pals,' said Pearce, briefly glorying in the tragedy of his situation. 'That's me friendless the now.'

'But you'll have seen him on his last morning, will you not? On Thursday? I hear he was about the village in the morning.'

'I seen him indeed,' said Pearce. 'But he said he was gey busy, and never stopped to speak more than five words to me.'

'Did he say what he was busy about? For it must have been something important, for him to put aside his oldest friend for it.' Murray worried that he was laying the compliments on too obviously, but the Pearces seemed not to notice, or thought gentlemen were entitled to ask daft questions if they were hurting no one.

'Nah, he didna,' said Pearce, irked that he had no better story to tell. 'He bade me good day and went away up the hill like a lilty, for all he walked with a stick. My son has to help me get about,' he added, sorrowfully, 'and he's a gey busy man, with his job and all.'

'Of course,' said Murray. 'It must be very awkward for you.' He thought for a moment. 'Which hill was that he was climbing? For Mr. Coulter thought he saw him up behind the tannery near noon.' He apologised to his friend in his head for such a blatant lie.

'Did he now? I wonder what he was doing up there?' Father and son met each other's eyes, before old Mr. Pearce went on, 'Nah, it was the headland to the north I seen him heading for, the back of eleven. We live that end of the village so that Norrie here is handy for his work on the estate. I get a good view of the road there,' he went on, 'frae my windy, and I see all kinds going up and down that road. I seen yourself there yesterday, sir, and Mrs. Black, and Miss Pringle and all.'

'It was a fine day for a walk,' said Murray, refusing to acknowledge the hints in the old man's richly suggestive tone. It did make him wonder, though: could Newell have been in league with his old friend in finding any blackmail victims? And if they were partners in the business, did that mean that Pearce's life was also in danger? Or that he might know who had killed Newell? This was not the place to ask, but it was something he should certainly follow up soon, just in case. The old man did not seem in the least worried, but that was not to say that he was not at risk, all the same.

The young Pearce, who had been sitting between them but taking no part in the conversation, suddenly arose with a muttered apology.

'Have you any milk?' he called across to Innes. 'I have a gey sore throat on me, and I think milk would soothe it.'

'I hope it's nothing catching,' said the beadle from church, whom Murray had also recognised from the mutual improvement society. He pressed his lips together primly, as if protecting his own throat. Thomson, who must have been wandering amongst the mourners out in the lane for some time, made his appearance in the doorway and Innes, bound by the hospitality of a funeral, gave him ale and oatcakes as he stood, then fetched milk for Pearce.

'Tell me, Mr. Pearce,' Murray changed the subject, 'for you seem to know what goes on about here: who are these Irish peasants I've heard of? I had no idea they were such a problem.'

'Ach, they're like the students, only they're aye begging.' The old man took a great draught of ale, and licked his lips clumsily: his speech, however, was only slightly mumbled. 'They come over looking for work, but there's none around here, nothing to spare, now that half the army's come home again. Some of them are old soldiers and all. They take boats to Portpatrick and then start walking, thinking they'll maybe find work in Glasgow – I hear Glasgow's full of them - but there's plenty only gets as far as Stranraer on the first strike, and they've been a dire burden on the poors funds, so they say. So then the minister there tries to make them move on and they come through here next, so the ones that's no so good on their feet or who are just lazy stop and try again to beg. And there's some like to make it easy for you, and just take your money when your back's turned, or the washing off your bushes. I'd take my son's gun and make a few of them dance on up the coast, if it was me,' he said, adopting a confidential tone, 'but the laird and the minister here is more easy on them.'

'I see. I had no idea so many were coming over,' said Murray.

'Not that I blame them in some ways,' added Pearce, 'for I wouldna fancy living in Ireland myself, always rebelling and chasing each other round the country, sometimes the Papists, sometimes the Episcopalians, sometimes hanging good Presbyterians for who kens what?' He ignored his own country's not unblemished history in this regard. 'But I'd sooner have a dozen of them than two dozen, for all that. Let them move on to Glasgow: there's mair room for them there, and with their ain sort, and all.'

'Well, thank you for this information,' said Murray. 'That was extremely interesting. Oh, here's the minister for the kisting.' Through the open door he could see the crowd in the lane making way for Coulter, pallid but dutiful. Murray wondered if this was his first funeral since his wife's.

'Aye, aye – he'll be kisted without me and not lose a'thing by it,' said Pearce, 'for I canna stand out there on my own.'

'Up you get, Father,' said Norrie, returning at that moment, and grabbed him under the arms with a jolt. Murray followed them out into the lane where they were just in time to see Coulter disappear into the crowded cottage. The carpenter, carrying the appropriate tools, followed. Silence fell, so that all that could be heard in the lane was the cry of gulls high above the village streets and the ever-present hushing of the waves in the loch. They bowed their heads, sensing the prayer rather than hearing it. After a few minutes there was a stir at the cottage door, and Innes led out the four bearers, carrying the coffin at hip height. They raised it, then the men replaced their hats and followed the coffin up the lane and around the corner towards the church, leaving the women and Coulter behind. Norrie Pearce helped his father along slowly, and Murray let them drop behind, finding himself walking along with the students. He nodded to them.

'You made it in time, then?'

'Just about!' said McCullough in the same low voice. 'Adair can be hard to shift in the mornings!'

'Many apologies,' said Adair, with a grin that would have seemed wolfish in his long grey face, were it not for his soft brown eyes. 'Once I fall asleep I need something in the nature of a small earthquake to waken me.'

'We know that,' said Nugent grumpily.

In the kirkyard they gathered about the open grave and waited, heads bowed, for the coffin to be lowered. No more spying on his neighbours for Mr. Newell: no more secret stores of money, or filching meat or spirits from his lodgers. The coffin was covered in the plainest black cloth and the parish's lowest grade of mortcloth had been used to cover it for the short journey. Murray wondered if whoever had taken his savings was here, feeling a twinge of guilt for allowing him to go to his grave like a pauper. He glanced around: the four students stood solemnly beside him, probably less familiar with funerals than their elders; Pearce and his son were stony-faced behind them; Herkless had appeared on his other side, also examining the crowd with his quick dark eyes, and Thomson watched them all unabashedly, perched, to improve his view, on an adjacent gravestone. Innes and some of the other scientists Murray had seen on Saturday made the inner circle, helping to cover the coffin before Innes passed a bottle to the chief grave digger. The digger held it suspiciously.

'Thanks,' he said, without looking up at Innes, and set it carefully to one side. In Murray's experience that was unusual: grave diggers were notorious for sustaining their work with steady drinking, and a bottle would scarcely touch the ground unless it was empty. Innes pursed his lips, his cheeks a little flushed, but said nothing, and walked away back to the kirkyard gate and home. The mourners dispersed slowly, talking amongst themselves.

'Well, that's that,' said Herkless to Murray and the students. 'And still no answer as to how he died, though it seems as if whisky is not to be trusted any more.'

'I wonder if Mr. Thomson will let us go now?' said McCullough. Nugent grunted.

There was a shout from beyond the kirkyard gate.

'What on earth?' asked Murray, staring ahead. Herkless turned, too.

'Oh, it's some of the Irish.'

'The what?' asked McCullough.

'The peasants. I'd better see to it,' Herkless added, and strode across to the gate. Innes was standing with his hands up defensively, while around him stood five or six men and women, poorly dressed, with bundles bound on to their backs.

'I've nothing for you!' Innes was saying, crossly.

'Ah, come on, sir,' said one of the women. She wore a red shawl and had a face as wrinkled as the skin on a rice pudding. Her pack was patched and grubby, and her voice was high-pitched, grating on the ear. 'You've just come from burying your loved ones, surely you'll take pity on those so starved we might be next?'

'For the luck of the journey of the dead one,' said the man next to her, as if it were only reasonable. 'You wouldn't want to be uncharitable, sir, and him only in the ground?'

'I mind the time we were here before,' said the woman, 'and that man was the most generous and kindly gentleman that ever I met. He showered food and money on us, so he did, like the blessed rain from heaven!'

'I can tell you you definitely have the wrong man there!' said

Innes, with some force.

'Ladies and gentlemen,' said Herkless quickly, and Innes looked round at him with relief. 'Come with me and we'll find you a hot meal and somewhere to sleep tonight.'

'Oh, sir, sir, you're an angel sent to earth to care for us poor innocents, sir!' said the woman in the red shawl. She slid forward to Herkless, and fastened herself on his arm. 'I see fine you're an angel! Your mother and all the saints in heaven will be praying for you tonight!'

'That is excellent news, dear lady,' said Herkless, his mouth twitching, 'but I would not wish to make your good man jealous by this intimate contact. Make your way down to the main street and then ask for Kirkwelland House: the housekeeper will see you are attended to.'

'Kirkwelland House? Isn't that fine, now?' The man gently detached the woman from Herkless' sleeve and led her off as if they were going to a fair, the others following in much the same manner. Only the last man, a thin, bony character with large eyes, gazed back silently at Herkless and the others, made a little gesture with his hand, and followed them out of sight.

Chapter Ten

'I'd better mention to Coulter that there is a party of Irish in the town,' said Herkless to Murray. 'And I should fetch my daughter, too, I daresay. What are your plans for the rest of the day? And did Coulter receive the note about the picnic tomorrow?'

'I believe he sent a reply accepting the invitation,' said Murray.

'He seems a little more cheerful, would you say?'

'That is my impression too, sir.'

'Good, good. Of course he sustained a terrible loss, but I must tell you, Mr. Murray, that for a while there several of us thought we might lose him, too.'

'So I understand.' They were near the end of the lane and Newell's cottage again.

'We cannot really afford to lose him, Mr. Murray. There is plenty of valuable work for him to do here.'

He turned and fixed Murray's gaze, as if he had said something of particular significance.

'Yes, yes,' said Murray, imagining Herkless meant Coulter's parish work. 'I can see that. I think he will do what he has to do.'

'Excellent.' Herkless gave Murray a brisk tap on the arm. 'You're doing him good, you know.'

'If I am, I'm delighted.'

Herkless seemed as if he might say something more, but at that moment Mrs. Black emerged from Newell's cottage, Coulter behind her. She was adjusting her black shawl with quick little flaps, movement constricted by her bonnet in one hand.

'May I hold that for you a moment?' asked Murray, and took the bonnet. Mrs. Black beamed.

'Oh, Mr. Murray, how thoughtful! Just let me –' She gave the shawl a final flap, and took the bonnet back with a curtsey. Murray noticed that she was watching Herkless out of the corner of her eye, and hoped he had not overstepped any mark. It made him think of something, and he decided to risk things further.

'Are you on your way home?' he asked her. 'I intend to walk that way: perhaps I can escort you?'

The bonnet bobbed, half-fastened.

'That would be charming! How lovely.' This time Herkless was definitely on the receiving end of a very pointed look, and Murray himself caught an amused wriggle of Herkless' eyebrows. He felt safe enough, then, from that quarter: if Mrs. Black was trying to make Herkless jealous, Herkless was not taking it terribly seriously.

'I'll see you later, Coulter?' Murray caught his host about to leave.

'Oh, yes, of course, Murray.'

'But before you go, Coulter,' said Herkless, as Mrs. Black hooked her hand securely under Murray's arm, 'there are some Irish beggars in the village. I've sent them up to the house for a meal and a bed for the night. I wonder if you could ...'

Their voices faded as Mrs. Black marched him down the street. She must have been used to walking with men much taller than she, for she had a way of skipping every five or six steps to keep up, even though he tried to moderate his pace to suit her.

'Will you be coming to Mr. Herkless' picnic tomorrow?' she asked. 'If the weather holds, of course. But it has all the appearance of being good.'

'Yes, I do hope to,' said Murray. 'It is a thoughtful idea, to keep the poor students amused while they are stuck here.'

She frowned.

'Surely it cannot take long to find out who killed Newell, if anyone did,' she said. 'He was not a very nice man, but there cannot have been very many people eager to murder him.'

'I understand you were kind enough to have him as a customer of yours, though?' Murray asked tentatively.

'A customer?' She did not seem to be offended. 'Oh, you mean my little sweetmeats! Goodness, how did you hear so quickly about those?'

Murray smiled.

'My manservant – well, he is only a boy – is delighted with them. He says, and he should know, that they are better than anything found in Edinburgh.'

'Well!' Mrs. Black blushed in delight, her face glowing in the nest of her black bonnet. 'That is most kind of him. You must send him along again and I shall have him test one or two new things I am trying. I should value the opinion of such an expert!'

'I'm sure he'd be delighted,' said Murray. It would no doubt appeal to Walter's scientific mind. 'Newell, I believe, was a regular customer?'

'He was, unfortunately. Oh, I should not say that,' she said quickly. 'It is very gratifying when someone enjoys your work, of course, and the poor old man … well, I daresay he could not help being as objectionable as he was. I just hoped, I must confess, that he drove no one else away, for he would hover around, you know?'

'What was his favourite?' Murray asked lightly.

'Oh, anything with mint in it,' she replied after a moment. 'I suppose he was trying to sweeten his breath.'

'Was he there every day?'

'Well, not Sundays, of course. But every other day, yes, I think so. He rarely missed.'

Murray laughed.

'Your wares must indeed be as enticing as Walter says! Was he there last Thursday?'

'Last Thursday? Oh! You mean the morning of the day he died?' She considered, suddenly a little breathless. 'Mrs. Innes said you were asking questions, along with that sheriff's man with the shiny whiskers. Yes, he was there: it must have been about half past ten, I believe, if that is helpful, for Mr. Burns had just come along to collect some bits and pieces to sell in his shop, and he is always there about ten, and stops to gossip.'

'That is indeed helpful.' Murray thought: the old man Pearce had said Newell passed him after eleven, and now he had another fragment. 'How long did he stay with you?'

'A quarter of an hour or more,' said Mrs. Black, with the slightest shiver. 'Miss Pringle had come in for sugared almonds for Mr. Pringle, and she did not wish to leave in case Newell followed her home. I don't know if he would have, but he was the kind of person you always felt might be watching you, you know?'

'He never caused you any – anxiety?' Murray asked, trying to give her as broad a field as possible.

'Anxiety? I'm no young lass, Mr. Murray: if he had followed me I should have told him what I thought of him!' She looked up at him, laughing, but he felt there was more she could have told him, if she had wished. Maybe he should have narrowed the field, instead of broadening it. 'Did he ever blackmail you?' he could have asked, but would she have answered?

Once he had seen Mrs. Black to her front door he turned down towards the shore and perched on a rock, considering the blue loch in front of him. So far he did not have a great deal else to consider. A blackmailer had died, in a manner which might or might not have been accidental, and which involved a compound of mercury, which could be obtained from the schoolhouse and possibly elsewhere. He had so far failed to identify any of his victims. On the day of his death Newell had left his cottage shortly after dawn - no, he had sent the students away shortly after dawn, and sometime after that he had gone out himself. Around half past ten he had appeared at Mrs. Black's in the north of the village, and lingered there for a quarter of an hour. It then seemed that he had walked, without much delay or detour, to his friend Pearce's cottage where they exchanged a few words before he went on to climb the headland, using his stick.

Where was he going? Where did he spend the rest of his time out that day, and when had he returned to his home with, or to, his whisky? Where had he been between dawn and half past ten? When had his money disappeared? Had someone given him the whisky while he was out – in which case presumably he was expecting to receive it, or he would not have taken his stone bottle with him – or had it been left in his house? And if so, had that happened at the same time the money disappeared?

There was only one place he had seen in the village that might sell whisky, a small provision merchant on the main street. He pushed himself off the rock, brushed down his breeches, and went to inspect it.

The man with springy grey hair at the counter of the shop was already familiar: he was the beadle at the church and Murray had also seen him at Newell's funeral and at the meeting of the mutual improvement society. The man seated at ease in the customer's chair was also now a kent face about the village, for it was Thomson, boots polished to his customary glare in the sunlight from the door.

'Aye, Mr. Murray,' said Thomson, 'I was beginning to miss you.'

'I daresay,' said Murray. 'Are you asking this good gentleman – Mr. Burns, is it? - anything about Mr. Newell, or are you here to buy feed for your horse?'

'I'm asking,' said Thomson with drawn-up dignity, 'if Newell bought his whisky here.'

'And I'm telling him,' said the grey-haired man, 'that I sold a fill of whisky to Newell maybe once in two months.' He folded his arms obstinately. The questioning had evidently not been sympathetic.

'And not on Thursday, I take it?' asked Murray, with an understanding nod. The merchant squinted at him.

'Newell would never pay for a drop of whisky if someone else would buy it for him. The last time I saw him buy whisky in here would have been just before the Easter communions, maybe a month ago.'

'Was he in here at all on Thursday, though?' asked Murray, and Thomson pursed his lips, seeming to wonder what Murray was seeking.

'Thursday ...' Finding this a more reasonable question, the merchant was prepared to answer it properly. 'I've a notion he was in for something. Now, what was it?' He looked around the packed shop as if he might be able to work out what was missing. Murray thought it would be difficult. The room they were in was packed from floor to ceiling with goods of all kinds, from seeds to shears to ropes to cloth to jars of spices to loaves of sugar, not much of any one thing but everything one could think of, a patchwork quilt of merchandise.

'Do you remember what time of day he came in?' Murray tried.

'It would have been the morning.' The merchant considered. 'Maybe about nine? I'd the shop open and my breakfast ate, anyway.'

'About nine,' Murray repeated, fixing it in his head.

'It wasna baccy,' said the merchant, thoughtfully, 'for he aye bought that on a Monday. Ah, d'ye ken what it was? It's come to me the now. It was a sheet of paper.'

'A sheet of paper? Interesting,' said Murray quickly, seeing Thomson open his mouth for a sharp response. 'Had he bought paper before?'

'Once or twice. Not often at all, over the years.'

'Do you happen to know if he could read or write?'

'Aye, he could do both,' said the merchant. 'There was a gey strict dominie when we were at school.'

'You were at school with him?' Murray asked. Had he found another crony?

'Well, he was that much older nor me,' said the merchant. 'Forbye he was no a likeable man even then. Close, he was, always close: always had his eyes open for more money and his hand shut on it when he got it.'

'Yet you were at his funeral today, were you not?'

'I was. I'm friendly with his son-in-law, Innes. I saw he kenned you there, anyway. He let you to the mutual improvement society last Saturday.'

'That's right. It's an impressive society,' said Murray. 'I'm thinking of maybe helping start one in my home village.'

'Well, if the laird, the minister and the schoolmaster are willing, it's a gey good start,' said the merchant. 'Would you be one of them?'

'I'm the laird,' said Murray, taking no offence.

'And you're an educated gentleman yourself, too,' said the merchant, regarding him closely. 'I'd say it would do well. We're lucky here ourselves.'

'I'm not sure I could contribute as interesting a talk as your laird here,' said Murray, remembering Herkless' speech on geology.

'I'm sure there's few could,' acknowledged the merchant, proudly. 'As I say, we're gey lucky.'

'What interests you on the scientific side?' Murray asked, ignoring Thomson's glare. Mr. Burns turned down the corners of his mouth, considering.

'I like the weather, like Innes. All these soils and stones are interesting, but they dinna affect me much. But the weather, that's aye around, isn't it? Whiles I take a walk up through the laird's woods on the headland and see where he has his wee thermometers set up, and all the temperatures is different in different places. And clouds, I like clouds.'

'Oh, yes, you can see a great deal in clouds,' Murray agreed, though he hoped they were not to have a whole conversation on them. 'You have a grand shop here, Mr. Burns. Had you many in last Thursday when Newell was here?'

'Thursday's no one of my busy days, on the whole,' said Burns. 'In fact, I was able to go out myself up to Mrs. Black's later in the morning to bring back some of her sweeties – see, I sell a few for her here sometimes, particularly if a'body's passing through the village.' He had a small tray of the sweetmeats on his counter, half-full. 'Aye, she's a fine cook, Mrs. Black,' he went on, with a sigh. Perhaps Mrs. Burns was not so gifted.

'And when Newell was in for his piece of paper?'

Burns frowned hard, focussing his mind.

'He come in with young Pearce. Norrie, the gamekeeper.'

'Oh, did he? Yes, I've met Norrie. And they came in together?'

'I think they'd just met, though. Newell was asking after Pearce's faither. They were at school together and all.'

'And did they leave together?'

'No, they didn't, for Newell said he was in a hurry, though he never moved that fast, I can tell you, and Norrie let him be served first and waited on for what was it? Gun oil, that was it, and a new cloth.'

'Was anybody else here at the time?' asked Thomson, who seemed to feel he should have more of a role in the conversation. He stood up to be noticed.

'Nah, nah. That's how I could serve Newell straightaway. He never paid me for it, neither,' said Burns sadly. 'I wonder if I'll ever get that back? Paper and all – nothing cheap.'

'So you still dinna ken where the whisky came from,' said Thomson in satisfaction when they were both out on the street.

'No, but I'm putting together a pattern of where Newell was on the day of his death. I still need to know where he was between dawn and here, and where he was after he passed old Mr. Pearce's house and went up on the headland, up to the time he was found dying. Have you any idea?'

'I was seeking the whisky,' said Thomson.

'Fair enough. Well, he seems to have been moving north: the shop here on the main street, then Mrs. Black's in the north of the village, then Pearce's house, then the headland. Perhaps he started further south?'

'There's gey little to the south,' said Thomson dismissively, 'barring the tannery and the smithy.'

'Then perhaps we should ask there.'

'What use is there?' asked Thomson, turning away. 'We ken where he drank the whisky and we ken where he died. We ken where his money was before someone took it. All we need to know is where the whisky came from and where the money's gone, and we have the man. And who buys whisky at a tannery or a smithy?'

'From what I can hear, I don't think Newell bought whisky at all, if someone would give it to him.'

'You think someone at the tannery or the smithy gave him a bottle of whisky?' Thomson was unconvinced.

'It's possible. Or someone down there might have been being blackmailed by him and thought it worth their while to go and put mercury compound in his whisky at his house. The smith is connected with the mutual improvement society, anyway. He makes some of their equipment. He may well know about the compounds.'

'But why would he blackmail the smith? What could a smith have to hide? Never mind a tanner?' asked Thomson.

'Lots of people have something to hide, I'd have thought,' said Murray with a smile. 'And some people will pay to keep it hidden, even if they haven't much to pay with. Let's see if the smith or the tanner is in that position.'

The smith was not.

Raffan was a forthright man, choosing his words with as much restraint as one might expect from such a large and muscular individual.

'I never met anyone who deserved poisoning more,' he said firmly.

'What did he do to you?' asked Thomson, pretending that he was used to that kind of bald statement.

'He threatened me, the wee nyaff,' said the smith, and spat on the stone floor. 'Said he'd seen me with Burns' daughter up in the woods on the headland, and he'd tell her faither if I didna pay him money. I chased him out of the place with a spade. Then the wee limmer went to Sarah herself and tried again, and she came and told me and so when he come round again I went and told him that if he went near either of us again I'd pin him to the floor and use him as an anvil. He didna bother us after that.'

'When did all this happen?'

'He came to me first a couple of weeks ago, and then he tried Sarah last week. Then he came back here a few days ago. It would have been the day he died,' said the smith, nodding to himself. 'I canna think of a better use for whisky, and I like a drop of the stuff myself. He was here about a couple of hours past dawn, and that was when I told him he had no hope of profit from either of us.'

'So you didn't pay him, and nor did Miss Burns?'

'Away and catch yourself on, sir. Who with any sense would give money to that wee skite?'

'Well, at least it's more evidence that he was trying to be a blackmailer,' said Murray, as they left the road on the path for the tannery. The air was rich with the stink of animal skins in their curing process, and he tried not to breathe in too much through his nose.

'It's no evidence that he was successful. I canna see yon smith poisoning him, anyway,' said Thomson, who had clearly been impressed by the smith's close reasoning. 'He'd just have walloped him with a hammer.'

'I think you're right, there,' Murray conceded. 'And we know he was here two hours after dawn on Thursday. What would that have been – seven? Eight in the morning?'

'Between the two,' said Thomson.

'So he was out and about by eight, and down here. We still have a gap later, and a gap between the smith and Mr. Burns' shop.'

'He'll no have spent two hours in a tannery,' said Thomson firmly. 'I think he still had his sense of smell.'

But it turned out that Newell was less fussy than Thomson imagined.

'Aye, he was here, drinking ale with the oul fella,' said one of the brothers who ran the tannery. 'I'll take you in.'

If old Pearce guarded the road to the north, it seemed that there was an equivalent for the road to the south. The three brothers who owned the tannery had an aged father, a Mr. Craig, who sat by his window in the house they all shared with their wives and families and watched the comings and goings outside. A well-worn chair opposite him showed where his friends would come and gossip with him, but it was Mr. Craig who had the best view.

'Faither, there's gentlemen here to see you!' said the tanner who had brought them in. Mr. Craig turned sharp eyes on them, but did not rise.

'Here,' he said, 'bring them some ale, then.'

A youngish woman brought ale to Murray and Thomson, curtseyed politely, and turned to busy herself with several children by the door. All of them were neatly dressed, and the house was well kept with a stone floor, but the pervasive scent of the tannery must have curtailed their social lives considerably.

'Sit yourselves down,' said the old man, waving to the worn chair. 'You're a young man: you can manage a stool, can you, sir?'

Thomson took his place on the worn chair with a smug expression, while Murray perched on the stool. Now that they were nearer, Murray noticed the distinctive scent of old man nudging through the tanning smells.

'What can I do for you?' Craig asked when they had introduced themselves.

'It's about Mr. Newell, a friend of yours, I believe?'

'Aye, but he's dead this week,' said Craig, blue eyes wide. 'They're saying he was poisoned – is that why you're here?'

'That's right. We're trying to find out where he was the day he died, before he went home.' Murray took the lead.

'We dinna ken yet if he was poisoned, mind,' said Thomson quickly. Murray glanced at him and tried not to roll his eyes.

'He was here that morn, right enough,' said Craig gently. 'Aye, I'm that grieved about it. He often came here to see me. I canna move frae this chair, see, so company is a grand thing. I couldna go to his funeral at all, at all.' His face was resigned, the face of a man long housebound. 'And now that's him away. I'll no have a gossip with him again.'

'Was he here often?'

'Aye, twa three times a week,' said Craig. 'He was awful good to me. There's not many will come out this far just to sit, and some dinna like the smell, of course. But Newell would come often, and I was gey grateful.'

'What did you chat about?' asked Murray, with a sympathetic smile.

'Och, a'thing and everything,' said Craig, smiling back. 'He would bring me any news frae the village, what students were coming through, who was courting who, what the laird or the minister was saying. You're staying with the minister, are you no, sir? You kenned him at college, or so Newell says?'

'That's right. We're old friends.'

'Aye, aye. But he was a good listener, too,' added Craig. 'He was always interested in who was coming along the road, who I saw going south or north. It made me feel as if I had news to give him, too. He was gey good to me, so he was. He had nothing but his time to give, for he wasna a well-off man himself, but he gave it generously to me.'

'You can't think, then, of anyone who might have wanted to poison him?'

'Deliberately, you mean?' Old Craig's eyes opened wide. 'Who would want to kill him? That'd be daft.'

'Well, maybe so,' said Murray, rising from the stool as Thomson stood to leave. 'It's an odd thing to find in your whisky. Are your sons members of the mutual improvement society in the village, by the way? It seems a grand thing.'

'No, they havena the time,' said Craig. 'They're aye working hard here and a Saturday night is their time to rest and sort themselves out for the next week. Thomas Newell said it was a lot of men getting out of their wives' hair and fiddling round with things that didn't concern them.'

'Ah, well, perhaps he was right,' said Murray with a smile. 'Thank you for your time, Mr. Craig.'

'Not at all, not at all, sir. Come back, come back any time if there's anything else you want to ask me!' He craned round the chair, watching them to the door. The woman was in the kailyard, hoeing while the children played around her. They waved farewell, and left.

'That's the first person with a good word to say about Newell,' Murray remarked.

'And even he may have been deceived,' said Thomson darkly. 'Newell was only there to get the gossip, even if the old man didna realise it.'

Chapter Eleven

'Are you going back to Stranraer now?' Murray asked hopefully. 'Newell is buried – can the students go on their way?'

Thomson gave a twisted smile.

'Now, now, Mr. Murray, you've put me in mind of doing my proper duty on this one, even if it turns out that Newell died by accident after all. I'm determined to do a thorough job here. We ken now that he went from his house to the smithy to the tannery to the shop to Mrs. Black to the headland,' he marked them off on his gloved fingers, 'and at Mrs. Black's he saw Miss Pringle. I think we need to talk to her now, see if she can tell us a'thing. I always liked a redhead,' he added, smacking his shiny lips unappealingly.

Murray was not sure that they had indeed established that Newell had gone straight from his cottage to the smithy, but he let it pass. He was distracted by the idea of Thomson interrogating Miss Pringle: he could not quite decide if Thomson was just by nature rude, or whether there were grades in society here of which he was not yet aware. Perhaps it simply resulted from life in a village that was considerably smaller than Letho.

He noted that Thomson had said 'we need to talk to her', so that, at least, gave him the opportunity to smooth any ruffled feathers. Perhaps as sheriff's officer Thomson had had dealings with Pringle, as a man of law, and by extension knew his family. He would see.

It seemed that Thomson at least knew where the Pringles lived, which Murray did not. Thomson led the way to a house on the northern edge of the village, not quite as grand as Mrs. Black's home but respectably sized with two floors and three bays. The little portico over the front door appeared to be a new addition, for the earth around the base of the pillars was still rough with spilled plaster. It was slightly too large for the proportions to be entirely pleasing.

Thomson rattled at the risp with an air of familiarity, and a maidservant who seemed to recognise him let them in and announced them at the parlour door. Mrs. Pringle and Miss Pringle stood to curtsey as they entered: Murray had to stoop a little to get through the doorway. The ladies had changed out of their funeral black from the morning's ceremonies, and were both in blue: Anna's hair caught the light from the window to their little garden, and glinted gold amongst the red. Murray hoped Thomson would not openly lick his lips.

'We're here to ask you,' Thomson began, 'about the morn of Newell's death. Miss Pringle, I hear you saw him at Mrs. Black's.'

'Did I? I can't remember!' Anna's eyes shot open in horror.

'Now, don't make yourself anxious about it, Miss Pringle,' said Murray as calmingly as he could. 'It's simply this: Mrs. Black said you were buying sweetmeats from her that morning, and that you were reluctant to leave, she thought, in case Newell followed you. Does that sound likely?'

'It certainly does,' said her mother. 'You know you came home in a state, Annie, for you were convinced he was hiding behind the hedge, you goose!'

'Was that the morning of his death? Oh, but that's terrible!' said Anna. 'I thought the poor man was up to no good and all the time he was about to die!'

Murray pressed his lips together. Thomson laughed shortly.

'Maybe the twa things are connected, Miss,' he said. 'He wasna a very nice man, now, was he?'

'No, no he wasn't,' said Anna firmly. 'But one mustn't speak ill of the dead, must one?'

'I think in this case, dear,' said her mother, 'it would be all right. Mr. Thomson is trying to find out who might have killed Newell – if anyone did – would that be right, Mr. Thomson? I'm quite sure that suspecting you is the last thing on his mind, but we must try to help him find the right person. Because however much we might have disliked Newell, the whole thing is very distressing for the poor Inneses. And someone who kills once might even kill again, is that not the case?'

Murray was impressed at Mrs. Pringle's good sense.

'That is quite true, Mrs. Pringle. We need to find out who

could bring themselves to do such a thing so that they do not repeat it.'

She nodded to him, a tiny smile on her lips, as if she saw she had surprised him.

'So what we need to know is,' said Thomson, 'did you see anyone with Newell? Or following him?'

Anna Pringle thought hard, her round brows pressed together and her chin tucked in.

'I can mind no one,' she said at last. 'Mrs. Black saw me to the door, and Norrie Pearce was going up the road to his cottage, and Newell was lingering in the middle of the road but I think he went up after Norrie Pearce. Not with him, you know, just happening to go in the same direction.'

'Can you remember if he was carrying a stone whisky bottle?' asked Murray.

'Was that not what the poison was in? No! No, I never saw anything like that.'

'Are you sure?' asked Thomson. 'He might have had it on a string or a strap.'

'I'm quite sure, Mr. Thomson!'

'Does Norrie Pearce live with his father?' Murray asked.

'That's right, in the gamekeeper's cottage up the hill a little,' said Mrs. Pringle. 'Norrie isn't married, and Mrs. Pearce died a few years ago.'

That fitted together.

'Did you see Newell earlier in the day about the village?' Thomson asked, clearly now determined to be thorough. The ladies looked at each other.

'I was out earlier, at Mr. Burns' shop,' said Mrs. Pringle eventually. 'I didn't see him there, or on the way either way. I don't think you were out, were you, Anna?'

'Before going to Mrs. Black's, you mean? No, Mamma, I don't think I was,' said Anna, eyes still fixed on her mother.

'Right, well, that's that, then,' said Thomson, and rose to leave. Murray stood, but paused.

'Miss Pringle, we know Newell was not a pleasant man, but what made you think he would follow you?'

She did not answer, puzzled.

'Had he followed you before?' he persisted.

'Yes! Yes, he followed me once. Up on the headland.'

'Up on the headland? When was that?'

Anna blinked rapidly, staring at him as if she were trying very hard to see the purpose behind the question.

'It would have been about the New Year, or a little after. It is as fair a walk in the winter as it is in the summer.'

'I can imagine it might be. It is certainly fair just now. Do you usually feel safe up there? Were you on your own?'

'Yes, of course I was on my own,' she said quickly. 'Who on earth should I have been with, up there?'

'Thank you, Mrs. Pringle, Miss Pringle.' Murray bowed, and followed Thomson back into the street.

'I should think she could have been with almost anybody up on the headland,' said Murray irresistibly when they were clear of the house. 'But I'm sure she was not on her own. The question is, did her mother know?'

'What's that?' demanded Thomson.

'Was Miss Pringle meeting someone on the headland?' Murray explained. 'We know Newell was a blackmailer: we don't know that he was in the habit of following girls around and frightening them. If he followed her, the likelihood is that he found, or hoped to find, something to blackmail her over. Don't you think?'

'I don't see where any of this gets us,' said Thomson, pulling off his glove to excavate the contents of one polished ear. 'We still dinna ken where he got his whisky or where his money went or who poisoned him.'

'We have more evidence that he was a blackmailer and we know how he found out some of his information,' said Murray. 'One of his victims may have killed him, so who do we have now? Possibly the Pringles, possibly one or two of the students, but apparently not the smithy or the tannery or the Pearces, I assume.'

'It has to be someone who could get at the mercury,' added Thomson as they walked back down into the village.

'And the chemical to go with it, and the knowledge to mix them,' said Murray. Mrs. Black? he wondered. Might she have been a victim? What might she have done – assisted her husband to die? That was far-fetched – that was not to say it was not true, but

Murray had no evidence to support it beyond the fact that Dr. Black was dead.

'It's nearly dinner time,' he said, feeling suddenly weary. 'I'd better go back to the manse. What are your plans now?'

'I want to see if I can find a'body who saw him come home later,' said Thomson. 'We professionals canna just go and have our dinner when we feel like it, ken.'

'I'm sure you probably can, a man of your status,' Murray replied sweetly, and abandoned him in the middle of the main street to turn off for the manse.

'Well, I've spoken to Mrs. Black, the Pringles, the Craigs at the tannery, the smith – Raffan, wasn't it? and Mr. Burns at the shop, and I think we know most of what Newell was doing on Thursday morning, and where. We don't know who he met along the way, necessarily, and in some cases we don't know what he was doing even if we know where he was. Then he goes up past the gamekeeper's cottage on to the headland, and vanishes for two or three hours. The next we know, he's writhing on the floor of his cottage and never recovers.'

'You spoke to the Pringles? All of them? That was courageous,' said Coulter, stretching his feet out towards the parlour fire after supper.

'Not Mr. Pringle, just the ladies. Do they have just the one child?'

'No, there's a son, but he's apprenticed to a lawyer in Glasgow. The ladies are infinitely pleasanter to speak with than Mr. Pringle, are they not?'

'They're charming. And I note that Mrs. Pringle is a woman of sense,' Murray added.

'Unlike her daughter? Yes, indeed.' Coulter grinned. 'I'm afraid Anna Pringle has never been particularly bright. Nice girl, though,' he conceded.

Murray glanced sideways at his friend. It was far too early for him to think of a replacement for Bessie, but by her own account Anna Pringle was not going anywhere. Would Coulter be happy with a dim wife? Murray was not sure he would: by all accounts Bessie had been an intelligent, well-informed woman who shared Coulter's views and ideas, and was quite capable of discussing with him some of the more difficult of his readings.

'I was trying to find anyone who seemed likely to be one of Newell's blackmailing victims,' Murray went on eventually. 'Of course, no one is likely to admit to it, particularly if it might cause them to be suspected of murder. Raffan the smith was extremely forthright about his reaction to Newell's attempts.'

'Aye, he would be,' said Coulter, nodding. 'Was it to do with Sarah Burns?'

'It was, yes.'

Coulter made a face.

'Aye, they were up for antenuptial fornication last month. I daresay they've been at it again, but I reckon he'll make an honest woman of her soon.'

'Well, if everyone knows about it, I can't see how Newell hoped to make him pay to conceal it.'

'You pay more to the Kirk Session if you're caught a second time,' said Coulter simply.

'Of course.' Murray considered. 'Newell seems to have had outposts at both ends of the village, each manned with a crony watching out for movements for him. Craig at the tannery at the south end, and Pearce up at the north end, would that be right?'

'Sounds right. I heard he was visiting Craig a lot, which worried me a bit. The old man is an innocent at heart: I didn't want Newell using him badly.'

'I think he was completely unaware of anything but good in Newell's visits,' said Murray.

'Maybe that's as well.'

'Miss Pringle, however, was afraid of Newell following her and said he had done so once before, when she was up on the headland.'

'Really?' Coulter straightened a little. 'I had no idea he had that kind of reputation. This village has been mercifully free of any odd characters like that up to now.'

'She maintains she was alone on the headland, but she maintains it very vigorously,' said Murray. Coulter met his eye.

'You mean you think she was with someone? That would fit better with Newell's character,' he remarked, nodding to himself, 'if he was following her and marking who she was meeting. I wonder who it was?' he added.

'That's what I think. If she had been caught doing something she should not – or could be persuaded she should not – how likely would she be to pay up, do you think?'

'It depends,' said Coulter. 'If she was hiding something from her father, I'm not sure she would be very good at it. She would more likely tell him than wait for a blackmailer to do it. But if she took the matter to her father in the first place and Newell tried to blackmail the family, and Pringle chose to think the matter damaging to him personally, I suspect he would pay out a good deal.'

'Then, along with whoever might have been meeting secretly with Miss Pringle, we have another possible victim in Pringle himself,' said Murray. 'For anyone who has a position to maintain in a case like this is particularly vulnerable.'

'But what could Pringle have done to be blackmailed?'

'That I don't know,' admitted Murray. 'In the same way, Mrs. Black had the recipes for mercurial compounds at her disposal, and could probably lay her hands on mercury – particularly if she lied to me when she said Dr. Forbes had bought all her late husband's chemicals – but I cannot think of anything she might have done to lay herself open to blackmail, either.'

'And you still don't know where the whisky came from?'

'No.'

'These cases you've looked into before,' said Coulter, 'have they seemed as hopeless as this?'

'Not really, no,' Murray admitted.

'That's a shame,' said Coulter.

The carrier came smartly to the back door next morning and Mrs. Veitch, knowing how eagerly Mr. Murray had pounced on previous mail addressed to him, handed the letter to Walter and scurried him upstairs to deliver it to his master before he would come down and be breakfasting with his host. Murray was suitably grateful, and opened the letter straightaway.

'Gracious: Dunnet has made Augusta a gift of a kitten from the stable cat,' he remarked. Walter was dealing with soap and water in a manner he hoped looked professional.

'Our Dunnet, sir? The groom?'

'That's right.'

'I thought he only drowned kittens, sir. And he has had no great sympathy for babbies, either, in my experience.'

There were children all about Letho these days, so Walter would have seen a few of them come up against the truculent head groom.

'Mrs. Helliwell has a neat way of describing Augusta and the kitten together.' He laughed. 'I hope we go home before either has changed too much.'

'Can I help you investigate the murder today, sir?' asked Walter. 'I'm thinking Mrs. Black might have put the poison in some of her sweetmeats. Should I go and test some more? It would be scientific, like.'

'But what if you were poisoned, Walter?' Murray asked, teasing him.

'Aye, that's a thought, sir,' said Walter, seriously. 'But sometimes we have to face our fears and dangers, do we not, sir?'

Given that Walter had faced a few fears and dangers during his time in Murray's service, Murray felt a little reprimanded, and fell silent. Walter soaped his face for him, only dribbling about a Scots pint of water down his collar.

'It's the picnic today, so you'll be wanted up at Kirkwelland House, or wherever we go for the event,' Murray said when he had finished. His nightshirt was sticking to his back with soapy water, but he tried not to squirm.

'And this morning, sir?'

'Not sure yet. What's the weather like?' He craned to see out of the narrow window. 'It seems set fair. I still need to find out where Newell went when he climbed the headland, and when and how he came back. I'll have to talk to old Pearce, I fear.'

'Is he one of the scientific men, sir?'

'Only for want of any more entertaining way to spend his evenings, I believe,' said Murray.

'Do you need me to go with you, sir?' Walter asked, with the least emphasis on the word 'need'. Murray flicked soap off his razor and regarded him.

'Have you a previous engagement, then?'

'It's only that Mr. Innes said I could go and look at his wind gauge and his other things for observing the weather, sir.'

'When did you make this arrangement?' asked Murray.

'After the funeral, sir. You said you didn't need me so I had a wee chat with him but he said he was busy then and I should go back some morning.'

Murray, as frequently happened with Walter, felt that he was struggling to push an immoveable object. It was pointless to try.

'Very well, but don't wander any further, and be back here by noon. All right?'

'Thank you, sir,' said Walter politely.

It was indeed a fair morning. After breakfast, Murray tried to make a list of likely blackmail victims but continued to struggle, partly from the difficulties of making the list and partly because he wanted to be outside in the glittering spring air. He had already seen Walter head determinedly down the lane – then turn and try the other direction – to go to see Innes. In the end he abandoned the list, and snatched up his hat, gloves and stick, and set off.

The gamekeeper's cottage inhabited by Norrie Pearce and his father sat a little up from the north end of the village, and a little back from the road up the headland, giving the impression that it was peeping out of the woods like an animal in the undergrowth. Despite being half hidden under the trees it was well-maintained with a decent slate roof, and spoke clearly of how Herkless tended to his estate property. The front door was ajar to let in the fresh air, and a lass of about twelve was hanging a few cloths out to air on the bushes about the kailyard. She glanced up as she heard Murray's bootsteps on the sandy path.

'Is this the home of Mr. Pearce?' Murray called.

'Aye, sir. Old Mr. Pearce is within, sir,' she said with competence that was not matched by her attempt at a curtsey. Murray nodded his thanks, and knocked on the open door. A voice called to him to enter, and he found himself in a comfortable kitchen, a small fire bright in the hearth, a clean looking box bed in the corner, and well-ordered bins for flour and other foodstuffs lined on shelves. It was not quite what Murray had been expecting, he admitted to himself: the Pearces had not struck him as anything but a couple of careless men living alone in the kind of state that Newell had been in.

'Mr. Murray, is it no?' came a voice from the window, and he turned to find that old Mr. Pearce had been watching his arrival.

The old man was swaddled in blankets on a chair very similar to the one old Mr. Craig inhabited at the tannery, just where he could watch anything passing on the road, and for a moment Murray had the fancy that they were the bookends of the village, matching each other in form and function. 'Are you here to ask more questions about Thomas Newell?'

'If you don't mind. I'm sure you'd like to see his killer caught, if he was your oldest friend.'

'Aye, aye.' Pearce nodded, the slab of his grey hair unmoving on his forehead. 'He needs to be caught, right enough. But how can I help? He didna even stop to talk to me that last day.'

'But when he did last talk to you,' said Murray, 'did he say anything about his life? About anyone he had quarrelled with, or hurt in any way?' He did not mention blackmail: he was quite sure that unlike Craig at the tannery, Pearce was well aware of why Newell might have wanted information about passersby.

'He never got on with that son-in-law of his, nor his daughter either, come to that,' said Pearce. It sounded well-rehearsed. 'Innes was aye a bit above himself, doing his wee science things with the laird and all. My son Norrie sets up and checks half the thermometers in the woods for the laird, but does he put on airs? Not a bit of it.'

'Did he say he felt in any danger from them, though?'

'Nah, nah. He just didna like them. He said they never took care of him nor took his pains seriously. Not that his pains were a'thing like the ones I suffer, for I can scarce leave this chair, and he was all over the village every day.'

'And the day he died, you were sitting here and you saw him go up the road to the headland?'

'He jooked over here because he kenned well I would be watching, so he just came to the door and said hello and that he was in a hurry. What for did he have a reason to be in a hurry? You'd think he was a great man of business off to a grand meeting in Glasgow, the way he was talking.'

'Did you notice if he had his stone whisky jar with him?'

Pearce frowned.

'The one he was poisoned with? That would be a strange thing to be carrying up this way, unless he was bringing it here – and I'm damn' pleased he didna, for he could have poisoned the two of us and all. Let me think, though …' He frowned even more deeply, pressing yellow teeth into his broad thumbs. 'No, he didna. And do you ken how I remember? I mind he was holding his wee writing tablets in one hand, and fiddling with the string on them with the other, so he had no hand to carry that jar in. There! And Norrie says I can mind nothing anymore!' His face smoothed in his triumph.

'What would he be taking writing tablets up here for, any more than a whisky bottle?' asked Murray.

'That I dinna ken,' said Pearce, no longer interested in anything but his feat of memory. 'Maybe he was taking weather observations too. It might be catching.'

'Did you see him coming back down later?'

Pearce was about to answer, then stopped and thought.

'I dinna think I did! There's a thing. For he could have gone round more by the big house, and down into the village that way, but he didna usually do that: he stayed near the road, I believe, from all he ever said to me, so I would usually see him coming back down. Aye, you're right, I dinna believe I did at all.'

'And you'd have been here all day?'

'Aye, see, the lassie brings me my food to this wee table here and I only shift myself to the big table when Norrie comes home, and that's after dark. So – they found him in the afternoon, did they no?'

'They did – long before dark.'

'Then I'd swear on the Bible he never came back down this way. With the pains in my legs I never sleep much, so I'd know I'd have been awake and watching out.'

'That's very interesting,' said Murray.

'Is it no?' Pearce sat back, satisfied. 'What for would he have gone home the other way?'

Lexie Conyngham

Chapter Twelve

There was definitely more of a spring in Coulter's step as he and Murray walked up the hill to Kirkwelland House in the early afternoon. The day was continuing fair, and through the trees behind them the glinting blue of the loch seemed to glow with a light of its own. The afternoon sun was just beginning to warm the front face of the house and the people collecting outside the broad front door were bright with summer colours, making Coulter and Murray stand out in their black like a couple of cinders in a flower arrangement. Herkless, directing the operation, wore a deep green coat that Murray envied, with a neckcloth of yellow and turquoise. It would be another eighteen months before Murray could even contemplate such a change.

'We're off to the meadow above Kirkwelland Burn,' Herkless told them when he saw them. 'I rode up this morning to see how dry it was, and it seems to have drained well. The servants have gone on ahead with the tables and food and so on.'

'Do we walk there?' asked Murray.

'It's an easy distance, Mr. Murray!' said Kitty, curtseying with a welcoming smile. 'And a pleasant walk. We go through the gardens, follow a path by the woods, and there we are: the burn has cut through the rock there before it runs down past the village to the tannery, and it is very picturesque.'

'It sounds delightful. Are we the last to arrive?'

'Yes, but you are still in plenty of time,' she said reassuringly. 'Everyone else was early. Oh, except Mrs. Black – and here she is now! Good gracious.'

They all turned to see Mrs. Black, puffing a little, trotting up the drive. She was wearing a dress in a rich bright tan embroidered with green flowers, with a green shawl over it. They were obviously new.

'Of course, it must be two years since Dr. Black died,' Kitty murmured. 'I can only imagine she was very tired of wearing black! But that is a very fine cloth indeed,' she added almost to herself, with a little puzzled frown on her forehead. She bit her lower lip, and glanced at her father. Herkless was busy with the Pringles, and did not react.

'Good day, good day!' said Mrs. Black. 'What a delightful day we have for it! Kitty, I have brought some chocolate conserves, if you will forgive me.'

'Forgive you, Mrs. Black! I thank you: they will be delicious.' Kitty took the little basket. 'Let me carry them, though.'

'Miss Herkless, allow me,' said Murray quickly, eager for an excuse to be near her and very happy to do her any little service.

'How very kind,' she said, handing it over with an amused smile. 'You see how popular your sweetmeats are, Mrs. Black? We shall be lucky if there are any left to eat by the picnic.' She took Mrs. Black's arm and led her off, Murray and Coulter following behind. Walter, eyeing the basket longingly, attended closely.

'You must allow me,' Kitty was saying to Mrs. Black in a voice Murray could only just catch, 'to admire your beautiful gown! Such a rich colour!'

'Thank you, my dear,' said Mrs. Black, self-consciously tugging her shawl up over her shoulder, but not before Murray noticed that the gown was very closely fitted to her plump white back. 'It takes a little courage, I found, to appear in this after two years in black and white and purple, but the day is so lovely it seemed a shame to continue in dull colours. All the world knows I loved my husband dearly, but I do like a cheerful gown!'

'And it suits you tremendously well. May I ask, is the material from Glasgow? I don't remember seeing it in Stranraer.'

'It is,' Mrs. Black gave a little wriggle of pride. 'But Meg Innes made it up for me, of course. She is so clever!'

'Isn't she! I don't know what we should do without her,' agreed Kitty, though Murray thought he could still hear some puzzlement in her voice. He considered: Mrs. Black had not been left well off by her husband, and had to make the sweetmeats to bring in some money. Surely then she would not go to Glasgow for expensive cloth? Was that why Kitty was puzzled? Where had the money come from for that lovely new gown?

The party arranged themselves in a little procession, led by Herkless, and set off. It was indeed a very pleasant walk:

Kirkwelland House could boast a walled garden that caught the warm air very effectively, and Murray could see several plants he knew his gardener would never manage in the cold eastern climes of Letho. Herkless took them by a circuitous route to admire it all, and Murray was able to glance back and see the comfortable way the red-ochre house sat in its attractive setting. It was a house he would not mind visiting often, should the opportunity arise, even though it was quite far from home. Was Kitty the kind of woman who would mind settling far from her father? He had a feeling she would manage very well wherever she was, but he would prefer to know that she was happy. He pulled himself back from such contemplations: it was far too early for him to be thinking about remarrying, in the eyes of society, at any rate. Perhaps she would be prepared to wait? Good heavens! he said to himself, you have only known her a few days and have not the remotest idea of her feelings in the matter, barely having time to know your own! He gave himself an admonitory whack on the side of his calf with his cane. It did not hurt as much as he would have liked, for his boots were tough, but it caused Coulter to give him a bit of a look.

'Caught my cane on something,' Murray muttered, but he grinned, nevertheless.

At the far side of the garden they eventually reached a gate of wrought iron, elegantly made. Murray wondered if the brusque smith Raffan had made it. Through it they gathered on a sandy path that led between light woodland, the birch, oak and beech that were on the headland, too. The woods were extensive to their left, perhaps indeed part of that headland plantation, but they were only a few trees deep to their right, and the path was well lit, with birds flitting busily across it and a squirrel or two bolting along branches above their heads. Herkless still led the way but the path was broad enough that Mr. and Mrs. Pringle could walk arm in arm beside him, followed by Miss Pringle, Kitty and Mrs. Black, then in a changeable arrangement the students, McCullough and Gibson in front, Adair a little behind, and Nugent in between but as far from Adair on the path as he could be, it seemed. Then came Coulter and Murray, with Walter still following the basket in hope like an obedient puppy.

A low stone wall divided the woodland from pasture on their right, and as they walked they could see that the pastureland became narrower, with some kind of break between this field and the next to the south. They reached a rough track which was evidently used to move cattle in and out of this oddly-shaped field, left the woodland and made their way over a stile – Herkless with agility, turning to help Mrs. Pringle; Mr. Pringle complaining vocally; Miss Pringle glancing about her as if unsure, Kitty lithe and quick, then putting out a steadying hand for Mrs. Black, then the students held back to allow Coulter and Murray to go first. Murray handed Miss Pringle over though she still seemed uncertain of the whole procedure, and she hesitated again when they had crossed, at last moving on in front of the students.

They found themselves in a narrow pasture, as they had seen. The grass was luxuriant even this early in the year, sheltered on the west and north by the woodland, with a distant view of the Loch below them to the east, and to the south the gully cut by Kirkwelland Burn as Kitty had explained. The servants had set up two tables to hold the food, as well arranged as one might expect in a dining room, and another as a sideboard to enable them to clear away more easily. Baskets and hampers had been tucked behind the sideboard out of the way. Between the three tables were low seats covered in rugs and cushions, a compromise between proper seating and the rustic pleasures of sitting on the ground, though that, too would be comfortable enough on the rugs that had been laid out there. A large parasol offered some shelter for the ladies' fair skins, though they all, for the moment, seemed appreciative of the sun's spring warmth. Murray gave the basket of sweetmeats to Walter to take to the tables.

'This is charming, as always!' cried Mrs. Black, walking carefully towards the picnic area. There were no cattle in the pasture at present, but there was some evidence that they were not long departed. 'Mrs. Pringle, will you come and take a seat with me?' The two ladies sat decorously on one of the low benches. They provided quite a contrast, rounded and dark, slim and pale, and Mrs. Black seemed to think she was the one who benefitted, arranging herself prettily with her shawl just on the points of her shoulders to show off her throat to best advantage. She did not quite look at Herkless.

'Gentlemen,' said Kitty, glancing at Mrs. Black, 'allow me to show you the little glen here formed by the burn. If you were listening to my father's talk on Saturday night at the mutual improvement society, you will no doubt remember all about the local geology – and here you may see it displayed, or a great deal of it, anyway! No doubt he will ask questions to make sure you were paying attention.'

'And you thought you had left college!' Murray remarked to the students, as they followed her over to the edge of the little ravine, where a few trees and bushes concealed them from the rest of the party. Nugent was the first to reach the rough edge and stood in fascination, counting the layers of coloured sandstone and jutting ridges of harder rocks on the other side of the rift. McCullough and Gibson lined up beside him, and Adair stood, too, leaning a little on McCullough's broad shoulder, his face grey. Murray, a little behind, saw McCullough glance at his companion in alarm, then turn away. Kitty waved Murray forward for a better view.

'You are not afraid of heights, I hope, Mr. Murray?' she asked with a smile that would have made him deny it even if it had been true. She herself was right on the edge. The drop was a matter of twenty feet, nothing too frightening, but narrow and rocky, though the profusion of ferns made it appear almost soft and welcoming.

'Charming,' said Adair, and turned away.

Just as he did so, McCullough happened to move: Adair lost his balance, and flung out an arm to save himself though he was only falling forward, away from the edge. His arm, however, caught Kitty, and knocked her backwards. She did not even have time to cry out. Murray thought he would never forget her face, mouth open, eyes wide, as she seemed to lean in midair, before he seized her about the waist and pulled back. They fell to the grassy ground, Kitty floundering in bewilderment, before he jumped up quickly to help her to her feet.

'Good gracious, Mr. Murray! I fear I may owe you my life!' she exclaimed, her face quite pink, breath coming quickly.

'Not at all,' said Murray. His own heart was galloping, though he preferred not to analyse that. 'You may wish to brush down your gown before we return to the company, though,' he said, unable to think of anything more useful to say.

'Thank you.' She paused before she bent to brush her skirts, though, meeting his eye with what seemed to be a question. It remained unasked and unanswered, as McCullough took her arm to support her and Adair apologised over and over, and they returned to the picnic site to find that no one there had even noticed the near-tragedy. They were deciding whether to start to eat.

'Mr. Murray has just saved me from a quick drop into the burn, Father!' Kitty called.

'Really? Then I am truly grateful,' said Herkless, 'though ashamed that she was silly enough to put herself in danger. All well now?' he asked, but for all his casual response Murray could see the concern in his eyes.

'Yes, all is well,' she replied with something like her usual smile, and sat down on one of the benches.

'Mr. Herkless, do come and sit here! We ladies are in need of your guidance!' called Mrs. Black with a kind of desperate coquetry.

Herkless obediently settled himself on the rug at the foot of their bench, and examined a ladybird that had settled on Mrs. Pringle's shawl. Pringle waved Murray to his side imperiously.

'You will not have pasture of this quality in Fifeshire, sir.'

'Indeed this is particularly fine,' Murray agreed, smiling. 'I fear my sheep would find it altogether too rich.'

Coulter sat on his other side, removing his wide-brimmed hat to feel the sun on his fair hair. A lazy breeze licked at the grass like an unhurried cow.

'Such a delightful day! I hope it holds!' he murmured. Adair and McCullough passed by behind them to reach spaces, and Murray heard, just below the general hum of conversation, McCullough's anxious voice whisper,

'How could you have done it again? You have to stop this, so you do!'

'I'm sorry, I'm so sorry,' came Adair's more cultured tones, at the same low volume.

'You'll be sorry if I get you near that cliff edge again,' muttered another voice – Nugent, Murray reckoned. He did not look round, fearing to let them see they had been overheard, and by the time they came and settled themselves around the last empty bench McCullough was smiling, Gibson was as absent as ever, and Nugent and Adair seated themselves at either end of the bench with the other two a barrier in between. Adair seemed wretched.

What had he done again? Murray wondered. Had he knocked someone over a cliff before? But McCullough had made whatever it was sound almost habitual.

The company were all now seated, and in a moment the servants were distributing food from the table of savoury dishes behind Murray. He noted that Walter was lingering behind the table of sweet stuff, guarding the chocolate conserves as if he expected enemy attack: he was barely visible behind part of a mighty jelly shape which quivered on the table. Murray wondered what feat of engineering had ever brought it here safely, or if the cook had taken up residence in the meadow overnight to make it on site.

Mrs. Black was talking animatedly as if even her mind had previously been shrouded in mourning. She was a lively speaker when she started, Murray thought, watching her gesture with one hand and balance her plate with the other. He wondered if she were hoping the impact of her new finery would help her to win Mr. Herkless, for she seemed to be putting a great deal of energy into her conversation, her smiles, her gestures, as if she were working against the clock. Her bonnet, a light confection of Leghorn straw suitable for the day, tossed and twitched perilously close to the table holding the puddings.

'Something's going to be dropped soon,' Coulter murmured beside him. 'And there it goes.'

Mrs. Black's napkin slid to the ground, and she bent to retrieve it before any of the gentlemen or servants had a chance. There came a cry from behind the jelly shape, and Walter emerged, clutching his forehead.

'What's the matter, Walter?' Murray asked. Walter was not yet much practised at serving at table.

'Something hit me!' Walter complained.

'An insect of some kind?' asked Mrs. Pringle, peering over at him with concern.

'It will be a ladybird,' said Mr. Pringle with his usual assurance. Walter presented his forehead to Murray, who saw that there was indeed a red spot right in the centre. To have made such a mark through Walter's thick fringe must have required some strength.

'I think you have been stung, Walter,' said Murray.

'A bee sting, it must be,' said Mrs. Black. 'You'll need baking soda.'

'Alas, the one thing we have left at home!' said Herkless jokingly.

'I can see no sting,' said Murray, a little embarrassed at the attention his servant was attracting. 'May he have a little ice to soothe it?'

'Of course,' said Herkless. Walter retreated to find a small lump of ice, and the meal continued more peacefully. Mr. Pringle kept up a slow series of statements about the geology of Wigtownshire for Murray's benefit, though he was distracted by Coulter's low-voiced interjections of 'That's not right,' and 'No, it isn't,' on his other side. Nugent ate heartily, and McCullough's plate would have emptied faster if he had not tried to take so active a part in the conversation with Kitty and Anna Pringle: Anna was plying him with questions about Ireland, which he was doing his best to answer. Adair and Gibson spoke hardly at all, and ate only slightly more. Murray watched them out of the corner of his eye when he could: he had not yet, he felt, worked out the politics of the little group. Nugent had called them the odd ones, the ones no one else wanted to travel with. Why? Nugent himself was bad-tempered, yes, but Adair was very charming, Gibson was harmless, surely, and McCullough seemed like an ideal travelling companion, organised, caring, friendly. They had not been together the day of Newell's death: Gibson was on the shoreline, seeing his visions: Nugent and McCullough were walking south and Adair had gone back to the north, back along the path they had walked the previous day. It still seemed an odd choice. Murray turned very slightly to have a better view of Adair as he toyed with his food. He seemed to have eaten a little pie, and was a healthier colour, but as Murray watched, half hearing Pringle's ponderous dissertation on granite ('Sandstone is a major constituent of granite, sir, thus giving it its various colours such as rose and red.'), Adair set his plate down warily on the bench between himself and Gibson, and leaned forward to scoop something off Anna Pringle's skirts. Murray squinted. It was a large bee, which paced along his palm, waving its legs by turn in the air. Adair smiled at it, and as Anna jumped at the sight of it he waved his hand and let it fly off towards the woods, swerving through the air.

'It was on the tail of your gown, forgive me,' Adair was saying to Anna, his brown eyes warm. 'I did not wish it to sting you or you to crush it.'

Anna gave a little breathless laugh, and turned back to the conversation with McCullough, though Murray was fairly sure she was aware of Adair's every movement. Murray wondered if the fact they were both known to take walks up on the headland was a coincidence – but then it appeared that half the local population took their exercise up there. He tutted quietly to himself and turned back to Mr. Pringle.

Mr. Pringle had apparently reached the end of his lecture, and was now speaking across to Mr. Herkless, still sprawled at the feet of the ladies.

'Are you intending a visit to Stranraer this week at all, Herkless?' he asked. 'For if you are I should be happy to travel with you.'

'I did think I might go,' said Herkless, 'but I would not wish you to inconvenience yourself waiting for me, for I am by no means certain of it.'

'Nevertheless I shall wait,' said Pringle, bestowing the favour of his presence generously. Mrs. Black did not appreciate the interruption.

'Oh, Mr. Herkless! Are you to go in your gig? For if so I should be more than grateful if you could just squeeze me in?' She finished archly and gave a little wriggle as if of one being squeezed, and the seams of her gown creaked audibly. Mrs. Pringle's eyebrows rose slightly.

'Mrs. Black, you may be forcing me to make the unenviable choice between you and Mr. Pringle!' said Herkless. 'I fear I must avoid favouring either of you and ride, instead!'

'Oh, Mr. Herkless!' Mrs. Black swooped towards him with some new blandishment, which was never uttered. Something gave suddenly at the back of her gown: a servant behind the table of puddings let out a squawk, and the dish of eggs he was carrying flew into the air. Several eggs, finding themselves independently airborne, landed with heavy slurps in the massive jelly shape. The servant staggered, clutching his eye with one hand and the table with the other, and put his foot into another of the eggs which had fallen on to the grass. He slipped, lunged forward, and tipped the table. The company watched in horror, unable to move, as the puddings one by one slid off the table and landed on Mrs. Black and Herkless. As if sucked by their collectively indrawn breath the majestic jelly shape, complete with its cargo of pickled eggs, moved last, like a magnificent ship leaving the dock, sailed effortlessly past the servant's arms sweeping out to catch it, and picked up speed, slapping Mrs. Black resoundingly on the back of her head and enveloping her and Herkless in its sticky grasp. There was an awful silence.

'Sir, I've found a button!' said Walter suddenly. 'I think that's what hit me!'

He held up a little button covered in tan silk.

'Walter!' Murray's tone was warning, but the servant who had fallen was sitting on the grass with his legs spread out, still pressing the heel of his thumb into his eye, and holding up a twin of the button. Kitty suddenly stood up, setting her plate on the sideboard.

'Mrs. Black, do come back to the house and let us see if that jelly will come off,' she said with sympathy. She slipped her own shawl off and set it about Mrs. Black's shoulders, helping her up. Mrs. Black hid her face in the ruins of her straw bonnet, and allowed herself to be led back to the stile. As the two women made their way along the path back through the wood the company studiously looked the other way, as the servants did their best to scrape puddings off the carpet. Mrs. Pringle was mercifully unscathed, but Herkless was a mess and insisted on one of the servants pouring a bucket of water, brought to rinse the plates, over his head as he stood near the cliff edge, away from the picnic. McCullough, with an anxious smile, left his place to tend to the injured servant, and the Pringles, Murray, Coulter and the other students sat dazed, wondering what to do. Coulter stood abruptly and moved away towards the woods, scowling, and after a moment Murray noticed that his shoulders were heaving as he kept his back to the company. A minister, particularly one in mourning, should not be seen to find such a situation hilarious.

The minister's move, though, seemed to allow them all to stand and shift about, relaxing and moving out of the way of the servants' cleaning efforts.

'Poor Mrs. Black,' said Mrs. Pringle at last. 'Very

unfortunate.'

'Yes, indeed,' agreed Murray. 'I hope she will be able to rejoin us.'

'I fear her gown is ruined,' murmured Mrs. Pringle.

'She should have stayed in mourning,' said Mr. Pringle. 'There's no call for a widow to dress in bright colours at all. I know you never would, Ada,' he added to his wife. She did not quite respond.

'I'm not sure that wearing mourning would have helped, in the present situation,' said Murray.

'No,' said Nugent, 'that pudding was going, no matter what.' His face twisted, and he sank his mouth into his hands. Murray knew he was having the same trouble as Coulter and turned away, in case he caught Nugent's eye and set him off.

'Well, no puddings,' said Herkless briskly, returning to stand dripping at the edge of the picnic site. 'And I fear I should change. Would you all come back to the house and partake of more food there? Perhaps if I go ahead,' he wiped a smear of blancmange from his neck, 'and you can make the most of the pleasant weather here for a little before returning?'

'If you are quite sure,' said Murray, 'then at least it would be comforting to know that Mrs. Black is quite recovered.'

'Then let us adopt that plan.' Herkless bowed to them and strode off, squelching.

'I'd like to take a look at that ravine again,' said Nugent, pulling himself together. 'The geology is just great.' He turned and wandered off to the trees. McCullough had returned to Gibson and was tidying up his plate and cutlery as if he were a favoured child. Murray thought of Augusta, and smiled. He hoped he would see her again soon. Would Kitty Herkless like her? How could she not?

He walked over to Coulter, putting out a warning hand to his friend's shoulder before greeting him. Coulter's eyes were wet with laughter, but he seemed to have recovered.

'Dreadful for poor Mrs. Black,' he acknowledged, 'and I felt so sorry for her, and for Herkless. But every time I think of that jelly shape sliding inevitably down the table ...' His mouth twisted, and he drew a deep, wobbly breath.

'We're going back to the house shortly: Herkless went ahead

to clean himself up and presumably warn the rest of the servants – and Mrs. Black.'

'I doubt she'll want to see any of us,' said Coulter, shaking his head. 'But she'll have to see us sooner or later, and probably better sooner. Poor woman!'

Pringle hailed them from a few yards away.

'You have been in prayer,' he said to Coulter. 'We should go to the house. I note that the burn in the ravine is very low. There will be consequences amongst the cattle, and at the tannery.'

'Where are Mrs. and Miss Pringle?' Coulter asked. 'Are they ready to leave, or should we wait a little longer?'

'I left them at the ravine,' said Pringle. He stared about. 'They cannot have lingered there this long.' At that moment Mrs. Pringle appeared, but from the direction of the trees by the path to the house. She was alone.

'Where is Anna?' Mr. Pringle called.

'I thought she was with you,' said Mrs. Pringle. Murray glanced about. The servants had almost finished packing up, and he was pleased to see Walter making himself useful. Gibson and McCullough were standing up by the stile, gazing along the cattle road, their backs to the pasture. The rest of the pasture was empty.

'You left her at the ravine?' Murray asked, even as he set out towards it.

'She was just behind those trees, I'm sure of it!' called Pringle, as Coulter followed.

'He's sure of a lot of things, though,' said Coulter as they hurried across the pasture. 'And many of those are wrong.'

At the edge of the ravine, Nugent was standing alone, surveying the landscape with interest. He turned as he heard them approach.

'Have you seen Miss Pringle?' Coulter called.

'She went along that way,' Nugent said, waving to his right, downstream. The trees were thicker here, and it was impossible to see all the way along the cliff edge in either direction. Coulter began to make his way through them, followed by Murray. Murray glanced down into the ferny streambed.

'Look,' he said, 'the ferns are broken down there.'

Coulter stopped and stared down where he was pointing.

'That's not good,' he said quietly.

'Is there a way we can get down? She might be hurt,' said Murray.

'Further downstream,' said Coulter, 'but it's a bit of a scramble.'

'If you want to stay up on the top and direct me,' said Murray.

'No, come on.' Coulter led the way quickly through the trees to the west end of the pasture. There a stone wall came to the cliff edge, and they flung themselves over it. A few yards further on the cliff edge became less regular, and the cliff itself more of a stony slope. Coulter started down it, slithering and sliding sideways to keep his balance. Murray hurried after.

In a moment they were down by the side of the burn, which was a matter of five or six feet wide. They followed it upstream, beating their way through ferns as the sides of the ravine grew steep again and the sound of the running water echoed off the rocky face with the scrape of their steps.

'It's around here somewhere,' said Coulter, peering up.

'Yes, there: you can see where the fronds are bent and broken.'

There came a cry from high above them.

'Are you down there?' called Nugent.

'Yes, we're here!' Murray called back, and the sound thudded about the ravine.

'She's here, she's safe!' Nugent cried, and they could just glimpse his arm, waving. Then they could see Anna's head, peeping over the cliff edge.

'I'm here, Mr. Coulter!' she assured them. 'Quite safe!'

'Thank goodness!' Coulter called back. He turned and began to make for the place where they had climbed down. 'Now for the scrabble back up!'

Murray turned, too, trying to find a safe foothold amongst the ferns on the ravine's floor. He stepped back on to something soft, and jumped. A dead sheep, perhaps? That would explain the broken ferns. He bent down and pushed the ferns aside.

Adair lay there, face down, unmoving, his head and hand submerged in the stream.

Lexie Conyngham

Chapter Thirteen

'She's up here! She's safe!'

The voices continued to summon them out of the ravine, voices which floated away somewhere above the heads of Murray and Coulter, down by Adair's body.

'Is – is he definitely dead? Shouldn't we do something?' asked Coulter, starting to shiver. Murray pulled off a glove and touched Adair's graceful neck, long fingers feeling for the right point, but he found no pulse.

'He's dead, yes.' He sat back on his heels, and examined the ravine about him. 'Before we move him – and I think you and I should move him if we can, and not bring everyone else down here, too – can you see anything odd here? Any evidence of someone having been here apart from the three of us?'

'The three – no, no, I don't think so.'

They both stared about, upstream and down, Murray gently moving ferns aside to examine the ground. There was no trace of any footprints or disturbance of the foliage except for the line up the side of the ravine that they had noticed from above. It appeared that Adair had indeed fallen, alone, over the little cliff.

'He must have slipped,' said Coulter, his teeth now chattering.

'He stumbled earlier, when we were looking over the edge. When we first arrived in the pasture for the picnic.'

'I thought it was Kitty Herkless who nearly fell?'

'It was, but only because he turned and fell against her.'

'Are you still down there?' came another voice from above. It was Herkless, back to find his guests.

'They will not be down there now. They know my daughter is safe,' Pringle announced distantly.

'Yes, we're still down here,' Murray called back, and his voice sounded terribly loud over Adair's silent body. 'We have bad news, though.'

'Bad news? What do you mean? Anna Pringle is here.'

'But Adair is here,' said Murray, 'and he's dead.'

'Jamesie? Jamesie Adair? Dead?' McCullough must have rejoined the party too. 'Let me see!'

'The ferns are in the way,' said Murray. It seemed ridiculous, and disrespectful, to be shouting like this. 'Coulter and I will carry him downstream to the end of this narrow part, if a few others will help us bring him up the bank.'

'Oh, yes,' said Coulter, at a normal volume, 'I don't think we could manage that between the two of us.'

'How can he be dead?' McCullough was still crying out his bewildered shock above them. 'How could that happen?'

'We think he fell over the edge, and probably knocked himself out.' Murray saw Coulter glance at him, not understanding. 'Well, if he was conscious when he fell, he would not willingly have lain with his head in a stream, would he?'

'Oh, yes.'

'Now, one last look: right hand in the water, left hand behind him, face down, legs … knees bent, feet upwards, as if they trailed behind as he fell. No mud apparent on his clothing: it seems as if he simply toppled forward and fell head first.'

'That's a kind of mercy,' said Coulter. 'I should not have liked to have thought of him slipping but unable to pull himself back up, with all of us no distance away and unaware.'

'Rub your arms: it'll help with the shivering,' said Murray. 'I'll just turn him over. Come, now, Adair, I'll be gentle,' he murmured, feeling it only polite. He pulled Adair's shoulder out of the water and pushed him on to his back, tugging his legs out to make him easier to pick up. There was no stiffness, but then it was not that long since Adair had been sitting eating his picnic, or trying to. 'Look, there we are.'

Coulter stepped closer, still rubbing his arms vigorously.

'What is it?'

Murray indicated Adair's temple. It seemed odd, at first, until you realised that it curved in where it should curve out. His eyes and mouth were half-open, as if he were about to rouse himself and speak, to object to his treatment.

'That's where he hit something – that rock, I should think.'

Murray pointed to a blunt lump of reddish rock in the middle of the stream. 'The water has washed both it and him, but the shape is about right.'

'Curious pastime you've found yourself, Charles,' said Coulter, but at least his teeth were under control again.

'He'll be heavy, I think. Are you ready to make a start?'

'I think so.'

'Then take his legs, would you, and I'll catch him under the arms. Ready? And lift.'

There was a moment's pause while Coulter tried to turn around so that he could walk forwards down the ravine. Over their grunts they could hear sobbing from the field above them – more than one voice, Murray thought. Someone was upset that Adair was no longer alive. Had anyone been equally eager to see him dead?

They stumbled slowly down the stream, slipping on the moist earth and stone, tripping on ferns, pausing now and again to adjust their grip. Above them the voices and the sobbing followed, eyes watching their seemingly endless funerary progress, hands ready to help when the moment came. When they reached the rough slope they had slithered down earlier, in their hunt for Anna Pringle, Herkless was already halfway down, and had brought a hurdle from the field to carry the body. McCullough, his face contorted with huge, wracking sobs, was ready despite them, and between the four of them they hauled Adair's long unwieldy corpse on to the hurdle and then up the hill to where the Pringles, Nugent and Gibson were waiting at the top.

'We'll take him back to the house,' said Herkless. 'He was our guest.'

'Oh, Jamesie, Jamesie! Why could you not stop?' McCullough choked as they laid their burden down on the rich grass of the pasture, and he fell to his knees beside his friend's corpse. Gibson, too, knelt on the other side, and closed his eyes in fervent, silent prayer. Murray glanced around. Nugent was nearby, squinting down at the body with an expression on his face that Murray could not read: confusion? Guilt? Regret? Relief? Mrs. Pringle held her daughter close: Anna Pringle was ash white, her red hair startling against her skin, her dry eyes fixed on Adair's wet, closed face. Pringle himself looked on with an expression of disgust:

presumably people of any breeding did not die untidily in Wigtownshire.

'We'd better tell Thomson,' Murray murmured to Coulter and Herkless, as they stood a little apart.

'Thomson? The sheriff's man? Why?'

'Just in case.'

'But you said yourself that he stumbled earlier,' said Coulter, starting to shiver again. 'Surely he just stumbled again and this time there was no one there to catch him.'

'There's another possibility,' said Herkless, his handsome face serious. He lowered his voice. 'What if he had something to do with Newell's death?'

Coulter gasped.

'And compounded murder by – by self-destruction? But that would be terrible!'

'Perhaps there was something accidental in Newell's death, but he felt himself responsible,' said Herkless. 'Mercurial compounds are no doubt available to purchase in Glasgow. Perhaps he was carrying one, and it somehow was introduced to the whisky bottle.'

'Perhaps,' said Murray, even more quietly and with a glance at the other students, 'he was being blackmailed.'

'Over what?' demanded Coulter, defensive of his students as ever.

'I don't know,' said Murray, 'but did you catch what McCullough said just now? "Why could you not stop?", he said. And earlier, I heard him say "How could you have done it again? You have to stop this!", to which Adair apologised, very contritely, I thought.'

'But what had he done? What was he doing?'

'I have no idea.' He looked back at the students. 'Maybe they'll tell us now.'

McCullough was past the first deluge of sobs now, and with an effort pulled himself upright beside the hurdle.

'Can we cover his face before we take him back to the house?' he asked, his voice thick.

'Of course.' Herkless brought out a clean handkerchief and spread it over Adair's face. 'Shall we take him now?'

Gibson moved back, letting Murray and Coulter lean in to pick the hurdle up by its corners. McCullough took the third one, but just as Herkless was bending to lift the fourth, Nugent stepped forward, his face wrenched.

'Let me, sir. After all, it's not as if we haven't done it before, eh, Jamesie?'

He eased his hands under the corner of the hurdle, they lifted, and set off, even managing the stile and the narrow garden gate, and bringing Adair back to Kirkwelland House with a reasonable dignity.

Herkless had managed to hurry ahead a little, to give warning to the household and to Kitty. She met them at the door, her face shocked and solemn, and led the way into the dining room on the ground floor where a thick cloth had been spread on the table. They set the hurdle on top of it, McCullough tidying Adair's restless limbs and straightening his head.

'I'll send for the local woman,' said Kitty gently. 'She is very kind.'

McCullough nodded, not looking at her, eyes on Gibson, eyes on Adair. Nugent was standing slumped, head bowed, at the end of the table. Gibson seemed exhausted, his fair skin almost transparent.

'We shall leave now,' said Mr. Pringle, who had come no further than the dining room door but stood there, as if inspecting the arrangements.

'Of course – but perhaps a cup of tea before you go? And a brandy, for the shock?' asked Kitty. Murray had seen her catch sight of Anna Pringle and blink. If anyone appeared shocked, it was Anna.

'I think that would be a very good idea, Mr. Pringle,' said Mrs. Pringle firmly.

'Then come with me to the parlour,' said Kitty. 'Mr. McCullough, I shall have brandy sent in here too: you should all have some.'

'I must send for Thomson,' said her father. 'Coulter, will you stay a little longer, too?'

They moved away, Herkless rehearsing reasons for summoning Thomson and speculating as to where to find him. Murray was left with the students in the dining room. For a few minutes no one spoke: McCullough pulled out a chair for Gibson to sit on, and stood behind it, comforting hands on Gibson's thin shoulders, cheek resting against Gibson's gingery hair. Gibson's eyes were closed. When Murray finally spoke, they all jumped, as if they had completely forgotten he was there.

'McCullough, when you asked Adair to stop what he was doing, what did you mean?'

McCullough stared at him, not hostile, simply wondering what Murray was talking about until his stunned mind could sort it out. He pulled out the chair next to Gibson's, and went to sink his head on to his hands on the table, then drew back hurriedly when he touched Adair's leg instead. He gestured weakly, and let his hands drop down.

'Jamesie Adair was a lovely man,' he said. 'There wasn't a button of harm in him from the day he was born. The only thing was, he liked a drink.'

'Oh,' said Murray.

'Aye. I mean he really liked it. And the one wouldn't do, either, it needed to be whatever, and however much, he could get his hands on.' McCullough sighed heavily, as if with that breath the whole story would come out. 'He came with us because he knew we knew and he promised me he wouldn't drink on the way and I promised to try to keep him away from it, but he was too clever for me. He was dead drunk in Cairnryan, and that's what held us back. We had to carry him out of the lodgings, and you'd nearly have said he was as dead then as he is now. When he came round he was desperate sorry. He always was, and he always promised he would never do it again, but I don't think he could help it. He was drunk last Saturday, and then I managed to keep him off it the Sabbath and yesterday, Heaven help us, even through Newell's funeral, but this morning he found brandy and that was him away again. You saw him nearly cowp Miss Herkless over the cliff this morning. I should have been watching him. I knew fine well he was drunk: I should have kept him away from the cliff.' Tears were welling in his eyes again, but Murray needed to plough on.

'Could he have been being blackmailed by Newell over this?'

McCullough nodded desolately.

'Aye, he was and all. Newell never asked that much, just wee bits you thought you could afford to start with, anyway. Newell said he would write to Adair's parents and his local minister.'

'Do you think he would have killed Newell?'

McCullough went pale, but he bit his lip thoughtfully.

'D'you know, I don't know?'

'I'll tell you, though,' said Nugent unexpectedly, 'he wouldn't have killed him that way. If Adair had found whisky in Newell's house, or anywhere else, it wouldn't have been in the bottle long enough to be poisoned.'

'That's true,' said McCullough sadly. 'That's true enough. And I'm sorry to say I'm glad of it this once.'

Murray let that thought lie a moment, willing himself to push on. He spoke quietly, as if it would make his question more acceptable.

'If Newell was blackmailing Adair, was he blackmailing any of the rest of you?'

There was a long pause. Nugent stared firmly at the floor. Gibson shook his head, vague. McCullough at last sat back, and whispered,

'Yes.'

'And was it wee bits you thought you could afford to start with?' Murray asked gently.

'It was,' said McCullough. His gaze darted to Gibson and away. 'But this last time when I paid him,' he added suddenly, 'he sort of laughed at it, as if it wasn't very much, and he said he wouldn't need many more customers – that's what he called us – like me, for he had gentry amongst his customers now.'

'Gentry?' The Pringles? Murray wondered.

'That's what he said. Words and glances, he said: it was remarkable what you could work out from words and glances. He didn't say anything else, just put the money in that bag he kept in his box bed.'

'It's missing.'

'Is it?' McCullough did not really care.

'Would you mind,' said Murray, in the same quiet tone that had worked before, 'if I took a look through Adair's pack?'

'Why would you want to do that, sir?' asked Nugent, with a touch of his old belligerence. 'What business is it of yours?'

'There will be talk about Adair and Newell,' said Murray, 'and whether Adair might have killed Newell and then himself.'

Well, there was talk already, he thought, but did not mention that. 'It would be good if we found anything that might help to quash that notion from the start.'

'It certainly would!' said McCullough. 'Well, his pack would be up the stairs.'

'Would one of you be good enough to come with me and show me?'

McCullough and Nugent exchanged shrugs, then glanced down at Adair as if asking him for his opinion.

'I'll go,' said Nugent. 'You two stay here.'

He led Murray out into the deserted hall. Murray suddenly had a vision of it warm-lit and welcoming the night of his first visit, and allowed himself a little sigh. He followed Nugent up the main stairs, then through several doors to a passage at the back of the house. Nugent passed one closed door and opened the second.

'This is us – was us, is me,' he said obscurely. 'Gibson and McCullough are next door.'

The room was small and old fashioned, with a lumpy half tester bed in the middle of the far wall and a couple of hard chairs at a small round table by the window. The fireplace was minuscule: a generously sized fir cone would have filled it, and it showed no evidence of recent use. There was a faint aroma of damp.

'Three steps up from the servants' quarters, but not as crowded as the manse,' Nugent commented, not ungraciously. 'The food is dead good.'

'Well, that's something,' said Murray absently. 'Which of these packs is Adair's?'

'Yon one.' Nugent pointed to the one open on the floor between the bed and the window. The one on the table, presumably his own, was neat with the contents folded or arranged in an orderly fashion, even if they were all a little old and shabby. Murray passed it by and squatted down to examine Adair's belongings.

It amounted to a few shirts, all in good repair if grubby; sufficient stockings to go a fortnight and a matching supply of nether garments and handkerchiefs, all of fine making; the usual candle and box of flints; a number of books, of a quality and type that spoke eloquently to the book lover in Murray, as well as a volume or two of sermons ('Those are in his own hand,' Nugent put in: 'he had a lovely hand, as you'll see, and a good memory for copying a sermon. I'll give him that.'); a flask which by its scent had recently contained brandy but was now certainly empty; three or four letters each of which had been written in two parts by 'Your Father' and 'Your ever-loving Mamma', all a few weeks old and containing nothing of significance on this side of the water; and a further letter, this one in a childish hand, unsteady and looping, and dated only 'Saturday'. Murray scanned the large letters.

'Dearest Mr. Adair,' it read, 'for so I must call you even now. You tell me that you are not good enoff for me but I think that is up to me to decyed. I see no falt in you that the loving care of a good wife will not cure, and so I wold be to you for all our lives together. You have never been less than kindnes itself to me and I must beleeve that you trewly do love me for the way you have spoken to me always. You spoke when last we met of not wishing to take me so far from my home but that is no distance when trew love is at ishew. I cannot bear that you think we shold not meet again, for at least we will see each other at church tomorrow so you see it will not be so easy as that not to see each other, and I cannot beleeve that you can look on without pitty at least.

'With all my love wich you have for always,

'A.Pringle.'

Murray folded the letter away again just as he had found it, and went on with his search, but there seemed to be nothing else. He sat back on his heels, contemplating the pack, while Nugent sat on the edge of the bed nearest him and tapped his toes on the bare boards.

'What was there between Adair and Anna Pringle?' Murray asked at last.

'Oh, is that who it was from?' Nugent asked. 'I think she was making all the running there. But I wonder – is that why he was always off for walks over the headland, every time we stopped here? Hm – good question.' He seemed to be searching back through his memories of staying in Kirkwelland, matching them against this new theory. 'It never occurred to me to wonder before, but I think it might fit.' He tapped his teeth. 'I thought when I saw them together, though, that there was a good deal more to it on her side than on his. Except when he was drunk, he was a sensible man: he wouldn't have put himself in an awkward position with her. McCullough might know more about it than I do, though.'

'I'll ask him. Was this all Adair's stuff? Except what he's wearing, of course.'

'Aye, I think so.'

Murray irresistibly straightened out the shirts, and as he did so something fell from the sleeve of one of them. It was a small leather sack, and it fell with a knowing thud and a faint jingle. Murray and Nugent looked at one another.

'Money?' said Nugent. 'He was always better off than the rest of us.'

Murray tugged at the drawstrings and eased the bag open, pouring the contents out on to the shirt from which it had fallen. There were quite a few coins there, mostly pennies and halfpennies, a few farthings, a few shillings. It amounted to around two pounds, all told, Murray reckoned. And then there were the writing tablets.

'These aren't his, are they?' asked Murray, picking them up cautiously. He opened them, but the writing inside bore no resemblance to Adair's beautiful hand, nor to Miss Pringle's laboured scrawl. "I mind he was holding his wee writing tablets in one hand, and fiddling with the string on them with the other," old Pearce had told him that morning. The string was indeed frayed, but not broken: the full set of tablets seemed to be there.

'"J. Adair, 6d.", it says on the first page. Then it seems to have been smeared, somehow. Here, can you read any of it?' Murray passed the tablets to Nugent, but he flicked through and gave up quickly.

'Makes no sense to me,' he declared, and handed them back. Murray squinted at them without success.

'I'll take them and see if I can make any more out of them. But I think we may say that this was Newell's store of money – and presumably of information, too. His daughter said his memory was failing him: he must have decided to write down all his customers in this.' He scooped the money back into the bag, added the tablets, and stood up. 'Let's go back down and see if Thomson has arrived.'

'That wee man again? Dear help us,' muttered Nugent, but he

pushed himself off the bed and followed Murray.

Downstairs all was still quiet. They went to the dining room, Nugent pressing his lips together before he entered as if steeling himself for the business within. McCullough and Gibson had been sitting side by side, apparently in silence, and looked up without much interest at their return.

'Can you tell me about anything there was between Adair and Miss Pringle?' Murray asked. 'We found a letter.'

'Well, there was nothing, really, that he said anything to me about,' said McCullough, touching Adair's arm as if in apology. 'I think there maybe would have been, but he knew himself he had a problem with the drink and he was a good man: he wouldn't have inflicted that on anybody. He liked her fine at one stage, I think, but then he tried to break away.'

'We found Newell's money bag in Adair's things.'

'What? But how would that have come to be there?' McCullough looked genuinely baffled.

'You've no idea?'

'Not a bit of it. What would Jamesie be doing with that, even if he'd killed him?'

'Well, it also had this in it. I should think if the person who killed Newell was being blackmailed, this is something they would have wanted to remove from the cottage.' He showed McCullough the writing tablet.

'This has been wiped or something,' said McCullough. 'But you can still see bits, so you can.' He held the tablet so that the light from the window, early evening though it was, swept across the writing surface. 'This here says "J. Adair" – I suppose that bit was easy enough. Then below that it says "A. Pringle", so maybe the oul fella followed them up on to the headland and thought they were getting a wee bit close. What's that bit – Burn, maybe? Burns? I can't make it out. And the rest's been really taken out.'

'Burns is the man who owns the village shop, and Newell was trying to blackmail his daughter – unsuccessfully, I believe. A. Pringle, though: that seems to show that he was blackmailing Anna, rather than just Adair. I think I need to talk to Anna Pringle again.'

Chapter Fourteen

By the time they had discovered definitely that Thomson, the sheriff's man, had in fact ridden back to Stranraer and not stayed the previous night in Kirkwelland, it was dusk, and the general view was that it would be time enough to set off in the morning. Coulter tentatively offered to go and as Murray offered to travel with him, partly to make sure that this time he did leave the village and do what he said he would do, Herkless offered them the loan of his gig.

'You will need to be a competent driver,' said Pringle, his whole expression showing how much he doubted this was the case.

'I've not yet turned my own gig over,' Murray said hesitantly, fully aware that gigs were a dicey form of transport and Herkless' own gig might well be higher set than his, making its balance even less certain. Mr. and Mrs. Pringle, having agreed to tea and brandy, had only moved from the comfortable seats in the parlour to eat a hearty supper at the table, where Herkless, Coulter and Murray had eventually joined them. McCullough, Nugent and Gibson were still with Adair's body in the dining room. Only Miss Pringle had not managed to eat, and Murray had so far failed to speak to her alone. Kitty, however, had come to sit in the little chair next to his end of the sopha, and after seeing that everyone had punch and biscuits she relaxed and turned to him.

'Are you quite well, Mr. Murray? It must have been a shock to discover poor Mr. Adair like that.'

'It was unsettling, certainly, though I had gone down there suspecting that something had happened.'

'He stumbled earlier, of course,' she said, looking away.

'He did.' Murray's voice was expressionless. She glanced back at him, her deep blue eyes examining his face.

'Am I the only one,' she said quietly, 'to feel just a little uneasy at this accident following so soon after Newell's unfortunate death?'

'No,' said Murray, 'you are not the only one.'

She smiled.

'I thought you would have it in hand. What do you think, then? Did Mr. Adair have something to do with Newell's death, and throw himself into the ravine in remorse? Or has someone been disposing of more than one person inconvenient to their comfort?'

It was his turn to smile.

'He left no note to confess his sins, that I have been able to find,' he said, 'but on the other hand, Newell's money bag was found amongst his belongings upstairs.'

'You searched his belongings?' She was not shocked, he noted, just curious.

'It seemed sensible. Nugent came with me.'

'That was also sensible.' She thought for a moment, pressing her lower lip under her upper lip in a way he found suddenly very charming. He grinned at himself, not unwilling to enjoy this apparently growing friendship.

'The trouble is,' she said, and the expression on her face made him instantly solemn, 'if Mr. Adair was pushed into the ravine so easily this afternoon, there were only a few of us around who could have pushed him, were there not? The Pringles, the other students, Mr. Coulter, you, Mrs. Black, Father and me.'

'Not you or Mrs. Black, I think,' said Murray hurriedly, 'for when you took her away Adair was still in his seat.'

'But I left her to change, poor woman!' said Kitty. 'Some of the servants may vouch for me – surely we pay them well enough to do so! – but I'm afraid I left Mrs. Black alone.'

'For how long?'

'You see, I don't even know. I brought her back here, took her upstairs, called a maid and found some garments that would see her home respectably, and left them to it. When I went back to see if she had everything she needed, she was gone, and the maid said she had been dismissed almost immediately. Of course she would have wanted to hurry if she was to have any chance of taking the puddings off the dress without staining,' she added reasonably.

'So she could have doubled back?'

'It's possible, though I struggle to picture Mrs. Black striding through the woods to knock Mr. Adair off a cliff, which she would have had to do to reach the pasture without any of you seeing her.'

Murray considered this. The gate into the pasture was at the east end, and from there the pasture widened with the ravine on one side and the wooded path, visible to the whole pasture, on the other, until the west end of the pasture met the stone wall near where he and Coulter had scrambled down into the ravine. On the west side of that wall the woodland was quite dense until it reached, presumably, the garden wall of Kirkwelland House. It would not be a long walk but he imagined it would not be an easy one in a gown.

'Poor Mrs. Black,' Kitty said. 'She was so dreadfully embarrassed. I must call on her tomorrow or I fear she will never appear in public again.'

'It was a very unfortunate series of events, though perhaps she will feel it has been sufficiently overshadowed by Adair's death.'

'I hardly think she came back and knocked him over the edge just to take the weight off her own shame!' said Kitty with arched eyebrows, but they both laughed a little.

'No, it seems unlikely,' Murray agreed.

'The trouble is she was trying so hard to impress my father. That gown was prodigiously expensive, for I have seen that material before, and I doubt she could afford it: it makes me wonder if she had to skimp on the yardage to be able to buy it, and her dressmaker consequently made it a little tight. Of course I should not say so to a gentleman,' she added with a modest downturn of her blue eyes, 'but I am trying to impress you with my deductions, too. Poor Mrs. Black!'

'I hope she will not return to mourning as a consequence,' said Murray, 'for she looked very splendid in that brown.'

'I shall tell her that people admired her greatly.'

'What happened to Dr. Black?' Murray asked, taking the opportunity to find an answer to at least one question.

'You mean how did he die? He drowned while out fishing, poor man. And poor Mrs. Black again, for she did indeed miss him terribly, both financially and otherwise. They were a very contented couple. It gave him great pleasure to be out on the loch and he had befriended some of the fishermen who would take him out now and again, but on this day a gust caught the boat and he toppled in. He was a heavy man, and they could not quite manage to haul him out in time.'

'Very sad,' agreed Murray. He could not see how Mrs. Black could have been responsible for that. Could Newell have been blackmailing her for anything else?

The next morning Herkless' groom brought the gig down to the manse and handed it over, with one or two notes of instruction concerning the horse, of which he seemed naturally very possessive.

'She doesn't like to see another vehicle close in front of her, sir, and she's not too keen on hearing hooves behind her, either.' He was an Irishman, as many good grooms were, and as he spoke he was reassuring the mare with a smoothing hand on her shoulder.

'I'll try to take good care of her,' said Murray, hoping that the road to Stranraer was not a busy one.

'You'll have plenty to do in Stranraer,' he remarked to Coulter as the minister settled himself in the broad seat. Murray sorted out the reins and the horse tested the harness. 'You've been telling me you intend going there for a fortnight now and you've never gone. Doubtless you were waiting for a lift!'

'I – I'm not sure what I was intending to do there,' said Coulter uneasily as they started off. 'Perhaps I shall remember when we get there.'

The road was not particularly smooth, and Murray kept the mare down to a brisk walk, aware of the groom watching them from the manse gate. Nevertheless both horse and gig behaved themselves admirably, and soon they were able to pass the tannery and head south into the fresh air of the loch-edge road, and unfortunately the fresh, chilling drizzle that was currently soaking it. They pulled up their collars and turned down their hats.

'I should like to find Dr. Forbes and have another word with him,' said Murray, 'after we've sent Thomson back, if he'll consent to being sent. He was telling me they have a good deal of trouble with Irish beggars in Stranraer.'

'There are more than the poors fund can cope with, and of course there is no obligation to use it for them,' said Coulter rather primly. Murray remembered that Herkless and Coulter had been dealing with the Irish peasants passing through Kirkwelland, and kicked himself for forgetting Coulter's sympathy for them. Coulter and his wife had always been towards the Whiggish side of politics and the liberal side of the church. 'The minister there and I have been trying to help them by setting up a soup kitchen, separate from the poors fund, to enable the people to have some nourishment without feeling the need to steal from the townspeople. The thefts make them very unpopular.'

'They would,' said Murray drily.

Stranraer, as they approached it, gave the impression of being a low-lying town, with only a few buildings more than a single storey tall. A couple of plump spires broke the skyline, one of which Coulter pointed out as being the town house, and the other as the town kirk. There was little in the way of smoke or haze although the town was of a respectable size.

'What is the local industry?' asked Murray, keen to leave the subject of Irish paupers.

'Well ... fishing, I suppose,' said Coulter. 'Though that used to be better, if you listen to the old men. The herring don't come into the loch in the numbers they used to, I gather. And everything else in the industrial line is difficult because, you see, fuel is very expensive. There's a bit of tanning here, too, I suppose, just as in Kirkwelland, but mostly the town just takes the benefit of being on the road from Carlisle to Edinburgh or to Portpatrick, so the inns do well enough and any merchants can bring goods in and sell them on easily.'

Murray slowed the gig as the traffic became more dense on the approach to the town, trying to keep a good distance between the mare's nose and the cart in front of them. The sea, green-grey and ragged today with a fuzz of little wavelets, lapped on their right side and a building like a secession meeting house loomed on their left. Ahead, beyond the usual cottages of various qualities that frill small towns, Murray could see newer houses, taller and more prosperous, lining what was by that point a street rather than a country road. He slowed still further.

'Which direction should I take?' he asked.

'Straight ahead for now: you'll want the town house and it's on George Street,' said Coulter. He seemed to be searching for something, looking from side to side. 'I don't know where Dr.

Forbes lives, so you'll need to get directions for him – Thomson no doubt knows, if he'll take the time to tell you. Murray, will you set me down here? I've remembered what business I had,' Coulter explained as Murray eased on the reins. 'When you are done with Thomson and the doctor, meet me in the Star Inn, all right? I should be there before you. In fact, you may find it easier to take the gig there now and have them stable the horse while you walk about the place.'

'That seems sensible,' said Murray. Coulter directed him on to the Star, then vanished into a side street. Murray blinked. Such speed of action was not at all what he was used to with Coulter, not in the last couple of weeks, anyway. He waited a moment, watching down the unpromising side street – no more than a narrow lane, really - wondering what might take Coulter down there. His soup kitchen business?

As he watched a familiar figure appeared, slinking out of the same side street, hunching his shoulders as if he could hide the suspicious glance he cast about the main street from beneath his slab of fair hair. He strode off down the street, thumbs tucked into his waistcoat pockets and elbows wide to make a path through the crowds. Murray frowned. What was a gamekeeper doing here, then? It could be anything, really, but for that suspicious examination of the street. He paused, then hunted about him, selecting a man who seemed like a prosperous tradesman without airs – someone likely to talk to anyone.

'Excuse me, sir!' he called. The tradesman glanced up, then came across to the gig easily enough.

'Aye, what can I do for you, sir?'

Murray thought fast.

'I've been directed to a Dr. Forbes' house, but I think I must have misunderstood the directions. I was told to go down that lane.' He gestured with the whip at the side street.

'Dr. Forbes down there, sir! I dinna think so!' The tradesman laughed, tickled at the thought. 'That's where the Irish tinks are living: there's all sorts goes on down there. You wouldna catch Dr. Forbes there. He's up along George Street beyond the town house – you canna miss the town house, sir.'

'I thought there was some mistake! Thank you for your help,' said Murray, tipping his hat. The tradesman was still grinning, his day made. Coulter must indeed have been off sorting out his soup kitchen, but what was Norrie Pearce doing there? He wondered what activities 'all sorts' encompassed.

He flicked the reins and drove on thoughtfully to the Star, where a lad of decent appearance led the gig away into the yard and a girl who might have been his sister, but with a smile that did much more for Murray's mood, directed him to the Town House.

The Town House was a little grander than Murray had expected, with a heavily pedimented doorway and a creamy layer of render so that it reminded Murray of the ill-starred jelly shape at the picnic. Inside he found Thomson sharing a small, dark office with two clerks, all on stools at high desks. The clerks' pens did not pause when Murray came in, but Thomson, glinting in the dim light, looked across from his perch and sat back.

'Oh, aye, ye've found us, then. Tell me you've found Newell's killer and I'll take ship for the colonies.'

'I haven't, but there's been another death,' said Murray. At this the clerks did falter, but a glare from Thomson set them back on track instantly.

'Who's taken the whisky this time, then?' he asked.

'James Adair, one of the students, fell to his death in the burn. Where it cuts through pasture land, and the banks are steep.'

'Drunk?'

'I believe so.'

'Nothing to do with me, then. Or with Thomas Newell.'

'Perhaps not, but Newell's money was found in Adair's pack.' He almost did not say: he knew to what conclusion Thomson would leap, and he was sure, though he could not say why, that it was wrong.

'Then Adair murdered Newell and threw himself into the burn in remorse,' said Thomson inevitably. 'That's my job done, thank you very much, off you go.'

Murray wondered how such a rude man had managed to retain a senior post at all.

'I don't believe Adair did murder Newell,' he said. 'There was no note, and I believe those bent on self-destruction usually do leave a note – particularly as Adair would not have wanted, I think, anyone else to be suspected of a crime he had committed.'

'Maybe he didn't think of it till he got to the burn, and hadna a pen to hand,' said Thomson heavy with sarcasm.

'The other students also agree,' said Murray, 'that Adair would not have put poison in whisky: he would sooner have drunk the whisky.'

'That's a fine point,' said Thomson, unconvinced. 'If he was desperate enough to kill him – or if it was an accident –'

'An accident I could more readily believe,' Murray admitted. 'But he was showing no signs of remorse. He was in company until minutes before his death: it's not as if he was wandering and brooding. It just does not seem to fit with him,' he finished, aware that he was not arguing his case well.

'Where's the body?'

'At Kirkwelland House.'

'That's taking hospitality a bitty far,' Thomson remarked.

'It was nearest. We were all at a picnic near the house when it happened.'

'Did a'body see him fall?'

'Not anyone who's admitting to it. Of course if he was pushed they probably wouldn't say.'

'And who found him, then?'

'Mr. Coulter and I did.'

'Oh, aye?' Thomson eyed him glassily.

'We were walking up the ravine. We could hardly have reached up and pulled him down.' They had been walking up the ravine hunting for Anna Pringle, he suddenly remembered. She had not been seen for about the same time that Adair had been missing. Could she – had she even the strength – to push him over the edge? Repulsing an advance? No, more probably upset at his rejection, to judge by her letter. He had to talk to her soon.

'Och,' said Thomson, stretching and sliding off his stool with a thump, 'I suppose I'll have to go and see about it, or you'll no give me peace. Can you take me back? How did you get here?'

'I came in Mr. Herkless' gig, with Mr. Coulter,' said Murray, 'but I have to wait and take Mr. Coulter back.'

'Then I'll take the horse,' said Thomson unemotionally, knocked a speck of dust off his shiny hat, and left without looking back.

Murray asked the clerks for directions to Dr. Forbes' house, which they readily gave: once Thomson had gone they were chattily eager to be involved in any excitement available. Murray felt a little apologetic at leaving them behind in their pokey office. The doctor lived in a row of modern houses between the Town House and the Castle, which turned out to be a modest affair of whinstone with scaffolding around it and some kind of building work in progress. Murray had to rattle the risp a couple of times at the doctor's door to be heard over the shouts and rumblings coming from the workmen and their equipment.

A maid showed Murray in to a parlour stacked with books, where after a moment or two Dr. Forbes joined him and gestured him to one of the free chairs.

'What can I do for you, Mr. Murray? You were there when I was examining the fellow in Kirkwelland, I think?' The aroma of fresh ale was still about him, but his lick of hair was neat and his face and whiskers scrubbed.

'That's right: I'm helping Thomson look into Newell's death, and we've had a second death.'

'Oh yes?'

'One of the students who was staying with Newell at the time of his death. He fell into a ravine.'

'Tragic,' said the doctor, suiting his expression to the remark. 'And is there any connexion then, with Newell's death?'

'That is unclear. He had been drinking,' he added with a lack of emphasis. The doctor bowed his head and nodded, pursing his lips.

'Does Thomson wish me to examine the body?'

'He did not say,' said Murray. 'I wanted to find you anyway when I had the chance to visit Stranraer, and ask you something regarding Newell's death.'

'Please feel free,' said Forbes, leaning back and folding his arms comfortably. Murray glanced at him: whatever the alcoholic odours he found he had confidence in Dr Forbes' intellect. He wondered if Herkless had good reason to distrust him, since he had been the one to point out the evidence of drink.

'You said that it would have to be a compound of mercury to kill Newell: if it had just been mercury it would have passed straight through his body without harming him.'

'That's right: it needs to be mixed with something else to be either efficacious or harmful,' said the doctor. 'Or it could be gaseous. But mixing things with mercury is a difficult matter. Physicians in the past have tried the most extraordinary experiments – tying bottles of mercury with distilled water on to the sails of windmills, or the wheels of carriages. One moment ...' He looked about him, then reached one long arm and plucked a book from near the top of one of the many stacks, causing a near-collapse in the surrounding heaps. He balanced them against the book he had selected, then drew it away carefully and opened it. Murray could see that it was a copy of the *Edinburgh Dispensatory*, similar to the one he had borrowed from Mrs. Black. Dr. Forbes consulted the table of contents and flicked through the book. 'Here we are,' he said, after a moment's reading, 'this is what it made me think of. A mixture of vitriolic acid and alkali applied to mercury, making a strong turbith. It's used in severe cases of venereal disease, amongst a few other things.'

'Did you see, or did you know of any evidence that Newell might have been using it himself for one of those ailments? Rabies, I think, is also one mentioned.'

'You are familiar with this book, then? Splendid! You are not a physician yourself, though, are you?' he asked, suddenly wary.

'No, no: I borrowed a copy from Mrs. Black. She mentioned that you had bought over all her late husband's equipment and drugs after his death, is that correct?'

'I believe so. And quite a few of his books, but not the *Dispensatory* which as you see I already had. I love books,' he added sadly, 'but I do try not to purchase two copies of the same thing, or I should no longer be able to find the door.'

Murray could sympathise.

'So you think that someone mixed vitriolic acid with alkali and then with mercury.'

'Or bought it that way. He had vomited and also evacuated, and Mrs. Innes also mentioned a great deal of saliva. It seems the most likely mixture, but it does not have to be that you need to find someone able to mix it themselves.'

Murray left Dr. Forbes sitting amongst his books and walked back past the noisy castle to the Star Inn. It was the inn favoured by the daily mail coach from Carlisle to Ayr, but at this time of day it was quiet, and enquiry brought him the answer that Coulter had not yet arrived to meet him. He ordered a jug of claret and a dish of eggs, and sat in a quiet parlour that was divided only by a thick curtain from the section of the inn where local men seemed to be meeting to discuss the business of the day before going home for their evening meals. The food and drink were brought by the same pretty girl who had directed him earlier, and he was inclined to keep her talking if he could. Really, the standard of female features was extremely high in this part of the world, he thought.

'You'll do good business here with the mail coaches, then?' he asked. She seemed in no hurry.

'Aye, sir, it suits us well. Stranraer and the Rhinns is full of travellers these days, one direction or another.'

'I'm sure you enjoy hearing all their news, from the rest of Scotland, and England, and Ireland.'

'Aye, well, it depends, sir! There are travellers and travellers, and some are less desirable than others!'

'Oh, do you mean the Irish peasants?' Murray asked cautiously.

'That's right! They frighten me sometimes,' she said, with a dramatic shiver.

'How could they do that? I am sure that every man in Stranraer would leap to your defence if they so much as approached you!'

She giggled, as he had intended, then grew more solemn.

'No, but sir, it's not just the Irish. They say that the French are gathering again, and are going to bring Bonaparte back to France and invade Scotland and bring about revolution!' She was breathless with the idea. Murray had heard a few rumours, read a few speculative articles in the Edinburgh papers, but wondered at the practicalities of the idea. To invade, perhaps, was one thing, but to bring Bonaparte back from St. Helena, that remote island, or to invade without their beloved leader? It seemed unlikely.

The girl curtseyed and left, and Murray began to eat. The conversation in the public room beyond the curtain was not rowdy and its steady hum merely formed a carpet to Murray's wandering thoughts, until he heard a much closer voice, probably sidling up to the curtain for a private conversation, not thinking of what might be behind it.

'They're fine rabbits, sir, straight in from the country, skinned and ready,' said the voice, oddly familiar. It was not Norrie Pearce, though Murray's thoughts leapt to him and his unusual behaviour at the side street earlier.

'Whereabouts in the country?' came another voice, cautious.

'Up north of here,' said the first voice, airily. 'There's fine meat on them. And no many left, either.'

'I see that … Give me two, then,' said the second voice, and there was the chink of coins being exchanged. Then the first voice, louder than before. 'Oh, Mr. Coulter, sir, a fine day, is it no?'

Murray looked up, knowing whose the voice was now. If Herkless was wondering where his rabbits were going, he might do well to question his gamekeeper's old father.

Chapter Fifteen

Coulter was animated on the way back to Kirkwelland, more than Murray had seen him since his arrival, chattering about Pearce and the rabbits. Coulter himself had not seen the rabbits, but he had seen the swift movement of a piece of sacking and a quick glance pass between Pearce and his potential customer. He had greeted them and then been directed by the bright young lass with the pretty smile to the private room where Murray was waiting, so old Pearce had been spared anything that might embarrass him in front of the customer.

'I always thought he was a dreadful old scoundrel,' Coulter declared, 'but I had no evidence till now. I suppose they must be Herkless' rabbits.'

'I imagine so: Herkless did mention that they were going missing, and that Norrie Pearce was not much good as a gamekeeper.'

'Not if he's handing them to his own father to sell in the inns of Stranraer,' Coulter agreed.

'I wondered,' said Murray tentatively, 'if you might not rather be on Pearce's side? The poor man against the landowner?' He glanced around to see Coulter's face. A moment of shock was quickly replaced by a more thoughtful expression.

'I should be on Pearce's side if I felt that Herkless was paying him poorly, or wilfully allowing him to live in unhealthy conditions,' he conceded. 'But taking your employer's rabbits and selling them is theft, and I cannot in all conscience support that, can I? "Thou shalt not steal" is a commandment that most people know.'

'You seem to be in the fortunate position of being friends with your laird,' Murray remarked.

'Yes, Herkless has been very good to me and to the church. He is a sensible landlord, on the whole, too.'

'I noted the way you worked together to help those Irish paupers that were passing through the village.'

'What about it?' Coulter asked, a little sharply. Murray blinked.

'A laird and a minister would not always be of one mind on such matters, that is all. And a laird would not always be willing to give them accommodation and food at short notice on his own property. The Irish do not seem to have a good reputation.'

'As I say, he's a sensible man,' said Coulter shortly. Murray did not push the matter: what on earth was Coulter's problem with the Irish peasants? Was he being forced into helping them against his own judgement by the laird's charity, or by his fellow minister in Stranraer? Or was he encountering opposition in his work there, and felt Murray was not sympathetic?

They arrived back in Kirkwelland in the middle of the afternoon, and Murray drove the gig straight up to Kirkwelland House. Kitty Herkless was adjusting a flower arrangement in the drawing room when they were announced, and she turned to greet them, the front of her dark green gown flecked with white petals. She caught Murray noticing them.

'You find me at quite a disadvantage, gentlemen!' she rebuked them with a laugh.

'We were only bringing back the gig, and wanted to see how matters were,' said Murray. 'Are the students still downstairs?'

'They are,' said Kitty, turning solemn. 'And that dreadful Mr. Thomson is questioning them again. He is quite determined that one of them killed Newell, you know.'

'I'm afraid that finding Newell's money in Adair's pack did not help.'

'No: and yet I cannot imagine Mr. Adair killing anyone. He was always so kind and polite.' She brushed off her dress, then sat and gestured them to find spaces on chairs nearby.

'Did you know of any understanding he might have had here in Kirkwelland?'

'An understanding? Do you mean with a girl?'

'Yes, of course.'

'Well, it wasn't with me,' she said, 'but now you mention it

Anna Pringle has always seemed a little more excitable than usual when he was present. Is that who you mean? For I cannot think of anyone else.'

'It was Anna Pringle, yes. I know it is bound to be an unpleasant thought, Miss Herkless, but is Miss Pringle at all jealous? Or possessive?'

'What on earth do you mean, Mr. Murray?' He was sure she knew quite well what he meant, with that innocent look in her blue eyes.

'It would not have taken much to knock Mr. Adair down into the ravine: he was drunk and unsteady on his feet. Anyone he trusted could have approached closely enough to tip him over.'

'Anyone he trusted …' She gave a little shudder. 'I know we said that it must be one of us, Mr. Murray, but surely someone could have made their way up through the woodland and over the wall into the pasture? Perhaps they took a risk, but it would have been as risky for any of us. I do not like to think that someone he trusted could do such a thing.'

Murray opened his mouth to try some kind of reassurance, but at that moment the drawing room door opened and Herkless himself walked in. They stood to bow.

'Thank you for bringing my gig and horse back safely!' he greeted them. 'Not that I had any idea that you would not.'

'We bring some news with it, sir,' said Coulter, 'which I think you will want to hear,' and he recounted the discovery of old Pearce in the inn. Herkless frowned deeply.

'Well, that puts an end to that mystery,' he said. 'How very annoying. I shall have to scout around for another gamekeeper. It's a shame, for though he was no use at all as a gamekeeper he did help me record all the weather on the estate.'

'He mentioned that you had a good number of thermometers about the place,' said Murray. 'I wonder if any of them has been broken recently, like the one outside Innes' house?'

'Good heavens, that's a question!' agreed Herkless. 'I shall check them tomorrow. Though no doubt Pearce would have been quite clumsy enough to shoot one of them instead of a rabbit.'

'I spoke to Dr. Forbes when I was in Stranraer,' Murray went on. 'He confirmed that Newell was not killed with pure mercury but with a compound most likely of vitriol and alkali, both of which can be found in the kist that the mutual improvement society owns.'

Herkless and Coulter exchanged looks.

'If I discover that someone in that society has been improving their minds by the blending of poisons ...' said Herkless slowly.

'It could also have been bought already mixed,' said Murray hurriedly. 'It is used as a cure for – for several complaints. Asthma, for example,' he added quickly, remembering that Kitty might be shocked by the mention of venereal disease.

'I see. Presumably no one in Kirkwelland sells it?'

'Burns would be the only likely person, sir,' put in Coulter. 'We could ask him.'

'Indeed: we'd better. Amongst the rude mechanicals, the people most likely to have that degree of both interest and competence would be either Innes or Gourlay, the farmer. Have you met Gourlay, Mr. Murray?'

'I haven't, I don't think, but I have heard him mentioned.'

'He is growing prosperous through having scientifically drained and improved his soil,' said Herkless, 'and so has time and money to spend on further experiments. Optics are a particular favourite of his, I think.'

'But how would they even know what to blend and how to do it?' asked Coulter.

'Mrs. Black still has her husband's copy of the *New Edinburgh Dispensatory*,' said Murray. 'Perhaps someone borrowed it. She was happy enough to lend it to me. That would account for anyone in the village, and we do not know what the students might have been doing in their natural philosophy classes.'

'I'm sure we never did anything as interesting as that,' said Coulter, slightly wistfully.

'True, but times change,' said Herkless. 'It seems to me that universities nowadays are there chiefly to cram more and more knowledge into smaller and smaller minds.'

'Present company excepted, no doubt,' put in his daughter. 'Or rather, company downstairs.'

'Oh, they're bright enough, I suppose,' said Herkless, 'but they all seem so young! They'll be calling babes in arms to parishes soon!'

'And Mr. Thomson is back,' added Kitty, frowning at him. 'He's questioning the students again.'

'Oh!' said Coulter, 'you said that before and I did not take it in. Even now? Downstairs?'

'I believe so,' said Kitty.

'I must join them if I can,' said Coulter, leaping up. 'Thomson is capable of accusing them of almost anything and he'll have them arrested and taken away before they know what is going on. Excuse me.'

He left the room in a rush. Murray was torn: he should have gone too, but had not been quick enough, and he was very much inclined to stay and have conversation with Kitty Herkless, to help her, perhaps, with her flower arrangement or brush the petals from her hair. Still in mourning, he reminded himself sternly, and looked away. He had the impression, anyway, that Herkless had watched and understood his little moment of hesitation: perhaps he had undergone something similar himself elsewhere. How long ago had Mrs. Herkless died? he wondered. There was no sign of mourning here.

'This man Gourlay,' he said at last, 'would he have had any reason to be blackmailed by Newell?'

'He has given no sign of it,' said Herkless. 'What do you think, Kitty?'

'He seems a settled and happy man,' said Kitty thoughtfully. 'He has a young wife and two – no, three children, all healthy and well, and as Father says he is becoming prosperous through his own sense and hard work. He has a good standing in the village and the parish, but is not so protective of it, I should have thought, that he would be vulnerable to a blackmailer.'

'Unlike someone else?' Murray asked.

'I was thinking,' she admitted, 'of Mr. Pringle. I have no idea if he has anything to hide, but he seems to me to be the kind of person whose pride would demand him to hide something, don't you think?'

'He is undoubtedly proud,' her father agreed. 'But would he ever have laid himself open to any kind of temptation? I cannot see it. Perhaps I am merely prejudiced, but the idea of any woman, for example, wishing to engage in an illicit romantic attachment with him seems an extraordinary thought. And of course he would accept no arrangement that was not of the highest of standards.'

Murray and Kitty both smiled. Murray thought how comfortable he already felt in the company of both of them, and hoped that they both felt, as they seemed to, the same about him. But perhaps they were simply easy with everybody: after all, they seemed very well liked in the parish generally, by both their own class of people and the rude mechanicals, as Herkless called them. He wondered how Letho and Edinburgh would receive them.

He realised suddenly that he had been sitting in silence for some minutes, and untangled his long legs to stand.

'But I have trespassed on your time for too long. I think I might go and see if Mr. Gourlay is at home, and see if he can tell me of anyone interested in mixing compounds of mercury,' he said. 'How do I find his farm?'

'Walk past the church and take the lane up to your left,' said Kitty. 'When you come to the little bridge over the Welland Burn, look out for another turn to your left – the pathway is better made from that point, too. It's about half a mile up that road.'

'Thank you.'

He hoped, as he went, that he would not interrupt the farmer and his family at their dinner: from what Herkless and Kitty had said, Gourlay was moving up in the world and might have taken to dining at fashionable hours. The path was easy enough to find, anyway, with enough fine threading of wheel ruts to indicate regular use of a gig, and it was not long until he came to a freshly whitewashed farmhouse of a reasonable size, bigger than either the gamekeeper's house or Newell's lowly cottage, but perhaps not the size of the house at the tannery. The kailyard in front of it, which was very thoroughly cultivated, was cluttered with sundials and weather-related equipment, and a three-sided shelter to one side housed a stool and, to Murray's astonishment, a telescope on a stand. He wished he had brought Walter.

'Mr. Gourlay?' asked a maid of about ten who answered the door. 'Who shall I say, sir?'

Murray gave her his card, confident somehow that she could read. She disappeared and in a moment returned to usher Murray into a low parlour where Mr. Gourlay was sitting at a desk heaped with books and notebooks and ledgers. He stood up, puzzled, at

Murray's entrance, and bowed self-consciously.

'Will you take some refreshment, sir? Have you a horse needing attending?'

'No horse, thank you, and a cup of milk would be perfect, if you are not short.'

'Not at all. You heard the gentleman,' he added to the maid, who darted off again and returned at once with a tankard of that morning's milk. It was clean and delicious.

'How can I be of service, sir?' asked Gourlay, once they were seated. He fidgeted a little with the edge of a notebook, as if itching to get back to whatever he had been working on. Murray, reading upside down, thought it was lists of quantities of lime, presumably for adding to his fields. He had a round, outdoor face, with a thick head of black hair greying rapidly, and intelligent eyes. 'You're staying with the minister, aren't you?'

'That's right: we know each other from college. Both he and the laird recommended you as someone who might be able to help me. I know you are a keen member of the village mutual improvement society.'

'Oh, aye, sir. I saw we had the honour of your presence there last time, too.'

'Yes, that's right: I found it all very interesting, and hope to set up something similar in my own village when I go home. But I wonder – and here is where Mr. Coulter and Mr. Herkless thought you might be able to help – how do you keep track of things like the equipment and chemicals you have? You are an intelligent man: you will know, I'm sure, that the man Newell was poisoned with mercury and I am trying to work out which of the possible sources it came from. One of those is, of course, your wonderful kist in the schoolroom.'

Gourlay was thoughtful, and rubbed a thick thumb up the side seam of his breeches with a low grating noise.

'You'll have talked to Mr. Innes?' he asked.

'Yes, a little.'

'Innes wouldna have killed the oul fella, not by poison. He might have throttled him some days, but not poison. Mrs. Innes had good enough reason to hate her faither, too, but enough sense not to: I wish we could have women in the mutual improvement society,' he added, 'for Mrs. Innes would outshine us all!'

187

'Would she indeed?'

'Oh, aye, that woman has a good mind. But of the rest of them … I dinna ken that any of them would have the wit to use mercury or ken how to.'

'How well did you know Newell yourself?'

'Och, well enough. It's no a big village, is it? His wife was my own wife's cousin, but we werena close.'

'Did you see him at all, the day he died? He was out walking in the morning around the village, and then we don't know what he was doing after noon.'

Gourlay considered, pursing his lips.

'I dinna ken that I was in the village myself that day.'

'And he didn't come here?'

'I dinna think I ever saw him up here in my life! But I hear tell the mercury was in a jar of whisky: would he not have got that in the village?'

'No one saw him with a whisky bottle, no one that I've spoken to. We don't think it was already in his cottage that morning but we don't know yet where it came from, or where the mercury came from.'

At this Gourlay nodded eagerly.

'Aye, surely, sir, there are other places you could get mercury apart from our kist? A thermometer, maybe?'

'Yes, but you'd need other chemicals, too, to make the mercury poisonous. The doctor who examined the body thought that vitriol had been involved.'

'Mercury and vitriol?' said Gourlay, his eyes suddenly sharply focussed. 'You can buy that already mixed, can you no?'

'So I believe.'

'Now, who was it?' He rubbed the broad thumb up and down his breeches seam, staring past Murray's ear. 'That was it. I was in Stranraer, must be two weeks ago, and I was just going into the apothecary's there when the fellow coming out the door dropped his wee parcel on the ground in front of me. I picked it up to hand it to him, and he snatches it from me like I was trying to steal it, but I remember it said something on it ... turbith mineral, that was it. Is that not mercury and vitriol? You would take it to prevent rabies, I believe.'

'And who was it who had bought it?'

'Oh, it was Norrie Pearce, the laird's gamekeeper. And the look he gave me would have felled an oak tree, I can tell you.'

'Could Newell have walked round to Gourlay's house and back in the time we haven't accounted for?' Murray asked after dinner. He was growing quite accustomed to stretching his legs out to the manse parlour fire with a glass of brandy punch cradled on his stomach, though he was longing to see Augusta.

'Not by the road, I shouldn't think,' said Coulter, who seemed equally comfortable. 'There is a path if you go … well, round the back of the walled garden and past the south side of Kirkwelland House, along the bank of the Welland Burn, but I shouldn't have thought Newell could walk it, not with his legs. It's narrow and awkward, and steep in places. Otherwise he could have walked down that, around the back of the kirk and then over the bridge you crossed and up the lane to Gourlay's.'

'So what could he have done in the time available? He was last seen heading up the headland road, and Pearce swears he did not see him coming back down before dark, and of course we know that by dusk he was close to death in his own house. He couldn't have had more than an hour or so to walk up there and return by some route, not the road, to his cottage, possibly on his way acquiring a poisoned bottle of whisky.'

'He could simply have cut through the woods,' said Coulter. 'Supposing he met someone up in the woods – I was going to say either by accident or by design, but if they brought poisoned whisky with them it would probably be by design – and they talked, and he took the whisky, then he could simply have walked down through the woods, crossed the main drive of Kirkwelland House, and carried on across the common grazing there behind his own cottage to his own front door. That, with his legs, would have taken the hour or thereabouts.'

'That makes sense. I didn't realise one could do that. I suppose there are innumerable paths about here that the locals all know, just as there are at Letho.'

'The burn constrains things a bit, because it's too wide or too deep at most points to ford, and the sides are steep as you know further upstream. But the pasture behind the church, though it runs back into those outcrops between the church and the stream, that's either common grazing or Herkless', and everyone walks freely about it. It's just sheep there.'

'And Gourlay's land starts the other side of the burn?'

'That's right.'

'He says Newell's wife was his own wife's cousin, but even if he resented Newell's treatment of his wife, which you say was bad, that would not explain why he waited so long to do something about it. And then there's what he said about Pearce – that he saw him buy a compound of mercury in Stranraer.'

'But why would Pearce have wanted to kill his father's closest friend?'

'Newell spent a good deal of time up in the woods – perhaps he knew about the rabbits?'

They considered this for a moment.

'We only have old Pearce's word that Newell was even there, but suppose he was, and suppose old Pearce gave him that whisky?' said Murray.

'A gift of friendship,' said Coulter, his fair face dark, 'but he added the mercury compound too. And on the offchance that Newell offered him a companionable sip, he could just say no, no, it's all for you to enjoy!'

'There's a maid,' Murray remembered. 'She might have seen something.'

'She might ... do you know, I can't see Newell not being suspicious at the gift of a bottle of whisky from someone as mean as himself.'

'Unless it was part payment of the blackmail.'

'Aye,' Coulter reflected, 'that might work.'

'Anyway, tell me about Mr. Thomson this afternoon. How did the students fare?'

'Oh,' said Coulter with a sigh, 'as Miss Herkless says, he is determined that one of them is guilty. I think he favours Nugent at present.'

'Nugent was definitely there on the edge of the ravine,' Murray agreed, 'but I'm not sure he had the chance to do anything to Newell. He and McCullough were together that morning, as far as I can see.'

'He's the one most interested in the science,' said Coulter. 'He was fascinated by the geology of the ravine and also by the mutual improvement society's kist.'

'Yes, but that was the first he saw it. He would have had to bring the mercury compound with him from Glasgow.'

'That wouldn't be impossible. But why? He says he wasn't being blackmailed by Newell, whereas McCullough and Adair both were.'

'Not Gibson, I notice.'

'Not Gibson. Only because I suspect he would not have noticed nor cared, nor possibly understood. He spends his time in another world entirely.'

Murray nodded.

'Then what do you think?'

'I think Nugent has a temper, certainly. But as you say, why would he kill Newell? For what could he be being blackmailed? It has to be something Newell knew about, of course, which means something he saw around Kirkwelland. I cannot think of any scandal or crime that has been committed and unsolved until these murders, anything he could imagine would damage him if it were made known. And Nugent also has the air of one who would not submit to blackmail, but would simply punch the blackmailer and walk away.'

Murray laughed. 'I agree. But I cannot see McCullough either as a murderer, and as I remember it he and Gibson were visible and far from the ravine for most of the crucial time. He was angry with Adair for drinking again, but not to the point of pushing him over the edge, surely?'

'But he admits he was being blackmailed. Could he have poisoned Newell?'

'He would have had the same difficulties as Nugent, surely.'

'I suppose so. And surely he would not have risked carrying whisky if he knew that Adair would be likely to find it, so he would have had to buy the whisky here to put the poison in.'

'Are we going round in circles?' asked Murray. 'I think part of the trouble here is that although they are high on Thomson's list of suspects, you and I both have a soft spot for these students because they bring to mind our own student days, and in your case because they are intended for the ministry. But they are not the only suspects, and we have to make sure that Thomson remembers that, too.'

Lexie Conyngham

Chapter Sixteen

On Thursday morning, Murray rose at dawn and, sitting in his nightshirt and banyan, wrote out a list of the people who had attended the picnic, along with the few others prominent in the village who had come to his attention in the course of his questions. He put a star beside each one that seemed likely to have been blackmailed. It was not a promising list. It was a week today since Newell had been poisoned, and two days since Adair had been killed, and he was desperate for a little progress. The paper was uneven and his pen blotchy, his head hurt, and in general life seemed unsatisfactory.

He shaved in cold water, which suited his mood, and dressed without calling Walter. Walter had a great capacity to amuse him when he was in good form, and almost as great a capacity to annoy him when his temper was not so even. He crept downstairs and slid back the bolt on the front door, and stepped outside, his feet grating with unnatural loudness on the flag path.

The air, though damp, was fresh and pleasant, with the scent of both pasture behind the manse and the loch down in front. He breathed in and reluctantly slipped his hat on, and rubbed his face energetically to waken himself properly. The day glowed as though the sun were burning the clouds away from the other side and would soon burst through, a welcome portent for poor Adair's funeral. He sighed, and turned to the right at the garden gate, tracing his steps along the path that would lead to Newell's cottage once again.

The cottage stood dark and shabby as before, but this time he examined the outside, seeing how it backed on to the common pasture as Coulter had said the previous evening. Murray clambered over the stone wall and took a look. One or two goats were tethered near the back of the cottage, which had no door other than the one opening on to the lane. They ignored Murray and continued ripping away at the lush grass. Further away was a lone cow, more on the scale of the Fife black cattle he was used to, and beyond that were sheep working their way up the sharp, gorse-swollen slopes to the east of the pasture. Behind the cottage to the north, but still some distance away, was mixed woodland in twenty shades and textures of green, the woodland that must border the drive to Kirkwelland House and, beyond it, reach up to the headland and north east around the house's walled garden to meet the pasture where they had picnicked, where Adair had met his end. Murray could picture most of it in his head, as if it were on one of Herkless' estate maps, with little drawings on it for the houses: the gamekeeper's cottage, Mrs. Black's house, the Pringles' new porch out of scale, Mr. Burns' shop, the manse, the church, the smithy, the tannery. The schoolhouse with its deadly kist, the shoemaker's where Innes watched the weather, and the cottage here, festering in the middle like a sore, where the whole thing started. Or did it? Newell seemed to have his web spread wide, particularly if he had managed to find out about the Pearces selling rabbits in Stranraer: and he had his outposts to the north and south of the village, too. What about to the east? Where did the road lead that he had followed to get to Gourlay's farm? Had he had a spy there, too?

He turned back towards the lane, and noticed something tucked into the long grass by the cottage wall, round and grey-brown. He bent for a closer look, pushing the grass back with the point of his cane. It was a whisky flask, with the cork half in. It almost seemed as if it had been hidden there. Newell's secret hoard, buried when the students came? He pulled it out and lifted off the cork, peering inside. Then he found a flat stone and laid it on the ground, and tipped the flask carefully over it. A few drops of what smelled like whisky splashed on to the stone. They had an odd, silvery appearance.

He was scrambling back over the stone wall again, struggling not to drop the flask, when the door opened across the lane, and Innes appeared to assess the day.

'Good morning, sir!' he exclaimed, reasonably startled at the sight of Murray halfway over the wall.

'Good morning, Innes. Studying the day's weather?' Murray jumped down into the lane with what he hoped looked like dignity and purpose.

'That's right, sir, every day. See, the laird has gived me a new thermometer! And I was that sorry about the old one, and thought he would never replace it, but here it is.'

'That's very good of him: but I'm sure he knew it wasn't your fault,' said Murray, examining it as he was expected to. It was indeed very splendid, almost the size of the old one. It was already quite weathered: it must have been one of the thermometers from around the estate.

'And I've made a new bracket for it an all,' said Innes, showing him. 'That way if anyone hits a pack or whatever against it, the bulb won't be the first thing hit.'

'Very neat, yes.'

Mrs. Innes appeared behind her husband, keen to see who might be stopping for a gossip at this time of the morning.

'Oh, good morning, Mr. Murray, sir,' she curtseyed. 'Would you care for some ale and a bannock?'

He sniffed, remembering the excellent bannocks at Newell's funeral.

'That would be wonderful,' he admitted. 'I have not yet broken my fast. And I wondered if I could ask you something, both of you.'

Mrs. Innes drew him indoors and Innes, quickly making a note in his notebook, followed. He sat as directed on the great chair that had been given to Herkless at the funeral, feeling he was sitting in state, and slid his cane and the whisky flask under the seat.

'What was it you were wanting, sir? How can we be of service?' Mrs. Innes slid a bannock fresh off the girdle and laid it on a plate before him, with a pat of butter and a jug of ale.

'This is delicious,' he started. 'But it's this. First, have you a bit of sacking I could take this flask back in? I don't want to break it.'

Innes reached over to his workshop space and pulled back a small sack, and handed it to Murray.

'Thank you.'

'Another whisky flask?' asked Innes, trying not to sound inquisitive and failing.

'Yes: a little odd, so I'm going to show it to Thomson. Anyway, second: I'm trying to find out more about your father's movements on the day of his death, where he went, who he met, and where the whisky might have appeared from. I know he went from here to the smithy, to the tannery, to Mr. Burns' shop, to Mrs. Black's, to the Pearces and then up on to the headland, but there may be gaps I have not seen, and I do not know what happened between him going up on the headland and the students finding him already ill. From the timing he must have come almost straight down home, but Pearce says he did not see him come back by the road, so it seems he might have come back through the woods in front of Kirkwelland House and back across the common pasture. Does that make sense?'

'Aye, it does indeed,' said Innes, 'for I saw him coming back myself.'

'You did?' Murray nearly dropped the jug of ale.

'Aye, I was sitting here in the window at my work when he rolled himself over the wall, the same wall you come over yourself just now, sir. He always came over like a bundle of washing for his legs werena much use to him, though that never stopped him ganging round poking his nose in.'

'Aye, aye,' said his wife, in a tone that warned rather than agreed.

'Aye, well. I seen him come home that day and go into his house: it would have been maybe a quarter of an hour before you and the students appeared. Not long, anyway.'

'And had he a bottle with him?'

'Not and roll over the wall that way, no. He had his wee writing tablets, that was all, and his stick.'

'Good heavens. Did Thomson ask you if you had seen him?'

'Nah, Thomson hasna been near us for days.'

'And I didn't think to ask you, either. Did you see him go out in the morning, then?'

'No, I didna see that. It would have been early, see, and of course I do my observations early both out the front and out the back and I could well have been out the back at the time.'

'Of course. Has anyone else mentioned seeing him that day? I can find no one who saw him with a flask of whisky, and he did not buy one.'

'He wouldna buy one if he could help it,' said Innes swiftly, despite his wife's glare.

'No, no one has mentioned seeing him except for old Pearce,' said Mrs. Innes. 'I cannot think of anywhere else he might have gone, though it would not surprise me, either. He liked to call in to plenty of places.'

'Do you know why? Why he made so many calls?'

She sat on her stool by the fire, and slipped two more bannocks into a cloth, before she replied.

'I think he was asking people for money. Making them pay, I mean, because he knew things about them.'

'You mean blackmail.'

'That's a gey dirty word, sir. But yes,' she sighed, 'that's what I mean.'

'Yes.' Murray did not like to see the expression of angry shame on her face. 'I'm afraid he does seem to have been doing that.'

'I thought he couldna do worse than he has done,' she said, 'but I thought wrong. I'm only glad my poor mother wasna alive to find it out, too.'

'Do you think that was why he died?'

'I'd imagine so, wouldn't you, sir?' she replied bleakly.

'Do you know the names of any of his – victims?'

She shook her head quickly, eyes lowered.

'If we did we'd repay them out of whatever we can get for his scabbit belongings,' said Innes. 'We dinna need his money, but if we had it it could go back where it came from.'

'Apparently, so I've heard, he was bragging that he had secured gentry amongst his customers, as he called them,' said Murray. 'Do you know who or what he would mean by that?'

They both shook their heads.

'By gentry he would mean the likes of yourself, sir,' said Mrs. Innes. 'And the laird, and Miss Herkless, and the Pringles and Mrs. Black. And the minister, of course. Maybe one of the students? Though I never heard tell of it. But what could he find to blackmail any of them? The Herklesses and Mrs. Black are good people, and so is Mr. Coulter. And Mrs. Pringle is very kind. And Mr. Pringle is very proper, so that I cannot imagine him doing anything that he could be forced to pay over. I wondered sometimes if he used to make notes about them all in those writing tablets of his, for he always kept them gey close, but they're gone as well, as far as I can tell.'

'No, they've been found,' said Murray, 'but they have mostly been wiped blank. Do you know of any letters he may have sent recently?'

'Letters?' Innes gaped. 'That's news to me. I didna ken the oul fella could ever be bothered to write.'

'He had a good hand, when he would use it,' said Mrs. Innes in his defence. 'And he had learned spelling well, long ago. Could that be how he intended to deal with his gentry?' she asked, and Murray could see that she was indeed possessed of a sharp mind, as Gourlay had said.

'We only know that he bought a sheet of paper from Mr. Burns on the morning of his death,' he explained.

'And I thought he spent all his money on Mrs. Black's sweeties,' said Innes, making a face.

'Did you find any paper in his house?'

'Not a scrap. The place is empty the now except for the few bits we'll sell: the cottage belongs to the laird so we hope he'll put in decent neighbours now.'

'Aye,' said Mrs. Innes with a sigh, 'it's a sorry thing to say of your ain faither, but I'll no miss him. But whatever he did to my mother and me, and to his neighbours, he should not have had to die such a death. No one should.'

Full of delicious bannock and refreshing ale, Murray left the Inneses' house with the mysterious whisky flask swinging in its sack in his hand. He was not yet quite ready to go back to the manse, and so he walked on, drawn, as ever, by the north end of the town and the memory of his first sight of Kitty Herkless there. He passed Mrs. Black's house, and reproached himself for not having asked Kitty how she was after her terrible embarrassment at the picnic. The shutters were still folded shut, anyway. He hoped she was not so ashamed that she had stopped making her sweetmeats and selling them, for if nothing else Walter would be dreadfully disappointed. He wandered on, bumping the flask gently against his leg as he walked, as if he were setting out to irritate himself.

Once again he took the road up on to the headland, passing the little cottage in the woods where the Pearces lived. They would not be there for much longer, of course: he wondered where they would go, for Herkless was unlikely to give Norrie Pearce any kind of character. Glasgow? Ireland? He had not taken to the man, but at the same time he felt sorry for anyone having to up sticks and leave his home so suddenly, and go somewhere far enough away from his own reputation. He could see a figure at the window watching the road, and assumed that old Pearce was already in position for the day. Murray wondered how they had travelled to Stranraer.

He reached the top of the headland, enjoying the stretch of his legs with each steep step, and drew in deep breaths of the breeze blowing off the loch. The sun had almost completed its polishing job on the clouds and his shadow was starting to form at his feet: when he glanced behind him at the woodlands the sky's glare was so strong it hurt his eyes. He propped himself against his favourite boulder again and surveyed the bay before him. Black-headed gulls and kittiwakes flew almost around his feet, and below he could see the occasional cormorant, ragged sentinels on rocks by deeper water. Up here swallows screamed, whipped up higher by the breeze and bowled away behind him, another sign of good weather to come. The boulder was chilly still, its back to the sun, but his shoulders felt warm and he relaxed, taking off his hat and delighting in the tickle of the wind in his hair.

'Mr. Murray!'

The startled voice nearly made him fling his hat over the cliff. He spun about. Anna Pringle looked as shocked as he felt at finding him there, clutching her bonnet against the wind.

'Miss Pringle! I did not hear you approach.'

'I was not expecting to find anyone here so early.'

'No, nor I! Are you quite well, Miss Pringle? I have given you a shock, I think,' he said, but actually she gave all the appearance of having been interrupted in a good cry. Her face was lined and her eyes red, and even her beautiful hair seemed more dull than usual. In one white hand was a handkerchief, as soggy as if she had been bathing with it. He offered her his spare one.

'I am quite well, Mr. Murray, only a little taken aback.'

'Forgive me, Miss Pringle, I am intruding,' he said, and tried to withdraw and leave her to her private tears, but a great shudder ran through her and she burst into renewed sobs.

'Oh, Mr. Murray, I am so sorry, but I cannot seem to help it!' she cried, catching her breath every couple of words. 'He is gone and we never made up, and my father will not even let me go to his – his funeral!'

'Miss Pringle, please, allow me to lead you to a seat.' He found a rock of about the right height for her to sit on, and cast about for something to set across it. There was nothing, so he reluctantly took his coat off and laid it on the cool stone. The wind buffeted his shirt sleeves and he tried not to shiver. She sat, and bent over, sobbing, while tears dripped persistently straight into the thin-bladed clifftop grass. He patted her on the back, helpless.

At last she straightened, tired out, and the sobs died away. He crouched down in front of her, feeling over-tall.

'You speak, I take it, of Mr. Adair?'

He thought he had rashly set her off again, but no: after a gasp that seemed likely to turn her inside out she calmed, and nodded.

'We – we were engaged to be married.'

'Were you?' He tried to keep a note of disbelief out of his voice: he had seen that letter in Adair's pack.

'Nobody knew, of course. Nobody could know until he got his parish, and asked his father's permission, and then my father's permission. And every time they tried to leave for Ireland something happened and they were stuck! But we loved one another very dearly. He was … He was so kind …' She bent her head again, but it seemed she had run out of tears for now.

'But you said you had not made up?' he asked her gently.

'Oh! Mr. Murray, it is so cruel! He made me. He made me break off our engagement because he said he was not good enough for me. Can you believe anything so ridiculous? Of course he was good enough: he was wonderful. When he gazed at me with those great brown eyes … But he talked some nonsense about being ill, about drinking – it made no sense to me. And if he was ill it was my place to look after him, always. I told him we were still engaged, and that I would never release him because I loved him and I knew he loved me. And then we quarrelled …'

This time the sobs did return, though not with the earth-shattering strength they had had previously. Murray sat back.

Adair must have been aware that his drinking problems made him poor husband material – though perhaps he had other motives for asking to be released? He shook his head very slightly: just because he himself could not abide the idea of such a silly wife did not mean that Adair had not found her attractive, and there was that beautiful hair. He shook his head again. His own release from marriage with Lady Agostinella had made him shallow, he thought – and prone to the charms of every pretty girl he met, besides.

He waited until Anna's shoulders had slumped again, relieved of the tension of her tears.

'Miss Pringle,' he said, 'you said you met Newell up here at the turn of the year. Did he – did he ever ask you for money? Money, perhaps, so that he would not tell your father he had seen you with Mr. Adair?'

Her eyes shot open.

'How could you know such a thing? I never told anybody!'

'Did you pay him?'

'Only a very little, from my dress allowance. A very little, for Father likes to see Mamma and me nicely dressed. But Newell was so horrible. He talked for ages about how he would tell Father and how it would make us look, and how Father would be so cross he would never allow us to marry, and how he knew James' father and would tell him everything, too, and then if he knew he would cut James off without a penny and then we would be paupers and everything would be awful!'

Murray very much doubted that Newell had known Jamesie Adair's father, but it showed the old man's cleverness in playing on a weak mind. He might never even have had the nerve to go to Pringle, either, but they would not know that now, and it was something Anna had certainly not been prepared to risk.

'So when did you quarrel with poor James?' he asked her quietly, as if he were leading a nervous horse past something he knew would be alarming.

'On Tuesday.' Her voice wobbled alarmingly.

'The day before yesterday?'

She nodded.

'The day – the day he - he died.' She finished on a whisper.

'At the picnic?' Again he lowered his own voice, soft as a hand over her nose.

'No! No, earlier.' She had taken fright, and after a moment he sat back.

'When did you see him earlier?'

'Up here. We always met up here.' She spoke quickly now, her words skipping away so that he could not catch them. 'This is where we met, our particular place. Even after Newell found us up here, it was still our place. And then we quarrelled, and I told him I would tell my father and he would make James marry me, and that was a horrible thing to say to him because I knew he really wanted to marry me anyway and I was being mean, but I couldn't help it, he kept saying he couldn't marry me and I just knew that wasn't true! I knew we had to marry! I've loved him for four years! And I know he loved me too! And what am I going to do now? Father won't let me go to the funeral and James is dead and my life is over!' She bent and sobbed again, long, self-induced sobs, Murray thought with fading sympathy, though looking about at the society of Kirkwelland he had to admit that her prospects of a good and interesting marriage seemed faint. James Adair may well have been her only hope. But had they quarrelled here on the day of his death, or after the picnic? Had she been so frustrated at his demands for freedom, whether he asked for it for her sake or for his own, that she had pushed him into the ravine? Or faced with being forced to marry her, had he indeed jumped?

Chapter Seventeen

'It has been decided,' said Thomson, who glinted as if he had been polished for the occasion, 'that James Adair killed Thomas Newell, and then killed himself in remorse.'

'It has been decided, has it? You mean you have decided it?'

'I am the sheriff's officer placed in charge of investigating these deaths, so yes, I have decided it.'

'But if Adair had not died, you would have had to put this to a trial,' said Murray, not entirely astonished at what Thomson had done, but frustrated all the same. 'You could not just have decreed it like some Roman tyrant.'

'I'm no very interested in what they do in Rome,' said Thomson primly. 'I'm of the established church myself. And if Adair had not died, he would not have made what is close enough to a confession of his guilt, so I would not be in the happy position of declaring the matter closed. I admit,' he added, waving a finger at Murray, 'that Newell's death may have been accidental – Adair may have had the mercury compound for some medical condition of his own,' his tone making it clear what he thought that might be, 'and it somehow became added to the whisky, perhaps intended for Adair's own consumption. Nevertheless it seems very plain to me: Newell died at Adair's hands, whether intentionally or not, and Adair took his own life.'

The trouble was that there was little Murray could do at that point to prove otherwise. Adair did not seem like a murderer, but it could have been accidental. McCullough and Nugent could not think of any reason why Adair would have been carrying a mercury compound, and he certainly had not mentioned having one, but that was not proof. That Adair had shown no signs of distress or remorse in the days between Newell's death and his own told them very little, but it did make Murray doubt that

Thomson had found the right solution.

Thomson and the students had been waiting at Kirkwelland House when Murray and Coulter walked up there for the funeral. The contrast with Newell's funeral was marked: the premises were much larger but the attendance much smaller, with only the other students, the Herklesses, Mr. Pringle, Coulter, Thomson and Murray so far. Pringle sat very upright in the largest chair he could find with an expression on his face of extreme distaste, as though he wished to make it plain that only the duty owed by a Wigtownshire gentleman had caused him to be there at all. Kitty was busy seeing that guests had seats and the students were doing the duty of relatives in handing round oatcakes and drinks, and Murray slipped through them and sat on a low stool by Pringle's knees, in a suitably subservient attitude.

'You do Adair some honour by being here, sir,' he said quietly.

'Well, well,' said Pringle, assuming the little frown he thought appropriate to one doing honour. 'The boy was of reasonably good family, I understand.'

'Of course he must have been,' agreed Murray, 'for I understand he and your daughter ...?'

'He and my daughter what?' snapped Pringle, the little frown plunging into a scowl. 'What do you know about it? She came to me with some nonsense about an attachment, but of course that would be ridiculous! She is a silly romantic creature, and the very idea that my daughter would marry a student!'

'Well, he had graduated, sir: he was intended for a parish, I understand.'

'Students come to no good,' said Pringle darkly. Murray wondered briefly where he thought ministers came from, but it was no good trying to explain.

'I wondered if maybe you had seen him near the ravine on Tuesday, before he fell?'

'Me? No. I was nowhere near the ravine. I was looking, if you remember, for my daughter.'

'Of course. I just thought you might have noticed him. You see, Thomson there, the sheriff's man, is going to put it about that Adair killed himself, and I'm not sure that is just or fair. So if you had seen anything that might help to prove that he did not -'

'It seems more than likely to me that he did,' said Pringle firmly. 'If my daughter had told him – as she should – that she was not permitted to attach herself to him, then doubtless he did lose all hope. Foolish boy.'

Oh, dear, thought Murray, that did not go quite as I had hoped.

'Where did you find Miss Pringle, sir? Coulter and I, of course, had gone to hunt in the ravine, and then you all just appeared above us, to our great relief.'

'She appeared out of the little woodland at the bottom of the pasture,' said Pringle. 'I went in one end to look for her and she came out at the other, and Mrs. Pringle called me back.'

'Is there any chance that she could have been talking to Adair? She could, in fact, have been telling him that he had no hope of her?'

Pringle considered, drawing in his lower jaw to indicate intense thought.

'Yes, indeed, that would make sense. She was a little upset: at the time I put it down to the fact that she had worried us and was sorry for it, but now I think of it it would fit that she had been to tell him what I had said.'

And Pringle himself had been in the woods, too, then. There would have been nothing to stop him finding that importunate student on the cliff edge and tipping him over it for the audacity of courting his daughter. Or even for the audacity of asking for his freedom from the same daughter, though Pringle did not appear to know about that. It would have been a dreadful irony if Pringle had killed Adair for the opposite of what he intended.

He felt a hand on his shoulder, and turned to find to his delight that Kitty Herkless was smiling down upon him. Her father was behind her, and winked down at him, knowing he might need rescuing from Pringle's pontifications. Kitty, however, was more direct.

'Mr. Murray, I need you!'

'At your service, ma'am,' he said, with a bow to Mr. Pringle. He followed Kitty to the door of the parlour, while Herkless gravely sat where Murray had been sitting and engaged Pringle in conversation.

'Mrs. Black is downstairs, paying her respects to Mr. Adair. I wonder – I am anxious that she will lose her nerve before coming up here. Could you contrive to meet her in the hall and encourage her to join us? It is the first time she has been outside, I believe, since Tuesday.'

'Of course,' he said, and hurried downstairs. He lingered in the hall for a moment or two and managed, as Mrs. Black came out of the dining room, to seem as if he had just come through the front door.

'Mrs. Black!' He bowed. 'How lovely to see you, even if it is a sad occasion!'

'Oh, dear, Mr. Murray,' she curtseyed in a flurry of weary black muslin. 'I only came to pay my respects. I had no intention …'

'Will you allow me to escort you to the drawing room?'

She frowned, her gaze darting about the hall as if hunting an excuse.

'Yes, but perhaps – perhaps – but you have only just come in yourself.'

'If you would like a breath of air first, I can recommend it: may I accompany you?'

'Of course, of course.' Good manners did not allow her to refuse, though she obviously wanted to be alone. Murray reopened the front door and followed her outside to the little lawn that faced the lovely view of the loch. The weather was holding, and the water twinkled blue and grey, folded into its bay.

'It is a beautiful day, is it not?' Murray asked harmlessly.

'It is lovely, yes. It puts me in mind, though, of Tuesday.'

'Yes, indeed. Poor Adair.'

She sighed heavily.

'Yes, poor, poor young man. Such kind eyes and such pretty manners.' She gazed out at the loch, not meeting Murray's eyes at all. 'I've heard that the gossips say that he – destroyed himself.'

'And that he was responsible for Newell's death: yes, that is the story. I'm not sure it's true, though.'

'Oh?' This time she turned to look at him directly. 'Why not?'

'I have no proof either way. It's just a feeling.'

'Oh.' She was disappointed. 'I too feel that he could not have done such a thing – neither killed Newell nor killed himself. I believe he had – an illness, but he was such a likeable young man when he was in his right mind. I did worry about him. He would never have lasted long in a parish unless he had managed his problems: a congregation would never stand for that sort of weakness in their minister. Poor Mr. Adair.'

'I thought he had managed to keep his illness secret in the village.'

'That would be difficult, and besides, my late husband was an observant and experienced man. But I think his family did not know. It would be harsh if they found out now.'

'Self-destruction would be worse, though.'

'Yes: perhaps it could just be presented to them as an accident? The edges of the ravine are not very sound, are they? And his family do not need to know all the circumstances.'

'I believe Mr. Coulter is to write to them, and I'm sure he will be kind. He has made no bones about burying Adair in the kirkyard, after all.'

'Let us hope so.' She sighed again, her shoulders hunching with the depth of it. 'He seemed so peaceful there, in the dining room.'

'Of course the other possibility, which I'm sure you've realised,' said Murray after a moment, 'is that he knew something of Newell's death, and Newell's murderer pushed him into the ravine.'

She turned towards him, one hand out in shock as if to avert the possibility.

'That he was murdered too?' She stood with her mouth open. 'How could that be?' She blinked, her gaze back on the memory of the picnic field. 'With everyone there ...'

'Well, trees and plants hide the part of the ravine where he fell.' He was pleased to see that the idea that Adair had been murdered seemed to be a new one to her. 'Almost anyone could have left the party and followed him amongst the trees, or someone could have come up past the house through the woods, who was not of the picnic party.'

'Oh, yes, surely it was not one of the party,' she exclaimed, but she was still frowning, as if there had been something about the picnic party that made her hesitate.

'Unless one of them had a very good reason to kill Newell,' he added quietly. She was silent, then jumped as if she had only just taken in the meaning of his words.

'He – he wasn't a very pleasant man,' she said at last. 'But to kill poor Mr. Adair too … what could he have known that was so dangerous to the murderer?'

'That I don't know,' said Murray. But a thought occurred to him: Newell had been in the woods before he had died, up on the headland, and that was where he himself had met Adair that day. Newell had not been killed in the woods, and he had not, apparently, found the whisky there, but something had happened that had an impact on his death. Could Adair have seen something? Had the murderer seen him – and had Adair known?

Mrs. Black was starting to look uncomfortable and he was anxious that she should not leave just yet.

'You are growing chilly: the breeze is cold even in the sunshine. Shall we go in? Miss Herkless will be all alone with Mr. Coulter otherwise when the men go to the burial.'

'Oh! Are the Pringles not here yet?' Was he mistaken or was there a glint of hope in Mrs. Black's eyes? Meeting her neighbours again gradually would be easier, he thought, after her embarrassment.

'Mr. Pringle is, but I don't believe the ladies are coming. So do have pity on poor Miss Herkless, won't you?'

'Of course,' she said, and determinedly re-entered the house.

A few more mourners joined the procession through the village as McCullough, tears streaming down his round face, Nugent carved from stone, Murray and Herkless carried Adair's coffin from Kirkwelland House to the kirkyard. Gibson followed behind, with Pringle, Thomson, and a few other men of the village: Murray knew Mr. Burns of the shop, Innes, and Gourlay the farmer. He thought, too, that he caught just a glimpse of Anna Pringle as the mourners left the gateway of Kirkwelland House, but being a bearer he could not easily look more closely. When the interment was done, and the bottle had been passed around, Murray and Herkless drew aside to allow the three remaining students their moment at the graveside, McCullough nearly bent double with tears, Gibson with a hand on his shoulder, head bowed in prayer, and Nugent as ever a little apart. Pringle and Thomson had vanished.

'They seem ideally suited to one another,' Herkless remarked, seeing that they had gone. 'Each sustained in life by a notion of their own importance.'

Murray smiled.

'I was sorry that the Pringle ladies were not able to attend. Adair seems to have been very popular.'

'Yes, with Anna in particular, I believe,' said Herkless. 'It was perhaps unwise to leave them at home, but there, Pringle has never allowed himself to be guided by anything as plebeian as wisdom. Kitty would have enjoyed their company.'

'Mrs. Black came, though.'

'Yes. I find her altogether less alarming back in mourning.'

'She seems a very sensible, pleasant woman,' said Murray. 'And very handsome in that brown gown, until her unfortunate accident.'

'Ah, yes, the picnic, doomed on all sides. I fear your visit to us has not been as pleasant as we could all have hoped, Murray,' said Herkless, watching the students. 'I should like to assure you that this is usually a quiet, peaceable place, but I am not sure based on the past week or so that you would be inclined to believe me.'

'When one death happens, one unexpected death,' said Murray, 'often others follow. Old secrets come out, or new ones need to be hidden, or revenge is taken, or opportunities seized.'

'I forget you have such experience in these matters. Then you fear there might be more to come? Surely not: two deaths is plenty!'

'Two deaths and we do not know – we are not yet sure – that the killer has been safely identified.'

'If there are any more deaths I shall be forced to up sticks, take Kitty and move to Glasgow for a more peaceful life.' He sighed. 'Then you do not abide by Thomson's conclusions?'

'I'm not convinced. He might be right, but I'm not sure.'

'If he is right – and I'm not saying that I agree with him either,' added Herkless, 'it is at least to the advantage of our student friends.'

'They can go home?'

'Yes: directly this funeral is done. Thomson has given them permission.'

'Oh!' Murray considered that. If he was not sure that Adair had killed Newell and then himself, then was Thomson allowing

suspects to leave for freedom? McCullough, Gibson and Nugent ...
even if they had killed Newell, could they have killed Adair, their
friend and colleague? He stared about the kirkyard, as if seeking
inspiration. By the gate he noticed Norrie Pearce watching the
students. He was a suspect too, Murray thought: he must remember
to return and question him again before Herkless sent him away.
Herkless did not seem to have seen him.

'Their packs are still up at the house, though,' Herkless was
saying. 'If we can persuade them to move we can help them on
their way. Poor McCullough is going to flood the grave at this
rate.' He moved forward and put a hand on Gibson's shoulder, and
eased all three out of the kirkyard, with Murray following behind.

It was a doleful walk up to the house, and Murray had to resist
the temptation to become brisk and efficient. He did, however,
offer to help the students bring their packs downstairs, where Kitty
had provided food for them to eat or take with them. Murray once
again followed Nugent, along with Gibson and McCullough, up to
the plain landing and the two rooms they had reluctantly inhabited
for a week. The packs were ready, and it was a matter of minutes
to shoulder them, Murray taking Adair's, and return to the hall.

'I'll see you to the end of the village,' said Coulter, appearing
from the drawing room where, as custom had it, he had been sitting
with Kitty and Mrs. Black in prayer and probably gossip while the
coffin was removed to the kirkyard.

'I'll come too, if I may,' said Murray, 'and then you'll have
company back.'

'Thank you,' said McCullough. They had decided to take the
food with them, in order to pass through Stranraer before dusk, and
opened their packs again to find space for it. Then it was time to
retrieve their coats and hats and sticks and gloves, to make their
thanks to Kitty and Herkless, to be wished a safe journey home.
Then the packs were shouldered once again.

'I cannot quite believe we are actually free to leave,' said
McCullough. 'I expect at any moment to be stopped again.'

'Best away, then,' said Herkless, 'though it sounds ungracious
in me to say it!'

'Aye, sir, we should go,' said Nugent. He lifted Adair's pack
in his free hand.

'Here, one of us will take it to the end of the village for you,' said Coulter. 'No need for you to carry two.'

He reached for it, and Nugent swung it up to hand it over. The pack burst, blooming like a great dark flower in mid-air, and all the contents fell to the floor. Murray knelt quickly to help tidy them back in.

'Thomson took Newell's money,' said Kitty, 'and he was going to give it to the Inneses. I hope he remembers.'

Murray quickly folded the clothes, but stopped when one of the shirts crackled. He paused, and shook it out. A fold of cheap writing paper fluttered to the ground. They all stared at it for a long second, before Murray stooped and picked it up between long fingers.

'It's a letter,' he said. 'I wonder I did not find it the first time I searched his pack.'

'It's not large: you may have missed it,' said Herkless. 'What does it say?'

Murray unfolded it and skimmed through, before reading the large writing aloud.

'Dear Sir, I seen you in the woods with A.P. I sugest a meeting to discuss business. Your obed. servant Th. Newell.'

'Oh, dear,' said Kitty sadly. 'This does seem to add evidence to Mr. Thomson's theory, doesn't it?'

'Poor boy, poor boy,' murmured Herkless.

'I did not think he could have done it,' said Coulter.

'He was just so kind, it still seems impossible to me,' said McCullough. 'I don't think I'll ever believe it of him. He literally wouldn't hurt a fly, so he wouldn't, not if he could help it.'

'What if he had been drinking?' asked Herkless.

McCullough blushed red.

'Even when he was drinking he was gentle. You saw him that night after the mutual improvement society thing. He'd just flop about grinning and then fall asleep. I never even heard him say a harsh word in his cups, not one.'

Nugent muttered something, and turned away.

'Aye, right, time to go,' said McCullough. 'Do you want to keep the letter to show Mr. Thomson? I don't really think we need to take such a thing to his parents, do you?'

'I'll give it to him,' said Murray, and slipped the letter into his pocket. Then he finished rolling Adair's pack, and looped it over his own shoulder, and led the way out on to the drive. Kitty and Herkless followed, and waved the students off until they were out of sight.

Despite their sorrow, with every step they took towards the southern end of the village McCullough and Nugent, at least, seemed to grow lighter and more cheerful. Gibson remained his strange, aloof self, but at least he managed his own pack. Coulter chatted with them once again and reminisced about his own search for his first parish, and they talked of the parishes they might serve in when they returned to Ireland, finally able once again to consider the future.

'And I'll go and see Jamesie's parents in Hillsborough, and try to explain everything, and take his things back,' said McCullough. 'It's as handy for me as anybody, I suppose. And I'd like to see them and talk to them about him.'

'I'll come too, then,' said Gibson, and they exchanged a smile.

The scent of the tannery's ominous pools signalled the point of their parting, and soon the smithy came in sight, and then the little bridge over the Welland Burn that was the boundary of the parish. Around it, walling the road in and sheltering it here, were high boulders that sat unnaturally on the earth as if some careless giant had spilled them unaware from his pockets.

'The gates of the village,' Coulter joked. 'You've made it, gentlemen!'

'I hope you won't take it badly if I say I never want to see hide nor hair of Kirkwelland ever again!' said Nugent, an unaccustomed grin on his face.

'I can understand your feelings on the matter: I'll not take it ill,' said Coulter, and shook his hand. McCullough and Gibson followed. 'But if any of you is ever this way again and needs somewhere to stay, then come straight to the manse.'

'And if you're ever across the water, remember McCullough's drapery in Larne. My father will no doubt sell you enough for three new suits of clothes, but never mind that: my mother's a grand cook.'

The students at last edged away, then sped up, taking longer strides, and with a final flurry of waves they disappeared between the rocks and down the road to Stranraer.

'Well, for their sakes I hope we don't see them again tomorrow!' said Coulter, turning at last for home.

'Yet I am sure this is not the end,' said Murray. 'Whether it is simply that I do not trust Thomson, I do not know, but I am not satisfied.'

'It is because we all liked Adair,' said Coulter confidently. 'We don't want to think of him doing anything unpleasant. But it seems he must have. Come along, or Mrs. Veitch will complain if we're late. What on earth - ?'

Coulter broke off, as something heavy fell against him from the top of the nearest boulder. He staggered, and whatever it was tumbled off him, and hit Murray. Murray fell heavily on to his knees and then on to his face, winded. Then came a voice.

'You scoundrel! You've lost me my living and my home! Let me get my hands on you!'

Murray turned his head, and saw Norrie Pearce, standing on a low boulder by the bridge parapet and shouting down the stream while a black hat rolled a lazy circle on the road. Pearce leapt off the boulder and sprang away down by the riverbank while Murray struggled to his feet, testing his knees. Where was Coulter? He glanced about, and then saw, an unexpected distance away, his friend the minister, running for all he was worth straight for the tannery, with Norrie Pearce after him. Murray picked up Coulter's hat, and broke into a run, too. By the look on Norrie's face, Coulter would probably need some help.

Chapter Eighteen

It seemed a mile to the tannery, and it seemed a moment. The ground was grass and rock beside the burn, and slippery. The smell from the tannery was already intense.

Ahead Coulter vanished amongst the wooden frames around the pools, hidden by half-worked cow hides. Pearce plunged after him, still yelling. Murray sprinted in pursuit as best he could, but was brought up short by the maze of pools and frames. He glanced at the house. Craig, the old man at the window, was mouthing and gesturing to Murray's right, and Murray chose to take him at his word. He veered to the right, skirting the freshwater pool fed directly from the burn, where the hides were rinsed of salt. He heard footsteps. Coulter was doubling back, Pearce hot on his heels.

'Coulter!' shouted Murray. 'Over here!' He tried to find a path between the pools to reach his friend, but Pearce had his fists clenched now and was closing on Coulter. 'Look out!'

Coulter snapped around and Pearce lunged, but at that moment Murray jumped over the pool and crashed into both of them. There was a dreadful creak and crash as one of the frames, heavy with hide, folded and fell to the ground.

'What in the name of the wee man is going on out here?' came a new voice, and a man whom Murray remembered as the oldest tanner came out of the shed, aproned and proprietorial. He was followed at speed by another aproned man, younger and fitter. Pearce took advantage of the distraction to snatch up a bucket of liquid and fling it at Coulter. Coulter reeled as the bucket glanced off his head, tipping its foul contents slimily down his face. He began to choke, trying to wipe the filth off, but Pearce rushed up to punch him. His fist flailed out but his foot caught in the fallen frame and he fell. Murray seized him by the shoulder, dragging him to his feet in an effort to pin his arms behind his back, but at the same time a hand on his shoulder spun him, and the younger tanner punched him in the stomach. Murray doubled over but his height meant that he knocked the tanner off balance, and as they waltzed together on the edge of a stinking pool of hides and water, Pearce recovered himself and gave Murray a dunt in the ribs with his elbow before aiming another blow at Coulter. He caught him on the upper arm and Coulter in turn tripped over the fallen frame in his haste to run away. He grabbed at Murray's legs as he fell and Murray, already unsteady from Pearce's elbow, fell across the young tanner who scrabbled out from underneath and knocked down another frame, sending hides flapping over Coulter just as Pearce pulled him up again, drawing a knife from his belt. Murray rolled out of the way and kicked out at the young tanner, missed and hit Pearce's foot. Pearce found his foot in mid-air, and clutched at Coulter, both teetering narrowly between two ponds. Coulter, unaware of the water behind him, thrust at Pearce's desperate hands, and flailed back as he toppled. Pearce, a look of terrible shock on his face, fell like a stone into the pond behind him. The two splashes split the air and Murray and the young tanner sat back, panting. Old Mr. Craig in the window seemed to be clapping his hands in delight: he could not have had such excitement in years, sitting there.

'I think I'd repeat my question,' said the older tanner, stately in his apron. 'Up you get, the pair of you.'

The younger tanner sprang up, and Murray rolled to his feet, rubbing his head and wondering where his hat was.

'I – well, I think there are a couple of men in your ponds, Mr. Craig,' he said, not quite sure how to explain what had happened. 'My name is Murray: we met briefly the other day.' The niceties were automatic.

'Better get them out, then,' said Craig, who appeared to be a practical man. Coulter was already standing up and dripping in the freshwater pool, dragging hides away from his legs. He was starting to shiver. 'It's the minister!' exclaimed Craig, and hurried to pull him out. 'Where's the other fellow? I thought you said there were two?'

'It was Norrie Pearce,' said the younger tanner. 'I thought these two – er, gentlemen – were attacking him.'

'He attacked me!' said Coulter defensively.

'He fell the other way,' said Murray. 'Into that pond, there, I think.'

'Oh.'

The pond Murray had indicated was a deep, dark brown, and placid. Nothing could be seen in its mysterious depths, but a fair amount could be deduced from the smell.

'That'd be the dung water pond,' said the younger tanner.

Coulter had his handkerchief, wet though it was, over his nose.

'It is, isn't it?' he said in a muffled voice.

'Aye.'

'And that looks like the heel of a boot,' said Murray, trying not to breathe.

Towards their end of the pool, breaking the surface, was indeed the heel of a boot. It was not moving.

'That's not good,' remarked Craig, and fetched a stick with a hook on the end. He felt about in the water with it, hissing through his back teeth, and eventually said, 'Give us a hand, Jackie. And could I ask one of you gentlemen to put a bit of weight on the back of this?'

Murray and the younger tanner stepped forward and took the end of the stick, and between the three of them they hauled out their sodden catch by his belt. They all backed off as the body sagged on to the ground, and then Craig used the hooked stick to roll it on to its back. Pearce was as brown as the water, and as stinking, and quite dead.

'He must have hit his head,' said Coulter, shaking.

'Or had some kind of fit, perhaps. He seemed very shocked. His father has had a stroke, hasn't he? Perhaps it runs in the family.'

'But what was he doing here? What were any of you doing here?' asked Craig in a tone that was really very reasonable in the circumstances.

'Pearce attacked the minister,' said Murray, picking up Coulter's hat once again from where he had dropped it in his rush across the pond. He was wary about where he put his feet, not wanting a soaking, too. 'From what he said I think he thought Mr. Coulter had lost him his job.'

'Oh, aye, he'd been selling off the laird's rabbits in Stranraer,

I heard tell,' said Craig, nodding. Murray reminded himself that news travels through villages like smoke on a windy day. 'Mr. Herkless is a Justice of the Peace and all: nae doubt he'd have had him up for theft, too.'

'We were walking back to the village along the road when Pearce just ambushed us,' said Coulter, and gave a violent shiver. Drops sprayed from him as if he were a dog shaking itself.

'You took off like a laverock,' Murray commented.

'I had a fright,' said Coulter, his teeth chattering as much from shock as from cold.

'We havena had an accident here for years,' said Craig regretfully. 'I try to run a safe yard, but there's always some risk. It's no a place for haste. Here, I'm forgetting my manners,' he said suddenly. 'Come away into the house and dry off, and I'll get a blanket to cover Norrie Pearce. Jackie, get on ahead and tell the mistress.'

The younger tanner skipped off towards the house and Craig himself led Coulter away, and Murray gazed down at the hideously filthy body. It was impossible even to judge Pearce's expression in death. Had he killed Newell? It was too late to tell now. He stayed there like a lonely sentry amongst the tanning ponds until the woman he had seen in the kailyard before bustled out with a blanket. Together they covered the corpse, and he left her there with it and followed Coulter into the house.

The miasma of the tannery hung about them both like a cloak all the way back to the manse, and they were hardly in the door when Coulter ordered Mrs. Veitch to boil water for two large baths. Murray retired to his room to wait, stripping off his clothes and wrapping himself in his banyan. It did not entirely help: he suspected his hair and skin carried the smell, too.

His coat crackled a little as he took it off and he felt in the pocket to find the letter from Adair's pack. He curled himself on to the window seat and unfolded it to read it again.

'Dear Sir, I seen you in the woods with A.P. I sugest a meeting to discuss business. Your obed. servant Th. Newell.'

It certainly seemed to be Newell's writing, very similar to the hand used in the writing boards he had carried, the ones that had been so conveniently wiped. Except for Adair's name: whoever it was that had wiped them had no qualms about leaving evidence that Adair was being blackmailed. And was that likely to be Adair?

He read the letter again. 'Dear Sir …' Would Newell have addressed Adair as 'sir'? And yet it mentioned A.P. – who else might have been in the woods, that suggestive phrase, with Anna Pringle? From her attitude, no one: she seemed to have a heart only for James Adair. But that 'sir', like Adair's suicide, jangled somewhere in Murray's mind, off key, just not quite right.

Moreover, Adair was staying in his house: he had no need to write to him at all. He wished he had asked McCullough how Newell had first approached him to ask him for money. Murray was fairly sure it would not have been by letter. Mr. Burns had remembered Newell's purchase of a piece of writing paper as an unusual thing, and paper was expensive. He could not imagine Newell spending money on it when he could just have had a quiet word in private with Adair, maybe even on the headland.

And something had happened on the headland that day, he was sure of it. Not this demand for money from Adair, for that, if McCullough and Anna spoke truly, had been going on for a while. But there had to be some significance to the fact that Adair had been there, Newell had been there, and now they were both dead. Hadn't there?

The water arrived, and with it, Walter, self-importantly lugging one heavy bucket behind Mrs. Veitch with two more. They filled the bath and Murray dismissed them, but Walter lingered for a moment.

'Yes, Walter?'

'Sir, if you do not need me this evening, may I go out?'

'Out where?'

'Mr. Innes has offered to take me up to Mr. Gourlay's farm, to see all his scientific instruments, sir. He has a telescope to view the stars, sir.' Walter's face was solemn but there was a glint of excitement in his eyes. Murray reflected: he could spare him, and if he did not Walter would be distracted anyway.

'Very well,' he said, 'but don't get lost.'

'Of course not, sir. Thank you, sir.'

Bathed and scrubbed, yet still conscious of a lingering odour, Coulter and Murray dined and were about to settle in front of the parlour fire as had become their habit, when there came a knock at the door, and in a moment Mrs. Veitch appeared with a note.

'It's from Mrs. Black,' said Coulter in mild wonder. 'Just a moment – she is asking us to come down for a little supper. That's unusual.'

'She does not entertain much, then?'

'Not at all, since Dr. Black died. We had better go: I fear that after what happened on Tuesday she will need a little reassurance.'

'Anyone would, though at least she came to the funeral today.'

'I was glad to see it, but she was quiet while you were all at the kirkyard. Miss Kitty tried to make conversation for both of them, but Mrs. Black sat by the window. I had the impression she was thinking through some problem, though.'

'How to win her laird?' suggested Murray. Coulter grinned.

'Perhaps! But she left quite quickly when you and Herkless came back with the students, didn't she?'

'True. Shall we go, then?'

It was still daylight, though the sun was propped on the western side of the loch and cast long shadows amongst the houses of the village, and turned the water beyond them a tawny bronze. Summer seemed to be in the air: it was a lovely evening for a supper invitation.

If she was out of practice at entertaining, it did not show, for Mrs. Black had laid a pretty little supper table in her parlour with cold meats and pies and a jug of negus against the cold. She fluttered over them until they had seated themselves and begun to eat, but their expressions of satisfaction over the arrangements seemed to soothe her and she sat, too, and addressed herself to a pie with some enthusiasm.

'I hope,' she began eventually, 'that you will forgive any apparent impropriety in my asking two gentlemen here and no ladies, but I wanted very much to have a little word with you, Mr. Coulter, and Mr. Murray, I could hardly omit you for you are a very sympathetic man, I think.'

'You are very kind, ma'am,' he replied dutifully.

'Not at all! I found our little conversation this afternoon very helpful, and I believe you knew that you were helping me.'

'And if we can help you again in any way,' said Coulter,

wiping his lips with a well-pressed napkin.

'Oh, yes, yes.' She took a healthy draught of negus and coughed a little, then smoothed down her dress as if smoothing out her nerves. She was in deep blue this evening, not as striking as the unfortunate brown dress and clearly not a new gown, but a pleasant change from all her black, and, as far as Murray could see, better fitted. She breathed in purposefully. 'I fear – I perceive that I have made myself the object of ridicule.'

'Of ridicule? No, not at all!' cried Coulter.

'You mean the incident with the – ah, the jelly?' asked Murray carefully. 'That was an accident, and everyone knows that. Everyone was very sympathetic, and anyway, the dreadful incident which followed quite made everyone forget all about it.'

'Not the jelly – though that was very painful at the time,' Mrs. Black admitted, with a wry half-smile. 'I should not have attempted such a gown, I think, and my pride was very much wounded! But pride can recover, and I suspect that I may have been of service in causing some hilarity for the party, however sympathetic they might have been. It must have been a most amusing sight!'

'Um, yes,' said Coulter with quiet guilt. 'The jelly had been so splendid, and it flew so beautifully …'

'Yes, well,' said Mrs. Black. 'That is not strictly what I mean. I mean that I have been setting my cap at Mr. Herkless – yes, I use that shameful phrase as if I were a green girl – and only now have I acknowledged to myself that I have been setting it in vain. I have made a complete fool of myself. Mr. Herkless, kind gentleman though he undoubtedly is, cares nothing for me in that way.'

'I'm sure …' began Murray, trying to find words to be polite without admitting that he agreed with her. 'I'm sure he is a foolish man, then,' he finished awkwardly.

'Foolish maybe,' agreed Mrs. Black, smiling slightly, 'but his heart is engaged elsewhere, and I had not recognised it before, blind as I was. But now I am quite free, and I wanted to tell someone – someone who would understand, and that is why I invited you gentlemen this evening. I have cast all fondness aside, and cleared my mind and my heart, and I have remembered the love my husband and I had for each other, and I am content. There! Now let us try to talk of cheerful things, for there have been too many sorrows in Kirkwelland lately – and now I hear that Norrie Pearce has been caught selling on the laird's rabbits?'

'And there, I fear, is another tragedy,' said Coulter sadly, and explained the events of the afternoon. Mrs. Black was thoroughly shocked.

'I feel so sorry for the Craigs,' she said at last. 'As for Pearce, old Pearce, I mean, it is very sad but he must take some responsibility for it. But the Craigs are innocents in all this and still have the sorrow of a death on their premises. Old Mr. Craig is a sweet man, I've always found.'

'I think he quite enjoyed the excitement,' said Murray drily. 'He has a dull life there watching out the window.'

'Yes,' said Mrs. Black. 'While old Mr. Pearce has, I think, much more entertainment at his window.' She spoke innocently enough, but Murray surprised an expression in her eye that he found a little shocking – it was almost vindictive. He thought it must have been a trick of the light.

'So where is Herkless' heart engaged, then?' Murray asked Coulter once they were clear of Mrs. Black's.

'I can't imagine,' said Coulter. 'Unless it is someone in Stranraer, or perhaps Glasgow: he takes his carriage up there often enough. You've seen how small society is here in the village.'

'He would not have interested himself in Anna Pringle, would he?' asked Murray suddenly. A thought had occurred to him: Newell would certainly have addressed a letter to Herkless with 'Dear Sir'.

'Anna Pringle? I shouldn't think so: she's younger than Kitty,' said Coulter, slightly shocked. 'And I should have thought he would prefer a woman with more sense.'

'And then there's the idea of having Pringle as a father-in-law,' said Murray, with a slight shudder, though Herkless seemed quite capable of dealing with Pringle's pomposity.

'Yes, a prospect that does not appeal,' Coulter agreed.

'Yet even if it were the case that Herkless was interested in Anna, that would not be something to blackmail him over, would it?' Murray was thinking out loud, and Coulter stopped abruptly.

'Blackmailed? Herkless? Whatever are you talking about?'

'The note in Adair's pack,' Murray explained. He pulled it out of his pocket again and showed it to Coulter, who turned it towards their lantern to examine. 'It starts 'Dear Sir'. Would Newell have addressed a letter to Adair this way? It seems to me unlikely.'

'You are determined that Adair did not kill Newell, aren't you?' asked Coulter, a little grumpy. He peered at the letter, and bit his lips together. 'Why would Newell write to Adair at all? Why not just talk to him?'

'That occurred to me, too.'

Coulter read the letter through once more, then handed it back to Murray. He began to walk on thoughtfully.

'Add this,' Murray went on, pressing home his advantage, 'that Newell bragged to McCullough that he now had gentry among his clients. Who would he address as 'sir'?'

'Well, me,' said Coulter, 'and no, he wasn't blackmailing me nor had he offered to do so. Pringle, and Herkless. I can't think of anyone else in the village that he might write to or address so. But then think: if he is writing a letter perhaps it was for someone not in the village at all? He might have sent it by the carrier, or someone might have taken it for him.'

'Then why is it back here again?'

'Someone brought it back? Or perhaps he wrote it but never sent it.'

'But whoever it was was at least in the woods on the headland – he says he saw them.'

'It might not have been him that saw them. It might have been Pearce passing on information.'

'But they were still this close to the village, and the letter is here. He could not blackmail Pringle for meeting his daughter – or at least he would be unlikely to refer to her as 'A.P.', wouldn't he?'

'Let us not go any further with that thought,' said Coulter quickly, his face appalled in the lantern light.

'You say it was not you, so that leaves Herkless. Yet why should that be a blackmailable affair? Neither is married. What?'

For Coulter had slapped his hand on his forehead, and groaned.

'Mrs. Pringle,' he said. 'Mrs. Pringle is Ada.'

'Now that would be blackmailable,' said Murray. 'Shall we walk up to Kirkwelland House? It is still early enough to call.'

'I've had enough of today,' Coulter grumbled. 'I wish it would stop.' But he turned on reluctant feet and followed Murray and the lantern back to the gateway of Kirkwelland House.

Murray did his best not to think about the conversation ahead as they climbed the drive. He liked Herkless and had no wish to bring him any kind of discomfort, but his mind was deeply uneasy. He thought of the three students, finally free, and hoped they had found somewhere comfortable to stay that night with Adair's pack.

Herkless and Kitty were both sitting reading in the drawing room at Kirkwelland House, a peaceful scene which it gave Murray a pang to interrupt. Coulter looked as uneasy as he bowed to the Herklesses, and Kitty rang for refreshments.

'I wondered,' said Murray quickly before he could change his mind, 'if I might have a word in private, sir?'

Herkless raised his eyebrows and his mouth twitched as if he were hiding a smile, but he bowed and said,

'Of course – perhaps my study will be warm enough. Bring that candle, will you?'

Murray followed him across the landing and handed him the candle to light the sconces in the book-lined room. Scientific apparatus of different kinds littered a broad desk. The fire was unlit, but the study was cosy and Herkless ushered him to one of the well-cushioned chairs by the hearth. Murray fell silent, not sure where to start, but Herkless was ready with conversation to ease the moment.

'I hear that I no longer need to concern myself with Norrie Pearce, unfortunate man,' he said.

'Yes, I'm afraid so. I think he must have had a stroke: there is no sign of injury on him – that I could see through the filth. It was not a pleasant place to die.'

'No: nor do I envy the women laying him out. Thomson has left the village and gone up the coast in pursuit of his imagined French republicans, but he should be back tomorrow and we can present the facts to him them.'

'It was clearly an accident, though, while he was trying to attack Coulter for telling you about the rabbits.'

'Of course: he was not a pleasant character all round, and I suppose we had made him desperate. His father will feel his loss most keenly though, and of course he will have to go on the parish poors roll. Which he will doubtless augment with any stray rabbits he happens to find on my land or on others'.'

'I thought he found difficulty in walking.'

'Only when it suits him, I fear.' He regarded Murray with that glint of humour in his eyes. 'Now, how can I help you? Do you have a certain request to make of me? For if you have, I must tell you that though I think you are a little premature in your approach I shall not look with disfavour on any reasonable – er, bargain.'

'Sir?' Murray stared at him in bewilderment, then light dawned. 'Oh! I am not – I am not here to make an offer for your daughter, though indeed I should be honoured … I, too, think it a little early to be thinking of such things, and I have not even thought of making any offer …' He finished awkwardly, taken aback. He had made three proposals of marriage in the past: he had never had one accepted before it was even made.

'Oh, a shame,' said Herkless smoothly. 'But when the time comes – if things go along as at present – I must say that I think your offer would be sympathetically received by all parties.'

'Um, thank you, sir.' So Kitty did indeed look on him with favour! He forced himself to push the thought to the back of his mind for now, though it was difficult. 'No, I've come to ask you something much more awkward.' He drew a deep breath: this question could affect all those pleasant prospects, but it had to be asked. 'I've come to ask if you were being blackmailed by Newell.'

Lexie Conyngham

Chapter Nineteen

'Blackmailed? Concerning what?'

'Concerning a lady – well, in fact, concerning Mrs. Pringle.'

Murray held his breath. The little study seemed to have chilled. Herkless frowned, but then laughed out loud.

'Good heavens, has that surfaced again? Where on earth did you hear that?'

'Then it is not true? Forgive me, sir, it seemed it might be relevant.'

'I'll tell you what happened,' said Herkless, settling back comfortably in his chair. 'I was up inspecting the woodland on the headland one day – and of course noting the thermometers and so on – and I met Mrs. Pringle. Well, everyone in the village walks up there, as you've probably realised by now. I should charge admittance! She was seeking her daughter and I think we spoke a little about the worries that occur when one's daughter reaches marriageable age – to be honest I cannot fully remember what we spoke of for it was of little matter to me at the time. She went off one way and I went off the other and I thought nothing more about it. Then I received a letter from Newell threatening to blackmail me over it. I met with him and told him there was nothing in it and he would be making a fool of himself to try.'

'Would this be the letter in question, sir?' Murray asked, showing him the paper from Adair's pack. Herkless quickly read it through and handed it back.

'That's it, indeed! Ridiculous man. No wonder you came asking questions. Where did you find it?'

'In Adair's pack: it's the one we found this afternoon.'

'In Adair's pack?' Herkless looked confused.

'You were there at the time, sir.'

'Yes, I was, but it meant nothing to me at the time. We were talking of Adair, and I assumed it was a different letter. You can see that the whole thing made so little impression on me that I did not even draw a parallel between the two events – though of course it bears out Mrs. Pringle's concerns over her daughter, which she mentioned at the time.'

'Well, I am pleased to hear it,' said Murray, 'and I apologise once again for my intrusion. It is just that I am not satisfied over Adair's death and Thomson's assumption that Adair killed Newell.'

'Why not? Surely it should be enough that that odious individual cannot bother anyone else with his ridiculous demands? And even if Adair did kill him and then kill himself, I don't know that anyone thinks the worse of him for it.' He smiled. 'In another society, he might even have been praised for it.'

Murray returned the smile automatically, though he was still frowning.

'I don't know, but something still makes me doubt.' They rose, and Herkless put a friendly hand on his shoulder, but the doubt persisted, even when they returned to the drawing room and the delightful company of Kitty.

Coulter chattered with relief on the walk home, but Murray was silent, his mind still chewing over the facts of the case like mouthfuls of tough beef. It was mildly annoying, for he had discovered the therapeutic benefits of playing pianoforte duets with Kitty, and he felt he should have been dwelling on that instead, but Adair's amiable face kept popping into his head in the middle of the pleasantest memories.

He had not expected to find Walter waiting up for him back at the manse with hot water – or rather, water that had been hot.

'You should see Mr. Gourlay's telescope, sir! We saw Venus!' He poured out the water for Murray and handed him a towel dutifully. He had obviously been waiting for some time just to talk about his evening, and Murray allowed him to give a full account of every piece of equipment he had seen.

'And Mr. Gourlay was cross but it wasn't with me, sir.'

'What was that?' asked Murray vaguely, in the middle of pulling his nightshirt over his head.

'Mr. Gourlay and Mr. Innes were arguing.'

'Oh, yes? About the mutual improvement society?'

'No, sir. Mr. Gourlay was accusing Mr. Innes of holding back money that Mr. Newell had left, because Mr. Gourlay's wife was due something from the estate. I think that was it. I was looking at the sundial, sir, with a lantern. Did you know you can change the time by moving the lantern around? But you shouldn't be deceived by it, sir, for it's not real time. It doesn't show up on a watch: Mr. Gourlay lent me his to see.'

'Mr. Gourlay's wife was Mr. Newell's wife's ... what? Cousin? Sister?' He could not remember. It had not occurred to him that there might be an heir besides Mrs. Innes. And Mr. Gourlay had expensive habits, with his scientific equipment. Where had he been on the morning of Newell's death? Where had his wife been?

'Beth Scott that's married to Gourlay was cousin to Isabel Scott that was married to Thomas Newell,' said Coulter confidently at breakfast. 'Isabel Scott had a bit of money of her own that was to go to Beth and to Isabel's daughter, Innes' wife, after she died, but Newell, being Newell, had always delayed paying it. Now Newell is dead, Gourlay wants it paid, of course, but Innes is holding back because he's ashamed of what Newell did, and the Inneses want to pay the money back to the blackmailing victims – or the ones they can find, anyway. Naturally Gourlay and his wife are not over-pleased.' He sighed. 'I love my parishioners,' he added.

'I can tell.'

'Don't tell me you're hunting there for a murderer now, are you?' Coulter demanded. 'Are you always so ready to reject the easy solution when it presents itself?'

'When I'm not convinced that it's the right one, then yes, I hope I am,' said Murray, trying not to sound waspish. It would be very easy to admit that Adair was guilty and go home to Augusta, even with the promise to come back and visit Kitty Herkless – he reflected again on the intimacy of those duets the previous evening - but he could not do it.

'You need not trouble yourself,' said Coulter after a moment's thought. 'The Gourlays were both in Stranraer last Thursday: I remember because they were to see his cousin off on the coach to

London. They were to be away all day, for Mrs. Veitch went up in the afternoon to see that the maid was managing all right. She's Mrs. Veitch's niece, you see.'

'Villages,' Murray grumbled. 'Everyone is connected with everyone else.'

He left Coulter beginning work on his Sunday sermon, and took a walk about the town. He called in at Mr. Burns' shop where he made enquiries about the sales of writing paper and the provision of compounds of mercury, which Mr. Burns flatly denied selling. Mr. Burns was in high good humour, and explained to Murray that he had just contracted a useful marriage for his daughter Sarah with the smith Raffan. Murray congratulated him and offered Sarah, who was helping in the shop, every good wish for the future, at which she grinned with open enthusiasm. Another very handsome girl, Murray thought: he would be very content to pay this place another visit.

He arrived back at the manse just as a familiar, depressed-looking horse was being watered by Walter at the front gate. The horse, seeing his distraction, stole a mouthful of lush foliage from the garden and flicked his head high as if to deny he had ever touched the stuff. The sheriff's officer's horse, a thief? Murray laughed to himself, and went into the manse.

'Mr. Thomson has just arrived,' Coulter explained as Murray entered the parlour. He was standing, uneasy, while Thomson had settled himself like a polished button in the armchair. 'He wants to ask us about Pearce, of course.'

'Of course,' said Murray. 'Good day to you, Mr. Thomson: I hope we are not dragging you away from your vital pursuit of the French by the distraction of a mere corpse.'

'Always delighted to meet you again too, sir,' said Thomson with a well-oiled bow, as sincere as his face. 'If I leave this village for a month, will there be anybody left, I wonder?'

'Even if we were all dead, no doubt you would find someone to blame.'

'No doubt I would, indeed, Mr. Murray. Now, when did all this happen?'

'Yesterday,' said Coulter quickly, 'in the afternoon. We were just seeing the students, you know, to the end of the village –'

'Dinna tell me the students were into this rammy too!' cried Thomson, thumping the padded arm of the chair in frustration. 'If I have to drag them three back again I'll no be best pleased!'

'No, no, they'd long gone,' said Coulter, soothing him reluctantly, though his own fingers were twitching, Murray noticed. Thomson was doubtful.

'I never want to see they three again here or elsewhere,' he said, with gritted teeth.

'Don't worry: they have no wish to see you or this place again, either,' said Murray.

'Grand.'

'Anyway,' said Coulter, 'they had disappeared round the corner, so they were neither in sight nor in hearing, when we turned round to come back. We had walked only a couple of steps when Pearce landed on us from the rock above.'

'He was up on the rock? Waiting for you?'

'He must have been. He landed quite hard.'

Thomson again looked dubious.

'So assuming he wasn't dropped by a passing kittiwake,' Murray put in, 'or perhaps kicked from a great distance by one of your legendary cattle, it seems likely that he was on the rock.' Thomson scowled at him. 'Pearce was at the burial,' Murray continued, remembering. 'He may have hoped to see Coulter there, but at any rate he could have overheard that the students were to leave, and guess that Coulter would want to see them on their way. And if not – perhaps he followed us, or perhaps he just took his chance.'

'And why did he have this strong animosity towards you, Mr. Coulter?' Thomson asked.

'Oh!' said Coulter hurriedly, 'I thought everyone knew that now. Mr. Murray and I caught his father selling Mr. Herkless' rabbits without permission in the Star in Stranraer.'

'And nobody tellt me?' Thomson's official dignity was put out.

'We haven't really had much chance,' Murray said, reasonably. 'You had gone up the coast to hunt for Frenchmen.'

Thomson scowled.

'So he jumped you. Then what happened?'

'Coulter ran,' said Murray. He was still astonished at the

single-minded speed of his friend's sprint: it was almost as though he had been expecting attack. 'Pearce ran after him. I ran after Pearce.'

'You didna catch him?' asked Thomson, a sly expression on his shiny face.

'Old knee injury,' said Murray defensively. 'It took me a moment to recover from the initial attack.'

Thomson gave a little smug smile, though Murray could not see him having much turn of speed.

'And then there was the rammy at the tannery. My, that sounds grand! I'm gey sorry I missed it, ken?'

'It was most unpleasant.' Coulter's lips tightened at the memory.

'Pearce attacked Coulter,' Murray explained, 'I attacked Pearce, then Mr. Craig and his young brother came out and didn't recognise anybody but Pearce – Coulter was a little muddy - and they thought he was being attacked by two strangers. Young Craig then attacked me.'

'He's a big lad,' said Thomson blandly, but the glint of glee in his eyes was as shiny as the rest of him.

'Yes. Anyway, the consequence was that Coulter ended up in the freshwater pond, and Pearce in the dungwater pond, and when we fished him out, he was dead. I think he was dead before he hit the water.'

'From a blow?' asked Thomson keenly.

'From a stroke,' said Murray. 'I'll be interested to hear whether or not your Dr. Forbes finds water in his lungs.'

'We'll see, maybe,' said Thomson. 'Where's the corpus?'

'Back at his own house,' said Coulter at once. 'Would you like us to take you? No doubt you'll want to look at it.'

'Nae doubt, nae doubt, but nae hurry either,' said Thomson.

'Well, perhaps not on your part,' said Coulter, standing up, 'but I need to go and pray with old Mr. Pearce and offer him comfort at this tragic time. So shall we go?'

'Oh, very well,' said Thomson. 'Can I leave the horse here for now?'

'Of course, of course,' said Coulter, who was already shrugging into his second best coat – now his best one, since the soaking yesterday. Murray seized his hat, gloves and stick from the hallstand and waited with emphatic politeness until Thomson was organised, then followed him out. Coulter was already at the bottom of the path: Murray wondered at his rush. Surely Mr. Pearce was not the kind of person to be that eager for the comforts of the kirk? But perhaps Murray had misconstrued him.

Coulter hurried them through the village, along the main street and among the prosperous houses of the north end. They passed Mrs. Black's house just as she opened her door: she was dressed in a round green day gown, simply cut, her whole being well and cheerful. She waved to them and Coulter flicked a wave back, while Murray hurried after with a sketchy bow and tip of his hat.

'Good day, Mrs. Black!'

'Good day, Mr. Murray!'

They were off up the road towards the headland already, and in what seemed like three more strides they were at the gateway of the gamekeeper's house, tucked under the trees. Old Mr. Pearce, as usual, was at the window, watching them approach, impassive, as Coulter gradually slowed down. Pearce waved them over to the window, opening it.

'Aye, the sheriff's man, I should think so. But yon fellas – why have you brought them with you?'

'Show some respect to your betters,' said Thomson unexpectedly.

'That's a bit of a change of policy, isn't it?' Murray asked.

'Mr. Pearce,' said Coulter, 'what happened to Norrie was an accident – well, falling in the pond was an accident, anyway. But Mr. Murray saw his face just before he fell: it seems he might have had a stroke, just as you did.'

'Did he?' Pearce blinked, and considered. 'A stroke, you say? My faither had a stroke at the age of fifty. I had mine when I was fifty-eight. Norrie was only thirty. Ha!' A small triumphant smile appeared on his face.

'Where's the corpus?' asked Thomson.

'Did you think we could have it in the house?' demanded Pearce. 'It'd be like having a midden in your bed. We'd never get the smell out.'

'So where is it?' asked Thomson again with tight-jawed patience.

'It's in the shed round the back,' said Pearce, as if he was admitting to something shameful. 'The lass is sitting with him, and the woman from the village.'

They skirted the house and found themselves in the sketchiest of yards, with two or three sheds huddled together for support under a tree. One had the door wide open, and smoke issuing from it: they tried that one first. Inside, Norrie Pearce was laid out under a sheet, only his head visible, while the girl Murray had seen there before and an older woman tended to a fierce little fire in the middle of the earth floor. The scent of woodsmoke fought with the lingering aroma of dung water, and the women looked up at their visitors apologetically.

'Why can you never get a fire to smoke when you want it to, and if you dinna want it to you're smoked out of house and home?' asked the older woman plaintively, as she curtseyed to the minister.

'This is Mr. Thomson, the sheriff's officer,' Coulter explained. 'He needs to see the body.'

'He's gey welcome,' said the woman with heavy irony, and waved Thomson in. He did not stay long.

'Aye, well, I'll ask Dr. Forbes if he cares to come and make an examination, but I'm glad I'll no be paying his bill if he does,' he said, moving with unaccustomed haste towards the door.

'We washed him, ken,' said the woman, 'but that smell just doesna shift, does it?'

'I'll fetch some ale,' said the younger girl, with canny hospitality. 'Come away into the house.' She led the way quickly across the weedy area again and hurried into the house, leaving the older woman shrugging.

'I canna blame her,' she said, almost to herself. 'I just wish I'd thought of it first.'

They followed the girl into the house and accepted a jug of ale each, sitting in a row on a bench to drink it opposite a set of shelves above a long table. Old Pearce, accepting that the entertainment might be better inside for once, turned to face them, smiling grimly.

'Well, how did you find him?' he asked.

'I daresay he hasn't moved much since you saw him last,' said Thomson. When the girl had gone, Murray took the chance to stretch out his legs, for the bench was a low one.

'And will you be getting your fine Stranraer physician to examine him, then?' asked Pearce. 'I'd like fine to know if it was a stroke or if the minister here killed him.'

'If I did it was an accident – he attacked me!' said Coulter, going rather pink. Murray stared up at the shelves, absently noticing pewter plates, a packet of gunpowder, some stone bottles not unlike Newell's, or the one he had found beside Newell's cottage. Presumably they all came from the same place.

'Aye, aye,' said Pearce, 'why would my Norrie attack a minister, then?'

'I think you know very well why, Mr. Pearce,' said Coulter. 'After all, you were the one selling the rabbits your son had stolen from the laird.'

So much for praying with the bereaved father, thought Murray, his gaze still idling along the shelves. He noticed a smallish white packet, and stood up abruptly. The bench wobbled and Thomson spilled ale down the front of his coat.

'Ca' canny, Mr. Murray!' he cried, 'or you'll have us all upset!'

'Sorry … Mr. Pearce,' he said, lifting the package, 'why do you have a compound of mercury in your house?' The label was clear: turbith mineral. It was the compound of mercury and vitriol Norrie had been seen with in Stranraer.

'Ha!' said Pearce, 'I wondered if you'd see that. Are you going to arrest me now, Mr. Thomson? Or is it my son you want?'

'Mercury?' Thomson himself had slid off the bench to see the package. 'Come on, now, Pearce, tell us why it's here.'

Pearce was unbearably smug.

'See, I told Norrie that his unhealthy habits would take him to an early grave. Thirty years old! And me not till I was near sixty!'

'Pearce!' snapped Thomson, waving the packet in front of the old man's nose.

'Ach, one of the Irish weemin in Stranraer glengoried him. Ken? Give him the Canongate breeks? He was all swelled up,' he began to laugh, 'so he could hardly pull up his breeks! Filthy living, filthy living – that's what killed him, minister, so don't go taking his death to your ain credit.'

Coulter sat with his mouth open, staring from the mercury compound to Pearce's cackling face. He shook himself and snapped his lips shut, then stood.

'Funeral at noon tomorrow, Mr. Pearce?'

'Aye, aye, if that suits you. He's no going anywhere,' said Pearce, and cackled again. Coulter bowed slightly and walked out to the yard.

'Was Newell blackmailing your son, Pearce?' Murray asked.

'What?' Pearce stopped abruptly.

'Was Newell blackmailing Norrie over the rabbits?'

Pearce's jaw dropped.

'Dammit, d'you know I think he was?' For a moment, his crooked mouth worked unevenly, his lips wet. 'My ain oldest friend, blackmailing my ain son! And him lying there stinking of fulyie, the poor bairn, that would never harm a fly!' Tears suddenly flooded his eyes and he began to weep, great noisy sobs that echoed around the little house. Murray and Thomson retreated, and left the cottage. Glancing back, Murray caught sight of Coulter back standing by Pearce at the window, flashing him a desperate look.

'I didna see much sign of Mr. Coulter going to pray with old man Pearce,' said Thomson, sourly, as they walked back down the hill into the village.

'Perhaps he was working up to it. It can't be that easy to pray with someone when you've been accused of killing their son,' said Murray.

'Terbith mineral, eh? I hope you're no going to tell me you think Norrie Pearce killed Newell, now?'

'Well, Norrie was being blackmailed by him. Why would he not want to kill him?'

'I hadna Norrie down as a subtle man, though,' Thomson objected, more reasonably than usual. 'I wouldna have thought he would go to the trouble of poisoning someone when he could as easily take a stick and thump him.'

'He had a knife,' Murray remembered.

'Aye, most do.'

'He was ready enough to draw it, too.'

'So why poison?'

'I know, it seems unlikely.' Murray swished his cane through some weeds by the roadside. 'If Norrie Pearce and the students –

and the smith – were his typical 'customer', why did he suddenly try to blackmail the laird?'

'Greed?' Thomson sniffed. 'If you had to come up with an example of a greedy person, you'd choose Thomas Newell.'

'Perhaps it was the Pringle connexion,' Murray mused. 'He blackmailed students, so he tried Adair, then from that he tried Miss Pringle, then Mrs. Pringle and the laird.'

'He was blackmailing the laird?' Thomson stopped and stared at him like a shocked beetle.

'That's what I said. Well, he tried to, thinking there was something between him and Mrs. Pringle,' Murray explained. 'It was a bit like the smith Raffan's case – the laird told him there was nothing in it and he could go and chase himself.'

'It would have been a step up for him, right enough,' Thomson agreed, walking on again. 'A higher class of blackmail.'

'Well, of victim, anyway. Are you satisfied about Pearce's death, then? Or will you be arresting Coulter?'

Thomson pursed his shiny lips.

'I'll have to go down and talk to the folks at the tannery, I suppose,' he said, his nose wrinkling in anticipation. 'I canna say that Mr. Coulter seems a likely murderer. But then nor did Mr. Adair,' he added, with a sly look at Murray.

'Well, don't let me keep you, then,' said Murray. 'Do enjoy the tannery. I think you'll find the dung water pond particularly congenial.'

'I'll give it your respects.'

'Oh, yes, do that. Watch you don't trip and fall in, won't you?'

Thomson bowed ironically, and took his odd bowed gait down the main street, while Murray turned up the lane that led past Newell's cottage and round to the manse. Thomson's horse still stood at the manse gateway, exuding mild depression. He went to talk to it, not quite sure where it could be taken for its better comfort, when he saw a small crowd of people with packs making their way up the road from the Stranraer direction, about half a dozen adults and a few children, with their eye on him and on the manse.

'Good day to you, sir, and blessings upon you and your good lady and all your fine family!' said the man leading the pack.

'Good day to you,' said Murray politely, his attention mostly on the horse. Unaccustomed to kindness, apparently, it was nuzzling his shoulder with heavy enthusiasm.

'That's a fine horse and all, sir,' the man continued. 'Would you be wanting to sell it at all?'

'It's not mine,' said Murray. The hair on the back of his neck was prickling. 'Are you horse dealers?'

The man laughed, and a few of the crowd who had stopped behind him chuckled, too. A little boy with a face as innocent as a cherub slid forward and manoeuvred himself behind Murray, causing him to shift in turn so that his back was against the garden wall and his pockets were covered. The boy eased away again.

'No, no, we're just passing through, sir, on our way to Glasgow. Poor Irish peasants we are, looking for honest work. Would you know of any round these parts?'

'I'm a visitor here myself,' said Murray evasively. He surveyed the crowd, taller than most of them. There was a woman towards the back who seemed vaguely familiar, but when he tried to focus on her she slid behind the man beside her. 'But I believe if you need a bed for the night and a meal, you'd do well to try Kirkwelland House – the laird is a generous man and will set you on your way.'

'Kirkwelland House, sir? Where would that be?'

'It's – I'll walk you there,' said Murray, on a whim – a whim mostly based on the possibility of playing duets with Kitty Herkless again.

Chapter Twenty

Murray chivvied the Irish crowd before him along the lane, convinced that if he were not the last to leave one of the little boys would nip back and steal the sheriff's officer's horse, and while the horse might appreciate the change he was not keen to encourage horsetheft. He tried again as they walked to see the woman he thought he recognised, but she had drawn her shawl up about her face and resolutely strode forward, not looking back. It was only when they reached the main street and the breeze from the sea caught her shawl that Murray had the chance to catch at least her profile clearly, and to remember where he had seen her before. He turned away before she realised he had seen her. Odd, he thought. She had been the talkative Irish woman they had met on the day of Newell's funeral, the one that had been pestering Innes for money. He was quite sure: now he thought about it, she was absolutely identical, down to a patch of orangeish fabric on the dull cloth of her pack. What could she be doing coming round again?

He studied the group surreptitiously as he took them to the gates of Kirkwelland House and up the driveway. None of the rest seemed like any he remembered, but he had not paid much attention to them except for the talkative woman and the man who had drawn her back. He was not here, anyway. Oh, and there had been the little dark man at the back, who had nodded so significantly. Was he here? He scanned them as if making sure no one was falling behind. There! Was that him? A small, dark-haired man was towards the back, keeping in amongst the others, head down. But even at that he could see that it was a different man, with a different shape of head. No, there was no one else that was familiar, but he was positive about the woman.

Why would she be travelling through again? And so soon? He calculated: it would have been four days ago that he had seen her first. She could barely have reached Glasgow, on foot, before she had turned and come back again. Was she making a living out of the charity she might receive, walking back and forth to Stranraer? It seemed an unchancy way to live. Perhaps she had forgotten something, and gone back?

They turned the corner of the drive, and up ahead Murray was pleased to see Herkless himself approaching on horseback. The laird dismounted when he saw his visitors, and grinned at Murray.

'I see you've acquired a small following of your own!' he remarked.

'I hope I'm not taking a liberty, sir,' said Murray, 'but I remembered that you helped a party of Irish people before.'

'Quite right, quite right,' said Herkless genially, casting an eye over the group. The leading man moved forward immediately.

'May the good Lord bless you and all your household, sir!'

'I'm sure he will,' said Herkless with absent irony. 'If you follow the path round to the back of the house, you'll find the kitchens – there will be food and a bed for the night, if you wish it.'

'Ah, sir, you're a saint on this earth and a true gentleman!' cried the man, waving his hands expressively. The others echoed his sentiments, and Murray watched as they all trooped off round the corner of the house, the woman and the dark-haired man taking care to be amongst the thickest of the crowd.

'It is very good of you to help them like this,' he said to Herkless. 'It must be difficult to find space to put up so many so often.'

'Ah, well, if you're interested I shall show you how we do it,' said Herkless, turning his horse back towards the house. He led Murray along the path where the Irish had already gone: at the back of the house there were the usual kitchen entrances, and a separate door set into the wall of the building which seemed thicker than the average house door. Herkless looped his horse's reins over a nearby bush, produced a large key from his pocket and applied it to the keyhole.

'No doubt you have something like this at your own house,'

he said, ushering Murray inside, 'the concomitant of acting as a local magistrate. Well, we don't use them very often, for there is not much crime in Kirkwelland - or there wasn't before you came to visit us! – so I can offer the cells to these passing bands of peasants.'

Inside was a set of steps leading down to a dark and narrow corridor, where the only light seemed to be from small unglazed windows set high in the three cells on the right hand side. Their doors stood open, and inside were fresh mattresses and blankets, neatly folded, and evidence of recent fires. Three more cells lined the left hand side, but they were windowless and smelled damp. No cell was more than six feet square, though the ceilings were high, but no doubt it was better than sleeping in a ditch.

'Hot broth tonight and porage in the morning and they go upon their merry way,' Herkless explained. 'It costs little, and if I am honest it encourages them to go on out of the village and not help themselves to anything else on their way. Coulter and I arranged it, so there is sometimes help from the poors fund, too, to see them off.'

'Worthy on all counts, then – peasants helped and village protected,' said Murray.

'Everybody is happy,' Herkless nodded with a grin. Murray pursed his lips, remembering the woman in the crowd.

'Do you often see the same people returning?'

'Returning?' Herkless stepped into the nearest cell to tidy a blanket.

'Yes ... There's a woman in this party I'm sure I saw the day of Newell's funeral. She was very talkative that day, but she's quieter today – almost as if she were hiding.'

'Seems strange. Why would she come round again?' He turned back to Murray and spread his hands wide. 'I don't think this accommodation is that appealing.'

'Perhaps she had to return to Stranraer for some reason,' said Murray. 'There's a man with her, too, that I thought I recognised, but now I'm not so sure.'

'I suppose you didn't see them for very long on the day of Newell's funeral. Poor Innes was keen to be rid of them, as I remember. Now, Kitty's in the house, I believe – I want to catch Thomson before he leaves the village again, so if you'll excuse me

…'

'Of course – Thomson was heading down to the tannery, but he's left his horse at the manse so he'll have to come back for it.'

'Perfect, thank you.' They climbed back out of the little jail, and Herkless unwound his horse's reins, remounting smoothly. 'Perhaps you'll still be here when I return? No doubt we shall meet again soon, anyway.'

'Sir,' Murray bowed, and Herkless tipped his hat and rode off. Murray returned to the front of the house as if drawn by a string, and rang the bell.

'Mr. Murray!' Kitty seemed gratifying pleased to see him when he was announced at the parlour door: she and Anna Pringle rose and curtseyed. Anna was still pale, not the creamy pale that usually went with her stunning red hair, but a greyish, mournful colour. Kitty beside her glowed. 'I was just persuading Miss Pringle to take a turn with me in the garden, Mr. Murray. Will you join us? Or are you in urgent need of refreshment?'

'I can certainly survive a walk in the garden without starving,' Murray reassured her with a smile.

'Then let us go, by all means, before the rain starts.' Anna still seemed quiet and reluctant, but Kitty bustled round her, arranging her shawl around her thin shoulders and tying her bonnet strings in a neat bow. She prodded her gently towards the parlour door, managing to tie her own bonnet at the same time and flick a slightly pleading glance at Murray behind Anna's back. Murray held the door open for the ladies, then followed them outside.

'The formal gardens or the lawns, Mr. Murray?' Kitty asked over her shoulder, catching her shawl as the breeze snatched it.

'The wind is a little fresh,' said Murray. 'Perhaps the formal gardens today?'

'Of course.' A moment's walk brought them to the shelter of the pretty walled garden they had wandered through on the day of the picnic. Out of the wind, the temperature was noticeably higher. Murray wondered if Herkless monitored it here, too.

Three was an awkward number, he decided, as they began a slow perambulation of the gravelled paths. He could have a private conversation with neither girl: he would have liked to ask Anna Pringle more about Adair and Newell's attempts at blackmail, and he would very much have liked to speak about much less, and much more, important things with Kitty, but neither could be accomplished in this situation. He walked a few paces behind them on a narrower part of the path, eyes on Kitty's black curls and neat figure, reflecting on how unalarmed he had been at Herkless' assumption that he had come to ask for Kitty's hand. A misunderstanding like that would usually have sent him running for the hills, in the days when he had been free before his marriage. He was interested to find himself almost ready for another marriage: he would have expected to have been scared off the whole institution. But would Kitty wait until he could reasonably ask her?

'Mr. Murray,' she called back to him, moving aside to let him walk with them as the path widened. 'Have you had any further news of your little girl?'

'I had a letter this morning,' said Murray, with a grin. 'She was perfectly well when it was written, except that she cannot understand why her new kitten cannot share her bed with her at night.'

'You seem so happy when you speak of her,' said Anna wistfully. 'She must mean a great deal to you.'

'Daughters always mean a great deal to fathers, do they not?' asked Kitty, secure in her father's affections. Anna was less convinced.

'To your father, I am sure,' she agreed. 'But as for mine ... When I saw them together in the woods after the picnic, it struck me so clearly how fine your father is, Kitty. Mine, alas – I do not believe anybody likes my father, or even respects him as he feels they ought.'

'Well ...' said Kitty, not quite sure how to respond to this except with the painful truth. 'Oh!' she said suddenly, 'Look at the stableyard clock! It is past four already! Anna, did your father not say you would have to be home by four?'

'Oh,' said Anna mournfully, 'for once my father will not be angry. His mood has been so cheerful these last few days that I hardly recognise him. Would that – that I still had a reason to wish him cheerful, for if he had been like this before then my Jamesie – my Jamesie could have gone to speak with him with some hope of success!' She pressed her lips hard together, but tears still began to trickle down her pallid cheeks. Kitty regarded her helplessly, and caught Murray's eye.

'Perhaps I should walk you home safely, Miss Pringle,' said Murray quickly, knowing from the twinkle in her eye that he had read Kitty correctly. 'I suspect you have overtired yourself in these last few days.'

Anna managed a small smile as she sniffed and wiped her eyes.

'Thank you, Mr. Murray: it has been a very difficult time, whatever my father thinks.'

He gave Anna his arm, and bowed to Kitty. Mr. Pringle was a most unsympathetic character, he thought. And was it Adair's death that had made him so cheerful?

'I met another party of Irish peasants today. There do seem to be a great number of them passing this way, don't there?'

'Was Thomson with you when you met them?' Coulter asked. He seemed a little breathless.

'No, we had gone our separate ways, he to the tannery. I was outside here when they passed. A shilpit gathering, I'm afraid: I was worried that one of them might steal Thomson's horse.'

'You think they are not honest, simply because they are poor?' snapped Coulter, glowering suddenly at Murray.

'No! Not at all!' Murray was taken aback. 'I've known plenty of poor and honest people – and rich and dishonest ones, too, if it comes to that. It was just a couple of the young lads had that way of constantly moving around that distracts you from what they're really up to – haven't you noticed it in others?'

'I don't know what you mean,' said Coulter, sulkily. 'I have always found them perfectly honest, except when their needs are greatest.'

Hm, thought Murray, but he had no particular wish to provoke his friend further.

'Anyway, I took them up to Kirkwelland House, and the laird received them very hospitably. He showed me the quarters where they can sleep: he has made them very comfortable, I think.'

'And you feel they do not deserve that, do you?' asked Coulter.

'I never said that! You are both clearly doing your Christian duty. I wonder, though,' he added, for he did not like to think that his friend's Christian duty might be taken advantage of, 'if some of them do not find it too comfortable here.'

'What do you mean?' Coulter's question was low and wary.

'There was a woman in the group, older, with a red shawl and a pack that had been patched in orange. I am positive that she made one of the group that approached Innes after Newell's funeral, just outside the kirkyard.'

'What if she did?'

'It's just – what was she doing here again? Surely they are all passing through on their way to Glasgow to find work, not wandering up and down the coast in perpetuity living off innocent charity?'

Coulter sprang from his chair, face flushed.

'And what if she is? What business is it of yours? Who asked you to concern yourself in our affairs, whether feeding the poor or trifling with murders?'

'Good heavens, Coulter, I had no intention of upsetting you so, and I very much regret it. I had no idea you had so much concern for these people.'

Coulter breathed in and out several times, sharply, through his nose, before speaking again.

'It was a matter very dear to my darling Bessie's heart,' he said, with an effort. 'It was something we always did together, tending to the Irish peasants, seeing them safely on their way.'

'I see,' said Murray, gently. 'Then of course you are much affected by it. What a legacy to leave behind, the memory of such charity.'

Coulter nodded abruptly, close to tears. His face was blotchy, his thin lips pressed tight, and he looked away, down at the carpet. Murray frowned. He was not quite satisfied that Coulter had told him everything on the matter. Strong emotions often went with vulnerability. Could there have been something in this over which Coulter himself could have been blackmailed? If so, should he ask him now, when he was upset anyway, or wait until a quieter time when he was almost certain to upset him again?

Distantly he was aware of a knock at the front door, and the footsteps of Mrs. Veitch going to answer it. There was silence in the parlour, punctuated only by Coulter trying to regain control over his breathing. In a moment, the parlour door opened, and Mrs.

Veitch came in.

'Ah, sirs, we have a visitor,' she said, curtseying even as she took in the atmosphere in the little room. 'Shall I show him in, sir? It's Mr. Nugent.'

'I came to clear my conscience,' said Nugent, with his head bowed.

'Clear it of what?' asked Coulter, sitting neatly in the opposite chair at the parlour table. Murray remained standing by the fireplace. Coulter had recovered well, presumably a useful technique in a minister required to deal with other people's problems in the midst of his own. If he looked self-assured, Nugent did not. The confrontational student did not seem to have slept for several nights, though he and his friends had only left the village yesterday. He clutched his hands together on the table, as though forcibly preventing himself from fidgeting. The knuckles were yellow.

'Of ... of the hatred I felt for Jamesie Adair. It's not right, so it's not. I should never have let it grow so bad.'

Coulter said nothing, and Murray followed his example. Nugent was there to talk, and he would – in his own time.

Nugent breathed out heavily through his nose at last, and filled his chest again.

'You'll have heard of the Rebellion? Back in 1798?'

Murray and Coulter both frowned: they would have been young men at the time, at university, but both remembered one or two Irish students who had been much affected by it. They nodded.

'Aye,' Nugent acknowledged their uncertainty. 'The Irish are dead good at remembering things like that. Too good, usually.' He sighed. 'The United Irishmen wanted independence and as a part of that they wanted all the troubles between the Presbyterians and the Episcopalians and the Catholics all over with – all the bad memories washed away, a clean slate. But it was mostly students from Trinity – Trinity College, Dublin, that's all Episcopalian - that started it all, and the Presbyterians were agin rebellion of any kind. The North was divided, so it was, with Belfast the place the rebels called home, and Derry gone the other way. Well, even in the Presbyterians there were rifts. My own father was a minister – he had a good congregation, a first class one.'

'That means he had a good share of the King's bounty, is that right?' asked Coulter quietly. Nugent nodded, and Coulter half-turned to Murray. 'The King's bounty, the Regium Donum, is there to encourage the Presbyterian ministers to settle in Ulster. Some of the congregations couldn't survive without it.'

'Aye, that's right. He was in Hillsborough, a wee village in County Down. A prosperous place, these days, and all.'

'Is that not where Adair was from?' asked Murray.

'Aye,' said Nugent, with a grim look. 'It was. His father's a big merchant there, in the linen, oh, aye, very nicely off. And he and my father had been friends until this whole thing happened. But my father had been sickened for years with the troubles between the Episcopalians and us, never mind the Papists: we're all the sons of God, he said, and acknowledge Him as our Father, wherefore should we be fighting all the time? Ach, the church was awful political in those days anyway.

'Well, the rebellion was not a success, as you might recall, and my father was all set to get out of Ireland and off to America with a couple of his pals who had fought at the Battle of Ballynahinch. There were ships in Belfast harbour he'd get on to, no question, but he was betrayed at the last minute, and he was hanged.'

'Hanged!'

'Aye, that's right. He was hanged, with his two pals. He never did more than sympathise with them.'

There was a silence. It was over seventy years since there had been civil unrest like that in Scotland, yet it could be happening just the other side of the sea they could see from the window, in this young man's lifetime. Hangings happened, of course, but not with this wholesale feeling of disposal, like a scaffie sweeping the street.

'My mother told me all about it when I turned twelve,' Nugent said eventually. It seemed as if the words were being squeezed out of him. 'My mother's a saint. She loved my father, but she remarried when I was a wean, moved away from Hillsborough to Portaferry by the lough, with a man, a schoolmaster, who could rare me and my brother, and in due course my wee sister, too. When she told me, it was to warn me of what comes of religious division, of hatred, of betrayal. She told me who had told the soldiers about my father and his pals – and it was Mr. Adair,

Jamesie's father. She said he hadn't meant to, that he was a kind man in himself who had his own problems, that it just slipped out, but however she meant me to take it, I took it ill. She wanted me to train for the ministry, to go to Glasgow like my father before me, and I did – my stepfather agreed but we had to save the money, and so it chanced that though I was later going to college than some, I matriculated on the same day as Jamesie Adair from Hillsborough, and of course my ears pricked up.

'Jamesie Adair from Hillsborough: a handsome, decent creature, well off, with a loving father that was paying his fees. I hated him.

'Aye, right enough, I deserve it when they call me Ishmael. Ishmael was Abraham's son by Hagar, the concubine, aye? The one the Lord said would be a wild ass of a man, with his hand against everyone, and everyone's hand against him, and he shall live at odds with all his kin. That's what I've been like all my life, and it's nobody's fault but my own. And I've spent the last four years at Glasgow college, angry and resentful, making no friends, with only McCullough and Gibson that would tolerate me, and hating Jamesie Adair the way other folks might love, with nearly my whole being. It has sucked the energy from me day by day, and blackened the very soul of me, and if I died this night the Devil himself could claim me as his own.

'And then I realised that he was a drinker.

'It took me long enough, for for a long time I just thought he was determined to spend his father's money and enjoy his freedom, but at last I realised that he couldn't remotely help it. He was just wearing away. And yet, even when the man was halfcut and making little sense, and we had to carry him from our lodgings to give the landlady a bit of peace, yet he was always – decent, d'you see? I finally had to admit that he had his problems, but even with them he was a better man than I would ever be. He only had to smile at you and you felt the world was a better place, and though he was a drunkard he still did his work and read his books and studied as hard as he could, where I was so busy devouring myself with hatred for him that I couldn't concentrate half the time, imagining his father and my father, imagining how I might do something that would injure him as much as he had injured me.' His eyes grew distant, remembering himself and Adair, years wasted in destructive emotions when they could have been friends.

'So,' said Murray carefully, 'what are you trying to tell us? You hated Adair – did you kill him? Did you kill Newell hoping that Adair would be blamed?'

'I knew you would think that,' said Nugent, his shoulders sagging. 'I can only say that I didn't do either – but Newell did try to blackmail me, seeing how much I hated Adair, thinking there might be more to it that he could get me for. I think he chanced his arm with near everyone. But you can't blackmail someone for just how they feel, and I never did anything to Adair, I never. I just needed to tell you ...'

Murray watched the big hands as they clenched together, the shoulders hunched again, as if expecting a blow, the bowed head. If Nugent was guilty, why would he have come back to Kirkwelland? Unless, as he said, he was trying to clear his conscience, in which case why not confess? The only logical conclusion was indeed that he had not killed Adair, and there did not therefore seem to be a motive for him to have killed Newell. He frowned. The man's tension was almost palpable, much more than could be expected from a penitent awaiting forgiveness. There was something more, something he had not yet told them.

'The day Jamesie died,' said Murray, 'you were on the edge of the little ravine.'

'I was fascinated by the rocks, the geology,' murmured Nugent. 'I always loved natural philosophy – much more than divinity, to tell you the truth.'

'But there was more than rocks to be seen, wasn't there?' Murray persisted. 'You were there at the edge, while just downstream Adair fell - or was pushed - over the edge, weren't you?'

'I couldn't see him,' said Nugent, staring at the tablecloth. 'There was bushes and things in the way.'

'So you didn't see him. Did you perhaps hear him?'

There was a long pause.

'I might have.'

'What did you hear?'

'I heard someone talking to him. Someone arguing with him.'

'Just before he fell?'

'Well, it must have been, mustn't it?' Nugent looked up, cross that his information was being challenged. 'I've said before he was a decent fellow. How many people could he argue with in the one afternoon?'

'Well, he had already argued with McCullough, and it wasn't him because I quite clearly saw McCullough and Gibson by the stile all that time,' Coulter put in, as if he had spent some time considering it.

'It wasn't McCullough!' Nugent shouted suddenly. 'And it wasn't Gibson. And it wasn't me, either. It was Mr. Pringle.'

Chapter Twenty-One

'Do you believe him?'

'That he's innocent, or that Pringle killed Adair?'

'Well, either.'

Nugent had been packed off to bed, exhausted, with a bowl of Mrs. Veitch's broth inside him. Coulter and Murray, their earlier dispute forgotten in the face of this new information, sat comfortably by the fire in the parlour as they had before, wondering what to make of it.

'I think he's innocent of the murder. He seemed angry enough with himself for not going to Adair's aid when he heard the quarrel.'

'True, I think that will weigh on his conscience for some considerable time,' Coulter agreed. 'But I wondered if he hated Adair enough to kill Newell and have Adair blamed, and would have perhaps pushed Adair over the cliff himself if Pringle had not done it first?'

'Dear me!' said Murray. 'I think you have been spending too much time with me discussing murders: that is a devious theory indeed! No, I think if he had killed anyone he would have taken his opportunity to leave Kirkwelland, sail across the sea and never think of the matter again. He feels guilty enough about not helping Adair and perhaps preventing his death, but now he has told us, he will feel better, I think.'

'He did seem as if a weight had been lifted from his shoulders,' Coulter agreed. 'I shall ask Herkless if he will take Nugent and me into Stranraer tomorrow in his gig. Nugent can make his deposition to Thomson and I can set him on his way.'

'I should like to come too, if I can,' said Murray. 'If Herkless will lend us the gig again I can drive and save the laird the journey.'

'I cannot imagine that Stranraer has that many attractions for you!' said Coulter, startled. 'I'm sure Herkless will be perfectly happy to take us.'

'The place still has a novelty for me,' said Murray, 'and I should like to see Thomson again myself.'

'Really?' Coulter seemed unconvinced. 'I should have thought you would have been pleased enough not to see him at all for a few days.'

'No doubt if we do not beard him in his den he will be back up here interrogating us about Nugent's appearance,' said Murray, wondering at Coulter's apparent reluctance to take him to Stranraer. 'We might as well get it over with. I'm sure Thomson will be back up here looking for his imagined French invaders again all too soon, but at least we can spare his poor horse one visit.'

'Well, there is that,' Coulter acknowledged at last. 'Very well: if Herkless will lend us the gig, you can drive Nugent and me there in the forenoon. But it is Saturday, so we shall need to be back in good time for me to write my sermon.'

'And to attend the Mutual Improvement Society's meeting: I have promised Walter he may go, but I'd like to see what he's learning.'

'You approve of educating your servants, then?' asked Coulter, pleased.

'All my servants can read and write,' said Murray proudly. 'Most can add figures.'

'I'm delighted to hear it,' said Coulter with a warm expression. 'There is no benefit in keeping the working classes ignorant, whatever some may say about revolution.'

'Young Walter, however, is displaying an aptitude for science - more of an aptitude for science, to be truthful, than for any aspect of service. Quite apart from any ideals of universal education, which I know you are keen on, there is the practical question of settling people where they can be most useful. What could Walter do with science? Not, I imagine, shave me any better or remember where he left my hair brushes. Perhaps he could concoct better fertilisers for my lands, or advise me on the breeding of my cattle.'

'Ah, no, you need to consult Mr. Pringle on that kind of thing!' said Coulter with a grin.

'Ah, yes: Mr. Pringle.' Both their faces grew abruptly solemn again. 'Now, what are we going to do about that?'

They had talked over the several aspects of the matter long after supper, vaguely aware of Mrs. Veitch locking the front door and the other soft sounds of the house being settled for the night. The effect on Mrs. and Miss Pringle, the options if Pringle were not guilty after all, the possibility of Thomson's partiality in the matter, all were turned over and considered, but they were both tired and Murray felt he was not giving the facts his best analysis. He decided not to disturb Walter when he retired upstairs, but washed his face and hands in cold water and contemplated the village from his unshuttered window. The sea, glimpsed between the houses, glinted in the moonlight like mercury.

Could Pringle have murdered both Adair and Newell? He was confident enough for a killer, full of his own importance. Murray had noticed in the past that many killers shared that same focus on the paramount virtues of their own interests. No one had mentioned seeing him near Newell's cottage on the day of Newell's death – and Murray could not quite see him clambering over the wall from the field behind the cottage with a stone jar of whisky, as he had pictured the murderer doing. But he need not have done so – he would certainly have attracted attention if he had done.

His motive? Presumably Newell had approached him about Anna Pringle and her assignations with Adair on the headland. Would Pringle have considered paying him blackmail? Would he have thought even a preliminary payment, while he thought the problem over, beneath his dignity? He was not the most intelligent of men, Murray reminded himself. But of their suspects, he was certainly one that Murray could easily see resorting to poison, out of sight, out of mind, rather than bringing Newell down in a moment of physical violence. Though if he had then pushed Adair over the cliff … And where had Anna been while her father was quarrelling with Adair? Was this before or after she had reappeared from the woodland?

He wished that he and Coulter had not been down in the ravine at this point. What might they have observed, if they had been back in the picnic field? But then surely Adair had fallen before they went down there? He swore mildly, theories swirling in his head.

Where would Pringle have obtained the mercury? And the whisky? He might have bought both in Stranraer a month ago, and saved them for the appropriate opportunity. He had no particular reason to rush as long as he kept up payments, presumably. There was no danger of Newell making anything public while he still thought he could make money out of it. But would Pringle really have killed him to stop him revealing such a small thing? Adair was a respectable man, whatever Pringle thought: the village as a whole would have heartily approved a match between Anna and a well-to-do, well-educated Irishman of whom they were all quite fond. Even if there was a suspicion that the two young people had anticipated the wedding, which there did not seem to be, no doubt a little pressure could be applied to bring the business forward: there was no need to do more than send Newell packing with confirmation of the wedding date.

But then Adair had asked to be released from whatever understanding there had been between him and Anna – presumably because he knew his drinking would make Anna unhappy. Such a motive fitted in with his reputed kindness, certainly. But would Pringle understand such a request? If Anna was not to marry a decent student passing through the village, where was she to find a suitable husband, anyway?

So many people did seem to pass through Kirkwelland, back and forth. His mind wandered back to the Irishwoman he had seen passing through twice. Had she simply had to return down the coast for some reason? Or was she trying to live off the charity of the parishes she passed through? Murray imagined that not all of them were as generous as Kirkwelland. If she was innocent, why had she appeared to be trying to hide from him? Particularly when she had been so outgoing the previous time? Perhaps that was just because she knew her behaviour looked odd, and thought that as an Irish peasant she might be suspected of all kinds of devilment. Was it simply a vicious circle?

His eye was caught by the shadow of a movement outside in the lane. He pulled back a little into the shade of the narrow window, and focussed on it. A figure was making its way cautiously, flickering between moonlight and darkness, along the

lane from north to south. Who on earth would be out at this hour?
It was a short, bulky figure, and after a moment he realised that it
was a small man carrying a pack over his shoulder. Not, then,
presumably, someone out for a midnight stroll, or slipping back
from an evening's drinking. As the figure slowly approached the
manse's garden gate, he finally had a good chance to see the face
in profile. He had seen it before ... of course. It was the little dark-
haired man who had been so careful to walk amongst the thickest
parts of the crowd of Irish he had taken up to Kirkwelland House
earlier. Another man heading back down the coast again? But why
would he go before he had had the chance to take full advantage of
the laird's hospitality?

He watched the figure slip through the shadows past the
manse and the kirkyard gate, and along the lane. As soon as he
could, he slid the sash window open quietly, and leaned out to see
where the man was going. The man paid no attention to the church
or any of the cottages on the shore side of the lane, stepping
slowing and deliberately straight ahead. Past the church the lane
dipped to the crossroads where the road to Gourlay's farm crossed
the bridge and rose to the left and another lane led down towards
the shore. The figure disappeared into the dip, the moonlight
giving a strange, liquid impression as if he were sliding into water.
The lane was visible again beyond the dip, heading on to meet the
Stranraer road, and Murray waited, braced against the windowsill,
for the figure to reappear on it. He held his breath, blinking to keep
his eyes focussed, but no figure appeared.

Where had he gone? Up towards Gourlay's farm, or down to
the shore?

He hesitated a few more minutes, then gave up, sliding the
window closed. He had wondered before where the road past
Gourlay's farm went to: tomorrow he would have to find out.

Coulter had sent a note up to Kirkwelland House the previous
evening, and after an early breakfast with Nugent, who was
naturally not ebullient, they were pleased to see the groom appear
with the gig and horse. Nugent strapped his belongings to the rack
at the rear, and they arranged themselves on the seat, a little more
cramped than the last time. The groom looked on as anxiously as
before as they set off and the horse seemed to notice the difference,

too, putting her head down to press her shoulders into the weight.

They passed down the lane and into the dip by the crossroads.

'Where does that road go?' Murray asked. 'I mean, after the turn-off to Gourlay's farm? I keep meaning to ask.' He had decided not to mention the mysterious figure in the night: there were things about the Irish peasants, he had finally acknowledged, that seemed to set Coulter's teeth on edge.

'Towards Newton Stewart,' said Coulter easily enough. 'Then you could go on to Dumfries from there.'

'They're both on the London road, aren't they?'

'Aye,' said Nugent, 'the one that comes into Stranraer. That's the one the soldiers all come in and out on, on their way to Ireland.' He made a face. 'Sorry: the soldiers always remind me of my father.'

And indeed the soldiers were very much in evidence in Stranraer itself, the last biggish town before Portpatrick. The roads were blossoming with redcoats, an English regiment, as far as Murray could see, from their white facings, but not one whose badge he recognised. It seemed that as they had arrived on the Saturday morning, footsore and eager to be rid of their packs, the officers had decided they would be billeted there until after the Sabbath and were demanding accommodation accordingly. They were lucky to slip the gig into the stableyard of the Star behind a quartermaster as he argued with the stableboy, and the laird's mare was the last horse into the stables. They stayed long enough to see her settled with hay and water, then betook themselves, Nugent with a look of unhappy determination on his face, to the townhouse to find Thomson.

Thomson was not in: a lad had been crushed when one of the heavy military wagons had been backed injudiciously into a wall, one of the clerks explained, but even as they were wondering whether or not to wait Thomson reappeared, glinting in the doorway with one leg in the building and one out. When he saw Nugent his face soured like a man unexpectedly finding he was sucking a lemon.

'What is it about you lot?' he demanded by way of greeting. 'Can you no leave a body in peace? Is there something wrang with your ain country that every time you say you're ganging back to it, you bounce back here like a gowfball off a stane dyke?'

'Mr. Nugent has returned with some information about Mr. Adair's death,' said Coulter politely.

'Aye?' Thomson maintained a hostile expression. 'Adair threw himself into that place, ken.'

'But just before that, he was heard quarrelling with Mr. Pringle,' said Murray. Was it his imagination, or did both clerks stop writing suddenly? In an instant they were both scribbling away again: it was impossible to tell.

'I heard him,' said Nugent, pulling himself upright. 'I heard them quarrelling. Violently.'

'And why have you no said anything about this afore?'

Nugent reddened.

'I had no great friendship for Jamesie Adair, for an old reason, and but for that I should have gone to help him against such threats. But I did not go to his aid, and he is dead, and it is on my conscience.'

'Threats? I thought you said it was a quarrel?'

'Mr. Pringle said he would make Adair pay for what he had done to Pringle's daughter.'

Thomson regarded him for a long moment.

'It bears investigating, don't you think?' Murray suggested.

Thomson flicked him a disparaging glance, and presented his stubby fingers to illustrate his thoughts.

'One, I ken my job, thank you for your kind advice. Two, if this fellow had "no great friendship" for Adair, who's to say he didn't tip the man over the edge himself? Three, if he's speaking the truth, it's no proof that Mr. Pringle – who is a fine, upstanding gentleman and a man who has taught me a great deal about the law – did the deed. Four, if he did happen, in a quite justifiable attempt to protect his daughter's honour, tip that drunkard over the edge, I'm not even sure it counts as a crime. And five, Adair threw himself into the ravine after killing Newell and I canna see how any of this helps with that at all.'

'Adair was not a suicide!' cried Coulter, upset. 'If he had been the means of Newell's death, I am certain he would have admitted it, not killed himself.'

'And he'd never have given Newell whisky,' said Nugent. 'He'd have drunk it - mercury and all, probably,' he added more quietly.

'It's the only answer that fits the facts,' said Thomson, quite unperturbed.

'Oh, come on, Nugent: there is no point in this,' said Coulter. 'You have tried your best. Your conscience is clear.'

'It's not really,' Nugent objected. 'I should have gone to help him. That's never going to be clear.'

'But this man can't help with that, can he?' Coulter was already halfway out of the door.

'Just a second,' said Murray, but Coulter was gone. Nugent hung at the doorway, half waiting for Murray, half watching Coulter. After a moment he disappeared into the street, and Murray turned back to Thomson.

'I think you're wrong,' he began cheerfully, 'but on another matter – why do you search up the coast for possible French insurgents?'

'Because we're told they're here, coming through from Ireland,' said Thomson, as though to an idiot.

'I realise that, but why up the coast? Where do the powers that be think they are going?'

Thomson opened his mouth, then shut it again, frowning.

'Well,' he said more slowly, 'they might be going to Glasgow. See, you'll ken we have a wheen of Irish peasants and all kinds passing through here and going north for work. I think the thinking is that the French could be following the same path.'

'But what would they be doing there? Would they not be better to travel south, into England?'

'Well ...'

'And if they did, they'd probably be best heading for Carlisle, wouldn't they?'

'I suppose ...'

'I'll leave that thought with you, Mr. Thomson,' said Murray. 'Oh, and what did you mean when you said that Pringle had taught you about the law?'

Thomson's face cleared.

'Mr. Pringle is a very fine lawyer, and he has been kind enough to take me under his wing in an – informal – apprenticeship, with a view to me taking over his clients when he retires.'

'I see – how generous he is. No wonder you are so supportive of him. Well, I'll bid you good day, sir.'

In the street, unexpectedly, he found Nugent waiting.

'No wonder he's keen to defend Pringle: Pringle's putting him in the way of a prosperous change of living,' said Murray sourly. 'Where's Coulter gone?'

'He said he'd meet you back at the Star later,' said Nugent. 'Do you think I've wasted my time, sir?'

'No,' said Murray thoughtfully. 'I don't think so. I may be wrong but I'm not happy with Thomson's attitude to this. Telling Thomson may have been a waste of time but I hope that telling us has not been. Now, is there anything else you need to do or shall we set you on your way again?'

'McCullough and Gibson are at Lochans, sir – it's a wee place a few miles south. It's cheaper than staying in Stranraer, particularly when the soldiers are on the move.'

'I'll walk to the end of the town with you, then,' said Murray, and took Nugent's pack again. 'It's good of them to wait for you.'

'They're in no hurry to get home, the two of them,' said Nugent, with the lightest touch of significance.

'McCullough seems to take very good care of Gibson.'

'He does ... Adair used to say that between them they would make the perfect parish minister: Gibson to preach and lead the way to God, and McCullough to tend the flock as they follow Gibson.'

'I can see his point.'

They set off. The morning was pleasant enough and the soldiers did not seem to have penetrated so deeply to this side of the town. They quickly left the narrow streets for country lanes, and fewer buildings to either side, and found themselves out in farmland to the south. Now Nugent had talked of his past, he seemed eager to spill everything out, and he told Murray in detail about his childhood by the side of Strangford Lough, watching the little ferries cross from the tip of the Ards Peninsula to the main Down coast, the fishing boats in the lough, the leafy shores, and his day-to-day studies in his step-father's little classroom with the village boys. Murray half-listened, thinking about Thomson and Pringle, and what to do next. Before he thought about leaving Stranraer they were already at the modest hamlet of Lochans, where McCullough and Gibson were waiting by the side of the road, sitting on a grassy bank in the faint sunshine. Behind them a tall meal mill groaned as it seemed to have done for a hundred years, wearily. McCullough rose with enthusiasm when he saw Murray, and Gibson eased himself to his feet.

'Good day to you, Mr. Murray, sir!' McCullough cried, waving his hat. 'I'm sorry you have to see our poor miserable faces again! But Nugent insisted, and I think he was quite right.'

'Yes, indeed he was,' said Murray with a grin. 'I'm not sure yet where it takes us, but I was very glad to have the information.'

'Well, we'll need to get on, then,' said McCullough, with a pat on Nugent's arm. 'They've asked Gibson to preach at Portpatrick tomorrow again, so I'd like to get there in good time for him to have a decent night's sleep.'

'And I'd better get back to Stranraer and find Coulter,' Murray agreed. 'I'll wish you once again a safe journey home.'

'Thank you, sir!' Nugent and McCullough bowed, and flung their packs up once again, McCullough with Gibson's, Nugent with Adair's. McCullough called Nugent over, adjusting one of Nugent's straps, leaving Gibson standing next to Murray. To Murray's astonishment, Gibson cleared his throat lightly, and spoke to him.

'You are not quite sure of us yet, are you, sir?'

'I'm prepared to believe none of you murdered Newell, or Adair,' said Murray, after a moment's thought. It was difficult to be anything other than honest to Gibson.

'No man is perfect. Only God is without fault.'

'Of course.' There was a thoughtful pause.

'Mr. Murray,' said Gibson, 'I've been praying over this. And what I would like to say to you, though it might not sound much, is this. Men do the wrong things for the right reasons.'

'Yes?'

'Aye, that's what it is. Men do the wrong things for the right reasons.' Gibson nodded, serious.

'Come on, now, Gibson, don't tire yourself out,' said McCullough, taking him by the elbow. Gibson nodded again, and then let himself be led away. Murray waved to them, and turned back to Stranraer.

It was not that long before he was back in the town again, and he headed straight for the Star, afraid that Coulter's patience might be wearing thin. But his friend was nowhere to be seen in the inn, and when he asked the serving maid with the lovely smile, she said he had not been seen that day. Murray went to check on the horse and the gig, worried that they might have been evicted by some bossy officer, and wondered where Coulter might have gone.

In the end he remembered the lane where he had left Coulter on their first visit together to Stranraer. He would have been visiting the Irish peasants there, the ones with whom he was helping the local minister. He hesitated. Coulter was very sensitive about the Irish peasants. Would it be better to leave him to get on with his work and simply await him patiently in the Star? Or would it go some way to reconciliation between them over this if he went to see Coulter at work, made an effort to understand what their needs were and how Coulter was trying to meet them?

He turned over the options, not eager to venture into the rough-looking area where Coulter said the Irish were constrained to stay, but at the same time reluctant to sit in a crowded inn fighting for space with army officers when his mind wanted to explore all his questions about Adair and Newell and Pringle. Herkless' mare was a sweet creature with a soft nose and an intelligent eye, and he stood with her for a long time, perhaps in the hope that Coulter would appear and the question would cease to be relevant. But in the end he sighed, gave the mare's nose a final pat, and stepped out into the street, turning back towards the dingy lane that Coulter had disappeared into on that first day.

At first he struggled to find it, but then he remembered seeing Norrie Pearce there, too, and that helped to fix the point for him. The alley was narrower and darker than he recalled, and he had to make himself walk confidently into it. Like many alleys, it began fairly well, with the back doors of shops facing the main street and the detritus that gathers around such commercial businesses, littering smooth slabs of old but well-cut stone. After a few strides, however, the slabs became more scattered, the mud thicker, the rubbish deeper and more unpleasant. The dogs and cats that lingered amongst it were thinner and dirtier, the hens less savoury. Laundry of an unclean appearance dangled above him across the lane, hopeless of either breeze or sunlight here. Children moved with suspicious purpose, while the adults sat in doorways, talking quietly across the lane, falling silent when they saw Murray approach. He pulled out a few pennies.

'I'm seeking a Mr. Coulter, a minister. Has anyone seen him?' he asked the nearest little group. A boy of about eight scuttled away as if Murray might snatch him off, and the adults shook their heads mournfully. They looked desperate, and starving. Why did they think things would be better here than they had been at home? Maybe at least Coulter's soup kitchen would nourish them on their way to find profitable work elsewhere.

'Do you know the man I'm speaking of?' he asked, dropping the pennies into the hand of a woman huddled in a red shawl on the step. She glanced up at him and for half a second her gaze flickered further down the alley.

'Ach aye, we do,' she said hoarsely. 'But he's never been here the day, sir.'

'All right, thank you.' He edged past them, and worked his way further down the alley. What was the doorway her eyes had found? The narrow one with traces of blue paint on the door, or the low one with a half door falling off its hinges? He tried the first one.

Inside was a narrow wooden staircase, which almost creaked as he looked at it. He stopped, listening intently. Somewhere he could hear Coulter's voice, he was sure. What was he saying?

Another voice replied, though whether Coulter and his friend were upstairs here, or through the thin wall in the house next door, was hard to tell. The other voice was a man's, low, hard to hear. What were the words? Murray concentrated hard, then suddenly caught Coulter's voice raised a little.

'On ne peut pas fermer la fenêtre?' he asked, as if he were trying to close it.

Murray's jaw dropped. Then he slipped quietly out of the house, made his way on down the lane to where it emerged on a track behind the houses, and found his way to the main street and the Star Inn. Why, he thought as he went, would Coulter be speaking French to an Irish peasant?

Chapter Twenty-Two

The inn was busy, with a brisk buzz that a distant part of Murray's mind recognised as the result of soldiers in town. There were no available private parlours – they had all been taken by the officers – so Murray found himself a space at the corner of a long table and when the serving maid appeared, he ordered a jug of wine, feeling like a student again. He hardly noticed when it appeared in front of him, his eyes fixed on something much further away, and the serving maid with her smile at the ready departed disappointed.

He should have seen it, he thought. Why had he not realised what was happening? He knew about Coulter's liberal sympathies, all that he and Bessie had supported in the way of reform and social advances over the years he had been aware of them. Even at university, Coulter had talked of Bonaparte and his military glories, but then so had quite a number of fashionable people, heads turned by the mysterious allure of the little Sicilian. Murray thought that he himself had supposed it a foolish notion of youth, something Coulter would grow out of, as they all at that time had ideas or habits best grown out of. To assist the Irish peasants, that was what he might have expected of Coulter, a charitable gesture, not necessarily a popular one, but work he saw needed to be done. Coulter had that commitment, that dedication, which Murray knew he himself lacked, to work devotedly for a cause however difficult it might be. But now Murray knew that Coulter was going further. He knew in his own heart that Coulter was hiding French – what? Sympathisers? Spies? Agitants? – in parties of Irish peasants, to see them safely out of Stranraer under Thomson's nose and as far as Kirkwelland. Then the next step seemed to be that they parted from the Irish and took the back road out of the village towards Newton Stewart, Dumfries and Carlisle, avoiding military movements on the toll road, and entering England from the north. In his mind's eye he saw again that dark figure striding along the lane, in and out of shadow, his pack on his back, and vanishing into the dip of the road.

He poured a cup of wine and swallowed it down quickly, hardly tasting it. Coulter seemed to be involved with the whole route, starting with his soup kitchen activities in Stranraer and going on to organising accommodation for the Irish parties in Kirkwelland. Did he know in advance that a Frenchman would be coming from Ireland, via Portpatrick presumably, or had he a set-up ready and waiting for any chance arrival? That woman he had seen, passing twice through the village – was she a kind of escort, travelling back and forth to help the French travellers as they came along the route? Presumably she would send them on their way in Kirkwelland and then spend the night innocently with the rest of the Irish party, then double back to Portpatrick ready to collect the next Frenchman. How many could there have been? Dozens? Hundreds? Surely not so many. How had he started? Innocently enough, perhaps. Murray suddenly remembered Gibson's odd words to him when he bade goodbye to the students in Lochans. 'Men do the wrong things for the right reasons,' he had said. Well, whatever his ideals, what Coulter was doing was against the law. The awful thought that had been lingering, waiting to pounce, at the back of his mind skipped to the forefront at last. If Coulter were breaking the law, had Newell found out? Was Coulter being blackmailed? Was he the 'gentry' that Newell was so proud of catching?

Another cup of wine followed the first, sharp and sweet. Coulter had been in the lane outside Newell's cottage on the morning of Newell's death. Murray had seen him there. He did not want to think it, but he had to: could Coulter have killed Newell? If he had done it, Murray had to admit that he would expect Coulter to use poison, perhaps even in the hope that it would not hurt. Well, that had not been the case with the mercury compound: Newell had died in agony. Could Coulter have done that to anyone? Murray doubted it, not deliberately, anyway. But he could have taken the mercury from the mutual improvement society's kist. No one would question the minister 'borrowing' something, would they?

Murray felt sick. He poured another cup of wine, and sipped it more slowly. If – he forced himself to consider it fully – if Coulter had killed Newell, could he also have killed Adair?

No, in that he was assuredly in the clear. He had been with Murray the whole time Adair was out of sight. And anyway, surely Pringle had killed Adair? Murray shook his head to clear it a little. Pringle ... Pringle had argued with Adair shortly before his death. Pringle had reason to argue with Adair, either because he believed that Adair was making advances to Anna Pringle, or because Adair had turned Anna down. The problem was, they only had one witness who claimed to have heard Pringle quarrelling with Adair, and while Murray found that person, Nugent, credible, Thomson did not and in any case was ill-disposed to think any harm of Pringle. They had no proof that, even if Pringle had quarrelled with Adair, he had pushed him over the edge. Without that proof, it seemed to Murray highly unlikely that Pringle would admit to anything untoward – even he could not be that stupid. And Thomson would not arrest him with anything less than full proof.

Similarly, he had no proof either that Newell had blackmailed Coulter or that Coulter had murdered the old man. He sighed, throwing his head on to his hands, his elbows propped on the slightly sticky fir table. What was he to do? There was still no evidence that Thomson's opinion was not the correct one: that Adair had killed Newell, whether accidentally or not, and thrown himself into the ravine in a fit of remorse.

He stopped, rubbed his eyes and frowned. Think about it, he told himself. How might Adair have killed Newell?

Everyone was agreed that Adair was much too kind to intend to murder Newell, so it must have been an accident. So how could Adair have accidentally poisoned Newell with mercury compound in his whisky? Adair could have bought the whisky and added the compound for reasons of his own. But where could he have bought the whisky? The only place in town that might sell it was Burns, and he denied it. Could he have stolen it? No one had reported whisky missing. Could he have stolen it from Newell? But then why would he have left it in Newell's cottage?

Could he have found it, already poisoned by someone else, for some other reason, up on the headland where Murray had met him that morning? Well, possibly: but then surely, knowing Adair, he would have drunk it himself, there and then, not brought it back to Newell's where there was a danger of McCullough finding him and taking the whisky from him. And if he had by some mischance poisoned Newell, why had he not admitted it? If he had killed himself because of remorse, why had he shown no sign of that remorse from Newell's death to his own? Nothing made sense. Murray was more and more sure that Adair had had nothing to do with Newell's death.

Could Norrie Pearce have done it? He had mercury compound, and he was being blackmailed by Newell. There were stone jars in his house that were very like the one the whisky had been in – but Murray imagined the same jars were in every house in the village. He was a bad tempered man, with a gun: would he have bothered poisoning Newell? Would he not rather have punched him, stabbed him or shot him? Lying in wait to attack Coulter had shown a degree of forward planning, but planning that still ended in fists and blades, not in poison.

His head was starting to go round a little. There was too little evidence, or too much: the mercury could have come from three separate places, four if one imagined Mrs. Black might have kept some of her late husband's stock; anyone could have entered Newell's house and left the whisky there while he was out that day, or he could have been given it while he was on the headland – no, he had not had it when Innes saw him climb back over the wall by his cottage; Adair's death and Newell's might be linked, or they might not. He had seen himself where one murder had led to another, not necessarily because they were intrinsically connected, but because the first murder had created the conditions necessary for the second one. There were no witnesses to Newell's murder. There was a smallish circle of people who might have had the chance to kill Adair, but the access through the woodland confused the issue. How many people other than the picnic party knew they were going to be there that day? How many people had a distinct motive to kill Adair, aside from any chance that he had found out something to do with Newell's death? Only Pringle, or Anna, surely. Or Nugent, and he had deliberately come back to tell them about his motive, thereby apparently ruling himself out.

Murray was so embroiled in all this circular reasoning that he was almost relieved to see Coulter's face at the inn door. Then he remembered that he had no idea what to say to Coulter, either, and took another large sip of the wine, gesturing to Coulter to join him. Whatever he said, it could not be said here, in the public room of an inn. Coulter sat and accepted a small cup.

'But remember, I still have my sermon to write!' he said cheerfully. 'How did matters end between Nugent and Thomson?'

'Unprofitably,' said Murray, thinking back. It seemed like days ago. 'Thomson is being tutored by Pringle in the law with a view to Thomson taking over when Pringle retires, so he is unwilling to hear any evil of his unofficial master. He is determined that Adair killed Newell and then himself. Coulter, I cannot see how Adair could have killed Newell even accidentally.'

'Tell me on the way,' said Coulter, draining his cup. 'This is no place for a conversation like this.'

'I agree.'

They went to see to the gig, which even in the time Murray had been waiting had inevitably been tucked into a corner of the stableyard behind a small mountain of military equipment. Fortunately the stableman had recognised it as belonging to Mr. Herkless and had at least seen to it that it was well-treated, but it took some time and a degree of pleading with a few passing redcoats to disinter it. The mare by contrast was very happy to see them again, and trotted out to ready herself for the journey home with all willingness.

Murray managed to spend most of the journey home outlining his argument that Adair must be innocent, and Coulter seemed finally convinced. Pringle, they agreed, was a knottier problem: unless Anna was willing to talk more to them about her father and her erstwhile lover, they had no more information to help them decide one way or the other, and no evidence with which to confront him. Murray suggested appealing to Pringle's conscience, but Coulter, world-weary clergyman, just laughed. A silence fell between them, broken only by the steady clop of the mare's hooves and the gritty roll of the gig's wheels, as they followed the coast road along the grey wrinkled shore of Loch Ryan back to Kirkwelland.

Murray left Coulter at the manse and drove the gig up to Kirkwelland House to return it to the laird. His head was clearing again, and the possibility of seeing Kitty was a pleasant one. The groom took the gig and the horse, casting a quick eye over the mare to check that she had not been taken advantage of in any way in her absence, and nodding to himself when he saw that she was happy.

Herkless must have seen him from the house, and came out to greet him outside the front door.

'Thank you again for the use of your gig,' said Murray with a smile.

'How was the eminent Mr. Thomson this time?' Herkless asked.

'He is resistant to the idea that Nugent might be a reliable witness.' He elaborated.

'Well, anyone with Pringle as their tutor is obviously steeped in reason and good sense,' Herkless admitted.

'It's true that even if what Nugent says is correct – which I believe is the case – it is no proof that Pringle did more than argue and leave him.' Murray sighed.

'But you are still convinced that Adair did not kill himself?'

'I'm convinced he did not kill Newell,' said Murray slowly. 'I think it still possible that he could have fallen off accidentally. He was, if not drunk, then at least unsteady.'

'Very true. Of course, that still leaves us with the problem of who killed Newell.'

'I know.' He sighed again. 'Perhaps with this puzzle I shall be forced to admit defeat. Yet I have a niggling feeling that there is something I have heard ... something that does not fit ...' He tried to catch the memory again in his mind, but it slipped away like quicksilver.

'Well, if you wish to challenge Pringle on the matter, here is your opportunity.' Herkless was gazing over Murray's shoulder. Murray turned. Pringle, followed at a pace by his wife, was hurrying up the drive towards them. 'That is not a speed consistent with his usual dignity,' Herkless remarked.

'Herkless! Herkless! Have you seen my daughter? Is she here?'

'I don't believe so,' said Herkless, 'but let me call for Kitty.' He stepped inside the house, gesturing them to follow.

'Is she missing?' asked Murray.

'We have not seen her since early this morning,' said Mrs.

Pringle quickly. 'She went out before breakfast and has not returned.'

Kitty appeared from the parlour, intelligent eyes wide.

'I haven't seen her at all today, but then I have only been as far as the garden. Could she be walking on the headland? I know she likes to walk there, especially since – especially when she wants to be alone.'

'The headland? Of course, of course,' said Pringle. 'I have just returned home to find her gone, so we came straight here hoping that she was with her good friend.' He bowed slightly to Kitty. 'But the headland – that makes sense. The silly girl has probably moped herself into a trance and not noticed the time.' Mrs. Pringle shot him a glance that should have hurt.

'Would you like some help looking?' asked Murray. 'I'm sure Mr. Pringle is right and she has just lost track of time.'

'Of course: I'll come too,' said Herkless. 'Let me fetch my hat and stick.'

'Should I come too?' asked Kitty.

'Best not, my dear,' said her father.

'Oh, if you wouldn't mind staying here, Kitty?' said Mrs. Pringle. 'In case she comes here?'

'Of course,' said Kitty, and set her hand on Mrs. Pringle's arm. 'I'm sure she'll turn up safe and sound, ma'am.'

Mrs. Pringle's smile was twisted, and she turned quickly and led the men back down the drive to the village, striding out in front of them. Pringle himself waddled in the rear, fast for him, but a drag to Murray and Herkless. Herkless fell back to encourage him, while Murray lengthened his stride and caught up with Mrs. Pringle.

'Mrs. Pringle, forgive me, but did Newell ever approach either you or your daughter? With a view to obtaining money from you?' he added in a low voice.

Mrs. Pringle gasped, but did not break her stride.

'Can't you leave that horrid man's death? I was never more glad to hear that someone had died.'

'But you cannot think that James Adair killed him, can you? And someone must have.'

'And did everyone a good deed.' She cast a glance behind her, but her husband and Herkless were out of clear hearing. 'Yes, yes, if you must know, Mr. Murray, Newell tried to extort money from me. He had seen me with – with a gentleman. We did not even touch: I do not know how he could tell there was anything amiss between us.' Words and glances, Murray thought. Newell was finely tuned to secrets.

'Was the gentleman Mr. Herkless?' Murray asked.

'Oh, do not ask me, Mr. Murray! I shall not name names!' But the flush that rose on her creamy face was not solely the result of her fast pace.

'Did you pay him?'

'A little. Just a little. I'm not – Mr. Pringle does not – '

'I understand. Mrs. Pringle, I am sorry to ask you such things, but as you said yourself if someone can kill once they can kill again. And the next person they kill might not be so deserving of death.'

She sniffed, though whether with emotion or disbelief it was hard to tell.

'It was – pleasant – to have someone appreciate me,' she said, almost inaudibly. 'It has not happened for a long time.'

Murray had nothing to say. Mrs. Pringle could only have his sympathies.

'What did your husband think of James Adair?' he asked after a moment.

'I don't believe he paid him any regard at all,' said Mrs. Pringle frankly. 'He has a low opinion of students.'

'But Anna was very fond of him.'

'Indeed she was.' She drew in a deep breath. 'If Mr. Adair had returned next year as a minister, or as an associate in his father's business, perhaps, no doubt my husband would have looked favourably upon him. It would only have taken a little time, I'm quite sure.'

'Even though he was a drunkard?'

'He was a respectable, well-to-do drunkard, Mr. Murray: my husband would only have considered that. Anna tells me that Mr. Adair himself tried to withdraw from their friendship because he knew his own failings, but Anna is foolish. She thought everything would be delightful, that such a little thing could make no difference to their love for each other. Poor girl.'

They had reached the Pringles' house, and were stopped by a

cry from Pringle behind them. He and Herkless hurried to catch up, Pringle panting and red.

'My dear, you would do well to go inside and wait. She may well be there already.'

'Then best to find out,' said Mrs. Pringle briskly, and opening the door she called for the maid. A few words were exchanged in the hallway, muffled by the outsized porch. Then Mrs. Pringle turned back, her hopes dashed again.

'No, no sign.' She swallowed hard.

'Then indeed stay here, madam, and we shall go and seek her,' said Herkless. 'No doubt we shall be back in half an hour with a very hungry young lady!' They exchanged the briefest of glances, and Murray turned quickly to Pringle, but he was propped against his own garden wall, catching his breath. Clearly, thought Murray, there was more to the relationship between Mrs. Pringle and Herkless than the laird had admitted, which was only gentlemanly.

'What was she wearing this morning, Mrs. Pringle?' Murray asked.

'She had her dark blue spencer on, over a light blue round gown, and a straw bonnet.'

'Dark blue spencer, light blue gown, straw bonnet. Right, we'd better get going,' he said. 'I think it might be going to rain.'

Indeed, pewter clouds had lined up above the loch, and gulls slashed white arrows against them, wheeling as if in anticipation of a storm. Pringle pushed himself away from the wall, and stood ready. Herkless adjusted his hat, and they set off.

The road up to the headland was sheltered, but they could already hear the wind rising around them.

'Where were you this morning?' Murray asked Pringle, to break the grim silence.

'Oh, I was with Mr. Gourlay all morning,' said Pringle primly. 'He is in the midst of making an important land purchase, and required my expert assistance for some hours.'

'I understand you are good enough to teach Mr. Thomson some of your skills,' said Murray.

'Mr. Thomson is a keen scholar when he meets with an accomplished teacher,' Pringle affirmed.

'He certainly made clear his sensibility of the honour you were conferring on him,' Murray agreed. He caught Herkless' eye and all but laughed out loud at his expression.

Despite Pringle's monumental pace they were soon at the top of the headland, holding their hats tightly.

'Surely she is not foolish enough to stay out in this weather?' Pringle demanded.

'She may have taken shelter in the woods,' said Herkless, struggling as the wind whipped his words. 'Perhaps she has turned an ankle, or something.'

They dived into the woodland, eager for the shelter themselves.

'Where might she have gone, though?' Murray asked, poking the undergrowth tentatively with his cane. It was as noisy in here as out exposed on the headland, for the wind was tossing and shaking the treetops above them.

'I'm not sure, though this is a popular path,' said Herkless, leading the way along a broadish gap between the trees. They walked slowly, examining every bush and hollow, and calling Anna's name. There was no sign.

'Perhaps we should take different paths,' suggested Murray, and the others agreed – partly, Murray thought, because Pringle was again lagging behind. They selected a direction each, and set off again. Murray could hear the occasional call from the other two, even above the wind. He peered around through the leaves. Dark blue spencer, light blue gown, straw bonnet. There was nothing but green and brown and the silver trunks of the birches. He moved on again. Dark blue spencer, light blue gown, straw bonnet. And that glorious red hair. Surely if she were anywhere near here she would have heard them or they would have seen her by now?

Dark blue spencer … Something caught his eye but when he concentrated he saw it was only Herkless, in his dark coat, somewhere up ahead. Light blue gown: there was nothing light blue up here today, not even the sky, which was growing more leaden by the minute. Straw bonnet … that was a more difficult colour to spot out of doors, in woodland. There were plenty of things not far from that colour – like that patch over there, he thought, focussing again. That looked remarkably like a straw bonnet. He moved closer. It looked like a straw bonnet because it was a straw bonnet, upside down and hanging by its ribbons from a bush. He called out, and Herkless came running, Pringle more slowly after him.

'Is this hers?' Murray asked, swinging it in their direction.

'It's a straw bonnet, anyway,' said Herkless, eyes darting about to see if there was anything else. 'Is it Anna's, Pringle?'

'It could be, well enough,' said Pringle, somewhat dismissively. 'What's it doing hanging there, if it is?'

'On a day like this it could have blown in here from somewhere else, though,' Murray muttered, even as he investigated the area around the bush. 'There's nothing else here.'

'Perhaps it's a start? A good sign?' suggested Herkless. 'She was startled by something, perhaps, and ran, and the bonnet was snatched off by the bush? Perhaps if we try this way ...' He pointed beyond the bush.

'Why don't you go that way, for you know the land better anyway,' said Murray, 'and I'll try my theory of the bonnet being blown into the woods. The wind is coming from that direction, I believe: I'll follow it back, as it were.'

'Very well,' said Herkless. 'Pringle?'

'I'll just wait here,' said Pringle, who was out of breath again. He found a log and laid his handkerchief over it, and perched on it with as much grace as he could muster. Murray and Herkless glanced at each other, nodded, and went their separate ways.

The path the wind had followed into the woods led Murray back on to the headland, not far from the rock from which he had several times admired the view over the loch. It was not so appealing today, growing misty and grey. The opposite side of the bay was a flat dark green, and the few fishing boats visible were scurrying for harbour. The sweep of the wind was knitted with gulls' cries.

He searched amongst the boulders there by the cliff edge, where the grass was short and sharp. There was no sign of Anna, until he came to almost the very lip of the cliff. Two round indentations cut into the sod, showing dark crescents of moist earth. He knelt beside them. It appeared very much like two heel marks, from boots of a size that would not seem out of place on Anna, though he had never paid any attention to her feet. He bit his lips together. Someone making these marks would have had their back to the sea, and would moreover have been leaning backwards.

His heart beating quickly, he lay flat on the turf beside the marks, and slid forward to see over the cliff without giving himself up to the mercy of the wind.

The cliff was not a smooth drop, and it took a moment before he could sort out the mixture of close-clinging plants and distant waves that cluttered his view. Then he saw movement amongst the foam nearest the shore, long, dark red tendrils, curling and stretching with every wave. An inch further, and he could see her face, staring up at him, but heedless of the water running over her from head to foot, shifting hair and dark blue spencer and light blue gown. Anna was dead.

Chapter Twenty-Three

His shout brought Herkless running and Pringle waddling after.

'She's down there. Mr. Pringle, I'm so sorry.'

Herkless peered over the edge warily.

'I had to lie down to see her, but she's there,' Murray explained.

'She must have lost all hope,' said Herkless sadly. 'Poor girl, poor girl.'

'Anna?' Pringle seemed stunned. 'Anna's down there? In the sea?'

'Partly,' Murray said. 'What's the easiest way down?'

'There's a path there.' Herkless pointed to the north of the headland, where a pebbly track led downwards towards the beach. 'It goes down to the shore and then you can turn back under the cliff.'

'Anna?' Pringle repeated. 'Anna's down there?'

'Sit down on that rock, Mr. Pringle. You look as if you're about to pass out.' Murray took him by the elbow. 'Herkless, do you think we can manage between us?'

'She's no weight, surely,' Herkless nodded. 'Murray's right, Pringle: stay here and we'll deal with this.'

Pringle sat heavily on the rock like a sack of grain. His face seemed to have lost consistency.

'Anna?' he said again.

'We'll fetch her body,' said Murray firmly, choosing his words deliberately to help Pringle take in the fact of his daughter's death. 'Stay here.'

Herkless led the way down the path, no more than a foot-width across in the sharp grass, brushing between gorse bushes quickly to avoid the prickles. It was steep and they were on the crunching shingle in a few minutes.

'This way,' said Herkless, needlessly. The headland from here was pretty, not a straight drop but ledged with shelves of scurvy grass and thyme and even the occasional gorse bush clinging to a corner. Could she not have caught one as she fell? She fell backwards: she would have seen the wall of rock pass her as she tumbled over. Or was she gazing at the grey sky instead? Did she have time to realise what was happening, or did it all happen too fast? Backwards: no one throws themselves off anywhere backwards, surely. Murray shook his head, trying to concentrate on where to put his feet on the scramble of rocks at the foot of the cliff.

'Here she is,' said Herkless flatly.

She lay, as Murray had seen, in a little inlet between the rocks, half in the water and half out, but the tide was rising. If they did not take her back now, she might be washed away. Her glorious hair spread like seaweed, her face pallid as the cockle shells on the beach, eyes still staring wide, hands floating light beside her as if calming them as they approached. Murray found his mind tangled between sorrow, and respect, and wondering how best to rescue the corpse from the greedy waves.

'If one of us wades in each side,' he suggested, 'and we take her up that way?'

'I can probably lift her on my own,' said Herkless. 'A shame to ruin two pairs of boots, and these are old ones.'

'Well …' Murray was torn. It made sense. 'Then if you lift her out, and we'll take her together up the hill. She's wet, she'll be heavier than she would be otherwise.'

'True. I'll lift her out, then, and if you take her arms and I'll take her ankles … It doesn't seem right, does it, but Pringle couldn't do it even if he was in his right mind, which I suspect he isn't just now. And you go first up the hill – you could face forwards to watch your step, couldn't you, and still hold her under the arms?'

'I think so. It would be awkward to fall with her.'

'Right.' Herkless skirted round a rock to the little inlet. Only Anna's calves and feet still remained on the patch of shingle, edging now towards the loch with every insistent wave. He stepped into the water beside her, paused slightly, stooped to close Anna's eyes, then bent quickly and scooped her up. Despite what they had said, the weight of her wet clothes seemed to take him by surprise and he staggered for a second, then lifted her and turned carefully back towards Murray. The red hair dangled, flowing with seawater, and her arm slid down as Herkless felt his way back over the rocks. As soon as he reached Murray, Murray slid his hands under her arms and took his share of the burden. Herkless caught his eye.

'You were right about the weight, eh?'

Murray nodded. They began their slow progress across the shingle, Murray turning clumsily to walk forwards, boots sliding on shells and pebbles. It was almost a relief to reach the more stable footing of the path up to the headland, but here they had to stop and lift the corpse at each gorse bush, to stop the wet gown and spencer catching on the thorns. It was remarkably slow going, and they were both breathless by the time they reached the rock where Pringle still sat, his mouth open, slapped by the wind. They laid Anna at his feet, and Herkless quickly felt for a handkerchief to cover her face.

'She's all wet,' said Pringle dully. 'She'll be cold, silly girl.'

'Wait,' said Murray. He knelt beside her. Herkless on her other side set the handkerchief over her face, tucking it in to the top of her high-necked chemisette to stop the wind snatching it. 'Let me see for a second?'

'Oh, I've just got it secure ...' Herkless objected, but Murray was already pulling the handkerchief back from Anna's grey-white throat. He swallowed: he glanced up at Herkless, who caught his eye and made a curious face.

'Look,' said Murray, though his voice sounded strange even to him.

'What is it?' asked Herkless, and even Pringle seemed to focus.

'Thumbprints,' said Murray, pointing to two dark bruises.

'Surely not. Bruises from the fall, perhaps?'

'But she fell backwards ...'

'Thumbprints?' asked Pringle, thick with confusion. 'What do you mean?'

'I mean she didn't jump, or fall by accident. She was strangled,' said Murray, as if in a dream. 'We need Mr. Thomson back again.'

'Strangled? How did she …' Pringle opened and closed his mouth a few times, soundlessly. Murray and Herkless both sat back, avoiding each other's eyes. Murray tucked the handkerchief back, and lifted the soaking tails of the dark blue spencer to cover the skirts of the pale blue gown. The heels of her little boots, he saw, were black with mud: they matched the heel prints he had noticed earlier. Someone had grabbed her throat and held her, with her back to the cliff, to the breezy sea, and choked her, and let her drop to the rocks below. He swallowed hard.

'We need to take her home.'

'Aye,' said Pringle after a moment. 'She needs to come home now.'

He stood, and Murray and Herkless slowly followed. Murray bent and lifted Anna on his own. Herkless made a little sound, as if in protest, then stopped. Murray did not glance at him, but set off, leading the way back to the road and thence down, with his sorry, sodden burden, to the Pringles' house under the headland, where Mrs. Pringle would be waiting.

He had not stayed long at the Pringles', only long enough to see that Mrs. Pringle had good servants to help her with both her daughter's body and her stunned husband. Herkless in his wet boots headed quickly back to Kirkwelland House, promising to send a man to Stranraer for Thomson, and Murray, his coat filthy and wet and his mind spinning, walked slowly back to the manse. Mrs. Veitch was serving tea to Coulter, and hurried to fetch another cup and saucer, while Murray went upstairs to change. Walter came to help.

'Sir! Sir, do you remember you said I could go to the mutual improvement society this evening, sir?'

'What?'

'To do the science, sir. There's a man going to talk about water and watermills and springs and the like. May I still go, sir?'

'Yes, yes, of course. Are you sure you can find the way?' he added automatically.

'Aye, sir. Well, no, sir, but I can find my way to Mr. Innes' house, and he'll take me the rest of the way.'

'Fine, fine.' Murray sat on the bed and stared out of the window. Between the cottages, he could see the grey waters of the bay endlessly flickering with white spume, and seabirds wheeling above them. Walter handed him a clean shirt, and he slid into it without thinking about it, then added the usual black waistcoat and coat. Walter approached with a neckcloth, and Murray allowed him to try tying it a couple of times in silence before dismissing him kindly and retying it himself. A cup of tea would most likely help, he thought distantly, and returned to the parlour and Coulter, who poured it for him and handed it to him as he slumped in an armchair. The hot liquid made some impact, and he pulled himself straighter. Coulter was gazing at him expectantly.

'Anna Pringle is dead,' Murray said flatly.

'What?'

Murray took another sip of tea, and stretched, suddenly weary.

'When I took the gig back, the Pringles arrived to say Anna was missing. Pringle and Herkless and I went to seek her on the headland, and we found her – I found her – in the sea under the cliff.'

'Oh, not again!' Coulter gasped. 'Just like poor Jamesie Adair.'

'Not quite like Adair,' said Murray sourly. 'Anna had been strangled first.'

Coulter's jaw dropped.

'But – but – who? Why?'

'I think it tells us one thing, anyway,' said Murray. 'It tells us that this business is not over, and that, if nothing else, is proof that Adair was not Newell's murderer.'

'Surely you don't think that Pringle murdered his own daughter?' Coulter's voice dropped, in awe of the very words.

Murray pursed his lips.

'Look, I don't know. I want to make sure. He says he was with Gourlay this morning, since breakfast, and Anna left the house before breakfast. I need to check with Gourlay before anything else.'

'Yet surely the same person killed all three, Newell, Adair, and – oh, poor Anna! There cannot be two killers in Kirkwelland, can there?'

'I don't know.' He ran a hand hard through his hair, as if his fingernails could reach in and straighten his thoughts. 'But Coulter …'

'Yes?' Coulter was plainly distressed, but eager to help.

'Coulter, I need to tell you something, and I need to ask you something.'

'Anything!' said Coulter, confident. Murray sighed.

'I need to tell you that I heard you talking this morning with a Frenchman in Stranraer, down the alley where the Irish live. And I think you know what that means, don't you?'

Coulter went white, his freckles suddenly stark.

'What – what were you doing there?' he asked, not even denying it.

'Looking for you: you hadn't turned up at the inn and I thought I might have missed you with my walk out to Lochans. But you were still busy, weren't you? You are helping French dissenters enter the country from Ireland and travel towards Carlisle, isn't that right?'

Coulter nodded slowly, and set down his teacup and saucer on the table. He pulled his coat straight before starting to speak, as if he were addressing some kind of court.

'It seemed … it seemed to Bessie and me like a good thing to do. They swore to me they were intending no harm, just working away quietly to persuade people, and I think that's true, for there has been no news of any violence perpetrated - yet … I mean, they couldn't bring Bonaparte back from St. Helena, could they? There wouldn't be another war, or anything. But they could help persuade people, all kinds of people, to think – differently, more mercifully. To change the politics of this country, even, but at least to change people's attitudes. Universal education, now,' he said, growing enthusiastic. 'You can see here how well that works, and you've said yourself you want to help educate the people in your village. But so few places have the chance, so few lairds support such movements. They would rather have the lower classes available for work, and not helped to read things that might stop them working so cheaply, or such long hours. Can that be right? And Bessie and I – we wanted something better for our family, a happier world …' He blinked. 'Surely you can't disagree with that?'

Men do the wrong things for the right reasons, Murray thought. Gibson saw more than his visions of heaven: he saw things in this world, too. Poor Coulter. Reform might be the path ahead, but perhaps the French were not the best example to follow.

'That's not the point,' said Murray at last, 'though you know I think the mutual improvement society is a good idea. The point is you were acting against the law, which is not a wise thing for a minister. It lays you open to all kinds of trouble. Coulter, please tell me honestly: was Newell blackmailing you?'

Coulter pursed his thin lips, frowning. For a moment Murray thought he was going to cry. Then his face cleared and his shoulders sagged.

'Yes. Yes, he was, just a little.'

Murray sighed heavily.

'And please, let me ask this. I know you were in the lane outside his cottage the morning of the day he died. Did you poison his whisky? Did you kill him?'

The colour in Coulter's face washed in and out again.

'No,' he said firmly and with precision. 'I did not kill him.'

Murray nodded, acknowledging that he believed his old friend. Then he shifted in his chair, knowing he had to press on.

'Tell me another thing,' he said, feeling his voice catch. 'You and Herkless have been co-operating in helping the Irish peasants, feeding them, giving them shelter and charity. The Irish peasants were shielding the French sympathisers, weren't they?'

'Not wittingly,' Coulter said hurriedly. 'There were one or two who led the Frenchmen up here in parties of Irish travellers, but the party in general would not know who they were. They were innocent: do not blame them.'

Murray nodded again.

'But Herkless: did he know what you were doing?'

Coulter, taken aback, squirmed. His gaze fell to the floor, and he snatched up his tea cup and took a larger mouthful than was wise, coughing and spluttering for a moment. Murray kept his eyes on Coulter's face, though he wanted to avert his gaze.

'Herkless?' he prodded again. Coulter, recovered, nodded his head.

'Herkless knew. He gave them food before they went on their way.'

'Up the road past the turn to Gourlay's farm, off towards Newton Stewart and Carlisle?'

'How do you know?' Coulter's eyes widened. 'By the back

roads, so that they did not come across any regiments that might be marching, like that one yesterday. That's why I was visiting Monsieur – ah, the Frenchman in Stranraer. I was telling him to lie low because of all the soldiers there.'

'So Herkless knew. Herkless was a part of it.' Murray's heart felt suddenly heavy. 'Was he being blackmailed, too?'

'I don't know,' said Coulter, and it seemed he did not. 'I can't imagine Herkless allowing himself to be blackmailed, can you?'

'No,' said Murray, and that was the trouble.

He finished his tea and set out again, determined to tidy up the details. Coulter had gone to visit the Pringles, an unwelcome task. A thin rain was falling, or perhaps just hanging in the air, attaching itself to coat and breeches as he strode down the lane to the crossroads. The turning towards Newton Stewart was busy enough now with a few carts rumbling back and forth, but no Frenchmen were to be seen. He turned left and left again after the bridge, and made his way up the hill towards Gourlay's farm.

Gourlay was at dinner with his wife and children. Murray apologised for interrupting.

'I bring bad news, I'm afraid, though not such as to touch you directly, I think. Anna Pringle has died.'

'Anna Pringle? Dear heaven!' exclaimed Mrs. Gourlay.

'Aye, she was gey owertain when yon student died, was she no?' responded her husband. 'When was this? For her faither was here this morn, on business,' he added, with some pride.

'She set out before breakfast and was not seen until they found her body under the cliff an hour or so ago,' said Murray, distancing himself from the business. 'Her father was there when they found her.'

'Poor man, poor man,' said Mrs. Gourlay, a hand unconsciously on her little girl's shoulder.

'I suppose he must have gone straight there from here,' Murray mused.

'I dinna ken. He was here by eight of the clock this morn, and away the back of twelve.'

'My, a good deal of business, then!' said Murray admiringly. Gourlay acknowledged it with a slow nod.

'We gave him his breakfast and all,' he added reasonably.

'Anyway, can we be of service, Mr. Murray?' asked Mrs. Gourlay politely. 'I'm sure you did not come just to bring the claik.'

'No, no indeed,' agreed Murray, as if he had just thought of it. 'I came to ask if you had seen any Irish peasants passing this way? Maybe on the main road at the end of your lane?'

'One or two,' Gourlay said, after a glance at his wife for confirmation. 'No gangs of them, like you see going up to Glasgow. Is that what you mean?'

'That's exactly it. One or two,' he repeated. 'That's what I wanted to know.'

Though what he had really wanted to know he had also found out: it seemed extremely unlikely that Pringle had murdered his daughter, and if he had not, then it made little sense for him to have murdered Adair, either.

He walked back to the manse, irritably swishing his cane into the grassy banks at the side of the lane. What could he do? He reached the gate of the manse, and paused, half-expecting to see Thomson's miserable horse already tethered there, back for the next death. But there was no horse, and no sheriff's man: he was alone, and something had to be done. He took a deep breath, breathing out through his nose, half-facing the gate, half-hesitating, cane flicking. Then he snatched himself up and strode off, towards the other end of the lane.

He turned the corner, picturing as well as he could that morning nine days ago. Coulter had been talking with Herkless just here, halfway down the lane. Neither – he screwed his eyes shut and forced himself to see them again – neither had anything in their hands except for Herkless' cane: definitely there were no whisky jugs. He peered over the wall, remembering the jug by the side of the cottage. He had not yet given it to Thomson.

'Evening, sir,' came a voice from behind him. Innes was leaning in his own doorway, taking the air after dinner.

'Evening, Innes. Ah, off to the mutual improvement society this evening, then?'

'That's right, sir. Young Walter is to come too, with your permission, sir.'

'He has it: he should be along later.'

'Sad news of Miss Pringle,' Innes added.

'Very sad.'

'She and Mr. Adair … Well, they never killed themselves, did they, Mr. Murray?'

Murray blinked.

'No. No,' he said again, 'I don't believe they did.'

'Whoever murdered them probably murdered the old man as well, do you think?' Innes went on, cautiously.

'I think that must be the case,' Murray agreed.

'Aye, aye. The wife and I were talking about it. She reckons – but there, I can't go telling you that, Mr. Murray. And anyway, I think maybe you know as much as we do, would I be right, sir?'

He met Murray's eye, and then his gaze slid almost involuntarily round to the great thermometer suspended again by his door. Murray frowned, and Innes jumped.

'I didn't mean any disrespect, sir!' he said hurriedly. Murray shook his head.

'No, no, I didn't think that. It's just – difficult,' he added.

'Aye, sir. Well, I'll bid you good evening. I hope we might see you at the mutual improvement society later, then, sir?'

'I hope so. Perhaps,' Murray said, and carried on down the lane.

The drive to Kirkwelland House was shady and damp, the light starting to fade as if the rain were washing it out. When he knocked, the maid showed him up to the drawing room where Kitty, in the green gown that he so liked on her, was alone with a book. She jumped up with a smile when Murray entered the room.

'Mr. Murray! I'm very glad to see you, and I beg if you are not otherwise engaged that you will flaunt convention, come to my rescue and stay for dinner!'

'Come to your rescue? Why, are you left entirely alone this evening?' He could not help smiling when she did, as if it were contagious.

'Not alone as such,' she admitted, waving him to a seat near hers, 'but Papa is in such a strange mood that I cannot look forward at all to the meal. You will stay, won't you? You always seem to cheer him.'

At any other time Murray would have been thrilled to hear it.

'I came to speak with him, actually,' he said, though he could not resist sitting down with her. 'I should not impose myself upon you.'

'Please do not think of it as an imposition! Think of it as a favour!'

'Then I cannot refuse. But can I speak with your father?'

'Not at the moment,' Kitty said, 'for he is arranging something in the prison – you know, the little cells where we accommodate the Irish peasants when they come? He wants to make the other cells less damp, though how that is to be achieved, even as a charity, is beyond me, I have to say. He's there with some of the outdoor servants just now, and not to be disturbed, he told me.'

'He's very good to the Irish peasants, isn't he?'

'I suppose,' Kitty agreed. 'He has been doing it since I was small, so it seems quite everyday to me. But yes, if one thinks about it, not everyone would be so accommodating. But then, we have the space and the ability to feed them, so why not?'

'True. I'm afraid I have no advice to offer him on damp cellars, having had problems of my own in that respect, so I shall obey his instructions and stay clear until he is ready.' Already her company was easing his spirits and he had started to relax.

'So what did you do with your own damp cellars?' asked Kitty. 'Was this at the lovely Letho? For I am quite sure from your descriptions that no house in Fife is lovelier.'

'It was, and I did nothing to begin with,' Murray explained, still smiling. 'Then when I tried something, it ended in disaster.'

He told her the sad story of his servants' wing, now completely rebuilt, but tried to make it more entertaining and less horrific than it had been at the time. He was delighted to make her laugh, and in a few minutes she had easily persuaded him to stay to dinner and sent a servant down to tell Mrs. Veitch at the manse, to return with appropriate slippers and waistcoat, at least.

The servant reappeared all too quickly with a full suit of evening clothes, and Murray had to leave Kitty to go to a spare room and change. Hot water and towels had been left for him and he used them hurriedly, reluctant to allow himself time to think too much. The surface of his mind dwelt on Kitty, her intelligent eyes, her trim figure, her shining black hair, her delicate lips. What went on under that surface was something he was trying very hard to ignore. He assessed his appearance in the long cheval mirror, and wondered what his chances were. Then he straightened his already straight waistcoat, and went back downstairs to the drawing room.

Chapter Twenty-Four

'Ah, Murray, I've been expecting you. Kitty says you are able to join us for dinner. Splendid.' Herkless had risen to greet him as he walked into the drawing room, and they bowed in as friendly a fashion as ever. Kitty, too, rose, smiling, making his heart skip.

'My father is determined to improve his mood just to please you, so you see, Mr. Murray, you are already doing us both a service. If you are ready, shall we go down to dinner?'

The meal passed for Murray in a tumble of confusion of thoughts and feelings. The Herklesses were both as charming and entertaining as ever, and Murray found himself laughing heartily at Herkless' anecdotes of the rude mechanicals, as he called them, of the mutual improvement society. His stories, though, were not unkind: here was a laird who cared for the people of his village, Murray thought, a good example to follow at Letho, and a good grounding for any future mistress of Letho … Kitty was so lovely in the candlelight that he felt physically bereft when she rose and left them to their brandy, and he was alone with Herkless. He allowed his thoughts to dwell a moment longer, hopelessly, on Kitty, then met Herkless' eye.

'I believe you wanted a word with me, earlier,' said Herkless lightly, but it was no light expression on his face.

'I did, sir.'

'And again, I suspect it is not to ask for Kitty's hand, more's the pity.'

'If circumstances were different, sir, I should jump at the chance. She is – everything one would desire, I believe.'

'But circumstances – and here we are not just speaking of your current state of mourning – are indeed different.' He cleared his throat, for once a little unsure of himself. 'What is it you need to ask me?'

'I think you know, sir. You killed Anna Pringle, did you not?'

There was a long silence, but Murray could be patient now: the question had been asked.

'I did.' Herkless breathed out, staring down at his brandy glass and his own strong fingers holding it. 'I wish I had not.'

'It defeated the object, didn't it? You killed her to make sure she would not give away any more information, about seeing you back at the picnic field just before Adair died. But when I saw how you were trying to hide the marks on her throat,' he remembered how Herkless had insisted on sending him up the steep path forwards, how he had tucked the handkerchief into the high neck of Anna's lace chemisette, 'I knew for certain that you had murdered her.'

Herkless made a rueful face, nodding slightly.

'What a terrible shame,' he said. 'I should have liked you as a son-in-law, a clever man like you.'

'I can't see it working, somehow,' said Murray. 'Can you?'

'No.'

'You killed Newell because he wanted to blackmail you. Not over your liaison with Mrs. Pringle – over which I suspect you have been more discreet than honest – but over your work bringing French agitators into the country from Ireland. Newell said he was including gentry amongst his 'customers', but you wouldn't pay him.'

'I was not going to be beholden to that dreadful old man, like some common villager bedding his lass before the wedding,' Herkless declared softly.

'But you met him on the headland – which might as well be the market square, with everything that goes on there – and perhaps told him you would pay him soon? Or that you had left something by way of payment at his cottage? And you had: in the morning I saw you in the lane but you had no whisky bottle with you then. Instead you had hidden it, already poisoned – with the mercury and other chemicals you took from the kist in the schoolhouse behind the wall by the cottage. Instead of being seen to climb the wall or risk being found with a whisky jar, you were able to wait until the coast was clear, slip into Newell's cottage and decant your poisoned whisky into his bottle, throwing your empty one over the wall again. Then all you had to do was wait until he drank it – which would not be long.'

'Nevertheless it took him an unconscionable time to die, by all accounts,' Herkless put in. 'I thought it would be quicker, which would have been better for both of us.'

Murray frowned.

'But Adair was up on the headland too that day, hoping to meet Anna Pringle, and he overheard your conversation with Newell, didn't he?'

'I believe he did. He mentioned it to me, in a kindly fashion, in one of his sober moments. He simply thought I should know I had opened myself to suspicion: I don't even know that he thought I was in any way involved.'

'Yet you decided to kill him. So after the unfortunate incident with the jelly, you came back through the woodland and took your chance, slipping away again when you had pushed him over the edge.'

'Yes: I had made sure that that fool Pringle hadn't seen me, but I didn't realise half the Pringle family were marching about in the woods. Anna mentioned something to Kitty the other day, which Kitty passed on – in all innocence, I assure you – to me. I suspected that you were more perceptive than Kitty on this occasion.'

'It took a little while to sink in, I have to confess,' said Murray honestly. 'But it was not good of you to place the money and writing tablets in Adair's pack – and the letter, later.'

'No, perhaps that was ungentlemanly,' Herkless admitted, dropping his gaze.

'And Innes' thermometer?'

'A whim,' said Herkless. 'To confuse things, I thought.'

'It would have been a clumsy way to obtain the mercury, certainly.' Murray fiddled with his brandy glass, feeling waves of disappointment wash over him from every angle.

'So,' said Herkless after a pause, 'will you be handing me over to Thomson?'

'I think I have to,' said Murray. 'If I don't, where will you stop?'

'And if I promised to stop?' Herkless asked with a kind of smile. Damn it, thought Murray, he was such a likeable man.

'That would not account for the people you have already killed. Think of the Pringles. Think of poor Jamesie Adair's family, and his friends.'

Herkless nodded.

'I know. But will you at least allow me to plead my case a little? On behalf of what you call the French agitators? There is one of them down in the cellar I showed you now, a most well informed and educated man. You speak French, do you not?'

'Yes, of course, but –'

'Oh, come and meet him, please. You need not implicate yourself in any of this so-called wrong doing. You can simply collect more information for the egregious Mr. Thomson.' Herkless stood, hands wide, willing him to come. Murray could not resist.

'Oh, very well. Let me meet him, but I cannot promise any degree of mercy for either of you.'

'Of course not – I only ask that you listen.'

Herkless led the way across the hall to the front door, where he lifted his cane from the rack there, and outside. The sun was setting behind the clouds and the sea below them was charcoal grey, the other side of the bay a black tongue of land against the western sky. Herkless ushered Murray round the corner of the house along the gravel path they had gone by before, to the door of the cellar. It was unlocked, and Herkless leaned past Murray to push it open.

'He's in the second cell on the right: it's the driest, most comfortable one,' he explained, letting Murray go first. Murray descended the few steps to the cellar floor, and went to the wooden door of the cell. It was slightly ajar, and he pushed it open. Inside the light was very dim, though he could just make out a large, squarish shape in the middle of the floor.

'Don't you let your tenants have candles?' he asked with a laugh, half-turning back to Herkless.

'Sorry, Murray,' said Herkless, and Murray felt a heavy thump on the back of his head. The darkness became complete.

When he woke, he was baffled. Had he squirmed in his sleep and tangled himself in the bedclothes? He seemed to be curled up in a ball, unable to move. He opened his eyes, blinking, but there was no light at all: still the middle of the night, then. He closed them again: it felt better, for his head was aching. He must have drunk too much brandy in the manse parlour … no, he had been at Kirkwelland House, drinking with … oh.

He muttered a few creative curses at himself for his own stupidity. How could he have imagined that Herkless would submit easily?

But where was he, and what was happening? He thought hard, trying to bypass the pain in his head. He felt sick. He was probably still in the cell, for why lure him down there and then go to the trouble of carrying him somewhere else? And he was still alive. That was interesting. Why was he not dead?

He wriggled carefully. His wrists and ankles were tied, and he seemed to be in some kind of chest or trunk. It smelled of damp, and ancient lavender, as if it had been used to store linens at some time in the past. It had not been designed for someone of his size, clearly: his neck was already cramped. Well, he was not going to escape from the chest tied up, so the first priority was to try to undo the bonds. Was anyone guarding him, outside? If so, he needed to be quiet. He began to investigate the ropes with his fingers. They were tied with some skill, of course. He sighed. Why had he been so stupid?

He continued to work his wrists back and forth, hoping to loosen the ties, and after a moment he brushed against something on the side of the chest. He felt carefully around it. The trunk was clearly an old one, and it felt as if a metal stave had somehow come loose and bent into the body of the trunk. Cautiously, he tried to rub the rope along the stave, and at the third or fourth stroke he could feel just the least fraying on the outer edge of the rope. He worked on with more enthusiasm, and in a few minutes he had one rope free. His hands were still pinned behind his back but he freed his wrists, then reached awkwardly further down the trunk to reach his ankles. His arms had to stretch further than he thought possible, and his shoulders and neck screamed warnings about unnatural angles, but at last he managed to grab an end of the ankle rope and work it free. He could not reach far, but the rope was thick and he could push it back on itself to an extent, and in less than ten minutes, he reckoned, his ankles were unbound.

Well, he thought, I'm untied, but how on earth am I to lever myself up from this?

It hurt, for he must have been lying there for some time, but at last he managed to shift his position in the trunk and contemplate the next problem: how was he to escape from the trunk?

That turned out to be surprisingly easy. Herkless evidently had more faith in his own knots, or the trunk was so old he had lost the key, but the lid lifted at Murray's push and no one sprang to stop him. He emerged slowly, looking about him. He was indeed still in the cell, a bleak moonlight now slipping through the high barred window. The clouds must have cleared, but how late was it? Had anyone missed him? Probably not: Coulter would just assume he was staying late delighting in Kitty's company, and presumably Herkless had told Kitty that Murray had had to leave early.

He stepped out of the trunk, wobbled almost to the point of vomiting, and immediately tripped on something on the floor. He bent and picked up Herkless' cane. Herkless must have used it to knock Murray out, and then dropped it when he lifted Murray into the trunk, then forgotten it. Murray weighed it in his hands, feeling its use as a weapon. He leaned it against the trunk, and investigated further.

The cell door was locked, so Herkless had taken some precautions. He went next to the window, but it was so high that he could just reach the bottom of the bars with his outstretched fingers. He examined the mattresses and blankets, but they were not thick enough, combined, to allow him to reach a useful height.

He had walked round the cell once more, kicking the mattresses in frustration, and returned to stare up at the little window, when he heard a light footstep on the gravel path above. He pulled back into the shadows but still managed to catch a glimpse of a small, steady pair of boots that he recognised, and he was back at the window in an instant.

'Walter!' he gave as loud a whisper as he dared. 'What are you doing here?'

Walter jumped, looked around, then down. He knelt solemnly by the low window.

'Sir? Is that you, Mr. Murray, sir?'

'Yes – where were you going?'

'Well, here, sir. Kirkwelland House.'

'Good heavens. And you found it safely?'

'Yes, sir. Well, to be honest, I followed Mr. Herkless home.'

'Mr. Herkless is here?' Murray hissed, wondering what the

man was up to now. All this staring upwards was making him
dizzy.

'No, no, sir. He didna see me follow him. Honest.'

'But why, Walter? What are you doing here?'

'Seeking you, sir. It wasn't right, what Mr. Herkless said at the
mutual improvement society, and I thought you might have kissed
the causey somewise.'

'Why, what did he say?'

'He told Mr. Coulter you were away home with a bad stomach
and the minister must just have missed you.'

'Why did that not convince you?'

'Well, sir, I've never known you with a bad stomach and
anyway, he had a cane with him, and when he set it down I saw it
was yours – you ken, it had your wee stars on the top of the
handle.'

The Murray mullets, engraved in silver: it had been his
grandfather's.

'You didn't say anything to him, did you?'

'I don't think he saw me at all, sir. I'm gey small,' he said
with a certain pride.

'Small but useful, Walter, and I'm very glad to see you,
however you worked it out. Well done.' He could feel, though he
could not clearly see it, a glow of self-satisfaction emanate from
Walter's prim outline.

'Are you locked in down there, sir?' he asked.

'I am. It's a cell in a cellar, and I'm not tall enough to reach
the window to any effect.'

'Well if you're not tall enough, sir, I doubt any man is.'
Walter was revealing a certain height bias this evening.

'Yes, thank you, Walter. Maybe you could go and fetch help?'

'Water displacement, sir.'

'I beg your pardon?' Murray was startled.

'Water displacement. The man this evening was talking about
water flow and water displacement. If I could get the water from
the pump here into your cell, and fill it up, it would lift you up to
the window.'

Murray glanced about him. It was not a large cell, but still …

'There's a gap under the door - I suppose I could block that
with a mattress. But I think it would take an awful lot of water,

Walter. You'd be exhausted pumping.'

'It looks like the kind of a pump that would clatter, too, sir. No doubt the laird would find me before I had the water much above your knees.'

Murray had the sneaking suspicion that Walter was quite enjoying the image of his master up to his knees in water.

'Well, I think it's altogether too dangerous for the possible results. Any other ideas? Or will you just go for help?'

'I'll take a wee scance at the door, sir, first.'

'Careful, Walter!' Murray urged him, but he was gone, soft footsteps crunching the gravel lightly.

It struck him that the moonlight had changed substantially since he had walked here with Herkless after dinner – and Herkless had been down to the village and back. Had there been something in the brandy? No wonder he felt so peculiar.

Eventually he heard a noise in the passage outside his cell, briefly, then nothing, then, alarmingly, a scrabble in a bush outside the window again.

'Sir?'

'Yes, Walter? Are you all right?'

'Aye, sir. That gap under your cell door – have you got something you could push through it to lie flat, sir? The tail of your coat, maybe, if you took it off.'

'There are blankets here: one of them would fit, if I pushed the corner through.' Murray was puzzled.

'Aye, grand, sir. A blanket might be better: it'll dull the noise.'

'The noise of what?'

'Well, sir, will you take this? It took me a wee while to find one the right size.'

He poked something through the bars, and Murray reached up to take it. It was a small stick, thin but strong and straight.

'What's this for?'

'Well, sir – and I think this is quite clever, sir – what you should do is push a blanket under the door so there's a good bit of it lying flat outside the door. Then use the stick to poke the key – the key's in the keyhole, sir – poke the key out of the keyhole so it lands on the blanket, then pull it back under the door, and use the key to let yourself out.'

Murray considered for a moment.

'It's a grand idea, Walter, but tell me this: if the key is in the keyhole, why did you not turn it yourself and let me out?'

There was a pause.

'Oh.'

'Never mind, it was a good scheme. Could you maybe go and let me out now?'

'Aye, sir, I will.'

He stood, then bent to brush off the knees of his breeches, which was probably what saved him. Murray heard a heavier step from the direction of the main door.

'Walter! Run!' he snapped. Walter straightened, confused, then must have heard something and left in remarkable silence. Murray leapt for the trunk, grabbing Herkless' abandoned cane, curled himself inside and shut the lid, praying he had made the right decision, and praying too that Walter would escape safely, for both their sakes.

It seemed he had. Herkless had brought a few servants with him – it was hard to tell how many, but probably more than Murray could have fought off even with the cane. In addition, it seemed that with the servants there Herkless had no wish to open the trunk to check on the contents. Sounds were muffled, but Murray concentrated hard.

'Take it out to the gig, will you?' said Herkless indistinctly. 'Watch, it's heavy. It's things for Mr. Coulter's soup kitchen down in Stranraer. I told him this evening I'd take it down to him at the manse.'

Murray felt the trunk lifting, tipping a little from side to side as the men adjusted their hold. He prayed they would not drop him. He wondered if he should try to attract the attention of the servants, as Herkless evidently had not taken them into his confidence. He hesitated, thinking that a man emerging from a trunk would likely cause the servants to drop it, and in that moment he felt the trunk settled on the uneasy rack at the back of the gig, and heard straps being fastened around it. Then he felt the jerk of the gig setting off. Where was he going to end up?

He pushed up against the lid of the trunk. There was a very slight give, as if the straps had not been pulled particularly tightly. It did not fill him with joy, as the thought of tumbling off the back of the gig was not an appealing one, but it might be useful. He continued to push against the strap, jiggling it as much as he could, and had the pleasure of seeing it loosening a little more with each push.

It was not a comfortable journey, and Murray was starting to feel rather queasy by the time he felt the gig ease to a halt. The trunk moved as presumably Herkless slipped down from the seat, and he tensed, but he heard the squeak of a small gate and knew himself to be back at the manse. What was Herkless up to? Surely he was not really intending Coulter to deliver him to the soup kitchen! But … what if Coulter had lied to him? What if he really had been involved in Newell's death? He remembered Coulter's precise enunciation – 'I did not kill him'. What had he meant by that? It had seemed so clear at the time. But now, was Herkless fetching his ally to help him dispose of Murray? He kept working at the straps, trying to be ready for any eventuality.

Footsteps approached, and he heard voices.

'Saucepans and such,' he heard Herkless say. 'I thought, since the night is fine, we might as well take them down to Stranraer tonight. Look at that moon! Isn't it splendid?'

'Well,' came Coulter's voice, dubiously, 'it's very good of you.'

He was lying to Coulter, then, so unless there was someone else listening, Coulter was not in on this scheme, at least. He felt again the change in angle as Coulter and Herkless climbed into the gig, and the wobble as Herkless turned the gig and horse in the narrow lane. They set off down the dip to the crossroads, then it was harder to tell where they were except that the noise of the wheels lessened when they reached the better surface of the main road out of the village. They picked up speed. He could hear no conversation, but the purr of the wheels would have obscured it, anyway.

He felt the gig round a corner – perhaps amongst the rocks where Norrie Pearce had attacked them? and then slow to a halt. The hairs rose on the back of his neck, and his ears seemed to stretch out, trying to hear anything that would tell him what was going on.

'… something odd with the reins,' he heard Herkless say. The gig moved as Herkless climbed down, then again as Coulter followed.

'Can I help?' Coulter asked, then there was a thump, and a heavy grunt. Murray's heart doubled speed. Had Herkless knocked Coulter out as he had Murray? If so ... The gig began to move, but not along the road: it was being shaken. What was happening? Then he realised, as the trunk started to tip from end to end, putting pressure on first his knees and then his neck. He clutched Herkless' cane, bracing himself in anticipation of the impact. The gig swung further, paused for a moment, then fell with a crash on its side. Murray breathed a small sigh of relief: he had fallen on his knees rather than his neck, and for a mercy it had been the final straw for the straps holding the trunk: both had snapped open. He rolled quickly out of the trunk and was on his feet before Herkless came round the back of the overturned gig.

'What?' Herkless was stunned to see him on his feet, which was good as his feet were not too steady after his cramped journey. Murray stepped towards him and before he could think about regretting it, landed a solid punch on Herkless' jaw. Herkless staggered back but at the same time brought his cane round – Murray's cane – and struck Murray across the shoulder, hard. Herkless took advantage of Murray's lurch sideways to try to get past him. Murray glanced round. Herkless must be trying to make for his horse, which was free of the gig. He stuck out Herkless' cane and Herkless stumbled over it, but did not fall. Murray followed up by grabbing Herkless' flailing elbow and pulling him round to meet another punch. It connected with Herkless' nose, which burst with blood. He lashed back, landing a fist in Murray's ear which left his head ringing. He shook it hard – he thought he heard hoofbeats, but it was probably just the blow. He kicked out, and made contact with Herkless' leg: he felt bone, but he was still in his evening slippers and he doubted the kick had done much harm.

Herkless had made another two strides towards the mare, which was edging away, alarming by all the quick movements. He seemed to be limping. Murray lunged after him and caught him again, less steadily this time, pulling at his coat, trying to drag him back. Herkless struggled to free himself, and struck back at Murray's slithering grasp. Then he broke free, and made, lopsided, for the mare.

Lexie Conyngham

Chapter Twenty-Five

Then there came a shout, and something hard hit Murray on the shoulder, making him stagger. At the same time Herkless fell to the ground with a cry of pain, and both of them, bewildered, stared up at a figure on a familiar, world-weary horse who was holding a stout baton above them with a warning glare.

'Quit that now, you limmers! Or I'll have you in chains in the jail this minute!'

'Thomson?' asked Murray, gasping for breath.

'Is that you, Mr. Murray? Well, I might have known. Who is it this time, then, eh?' Thomson peered into the shadows of the rocks. 'Is that Mr. Herkless and all? Wherefore were you attacking him?'

'He's the murderer.'

'Oh, aye?' Herkless was panting on the ground, clutching his leg and groaning. Thomson stared down at him, head on one side. 'What happened you?'

'Murray attacked me,' Herkless moaned, sounding quite pathetic. 'And I've hurt my leg.'

'He was going to kill me. He might already have killed the minister. Coulter? Where are you?' Murray straightened himself and peered around. 'Where have you left him?' he demanded. In his confusion, he was sure he saw Walter hurrying over to the capsized gig.

'Under the gig,' said Herkless. 'Thomson, the gig overturned – I was just going to see if Coulter was all right when Murray just launched himself at me. I don't know why.'

Murray hurried round the gig. Coulter lay on his back, his legs under one wheel of the gig, pinned down. He was very white.

'Coulter!' Murray crouched by him, slapping his face gently.

He pushed one glove down and felt for a pulse. 'He's alive!' he called.

Thomson, dismounted, stalked round the gig and gazed down at Coulter, whose eyes were flickering open. Walter squatted beside him next to Murray, staring.

'Mr. Coulter,' Thomson said, in a tone that implied he had caught him scrumping apples once too often. 'What happened here?'

'What?' asked Coulter. 'Ow, my legs!'

'What happened, Coulter? Do you remember?'

Coulter's face crumpled up with pain and concentration.

'We were going to the soup kitchen, I think. Murray, I should have listened to Walter. Were you following us?'

'In a manner of speaking,' said Murray wrily. 'I was in the trunk on the back of the gig.'

'Eh?' said Thomson, stepping back round the gig to look at the trunk. 'This one here?'

'That's right: Herkless told Coulter it was full of saucepans and such for his soup kitchen in Stranraer.'

'He must have hidden in there,' called Herkless. 'No doubt he was waiting to attack us.'

'But he didn't attack us, Herkless,' said Coulter suddenly. 'I remember: you said there was something wrong with the reins, and I got down to see if I could help, and you hit me! I remember now.'

'Och, don't be daft, Coulter,' said Herkless firmly. 'Why would I do that? You're confused: you must have hit your head when the gig overturned.'

'I don't think so,' said Coulter, struggling to sit up as Murray and Thomson between them righted the gig. 'I think I know what you were doing. You killed Newell, didn't you?'

'Eh?' said Thomson again, looking from the laird to the minister and back. Herkless was trying to stand, but his leg kept giving way.

'I saw you that day. I only remembered this evening, after Murray was asking me about you and the French.'

'The French?' repeated Thomson, now edging towards Herkless, his eye on him in puzzlement.

'I was coming up the lane towards the corner where Newell's

cottage is,' said Coulter, 'the morning before he died. Up ahead, I saw Herkless coming out of Newell's cottage and turn away for a minute, then he came down the lane and we talked for a little – about the French and the Irish, which distracted me. I only remembered this evening. I did,' he added, as if Murray might challenge him on it.

'And you knew he would remember,' said Murray, 'and though you had the matter of the French to hold over him –'

'What is this about the French?' asked Thomson crossly. He had picked up one of the ropes from the trunk, left over from Murray's imprisonment there, and was approaching Herkless with more confidence.

'You were staging a gig accident, then, with Coulter and me to die in the wreckage,' said Murray. 'That's why you didn't kill me earlier: you needed a fresh body, not a stiff one, if you were to tell people we had died at the same time.'

'I like to pay attention to detail,' said Herkless at last, dropping his head in defeat. 'But I should just have pushed Anna Pringle. The trouble was, she realised what I was up to – I had no idea she had that much intelligence – so I had to do it. Ah, well: there we are. I had a good run, I suppose.'

Thomson took Herkless, bound and lame, in his own gig to Stranraer, leaving Coulter and Murray by the side of the road with Thomson's own horse and the broken trunk. Murray pulled it off the road and squatted down beside Coulter.

'Are you fit to walk?'

'Aye, of course.' Murray tried to help him up, but he screamed hoarsely. 'Ah, no. Legs not quite right,' he gasped, hand over his mouth.

'Could we get him on to the horse, sir?' Walter suggested.

'I'll have to lie across it like a pack,' Coulter said, with an attempt at humour.

'That's a way for a respectable minister to come home,' said Murray, turning to bring the horse over. It seemed pleased enough to see him again. 'Walter, what are you doing here anyway?' Walter opened his mouth to reply, but was interrupted by a gasp of pain from the minister.

'Respectable? I doubt I'll be that any more, after Herkless has talked,' Coulter admitted, breathing hard. 'I may have to look for a new line of work, at the very least. Or I might hang for treason,' he added, almost as if it would not matter.

'Let's deal with that if and when it happens,' said Murray. 'First, let's try and get you up here.' Coulter leaned over and Murray, with difficulty, hoisted him up on his shoulder and, with Walter holding the horse steady, managed to manoeuvre him to lie, legs dangling, over the saddle. Coulter was not a healthy colour, but urged them on, between gasps, to lead the horse back to the village, swearing it was better than lying by the side of the road waiting for help.

Mrs. Veitch, roused from an apparent doze in the kitchen chair, rushed to the door to help Murray bring Coulter in and lay him on the hard sopha in the parlour. Coulter bit his lips so hard they bled, but made no complaint as they straightened him out.

'Both broken,' whispered Mrs. Veitch, as if handing down a death sentence.

'Then fetch whoever in the village is best at such matters.'

'I'll go for Mrs. Black,' she said at once, and seized her shawl.

Murray sat with Coulter, giving him a brandy. He sipped it gratefully.

'I should have known,' he said. 'Well, I did know. But I thought I might be able to help you,' he added.

'What do you mean? Are you growing confused?' Murray asked, concerned.

'No! Believe me, this pain clears the mind very nicely. No, I mean I suspected Herkless was up to something when he came to the door this evening. Walter told me where you were.'

'Walter told you?'

'Oh, yes. He came in at a great rate, and told us you were locked in a cell at Kirkwelland House, and that Herkless had had your cane at the meeting. Then he set off for Stranraer, he said, to meet Thomson and hurry him along. I know you said he couldn't find his way anywhere but he was very determined – and fast. He was out of the door before I had the chance to stop him.'

Murray rose, and rang the bell. It was time he did something about Walter. It was clear that he would never make a useful bodyservant. In a moment, he appeared at the parlour door, his jaw dropping when he saw Coulter's legs by bright candlelight.

'Aye, sir, what's your will?' he asked, never taking his eyes off Coulter's battered legs.

'Walter, I'd like to dismiss you from my service.'

'What, now?' Walter finally looked at him.

'Well, not till we get home, perhaps. How should you like to go back to school?'

Walter did not take long to answer.

'I'd like it very much, sir, except for the Latin. I dinna see how that can be a language.'

'Disregard the Latin for now. Mathematics, though, you like that?'

Walter's eyes shone beneath his chestnut fringe.

'Oh, aye, sir! But sir, how can my family afford such a thing?'

'I'll pay. And should you manage to pass the right examinations, I'll pay your fees at St. Andrews University. Would you like to do that? Or would you rather stay as a servant at Letho?'

'Would ... would anyone show me the way to St. Andrews?' Walter asked uncertainly.

'I'd take you there myself, for the service you have done me this evening.'

'Thank you, sir. Then yes,' he said, nodding with decision, 'I should like that very much.'

Mrs. Black arrived in a great bustle of bandages and poultices, and Murray stayed a little to help with the heavy work of adjusting leg bones and holding a patient in terrible pain. The brandy bottle was plied plenteously, and when the straightening was done, and Coulter half-conscious, Murray left him to the women's tender care and took his cane, and Herkless', and went out. It was near midnight.

Kirkwelland House was still lit, and though he had half-expected to find that Kitty had retired for the night, he was shown to the drawing room where she was reading again in front of a dying fire. She looked up expectantly when he came in, but frowned to see he was alone.

'I thought you and Papa had gone down to the rude

mechanicals together?' she said. 'He said you'd gone on ahead.'

'No, I was not there,' Murray said. 'Miss Herkless, I have some bad news for you.'

If he had had any doubts as to Kitty's innocence in the whole matter, they were put to rest by her complete shock at the news of what her father had been doing, not just the murders but even the sheltering of the French agitators. Murray rang for more brandy, and an extra shawl, and himself knelt to build up the fire a little. He stayed there, on his knees by the fireplace, his back half towards her, and let his bones rest for a moment in the warmth. He had been knocked out, drugged, cramped and battered, and he was feeling very tired. The maid appeared with the shawl and the brandy, and Kitty roused herself to wrap the fine paisley around her and sip at the glinting glass. At last she cleared her throat.

'You have suspected this for some time, I gather?'

'I was not sure until this afternoon, when he tried to hide the bruises on Anna's neck.'

She swallowed hard.

'How could I not have known?'

'He's your father, and a loving one: how could you even suspect?'

'He will hang for this.' Her voice was low, as if it might not happen if no one heard.

'Yes, I suspect he will.' He tried to be gentle. He turned, still on his weary knees, and took her hand as it lay in her lap. When he tried to formulate the words he felt suddenly reluctant to voice them, but he knew it had to be done. 'Miss Herkless, I had hoped that one day ... when my time of mourning was over, I had hoped that I might return and ask you to be my wife. If it would be of any service to you now, I make that offer, and the offer of my protection from – whatever is to come.'

She gave his hand the slightest pressure, and withdrew her own.

'Mr. Murray,' she said huskily, and started again. 'Mr. Murray, I believe that I might have accepted you, had things been different. But now I have duties to perform here, which will be onerous, no doubt, but have to be faced. I should stay in my own place. And whatever protection you might offer, and whatever evil he has done, I fear I should always think of you in my heart as the man who caused my father to be caught.'

'I understand,' he said, his own voice croaking. He rose stiffly to his feet. 'Then I shall leave you.'

'I think you must.' She would not meet his eye. He bowed, and left, surprised by the feeling of relief in his heart.

Murray and Walter walked along the path from Letho village to the big house, over the little river and through the pasture where his black cows and their calves munched the sweet Fife grass. They looked very small, he thought, with a smile.

'Will Mr. Coulter be able to walk again ever?' Walter asked, in his best scientific voice. He had been practising it all through the journey, but Murray found it tolerable.

'Yes, Mrs. Black thinks so. The breaks were bad, but they have set well, and there is no infection.'

'Mr. Thomson was not as good as our sheriff's officer, was he, sir?' was the next question.

'I don't know: he had his own ways.'

Thomson had come to collect his horse on the Sunday, when all was a guddle in the village with the schoolmaster having to preach, and the story of Anna's murder intertwining with tales of strange accidents on the Stranraer road by moonlight, and the rumours about where the laird could have gone.

'It was a pleasure working with you, Mr. Murray,' he said, solemnly and surprisingly offering Murray his hand, 'but it was very satisfying laying about you with the baton last night, all the same.'

'Have a care to your horse, will you, Thomson?' Murray had replied. 'It has enough to put up with bearing you round the place. Good luck to you,' he had added, and meant it.

At the soft golden sandstone steps of Letho House, he pushed open the white front door and rang the bell, greeting the dogs as they rushed excitedly to gather new scents from his boots. Walter slipped off to the servants' quarters as Robbins, the butler, appeared, a welcoming smile on his colourless face.

'All well?' Murray asked.

'All very well, sir,' Robbins agreed, but any further information was interrupted.

'Look who's here!' came a voice from the parlour doorway.

Mrs. Helliwell, kindly guardian, appeared, leading by the hand a tiny figure with dark, curling hair. 'It's Papa!'

'Papa!' cried the child, and scuttled over to be swept into his arms.

'Augusta!' cried Murray, tears in his eyes. 'Thank heavens: home at last.'

Scots and outlandish terms used in *Slow Death by Quicksilver*:

Argify – argue
Banyan – a type of large robe, often used as a dressing gown
Breeks - breeches
Ca'canny – go carefully
Claik - gossip
clyte
Coof
Crusie lamp – small primitive oil lamp
Cry – call, name
Dominie - schoolmaster
Dwam – daydream, swoon
Fulyie - excrement
Gey – very
Girdle – griddle
Give the Canongate breeks – give someone venereal disease
Glengorie –give someone venereal disease
Gowf - golf
Guddle – mess or muddle
Heritor – one of a committee who oversee the fabric of a
    parish, the church building, manse and schoolhouse
Idleset – idle, lazy
Jenny Meggy – cranefly
Jook – duck, make a sudden quick movement
Ken – know
Kiss the causey – come to grief
Kist – chest or trunk
Kisting – placing a corpse in its coffin, over which the
    minister would say prayers.
Laverock - lark
Limmer - rogue
Nyaff – worthless person
Owertain – over-affected, upset
Rammy – fight, scuffle
Rare – (Ulster) rear, bring up
Risp – a metal bar at a door to be rattled, in place of using a
    door knocker
Scabbit – lit. scabbed, dirty, unpleasant

Scaffie – street cleaner or rubbish collector
Scance - look
Scourie
Shilpit – unimpressive, rough, untrustworthy
Skite - rogue
Wean – wee one, child
Wheen – lots, a large quantity
Wud - mad

Thanks as always for the invaluable input of Kath and N, who generously pick their way through the newly-hatched text!

About the Author

Lexie Conyngham is a historian living in the shadow of the Highlands. Her Murray of Letho novels are born of a life amidst Scotland's old cities, ancient universities and hidden-away aristocratic estates, but she has written since the day she found out that people were allowed to do such a thing. Beyond teaching and research, her days are spent with wool, wild allotments and a wee bit of whisky.

The sequel to *Slow Death by Quicksilver* is at the planning stage. Follow her professional procrastination at www.murrayofletho.blogspot.com.

The Murray of Letho series:

Death in a Scarlet Gown
Knowledge of Sins Past
Service of the Heir
An Abandoned Woman
Fellowship with Demons
The Tender Herb: A Murder in Mughal India
Death of an Officer's Lady
Out of a Dark Reflection
Slow Death by Quicksilver

Stand-alones

Windhorse Burning
The War, The Bones and Dr. Cowie
Thrawn Thoughts and Blithe Bits (short stories)

Printed in Great Britain
by Amazon

83145927R00181